Mary Higgins Clark, number one international and *New York Times* bestselling author, has written thirty-four suspense novels; three collections of short stories; a historical novel, *Mount Vernon Love Story*; two children's books, including *The Magical Christmas Horse*; and a memoir, *Kitchen Privileges*. With her daughter Carol Higgins Clark, she has coauthored five more suspense novels. Her books have sold more than 100 million copies in the United States alone.

Alafair Burke is the *New York Times* bestselling author of eleven novels, including *Long Gone*, *If You Were Here*, and the latest in the Ellie Hatcher series, *All Day and a Night*. A former prosecutor, she now teaches criminal law and lives in Manhattan.

Loves Music, Loves to Dance
The Anastasia Syndrome and Other Stories
While My Pretty One Sleeps
Weep No More, My Lady
Stillwatch
A Cry in the Night
The Cradle Will Fall
A Stranger Is Watching
Where Are the Children?

BY MARY HIGGINS CLARK AND CAROL HIGGINS CLARK

Dashing Through the Snow
Santa Cruise
The Christmas Thief
He Sees You When You're Sleeping
Deck the Halls

BY ALAFAIR BURKE

If You Were Here
Long Gone

THE ELLIE HATCHER SERIES

All Day and a Night
Never Tell
212
Angel's Tip
Dead Connection

THE SAMANTHA KINCAID SERIES

Close Case
Missing Justice
Judgment Calls

MARY HIGGINS CLARK
& ALAFAIR BURKE

THE CINDERELLA MURDER

SIMON &
SCHUSTER

London · New York · Sydney · Toronto · New Delhi

A CBS COMPANY

First published in the US by Simon & Schuster, Inc., 2014
First published in Great Britain by Simon & Schuster UK Ltd, 2014
A CBS COMPANY

This paperback edition first published 2015

1 3 5 7 9 10 8 6 4 2

Simon & Schuster UK Ltd
1st Floor
Gray's Inn Road
London WC1X 8HB

www.simonandschuster.co.uk

Simon & Schuster Australia, Sydney
Simon & Schuster India, New Delhi

A CIP catalogue record for this book
is available from the British Library

Paperback B ISBN: 978-1-47115-685-4
Paperback A ISBN: 978-1-47113-850-8
eBook ISBN: 978-1-47113-851-5

Printed and bound by CPI Group (UK) Ltd, Croydon, CR0 4YY

Simon & Schuster UK Ltd are committed to sourcing paper that is made
from wood grown in sustainable forests and supports the Forest Stewardship
Council, the leading international forest certification organisation. Our
books displaying the FSC logo are printed on FSC certified paper.

For Andrew and Taylor Clark
The newlyweds—
With love

Acknowledgments

It is so satisfying to tell another tale, to share another journey with characters we have created and come to care deeply about—or not. And this time to have done it step by step with the wonderful writer Alafair Burke.

Marysue Rucci, editor-in-chief at Simon & Schuster, has been a marvelous friend and mentor. Alafair and I have so enjoyed working with her on this book, which is the first of a series.

The home team starts with my right hand, Nadine Petry, my daughter Patty, and my son Dave. And of course, John Conheeney, spouse extraordinaire.

Abiding thanks to Jackie Seow, art director. Her covers make me look so good.

And many thanks to my faithful readers, whose encouragement and support have made me write yet another tale.

Dear Reader,

My publisher had an idea I loved: with a cowriter, we should use the main characters in *I've Got You Under My Skin* in a series of novels. Working with Alafair Burke, a suspense writer I have long admired, we created *The Cinderella Murder*. In this novel and others to follow, the premise is that witnesses, friends, and family members from unsolved cases will be brought together to appear on a TV show years later in the hope of finding clues that were missed in the earlier investigations. I hope you enjoy the story.

Mary Higgins Clark

1

It was two o'clock in the morning. Right on time, Rosemary Dempsey thought ruefully as she opened her eyes and stirred. Whenever she had a big day ahead she would inevitably wake up in the middle of the night and start worrying that something would go wrong.

It had always been like this, even when she was a child. And now, fifty-five years old, happily married for thirty-two years, with one child, beautiful and gifted nineteen-year-old Susan, Rosemary could not be anything but a constant worrier, a living Cassandra. *Something is going to go wrong.*

Thanks again, Mom, Rosemary thought. Thanks for all the times you held your breath, so sure that the birthday upside-down cake I loved to make for Daddy would flop. The only one that did was the first one when I was eight years old. All the others were perfect. I was so proud of myself. But then, on his birthday when I was eighteen, you told me you always made a backup cake for him. In the single act of defiance that I can remember, I was so shocked and angry I tossed the one I had made in the garbage can.

You started laughing and then tried to apologize. "It's just that you're talented in other ways, Rosie, but let's face it, in the kitchen you're klutzy."

And of course you found other ways to tell me where I was klutzy,

Rosemary thought. "Rosie, when you make the bed, be sure that the spread is even on both sides. It only takes an extra minute to do it right." "Rosie, be careful. When you read a magazine, don't just toss it back on the table. Line it up with the others."

And now, even though I know I can throw a party or make a cake, I am always sure that something will go wrong, Rosemary thought.

But there was a reason today to be apprehensive. It was Jack's six-tieth birthday, and this evening sixty of their friends would be there to celebrate it. Cocktails and a buffet supper, served on the patio by their infallible caterer. The weather forecast was perfect, sunshine and seventy degrees.

It was May 7 in Silicon Valley and that meant that the flowers were in full bloom. Their dream house, the third since they'd moved to San Mateo thirty-two years ago, was built in the style of a Tuscan villa. Every time she turned into the driveway, she fell in love with it again.

Everything will be fine, she assured herself impatiently. And as usual I'll make the birthday chocolate upside-down cake for Jack and it will be perfect and our friends will have a good time and I will be told how I'm a marvel. "Your parties are always so perfect, Rosie . . . The supper was delicious . . . the house exquisite . . . ," and on and on. And I will be a nervous wreck inside, she thought, an absolute nervous wreck.

Careful not to awaken him, she wriggled her slender body over in the bed until her shoulder was touching Jack's. His even breath-ing told her that he was enjoying his usual untroubled sleep. And he deserved it. He worked so hard. As she often did when she was trying to overcome one of her worry attacks, Rosemary began to re-mind herself of all the good things in her life, starting with the day she met Jack on the campus of Marquette University. She had been an undergraduate. He had been a law student. It was the proverbial love at first sight. They had been married after she graduated from college. Jack was fascinated by developing technology, and his conversation became filled with talk of robots, telecommunications, microprocessors, and something called internetworking. Within a year they had moved to Northern California.

I always wanted us to live our lives in Milwaukee, Rosemary thought. I still could move back in a heartbeat. Unlike most human beings, I love cold winters. But moving here certainly has worked out for us. Jack is head of the legal department of Valley Tech, one of the top research companies in the country. And Susan was born here. After more than a decade without the family we hoped and prayed for, we were holding her in our arms.

Rosemary sighed. To her dismay, Susan, their only child, was a Californian to her fingertips. She'd scoff at the idea of relocating anywhere. Rosemary tried to wrest her mind away from the troublesome thought that last year Susan had chosen to go to UCLA, a great college but a full five-hour drive away. She had been accepted closer to home at Stanford University. Instead she had rushed to enroll at UCLA, probably because her no-good boyfriend, Keith Ratner, was already a student there. Dear God, Rosemary thought, don't let her end up eloping with him.

The last time she looked at the clock, it was three thirty, and her last impression before falling asleep was once again an overwhelming fear that today something was going to go desperately wrong.

2

She woke up at eight o'clock, an hour later than usual. Dismayed, she rushed out of bed, tossed on a robe, and hurried downstairs.

Jack was still in the kitchen, a toasted bagel in one hand, a cup of coffee in the other. He wore a sport shirt and khakis.

"Happy sixtieth birthday, love," she greeted him. "I didn't hear you get up."

He smiled, swallowed the last bit of the bagel, and put down the cup. "Don't I get a kiss for my birthday?"

"Sixty of them," Rosemary promised as she felt his arms go around her.

Jack was almost a foot taller than Rosemary. When she wore heels, it didn't seem so much, but when she was in her bedroom slippers, he towered over her.

He always made her smile. Jack was a handsome man. His full head of hair, now more gray than blond; his body, lean and muscular; his face, sunburned enough to emphasize the deep blue of his eyes.

Susan was much more like him in both looks and temperament. She was tall and willowy, with long blond hair, deep blue eyes, and classic features. Her brain was like his. Technically gifted, she was the best student in the lab at school and equally gifted in her drama classes.

Next to them, Rosemary always felt as though she faded into the background. That too had been her mother's appraisal. "Rosie, you really should have highlights in your hair. It's such a muddy brown."

Now, even though she did use streaks, Rosemary always thought of her hair as "muddy brown."

Jack collected his long kiss and then released her. "Don't kill me," he said, "but I was hoping to sneak in eighteen holes at the club before the party."

"I guessed that. Good for you!" Rosemary said.

"You don't mind if I abandon you? I know there's no chance of you joining."

They both laughed. He knew all too well that she would be fussing around over details all day.

Rosemary reached for the coffeepot. "Join me for another cup."

"Sure." He glanced out the window. "I'm glad the weather is so good. I hate it when Susan drives through rainstorms to get here, but the weather prediction is good for the weekend."

"And I don't like that she's going to be going back early tomorrow morning," Rosemary said.

"I know. But she's a good driver and young enough that the round trip won't be a problem. Though remind me to talk to her about trading in that car of hers. It's two years old, and already we've had too many visits to the garage." Jack took a final few sips of the coffee. "Okay, I'm on my way. I should be home around four." With a quick kiss on Rosemary's forehead, he was out the door.

At three o'clock, beaming with self-satisfaction, Rosemary stepped back from the kitchen table. Jack's birthday cake was perfect, not a crumb astray when she flipped it over and lifted the pan. The chocolate icing, her own recipe, was relatively smooth, with the words HAPPY 60TH BIRTHDAY, JACK, written carefully, word for word.

Everything is ready, she thought. Now, why can't I relax?

3

Forty-five minutes later, just as Rosemary was expecting Jack to walk in the door, the phone rang. It was Susan.

"Mom, I had to work up the courage to tell you. I can't get home tonight."

"Oh, Susan, Dad will be so disappointed!"

Susan's voice, young and eager, almost breathless, said, "I didn't call before because I didn't know for sure. Mom, *Frank Parker is going to meet me tonight*, about maybe being cast in his new movie." Her voice calmed a little. "Mom, remember when I was in *Home Before Dark*, just before Christmas?"

"How could I forget?" Rosemary and Jack had flown to Los Angeles to watch the campus play from the third row. "You were wonderful."

Susan laughed. "But you're my mother. Why wouldn't you say that? Anyhow, remember the casting agent, Edwin Lange, who said he'd sign me?"

"Yes, and you never heard from him again."

"But I did. He said Frank Parker saw my audition tape. Edwin taped the performance and showed it to Frank Parker. He said that Parker was blown away and is considering me for the lead in a movie he's casting. It's a movie set on a campus and he wants to find college students to be in it. He wants me to meet him. Mom, can you believe it? I don't want to jinx myself, but I feel so lucky. It's like it's too good to be true. Can you believe that I might get a role, maybe even the lead role?"

"Calm down before you have a heart attack," Rosemary cautioned, "and then you won't get any role." Rosemary smiled and pictured her daughter, energy exuding from every bone in her body, twisting her fingers through her long blond hair, those wonderful blue eyes shining.

The semester's almost over, she thought. If she did get a part in this movie, it would be a great experience. "Dad will certainly understand, Susan, but be sure to call him back."

"I'll try, but, Mom, I'm meeting Edwin in five minutes to go over the tape with him and rehearse, because he says Frank Parker will want me to read for him. I don't know how late it will be. You'll be having the party, and you'll never hear the phone. Why don't I call Dad in the morning?"

"That might not be a bad idea. The party is from six to ten, but most people linger on."

"Give him a birthday kiss for me."

"I will. Knock that director off his feet."

"I'll try."

"Love you, sweetheart."

"Love you, Mom."

Rosemary had never become used to the sudden silence that followed when a cell phone disconnected.

When the phone rang the next morning, Jack popped up from reading the newspaper. "There's our girl, bright and early by a college student's standards for a Sunday."

But the caller wasn't Susan. It was the Los Angeles Police Department. They had difficult news. A young woman had been found just before dawn in Laurel Canyon Park. She appeared to have been strangled. They didn't want to alarm them unnecessarily, but their daughter's driver's license had been retrieved from a purse found fifteen yards from the body. A mobile phone was clutched in her hand and the last number dialed was theirs.

4

Laurie Moran paused on her way to her office at 15 Rockefeller Center to admire the ocean of gold and red tulips blooming in the Channel Gardens. Named after the English Channel because they separated the French and British Empire Buildings, these gardens were always brimming with something lush and cheerful. Tulips were no match for the plaza's Christmas tree, but the discovery of new plantings every few weeks in spring always made it easier for Laurie to say good-bye to her favorite season in the city. While other New Yorkers complained about the throngs of holiday tourists, Laurie found cheer in the brisk air and festive decorations.

Outside the Lego store, a father was photographing his son next to the giant Lego dinosaur. Her own son, Timmy, always had to loop through the store to inspect the latest creations when he visited her at work.

"How long do you think it took them to make this, Dad? How many pieces do you think there are?" The boy looked up at his father with a certainty that he had all the answers in the world. Laurie felt a pang of sadness, remembering the way Timmy used to gaze at Greg with the same anticipatory awe. The father noticed her watching, and she turned away.

"Excuse me, miss, but would you mind taking our picture?"

Thirty-seven years old, Laurie had learned long ago that she came across as friendly and approachable. Slender, with honey-colored hair and clear hazel eyes, she was typically described as "good–looking" and "classy." She wore her hair in a simple shoulder-length bob and rarely bothered with makeup. She was attractive but un-threatening. She was the type of woman people stopped for directions or, as in this case, amateur photography.

"Of course I don't mind," she said.

The man handed her his phone. "These gadgets are great, but all our family pictures are from an arm's length away. It would nice to have something to show besides a bunch of selfies." He pulled his son in front of him as she stepped back to get the entire dinosaur in view.

"Say cheese," she urged.

They complied, flashing big, toothy smiles. Father and son, Laurie thought wistfully.

The father thanked Laurie as she returned his phone. "We didn't expect New Yorkers to be so nice."

"I promise, most of us are pretty nice," Laurie assured him. "Ask New Yorkers for directions and nine out of ten will take the time."

Laurie smiled, thinking of the day when she was crossing Rocke-feller Center with Donna Hanover, the former first lady of New York City. A tourist had touched Donna's arm and asked if she knew her way around New York. Donna had turned and pointed and explained. "You're just a couple of blocks from . . ." Smiling at the memory, Laurie crossed the street and entered the Fisher Blake Studios offices. She got off the elevator on the twenty-fifth floor and hurried to her office.

Grace Garcia and Jerry Klein were already busy at their cubicles. When Grace saw Laurie, she sprang up from her seat first.

"Hi, Laurie." Grace was Laurie's twenty-six-year-old assistant. As usual, her heart-shaped face was heavily but perfectly made up. Today, her ever-changing mane of long, jet-black hair was pulled into a tight ponytail. She wore a bright blue minidress with black tights and stiletto boots that would have sent Laurie toppling over face first.

Jerry, wearing one of his trademark cardigan sweaters, ambled from his seat to follow Laurie into her private office. Despite Grace's sky-high heels, long, lanky Jerry loomed over her. He was only one year older than Grace but had been with the company since he was in college, working his way up from intern to valued production assistant, and had just been promoted to assistant producer. If it hadn't been for Grace and Jerry's dedication, Laurie never could have gotten her show *Under Suspicion* off the ground.

"What's going on?" Laurie asked. "You two act like there's a surprise party waiting in my office."

"You could put it that way," Jerry said. "But the surprise isn't in your office."

"It's in here," Grace said, handing Laurie a legal-sized mailing envelope. The return address read ROSEMARY DEMPSEY, OAKLAND, CALIFORNIA. The seal had been opened. "Sorry, but we peeked."

"And?"

"She agreed," Jerry blurted excitedly. "Rosemary Dempsey's on board, signed on the dotted line. Congratulations, Laurie. *Under Suspicion's* next case will be the Cinderella Murder."

Grace and Jerry took their usual places on the white leather sofa beneath the windows overlooking the skating rink. No place would ever feel as safe to Laurie as her own home, but her office—spacious, sleek, modern—symbolized all her hard work over the years. In this room, she did her best work. In this room, she was the boss.

She paused at her desk to say a silent good morning to a single photograph on it. Snapped at a friend's beach home in East Hampton, it was the last picture she, Greg, and Timmy had taken as a family. Until last year, she had refused to keep any pictures of Greg in her office, certain that they would be a constant reminder to anyone who entered that her husband was dead and his murder still unsolved. Now she made it a point to look at the photograph at least once a day.

Her morning ritual complete, she settled into the gray swivel chair across from the sofa and flipped through the agreement Mrs. Dempsey had signed, indicating her willingness to participate in *Under Suspicion.* The idea for a news-based reality show that revisited unsolved crimes had been Laurie's. Instead of using actors, the series offered the victim's family and friends the opportunity to narrate the crime from a firsthand perspective. Though the network had been wary of the concept—not to mention some flops in Laurie's track record—Laurie's concept of a series of specials got off the ground. The first episode had not only aired to huge ratings, it had also led to the case's being solved.

It was nearly a year since "The Graduation Gala" had aired. Since then they had considered and rejected dozens of unsolved murders as none had been suitable for their requirements—that the nearest relatives and friends, some of whom remained "under suspicion," would be guests on the program.

Of all the cold cases Laurie had considered for the show's next installment, the murder twenty years ago of nineteen-year-old Susan Dempsey had been her first choice. Susan's father had passed away three years ago, but Laurie tracked down her mother, Rosemary. Though she was appreciative of any attempt to find out who killed her daughter, she said she had been "burned" by people who had reached out to her before. She wanted to make sure that Laurie and the television show would treat Susan's memory with respect. Her signature on the release meant that Laurie had earned her trust.

"We need to be careful," Laurie reminded Grace and Jerry. "The 'Cinderella' moniker came from the media, and Susan's mother despises it. When talking to the family and friends, we always use the victim's name. Her name was Susan."

A reporter for the *Los Angeles Times* had dubbed the case "the Cinderella Murder" because Susan was wearing only one shoe when her body was discovered in Laurel Canyon Park, south of Mulholland Drive in the Hollywood Hills. Though police quickly found the other near the park entrance—presumably it had slipped off as she tried to escape her killer—the image of a lost silver pump became the salient detail that struck a chord with the public.

"It is such a perfect case for the show," Jerry said. "A beautiful, brilliant college student, so we have the hot UCLA setting. The views from Mulholland Drive near Laurel Canyon Park are terrific. If we can track down the dog owner who found Susan's body, we can do a shoot right by the dog run where he was heading that morning."

"Not to mention," Grace added, "that the director Frank Parker was the last known person to see Susan alive. Now he's being called the modern Woody Allen. He had quite a reputation as a ladies' man before getting married."

Frank Parker had been a thirty-four-year-old director when Susan Dempsey was murdered. The creator of three independent films, he was successful enough to get studio backing for his next project. Most people had first heard of him and that project because he had been auditioning Susan for a role the night she was killed.

One of the challenges for *Under Suspicion* was persuading the people who were closest to the victim to participate. Some, like Susan's mother, Rosemary, wanted to breathe new life into cold investigations. Others might be eager to clear their names after living, as the show's title suggested, under a cloud of suspicion. And some, as Laurie had hoped would be the case with Frank Parker, might reluctantly agree to go along so they appeared to the public to be cooperative. Whenever whispers about the Cinderella case arose, Parker's handlers liked to remind the public that the police had officially cleared him as a suspect. But the man still had a reputation to protect and he wouldn't want to be seen as stonewalling an inquiry that might lead to solving a murder.

Parker had gone on to become an Academy Award–nominated director. "I just read the advance review for his next movie," Grace said. "It's supposed to be a shoo-in for an Oscar nomination."

Laurie said, "That may be our chance to get him to go along with us. It wouldn't hurt to have all that attention when the Oscars come along." She began to jot notes on a pad of paper. "Contacting the other people who were close to Susan is what we have to start on now. Let's follow up with calls to everyone on our list: Susan's roommates, her agent, her classmates, her lab partner at the research lab."

"Not the agent," Jerry said. "Edwin Lange passed away four years ago."

It was one less person on camera, but the agent's absence wouldn't affect their reinvestigation of the case. Edwin had been planning to run lines with Susan prior to her audition but got a phone call that afternoon informing him that his mother had had a heart attack. He had hopped immediately into his car, calling relatives constantly on his cell phone, until he arrived in Phoenix that night. He had been shocked to hear of Susan's death, but the police never considered the agent a suspect or material witness.

Laurie continued her list of people to contact. "It's especially important to Rosemary that we lock in Susan's boyfriend, Keith Ratner. Supposedly he was at some volunteer event, but Rosemary despised him and is convinced he had something to do with it. He's still in Hollywood, working as a character actor. I'll make that call and the one to Parker's people myself. Now that Susan's mother is officially on board, I hope that will convince everyone else. Either way, get ready to spend time in California."

Grace clapped her hands together. "I can't wait to go to Hollywood."

"Let's not get ahead of ourselves," Laurie said. "Our first stop is the Bay Area. To tell Susan's story, we have to get to know her. Really know her. We start with the person who knew her the longest."

"We start with her mother," Jerry confirmed.

5

Rosemary Dempsey was Laurie's reason for moving the Cinderella Murder to the top of her list for the show's next installment.

The network had been pressuring her to feature a case from the Midwest: the unsolved murder of a child beauty pageant contestant inside her family's home. The case had already been the subject of countless books and television shows over the past two decades. Laurie kept telling her boss, Brett Young, that there was nothing new for *Under Suspicion* to add.

"Who cares?" Brett had argued. "Every time we have an excuse to play those adorable pageant videos, our ratings skyrocket."

Laurie was not about to exploit the death of a child to bolster her network's ratings. Starting her research from scratch, she stumbled onto a true-crime blog featuring a "Where are they now?" post about the Cinderella case. The blogger appeared to have simply Googled the various people involved in the case: Susan's boyfriend was a working actor; her college research partner had gone on to find dot-com success; Frank Parker was . . . Frank Parker.

The blog post quoted only one source: Rosemary Dempsey, whose phone number was still listed—"Just in case anyone ever needs to tell me something about my daughter's death," she said. Rosemary told the blogger that she was willing to do anything to find out the truth about her daughter's murder. She also said that she was convinced that the stress caused by Susan's death had contributed to her husband's fatal stroke.

The overall tone of the blog post, filled with tawdry innuendo, left Laurie feeling sick. The author hinted, with no factual support, that Susan's desire to be a star may have made her willing to do *any-thing* to land a plum role with an emerging talent like Parker. She speculated, again with no proof, that a consensual liaison may have "gone wrong."

Laurie could not imagine what it would have been like for Rosemary Dempsey to read those words, written by a person she had trusted enough to confide her feelings to about the loss of both her daughter and her husband.

So when Laurie called Rosemary Dempsey about the possibility of participating in *Under Suspicion*, she had understood precisely what Rosemary meant when she said she'd been burned before. Laurie had made a promise to do her very best, both for her and her daughter. And she told Rosemary how she knew from experience what it was like not knowing.

Last year, when the police had finally identified Greg's killer, Laurie had learned what people meant when they used the word "closure." She didn't have her husband back, and Timmy was still without his father, but they no longer had to fear the man Timmy had called Blue Eyes. It was closure from fear but not from heartbreak.

"That damn shoe," Rosemary had said about the "Cinderella Murder" nickname. "The irony is that Susan never wore anything so flashy. She'd bought those shoes at a vintage store for a seventies party. But her agent, Edwin, thought they were perfect for the audition. If the public really needed a visual image to hang on to, it should have been her necklace. It was gold, with the sweetest little horseshoe pendant. It was found by her body, the chain broken in the struggle. We bought it for her on her fifteenth birthday, and the next day, she landed the lead role as Sandy in her high school's production of *Grease*. She always called it her lucky necklace. When the police described it, Jack and I knew we'd lost our baby."

Laurie had known at that moment that she wanted the murder of Susan Dempsey to be her next case. A young, talented girl whose life had been cut short. Greg was a brilliant young doctor whose life had been cut short. His murderer was dead now. Susan's was still out there.

6

Rosemary Dempsey juggled two overflowing brown paper grocery bags, managing to close the hatchback of her Volvo C30 with her right elbow. Spotting Lydia Levitt across the street, she quickly turned away, hoping to slip from the driveway to her front door unnoticed.

No such luck.

"Rosemary! My goodness. How can one person eat so much food? Let me help you!"

How could one person be so rude? Rosemary wondered. Rude, and yet at the same time so kind?

She smiled politely, and before she knew it, her across-the-street neighbor was at her side, grabbing one of the bags from her hands.

"Multigrain bread, huh? Oh, and organic eggs. And blueberries—all those antioxidants! Good for you. We put so much junk into our bodies. Personally, my weakness is jelly beans. Can you believe it?"

Rosemary nodded and made sure Lydia saw her polite smile. If Rosemary had to guess, she'd have said the woman was in about her midsixties, though God knows she didn't care.

"Thank you so much for your help, Lydia. And I'd say jelly beans are a relatively harmless vice."

She used her now-free hand to unlock the front door of her house.

"Wow, you lock your door? We don't usually do that here." Lydia set her bag next to Rosemary's on the kitchen island, just inside the entryway. "Well, about the jelly beans, tell that to Don. He keeps finding little pink and green surprises in the sofa cushions. He says it's like living with a five-year-old on Easter Sunday. Says my veins must be like Pixy Stix, filled with sugar."

Rosemary noticed the message light blinking on her telephone on the kitchen counter. Was it the call she was waiting for?

"Well, thank you again for the help, Lydia."

"You should come down for the book club on Tuesday nights. Or movies on Thursdays. Any activity you want, really: knitting, brunch club, yoga."

As Lydia rambled on about the various games Rosemary could be playing with her neighbors, Rosemary thought about the long road that had led her to this conversation. Rosemary had always assumed she'd remain forever in the home where she had raised her daughter and lived with her husband for thirty-seven years. But, as she had learned so long ago, the world didn't always work precisely as one expected. Sometimes you had to react to life's punches.

After Susan died, Jack offered to quit his job and go back to Wisconsin. The stock in the company that he had accumulated over the years and the generous pension and retirement benefits meant that they had plenty of money to take care of them for the rest of their lives. But Rosemary had realized that they had built a life in California. She had her church and her volunteer work at the soup kitchen. She had friends who cared so much about her that they kept her freezer full of casseroles for months, first after she said good-bye to Susan, then to Jack.

And so she'd stayed in California. After Jack died she did not want to stay in their home. It was too large, too empty. She bought a town house in a gated community outside Oakland and continued her life there.

She knew that she could either live with her grief or fall into despair. Daily Mass became a routine. She increased her volunteer work to the point where she became a grief counselor.

In retrospect, she might have been better off with a condo in San Francisco. In the city she would have had her anonymity. In the city she could buy multigrain bread and organic eggs and carry her groceries and check that urgent, blinking phone message without having to fend off Lydia Levitt's attempts to recruit her into group activities.

Her neighbor was finally wrapping up the list. "That's what's nice about this neighborhood," Lydia said. "Here at Castle Crossings, we're basically a *family*. Oh, I'm sorry. That was a poor choice of words."

Rosemary had first met this woman sixteen months ago and yet it wasn't till this moment that she finally saw herself through Lydia Levitt's eyes. At seventy-five years old, Rosemary had already been a widow for three years and had buried her only daughter two entire decades earlier. Lydia saw her as an old woman to be pitied.

Rosemary wanted to explain to Lydia that she had made a life filled with activities and friends, but she knew the woman had a point. Her activities and friends were the same as when she had been a San Mateo wife and mother. She had been slow to allow new people into her world. It was as if she didn't want to know anyone who didn't also know and love Jack and Susan. She didn't want to meet anyone who might see her, as Lydia apparently did, as a widow marked by tragedy.

"Thank you, Lydia. I really appreciate it." This time, her gratitude was sincere. Her neighbor might not have been tactful, but she was caring and kind. Rosemary made a mental promise to reach out again to Lydia once she was less preoccupied.

Once Rosemary was alone, she eagerly retrieved her voice mail. She heard a beep, followed by a clear voice that hinted at a tone of excitement.

"Hi, Rosemary. This is Laurie Moran from Fisher Blake Studios.

Thank you so much for sending back the release. As I explained, putting the show together depends also on how many of the people involved in the case we can sign up. Your daughter's agent, unfortunately, has passed away, but we have letters out to all the names you gave us: Frank Parker, the director; her boyfriend, Keith Ratner; and Susan's roommates, Madison and Nicole. The final call gets made by my boss. But your willingness to participate makes an enormous difference. I truly hope this happens and will get back to you as soon as I have a final answer. In the meantime, if you need me—"

Once Laurie began reciting her contact information, Rosemary saved the message. She then dialed another number from memory as she began unloading groceries. It was the number of Susan's college roommate Nicole.

Rosemary had told Nicole that she had decided to go ahead with the program.

"Nicole, have you made a decision about the television show?"

"Not quite. Not yet."

Rosemary rolled her eyes but kept her voice even. "The first time they made that kind of special, they ended up solving the case."

"I'm not sure I want the attention."

"It's not attention about *you*." Rosemary wondered if she sounded as shrill as she felt. "The focus of the show would be on Susan. On trying to solve her case. And you were close to Susan. You've seen how when someone brings it up on Facebook or Twitter, there are dozens of opinions, not least of which among them is that Susan was some kind of slut involved with half the men on campus. You could help to erase that image."

"How about the others? Did you speak to them?"

"I haven't yet," Rosemary said honestly, "but the producers will make their choice based on the level of cooperation they get from the people involved in the case. You were Susan's roommate for nearly two years. You know that *other* people won't want to cooperate."

She didn't even bother speaking their names. First up was Keith Ratner, whose wandering eye Susan had forgiven so many times. Despite his own transgressions, his possessiveness of Susan and unjustified jealousy had always made him Rosemary's top suspect. Next was Frank Parker, who had marched on with his fancy career, never giving Rosemary and Jack the common courtesy of a phone call or sympathy card for the loss of their daughter, whose only purpose in going to the Hollywood Hills was to see him. And Rosemary had never trusted Madison Meyer, Susan's other roommate, who had been only too happy to step into the role that Susan was supposed to audition for that night.

"Knowing Madison," Nicole was saying, "she'll show up with hair and makeup done."

Nicole was trying to defuse the tension with humor, but Rosemary was determined to stay on message. "You'll be important to the producers' decision."

The silence on the other end of the line was heavy.

"They'll be deciding soon," Rosemary nudged.

"Okay. I just need to check on a couple of things."

"Please hurry. The timing is important. *You're* important."

As Rosemary clicked off the phone, she prayed that Nicole would come through. The more people Laurie Moran could enlist, the greater the hope that one of them would inadvertently give himself or herself away. The thought of reliving the terrible circumstances of Susan's death was daunting, but she felt as though she were hearing lovable, wonderful Jack's voice saying, *Go for it, Rosie*.

Lovable, wonderful Jack.

7

Twenty-eight miles north, on the other side of the Golden Gate Bridge, Nicole Melling heard the click on the other end of the telephone line but couldn't bring herself to hit the disconnect button on the handset. She was staring at the phone in her hand when it started to make a loud beeping sound.

Her husband, Gavin, appeared in the kitchen. He must have heard the sound all the way from his home office upstairs.

He came to a halt when he spotted the phone, which she finally returned to its base. "I thought it was the smoke alarm."

"Is that a critique of my cooking?" she asked.

"Please, I know better." He gave her a kiss on the cheek. "You are absolutely the best cook—make that *chef*—I have ever known. I'd rather eat three meals a day here than go out to the finest gourmet restaurant in the world. And besides that, you're beautiful and have the disposition of an angel." He paused. "Is there anything I forgot?"

Nicole laughed. "That will do." Nicole knew that she was no beauty. She wasn't unattractive, either. She was just ordinary, her features unremarkable. But Gavin always made her feel like, in his eyes, she was gorgeous. And he was gorgeous in her eyes. Forty-eight years old, always trying to lose a few pounds, average height, starting to bald. He was a dynamo of brains and energy whose stock picks for his hedge fund made him a formidable figure on Wall Street.

"Seriously, is everything okay? It's a bit troubling to find my wife standing in the kitchen staring at a phone off the hook. Honest to God, you look as though you just received a threat."

Nicole shook her head and laughed. Her husband had no idea how close this joke came to the truth in her case.

"Everything's fine. That was Rosemary Dempsey."

"She's doing okay? I know you were disappointed when she didn't accept your invitation to join us for Thanksgiving."

She had told him about the possibility of this program. But she certainly hadn't told him the full story about where she was in her life when she had shared a dorm room with Susan.

She hadn't meant to conceal anything from him. She really had managed to convince herself that she was a different person now than she was before she met him.

If this program happened and someone dug deeply enough, would it be better to have told him the truth now?

"Do you know that show called *Under Suspicion?*" she began.

His expression was blank, then changed. "Oh sure, we saw it together. Sort of a true-crime reality show; the Graduation Gala Murder. Got lots of attention. It even ended up solving the crime."

She nodded. "They're thinking of featuring Susan's case for the next one. Rosemary really wants me to be a part of it."

He plucked a few grapes from the crystal bowl on the kitchen island. "You should do it," he said emphatically. "A show like that could break the entire case open." He paused, then added, "I can only imagine what it's like for Rosemary—not knowing. Look, honey, I know you don't like the limelight, but if it could bring some kind of closure for Rosemary, I'd say you owe it to her. You always tell me that Susan was your best friend." He grabbed several more grapes. "Do me a favor, hang up the phone at the end of the next call, okay? I was afraid you'd fainted."

Gavin took the stairs back to his home office. He had the luxury (and curse) of being able to run a hedge fund wherever he happened to be as long as he had a phone and Internet connection.

Now that she had spoken the possibility aloud, Nicole knew that, of course, she had to be part of the show. How would it look if Rosemary asked Susan's college roommate to help solve Susan's murder, and she refused? How could she sleep at night?

Twenty years was so long ago, but it felt like a minute. Nicole had left Southern California for a reason. She would have moved to the North Pole if necessary. In the Bay Area, with Gavin, she had a wonderful husband. With the marriage, she had also changed her last name. Nicole Hunter had become Nicole Melling. She had started over again. She had found peace. She had even forgiven herself.

This show could ruin everything.

8

"Good afternoon, Jennifer. Is he in?"

Brett Young's secretary looked up from her desk. "Yes, just back in from lunch."

Laurie had worked with Brett long enough to know his routine: telephone calls, e-mails, and other correspondence in the morning; a business-related lunch (preferably from noon to two); then back to his desk for creative work in the afternoon. Until a few months ago, Laurie would have needed to schedule an appointment to see her boss. Now that she was back on top with *Under Suspicion*, she was one of the lucky few who could pop in unannounced. If she was really lucky, he may have indulged in a glass of wine or two at lunch. It always helped his mood.

Cleared by his guard, Laurie tapped on Brett's office door before opening it.

"Got a sec?" she asked.

"Sure, especially if you're here to tell me you've decided to take on the little beauty queen case."

He looked up. Sixty-one years old and handsome by any standards, his expression was sealed in a permanent façade of extreme displeasure.

She took a seat on a recliner next to the sofa where Brett had been reading a script. Laurie thought her office was nice, but Brett's made it look like a cubbyhole in comparison.

"Brett, we went through that case. There's nothing new to say about that investigation. The whole point of our show is to get first-person accounts of people who were real players in the case. People who could possibly have been involved."

"And you'll do exactly that. Sic Alex Buckley on them and watch the witnesses squirm."

Alex Buckley was the renowned criminal defense attorney who had presented the first volume of the show about the so-called Graduation Gala Murder. His questioning of the witnesses had been perfect, ranging from gentle empathy to grueling cross-examination.

Since then, Laurie had seen him regularly. In the fall he'd invited her, Timmy, and her father to Giants football games and in the summer to Yankees baseball games. All four of them were ardent fans of both teams. He almost never invited her out alone, perhaps sensing she was not ready for a definitive progression of their relationship. She needed to complete the mourning process, to close the chapter on her life with Greg.

And she was too keenly aware that he was mentioned frequently in gossip columns for escorting a celebrity to a red-carpet affair. He was a very, very desirable man about town.

"Not even Alex Buckley could solve that case," Laurie insisted, "because we have no idea whom to question. DNA evidence has cleared the girl's entire family, and police never identified any other suspects. End of story."

"Who cares? Dig out those old pageant videos and glamour shots, and watch that Nielsen needle jump." It wasn't the first time Brett had lectured Laurie about the importance of ratings, and it wouldn't be the last. "You need something new? Get a scientist to conduct facial progression. Show the viewers what the victim would look like now."

"It simply wouldn't work. A technologically enhanced photograph could never tell the story of a life lost. Who knows what the future could have held for that girl?"

"Listen to me, Laurie. I happen to be a *successful* man. I know what I'm talking about. And I'm trying to help you keep your show on a roll. Some would say you got lucky the first time around and have just been riding it out since then." It had been nearly a year since the first *Under Suspicion* "news special" had aired. Since then, Laurie had been an executive producer on several of the studio's run-of-the-mill series, but Brett was eager to build on the *Under Suspicion* brand. "You gotta try to re-create the magic of the first time."

"Trust me. I went back to the drawing board and found a great case. It's perfect for *Under Suspicion*. The Cinderella Murder."

She handed him a photograph of Susan Dempsey, a professional headshot she had used for auditions. When Laurie had first seen it, she felt like Susan was looking straight through the camera, directly at her personally. Susan had been blessed with near-perfect features—high cheekbones, full lips, bright blue eyes—but the real beauty was in the energy of that stare.

Brett barely glanced at the photograph. "Never heard of it. Next! Seriously, Laurie, do I need to remind you of the flops you had before this thing came along? You of all people should know: success is fleeting."

"I know, I know. But you've heard of the case, Brett. The victim was a UCLA college student, found dead in the Hollywood Hills. Supposedly she no-showed for an audition that night."

Now he bothered to look at the headshot. "Wow, she was a knock-out. Is this the Frank Parker thing?"

Had Frank Parker not gone on to become famous, people might have forgotten entirely about the Cinderella Murder by now. But every once in a while, usually after Parker released a new film or got nominated for another award, someone would mention the onetime scandal in the director's younger life.

"The victim's name was Susan Dempsey," Laurie began. "By

every account, she was a remarkable girl: smart, attractive, talented, hardworking."

He waved his hand for her to get on with it. "We're not handing out medals. Why is this good TV?" Brett asked.

Laurie knew Brett Young would never understand her determination to help Susan's mother. Instead, she enthusiastically recited all of the features that made the case so appealing to Grace and Jerry. "First of all, it's a terrific setting. You've got the UCLA campus. The glitz of Hollywood. The noir of Mulholland Drive."

It was clear that Brett was now listening carefully. "You said the right word: 'Hollywood.' Celebrities. Fame. That's why people would care about that case. Wasn't she found near Parker's house?"

Laurie nodded. "Within walking distance, in Laurel Canyon Park. He says she never showed up for the audition. Her car was found parked on campus. Police never determined how she got from UCLA to the hills."

"Parker knew she was a student. If her car was at Parker's house, and he had anything to do with it, he could have arranged to move it back on campus," Brett observed slowly.

Laurie raised her eyes. "Brett, if I didn't know better, I'd say you're beginning to sound interested."

"Will Parker participate?"

"I don't know yet. I've got Susan's mother on board, though, and that will make a difference. She's motivated. She'll convince Susan's friends to talk on air."

"Friends, schmends. Family and friends won't get people to set their DVRs. An Academy Award–nominated director will. And get that actress, the one who landed the role."

"Madison Meyer," Laurie reminded him. "People forget that in addition to getting the role Susan was auditioning for, she was also one of Susan's roommates."

According to Frank Parker, when Susan failed to appear for

the audition, he called Madison Meyer, another student from the UCLA theater department, and invited her to audition at the last minute. When questioned by police, Madison vouched for Parker's timeline, saying she was with him in his living room at the time of Susan's death.

"Pretty strange he just happened to give the role to a novice actress who provided him a convenient alibi," Brett said, rubbing his chin, a sure sign that he was on board.

"This is a good case for the show, Brett. I feel it. I *know* it."

"You know I love you, Laurie, but your gut's not enough. Not with this kind of money at stake. Your show ain't cheap. The Cinderella Murder is just another cold case without Frank Parker. You lock him down for the show, and I'll give you the all-clear. Without him, I have a surefire backup."

"Don't tell me: the child pageant queen?"

"You said it. Not me."

No pressure, Laurie thought.

9

Frank Parker looked down at Madison Square Park from fifty-nine stories above. He loved New York City. Here, looking north out of the floor-to-ceiling windows of his penthouse apartment, he could see all the way to the top of Central Park. He felt like Batman watching over Gotham.

"I'm sorry, Frank, but you made me promise to nudge you about some of those to-do items before the day ended."

He turned to find his assistant, Clarence, standing in the entryway of the den. Clarence was well into his thirties but still had the body of a twenty-year-old gym rat. His clothing selections—today a fitted black sweater and impossibly slim slacks—were obviously intended to highlight the muscles he was so proud of. When Parker hired him, Clarence had volunteered that he hated his name, but everyone who heard it remembered him because of his god-awful moniker. So it worked for him.

The entire flight from Berlin, Clarence had been trying to get Frank's attention about interview requests, phone messages, even wine selections for an upcoming premiere party. On the one hand, these were the kind of nitty-gritty details for which Frank had no patience. On the other hand, the people who worked for him had learned by now the types of decisions that could send him over the edge if someone made the wrong call. He had a reputation as a micromanager. He assumed it was what made him good at his job.

But as poor Clarence had begged for Frank's attention on the plane, all Frank could do was continue reading scripts. The chance to read in peace on the private jet had been the only part of the trip he enjoyed. Though it made him sound provincial, he hated leaving the United States. For the time being, however, foreign film festivals were all the rage. You never knew what tiny gem you might find to remake into an American blockbuster.

"Don't you know by now, Clarence, that when I make you promise to interrupt me about something in the future, it's simply my way of delaying a conversation?"

"Of course I know that. Feel free to send me on my way again. Just don't snap at me tomorrow if the sky falls because you wouldn't let me relay these messages."

Frank's wife, Talia, paused in the hallway outside the den. "For Pete's sake, stop picking on poor Clarence. We'd probably have the lights cut off if he didn't keep life running for us. If you wait until we're back in Los Angeles, you'll end up getting too busy once again. Look out your pretty window and let him do his job."

Frank poured an inch and a half of scotch into a crystal highball glass and took a spot on the sofa. Clarence got settled into a wing chair across from him.

First up on Clarence's list was the studio's insistence that he sit down for a lengthy interview for a feature magazine article to promote his summer film release, called *The Dangerous Ones*. "Tell them I'll do it, but not with that wretched Theresa person." One of the magazine's writers was known for presenting her subjects in the worst possible light.

Next was a reminder that an option he had on last year's hottest novel was about to expire. "How much are we paying?"

"Another quarter of a million to extend the additional year."

He nodded and waved a hand. It had to be done.

None of this seemed urgent enough for Clarence to have been bothering him all day.

Clarence was looking down at his notes, but when he opened his mouth to speak, no words came out. He let out a long breath, smiled, and then tried again. Still nothing.

"What's gotten into you?" Frank asked.

"I'm not sure how to raise this."

"If I could read minds, I wouldn't need you, would I?"

"Fine. You got a letter from the producers of a television program. They'd like to meet with you."

"No. We'll do publicity closer to release. It's too early now."

"It's not about *The Dangerous Ones*. It's about you. The past."

"Isn't that what I just agreed to on the magazine article?"

"No, Frank, I mean the *past*. The show is *Under Suspicion*."

"What's that?"

"I keep forgetting that you're a genius about film but refuse to learn anything about television. It's a crime show. A news special, really. The concept is to reconstruct cold cases with the help of the people who were affected by them. You were involved in the Susan Dempsey case, and they want you to be part of their next special."

Startled, Frank turned his head and looked again out the window. When would people stop associating him with that awful event?

"So they want to talk to me about Susan Dempsey?" Clarence nodded. "As if I didn't talk enough back then to police, lawyers, studio executives—who, incidentally, were on the verge of dropping me . . . all I did was talk about that damn case. And yet here we are again."

"Frank, I had been waiting for a good time to speak to you about the letter. Now the producer—her name is Laurie Moran—has somehow gotten my number. She has called twice today already. If you want, we can say you're too busy doing edits on *The Dangerous*

Ones. We can even redo a couple of aerial shots in Paris if we have to make you unavailable."

The tinny sound of a pop song played from Clarence's front pants pocket. He pulled out his cell phone and examined the screen. "It's her again. The producer."

"Answer it."

"Are you sure?"

"Did I sound unsure?"

"This is Clarence," he said into the phone.

Frank had gotten where he was by trusting his instincts. Always. As he heard his assistant recite the familiar "I'll give Mr. Parker the message," he held out his palm. Clarence shook his head, but Frank leaned forward, more insistent.

Clarence did as instructed, voicing his displeasure with a loud sigh as he handed him the phone.

"What can I do for you, Ms. Moran?"

"First of all, thank you for taking my call. I know you're a busy man." The woman's voice was friendly but professional. She went on to explain the nature of her television show. Having just heard a similar description from Clarence, Frank was beginning to understand the reenactment concept. "I wanted to make sure you got my letter inviting you to tell your side of the story. We can work around your schedule. We'll come to Los Angeles or whatever other location is most convenient. Or if for some reason you're uncomfortable discussing your contact with Susan, we'll of course make a statement during the show informing viewers you declined to be interviewed."

Clarence had accused Frank of knowing nothing about television, but he was expert enough about entertainment generally to realize this woman could be bluffing. Would anyone really want to watch a show about the Cinderella Murder if he wasn't part of it? If he hung up now, could that stop the production in its tracks? Perhaps. But if they went forward without him, he'd have no control over their portrayal of him. They could place him at the top of their list of people who remained "under suspicion," as the show was called. All he needed was for ticket buyers to boycott his movies.

"I'm afraid I did not learn of your letter until just now, Ms. Moran, or I would have gotten back to you sooner. But, yes, I'll make time for your show." Across the table, Clarence's eyes shot open. "Have you spoken yet to Madison Meyer?"

"We're optimistic that all the relevant witnesses will appear." The producer was keeping her cards close to her vest.

"If Madison's anything like she was the last time I had contact with her, I'd show up at her front door with a camera crew. There's nothing more compelling to an out-of-work actress than the spotlight."

Clarence looked like he was going to jump out of his chair.

"I'll let you work out the details with Clarence," Frank said. "He'll have a look at the calendar and get back to you."

He said good-bye and returned Clarence's phone to him.

"I'll make scheduling excuses until she finally takes the hint?" he asked.

"No. You'll make sure I'm available. And I want to do it in L.A. I want to be a full participant, on the same terms with all the other players."

"Frank, that's a bad—"

"My mind is made up, Clarence, but thank you."

Once Clarence had left him alone, Frank took another sip of his scotch. He had gotten where he was by trusting his instincts, yes, but also because he had a raw talent for controlling the telling of a story. And his instincts were saying that this television show about Susan Dempsey would be just another story for him to control.

Talia watched from the hallway beyond the den as her husband's assistant left the apartment.

She had been married to Frank for ten years. She still remem-

bered calling her parents in Ohio to tell them about the engagement. She'd thought they would be happy to know that her days of
auditioning for bit roles and advertisements were over. They would
no longer have to worry about her living alone in that sketchy apartment complex in Glassell Park. She was getting married, and to a
wealthy, successful, famous director.

Instead, her father had said, "But didn't he have something to do
with the death of that girl?"

She had heard the way her husband had spoken to Clarence and
to that television person on the phone. She knew she had no chance
of changing his mind.

She found herself twisting her wedding ring in circles, watching
the three-carat diamond turn around her finger. She couldn't help
but think that he was making a terrible mistake.

10

Laurie was exhausted by the time the 6 train stopped at her local station, Ninety-Sixth Street and Lexington. As she climbed the stairs up to street level, her new Stuart Weitzman black patent pumps still not broken in, she quickly reminded herself to be grateful for her freedom to ride the subway without fear, like everyone else. A year earlier she wouldn't have dared.

She no longer scanned every face in every crowd for a man with blue eyes. That was the only description her son, Timmy, had been able to offer of the man who had shot his father in the forehead, point-blank, right in front of him. An elderly woman had heard the man say, "Timmy, tell your mother that she's next. Then it's your turn."

For five years, she had been terrified that the man known as Blue Eyes would find and kill her and Timmy, just as he had promised. It had been nearly a year since Blue Eyes was killed by police in a thwarted attempt to carry out his twisted plan. Laurie's fears hadn't entirely died with him, but she was slowly beginning to feel like a normal person again.

Her apartment was only two blocks away, on Ninety-Fourth Street. Once she reached her building, she gave a friendly wave to the usual weeknight doorman on her way to the mailboxes and elevator. "Hey, Ron."

When she reached her front door, she slipped a key into the top bolt first, then a second key into the doorknob, and then secured both locks behind her once she was inside her apartment. She kicked off her heels while she dropped her mail, purse, and briefcase on the console table in the entryway. Next was her suit jacket, which she tossed on top of her bags. She'd find time to put everything away later.

It had been a long day.

She headed straight for the kitchen, pulled an already-open bottle of sauvignon blanc from the refrigerator, and began pouring a glass. "Timmy," she called.

She took a sip and immediately felt the stress of the day begin to peel away. It had been one of those days when she hadn't had time to eat or drink water or check her e-mail. But at least the work had paid off. All the pieces for *Under Suspicion* to cover the Cinderella Murder were coming together.

"Timmy? Did you hear me? Is Grandpa letting you play video games already?"

Ever since Greg was killed, Laurie's father, Leo Farley, had stepped in as a kind of co-parent for Laurie's son, Timmy. Timmy was nine years old now. He'd spent more than half of his life with only Mommy and Grandpa to take care of him.

She couldn't imagine how she would have managed to continue working full-time if it weren't for her father's help. He lived one short block away. Every single day, he walked Timmy to and from school at Saint David's on Eighty-Ninth Street off Fifth Avenue and stayed with Timmy in the apartment until Laurie returned from work. She was far too grateful ever to complain, even when Grandpa allowed Timmy small indulgences like ice cream before dinner or video games before homework.

She suddenly realized that the apartment was completely silent. No sounds of her father talking through a math problem with Timmy. No sounds of Timmy asking his grandfather to repeat all the favorite stories he had already heard from Leo Farley's days with the NYPD: "Tell me about the time you chased a bad guy with a rowboat in Central Park," "Tell me about the time the police horse got away on the West Side Highway." No sounds of videos or games coming from Timmy's iPad.

Silence.

"Timmy?! Dad?!" She bolted from the kitchen so quickly that she completely forgot she was holding a glass. White wine sloshed onto the marble floor. She trekked through it, running into the living room with damp feet. She tried to remind herself that Blue Eyes was dead. They were safe now. But where was her son? Where was Dad?

They were supposed to be here by now. She rushed down the corridor to the den. Her father blinked at her from his comfortable leather chair. His feet were on the hassock.

"Hi, Laurie. What's the rush?"

"Just getting some exercise," Laurie said as she looked over to the sofa, where Timmy was curled up with a book in his hands.

"He was wiped out from soccer," Leo explained. "I could see his head dropping even on the walk home from school. I knew he'd fall asleep the minute he settled down." He looked at his watch. "Oh boy. We're going on two hours. He'll be up all night now. Sorry, Laurie."

"No, it's fine. I'm—"

"Hey," he said. "You're white as a sheet. What's going on?"

"I'm. It's just—"

"You were scared."

"Yes. For a moment."

"It's all right." He sat up in his chair, reached for her hand, and gave it a comforting squeeze.

She might have been taking the subway matter-of-factly like everyone else these days, but she still wasn't normal. When would things be normal?

"Timmy," her father said. "He said something about wanting takeout Indian food. Who's ever heard of a nine-year-old who likes lamb *saagwala*?"

At the sound of their voices, Timmy's eyes opened. He jumped up to give her a big bear hug. His enormous brown eyes, all expression and lashes, blinked up at her. She bent down to get closer to him. His head was still warm and smelled like sleep. She didn't need a glass of wine to feel like she was home.

Three hours later, Timmy's homework was done, the leftover takeout had been stored away, and Timmy—after enjoying his traditional "nighttime snack"—was tucked into bed.

Laurie returned to the table, where Leo was finishing a second cup of coffee. "Thank you, Dad," she said simply.

"Because I called for takeout?"

"No, I mean, for everything. For every day."

"Come on, Laurie. You know it's the best job I've ever had. Now, is it just my imagination, or were Timmy and I not the only people in this apartment who were a little tired this evening? I swear, sometimes I think you're right about that psychic connection you talk about."

When Timmy was born, Laurie was convinced that she and her son shared some inexplicable link that required neither words nor even physical contact. She would wake up in the middle of the night, certain that something was wrong, only to find dark silence. Invariably, within seconds, the baby monitor would crackle with the sounds of crying. Even tonight, hadn't she had a hankering for chicken *tikka masala* during the subway ride home?

"Of course I'm right," she said with a smile. "I'm always right, about everything. And so are you about my being a little tired. Only it's more than a little. I had a long day."

She told him about Brett Young's conditional approval of featuring the Cinderella Murder in the next installment of *Under Suspicion*, followed by her phone call to Frank Parker.

"Did he sound like a murderer?" Leo asked.

"You're the one who taught me that the coldest, cruelest creatures can also be the most charming."

He fell silent.

"I know you still worry about me, Dad."

"Of course I do, just like you worried about me and Timmy when you came home today. Blue Eyes may be gone, but the very nature of your show means you've got a good chance, every single time, of being in the room with a killer."

"You don't need to remind me. But I always have Grace and Jerry with me. I have a camera crew. Someone is with me at all times. I'm probably safer at work than I am walking down the street."

"Oh, that's really comforting."

"I'm perfectly safe, Dad. Frank Parker has a huge career now. He's not stupid. Even if he was the one who killed Susan Dempsey, the last thing he's going to do is expose himself by trying to hurt me."

"Well, I'd feel better if Alex were one of those people who was always around you at work. Is he available for this project?"

"I'm keeping my fingers crossed, but Alex has a law practice to run, Dad. He doesn't need a second full-time job as a television personality."

"That's all a story, and you know it. The more he's on TV, the more business he gets for his practice."

"Well, hopefully he'll be on board." Quickly she added, "And not because of your reason, but because no one could be better than he was on the show."

"And because you both like being together."

"I can't get past those detective skills, can I?" She smiled and patted his knee, temporarily putting the issue to rest. "Frank Parker said something interesting today. He suggested that the best way to get Madison Meyer to commit to the show would be to appear at her house with a television crew."

"It makes sense, like waving a needle in front of a junkie. You said her career is all but dead. When she actually sees how quickly she could be back in the spotlight, she might have a hard time saying no."

"And it's Los Angeles," she said, thinking aloud. "I can probably get a skeleton camera crew on a budget. With Madison, Parker, and Susan's mother on board, I can't imagine Brett not giving me the all-clear."

She picked up her phone from the coffee table and sent texts to Jerry and Grace: "Pack a bag for warm weather. We're heading to L.A. first thing in the morning."

The following afternoon in Los Angeles, Laurie pulled their rental van to the curb and double-checked the address against the one she had entered into the GPS. Jerry and the small production team they'd hired for the day—just a sound guy and two cameramen shooting handhelds—were already jumping out of the back, but Grace asked, "Everything okay? You look hesitant."

Sometimes it gave her the willies how well Grace could read her. Now that they were here, unannounced, at Madison Meyer's last known address, she was wondering if this was an insane idea.

Oh well, she told herself. This is reality television. She had to take risks. "No problem," she said, turning off the engine. "Just making sure we're in the right place."

"Not exactly Beverly Hills, is it?" Grace observed.

The ranch house was tiny, its blue paint starting to peel. The grass looked like it hadn't been mowed for a month. The weathered planter boxes beneath the front windows contained nothing but dirt.

Laurie led the way to the front door, Grace and Jerry at her heels, the camera crew close behind. She rang the bell, once, then twice more, before she saw a set of red fingernails pull back curtains from the adjacent window. Two minutes later, a woman she recognized as Madison Meyer finally opened the door. Based on the fresh lipstick that matched the fingernails, Laurie guessed that Madison had done a quick touch-up before meeting her newly arrived guests.

"Madison, my name is Laurie Moran. I'm a producer with Fisher Blake Studios, and I want to give you airtime on a show with more than ten million viewers."

The house was cramped and messy. Magazines were strewn randomly around the living room, on the sofa, on the coffee table, in a pile on the floor next to the television. Most of them seemed to be celebrity magazines with important features like "Who Wore It Better?" and "Guess Which Couple Is About to Split?" Two narrow bookshelves that lined the wall by the entryway were packed with memorabilia from Madison's short-lived success as an actress. At the center was the statuette she had received for her first role, the one Frank Parker had gifted her after Susan supposedly never showed up for her audition: a Spirit Award, not an Oscar, but still a sign of a budding career. But from Laurie's research, she gathered that Madison had gone nowhere but down after that one recognition.

"Did you get the letter I sent you, Miss Meyer?"

"I don't think so. Or maybe I did and I just wanted to see whether you'd be following up." She smiled coyly.

Laurie returned the smile. "Well, consider this the follow-up." She introduced Jerry and Grace, who both shook Madison's hand. "Have you heard of the special series *Under Suspicion*?"

"Oh yes," Madison said. "I watched the one last year. I even joked it was only a matter of time before someone came calling about my college roommate. I assume that's why you're here?"

"As you know," Laurie said, "there has been speculation over the years about whether you covered for Frank Parker. You said you were with him at his house at the time of Susan's death."

Madison opened her mouth to speak but then pressed her lips together and nodded slowly. Close up and in person, Laurie could see that Madison had retained her beauty. She had long, shiny blond hair; a heart-shaped face; and piercing green eyes. Her skin was still pale and clear. But Laurie could also see the changes that time had brought to Madison's face, as well as Madison's attempts to forestall them. A tell-tale stripe of mousy brown revealed she was due for another dye job. Her forehead was unnaturally smooth, her cheeks and lips plumped by fillers. She was still a gorgeous woman, but Laurie wondered whether she'd have been even more beautiful without all the intervention.

"That's true," Madison said. "I mean, the part about people speculating."

"You have nothing to say about that?" Laurie pressed.

"Am I the first person you asked? That letter you mailed seemed pretty generic."

"Ah, so now you *do* recall the letter," Laurie said, arching a brow. "You're right: we did ask others. We try to bring as many people who knew the victim as possible to—"

"So who are the other people? Who has committed?"

Laurie didn't see the harm in Madison's question. "Susan's mother. Your other roommate, Nicole Melling, is interested. Frank Parker."

Madison's green eyes sparkled at the mention of the director's name. "I assume your show pays?" she asked.

"Of course. Maybe not what a studio movie might pay, but I think you'll find the compensation to be fair." Laurie knew that Madison hadn't had any studio film offers for a decade.

"Then I'll have my agent call you to talk terms before I'll say any-thing on camera. Oh, and you." She looked directly at the two men with cameras. "When it comes time to shoot, the left is my good side. And no backlighting. It makes me look old."

As Laurie made her way back to the rental car, she allowed her-self to smile. Madison Meyer was playing hard to get, but she was already talking like the diva of the set.

11

Some people were just creatures of habit.

Not Madison. Heck, Madison wasn't even her name. Her real name was Meredith Morris. How old-fashioned was that? There wasn't even a cute nickname she could make out of it. She'd tried Merry, but people thought she was saying Mary. Then she tried Red, but that didn't even make sense for a blonde. But she always liked the alliteration. When she enrolled at UCLA to appease her parents, she changed her name to Madison Meyer, determined to get discovered by Hollywood.

In various stages of her life, she had been a vegetarian, a gun owner, a libertarian, a conservative, a liberal. She'd been married, and divorced, three times. She had dated actors, bankers, lawyers, waiters, even a farmer. Madison was constantly changing. The only constant was that she wanted to be a star.

But as Madison was to reinvention, Keith Ratner was to habit. Even back in college, he'd flirted, danced, and occasionally snuck off with Madison and other girls. But he always, always, always went back to his beloved Susan. He was loyal in his own crazy way, like a bigamist who insisted his only crime was loving his wives too much to disappoint them.

And just as Madison had always known Keith would never quit his high school girlfriend, she was confident she would find him at his usual haunt, a lounge celebrities liked called Teddy's, in the far front corner of the Roosevelt Hotel. He was even sitting in the same banquette where she'd last seen him here, about six months earlier. She should have called him Rain Man, that's how much Keith Ratner liked a routine. She was even fairly certain she could identify the clear liquid in his glass.

"Let me guess," she said by way of greeting. "Patrón Silver on the rocks?"

His face broke out into a broad smile. Twenty years later, and that smile still sent a chill up her spine. "Nope," he said, jiggling his glass. "I still love this place, but I've been a club soda guy for years. From here I'll hit Twenty-Four Hour Fitness for some cross-training."

Several years ago, at the height of Keith's television career, Madison had seen an interview highlighting his commitment to physical health, volunteer work, and his do-gooder church. It all seemed like a PR stunt to her, but here he was, in his favorite bar, sipping soda water.

"Still trying to convince everyone you're a reformed soul?" she asked.

"Clean body, clean mind."

She waved over a waitress and ordered herself a cucumber martini. "Vodka's clean enough by my standards."

"Speaking of standards," Keith teased, "how did the likes of you get past the red velvet rope?"

Madison's celebrity had taken off before his, thanks to her role in *Beauty Land*, Frank Parker's first major film. But Keith's career hadn't died like hers. If only he knew how close his comment cut to the bone. She had, in fact, slipped the bouncer a twenty to get in.

"I knew I'd find you here," she said.

"So this isn't a chance encounter?"

Keith obviously still knew the power he had over her. Madison recalled the first time she met him, as a freshman at UCLA. She'd shown up to an open casting call for some horrible musical based on the life of Jackson Pollock. Keith was there to audition for Pollock, she for the artist's wife, Lee Krasner. Madison could tell as they read their lines that they were both having a hard time suppressing laughter at the terrible dialogue. They finally burst into giggles when the casting agent declared that they were both "far too good-looking for this project." They headed straight from the audition to a nearby bar, where Keith knew a bartender willing to serve them despite their age. When he kissed her, it was her first taste of whiskey.

She didn't even know that he attended UCLA until she spotted him in Wilson Plaza, holding hands with a girl she recognized from her History of Theater class. Blond, pretty, a less primped version of Madison herself. Madison made a point of befriending Susan Dempsey the very next day, quickly learning that she'd come to UCLA with her high school boyfriend. Keith wasn't happy about his girlfriend's newest friendship, but there wasn't much he could say about it, was there?

Keith had Susan, so Madison moved on to other relationships, too. But they continued their dalliances. When Madison upped the ante by moving in with Susan sophomore year, it only seemed to make their secret rendezvous more exciting.

All that changed after Susan's murder. Keith stopped calling and brushed Madison off when she called him. Not long after she finished shooting *Beauty Land*, he dropped out of college. He told everyone he had landed a major agent who had big plans for him. But whispers in the theater department speculated that he was so broken up about Susan's murder than he could hardly function, let alone attend school or launch an acting career. Supposedly he had found Jesus. Other, less kind whispers suggested that his departure was proof that he'd had something to do with Susan's death after all.

Now, twenty years later, time had been easier on him than on Madison, as always seemed to be the case with men. Somehow the lines on his thin, angular face made him even more handsome. The dark, tousled hair that had pegged him as a rocker type when he was a college freshman now came off as comfortable and confident. He occasionally showed up as a featured guest on a one-hour network drama and had even had a small part in an indie film the previous year. But even so, Madison hadn't seen him in a regular gig since his cable sitcom was canceled four years earlier. Keith needed *Under Suspicion* almost as much as she did.

"Not a chance encounter," she confirmed, just as the waitress returned with her drink. She took a seat next to him and smiled.

"Uh-oh. It's been a while, but I know that look. You want something."

"Did you get contacted by a TV producer named Laurie Moran?"

"Oh, I get contacted by so *many* projects, I can't keep them all straight." Now he was the one smiling. He was still a ham, a completely charming ham.

"It's for *Under Suspicion*," she said. "They want to do a show about Susan's murder. They must have contacted you."

He looked away and took a sip of his drink. When he spoke, the lighthearted tone was absent. "I don't want anything to do with it. What's the point in rehashing everything that happened back then? They're really doing it?"

"Sounds like it."

"Do you know who else is in?"

"Susan's mother, Rosemary. Nicole, wherever she disappeared to. Apparently her last name's Melling now. And the person I think you'll really be interested in: Frank Parker."

When Keith heard that Madison had landed the role in *Beauty Land*, he had shown up outside her dorm. He was drunk and yelled, "How could you? That man killed my Susan, and everyone knows it. All you ever will be is a cheaper, lesser version of her!" It was the only time he had made her cry.

"I'm surprised they got anyone to go along with the show, other than Rosemary," he said.

"Well, I for one am doing it. If we play our cards right, it could help us both. Millions of people watch that show. It's exposure." She didn't add that she also hoped to persuade Frank Parker to find a role for her in his next project.

"I'll think about it. Is that it?"

"What I really need, Keith, is your word."

"And what word might that be? A secret, magical word?" The playful smile had returned.

"I mean it," she said. "No one can ever know about us."

"It was twenty years ago, Madison. We were all kids. You really think anyone will care that you and I played footsie on occasion?"

Was that all I was to him? she thought. "Of course they'll care. Susan was—perfect Susan: smart, talented, the whole package. I was—how did you word it? The other beauty, but *a cheaper, lesser version*. You know that the producers will portray Nicole as the good, loyal friend. I'll be the rival drama queen." Madison knew that the friendship between Susan and Nicole hadn't been nearly as perfect as the media had made it seem in the aftermath of Susan's death. "There are still people on the Internet saying I must have killed Susan or at least faked an alibi for Frank Parker, so I could get the role in *Beauty Land*. If the world finds out I was sneaking around with Saint Susan's boyfriend, they'll really think I did it."

"Well, maybe you did." She couldn't tell whether he was teasing or serious.

"Or maybe you did," she sniped, "just like Susan's parents always thought. It won't look good that you had something going with your girlfriend's own roommate."

"Mutual destruction," he said, staring at the empty glass he was now spinning in his hand.

"So I have your word?"

"Word," he said, pointing at her. "We never happened. Forget all our cozy little get-togethers. Our secret dies with us."

12

Once Madison was out of view, Keith pulled his cell phone from his jeans pocket, scrolled through his favorite contacts, and tapped on the entry listed as "AG." Very few people had this particular phone number. Keith had gotten it five years earlier, and that was after fifteen years of dedicated service. At the time, his career was on a roll. He chose to believe that it was the decade and a half of loyalty, not the fleeting appearance of fame or the financial rewards that came with it, that had led to this privilege.

"Yes?" the voice on the other line said. All these years later, and Keith still thought this voice was one of the strangest he'd ever heard. High-pitched like a child's, but completely confident and controlled.

"I have more information about the television show I told you about."

"Yes?"

"Apparently they are going forward with production. My understanding is that everyone else is getting pulled in: Frank Parker, Susan's mother, Madison Meyer, Nicole."

"Nicole. You're certain?"

With a source like Madison, how could Keith possibly be sure? That woman would lie, steal, cheat—maybe even kill—to get what she wanted. Wasn't that why he'd been drawn to her back then? She was dark and dangerous—everything Susan was not. But, as much as she'd been trying to manipulate him, seeking him out here at Teddy's, he didn't think she was lying about other people's signing on to appear on the show. "Yes, I'm almost positive." He knew to include the word "almost." You didn't get access to this phone number by withholding any tiny kernel of truth.

"Did they say anything else about Nicole?" the voice asked.

"Her last name is apparently Melling now. That's all I know."

There was a pause before the voice continued. "It will be better if you participate."

Keith had been afraid Martin would say that. Money in Keith's pocket meant more tithing, not to mention the help Keith could give to the church's reputation if he were back in the spotlight. Keith reminded himself that the church focused on fund-raising to advance its mission of helping the poor, but he really didn't want to do this show.

"Susan's mother has always suspected me of killing her daughter. I can only imagine what she'll say about me. And I've been public about my religion. It could make the church look bad."

"You're an actor. Charm the producers. And be sure to report back with any new information on Nicole."

"She's been off the radar for twenty years. Why the curiosity?"

"You let me worry about my own enemies."

When the line went dead, Keith Ratner was glad that he hadn't made an adversary of the man on the other end of the line. He intended to keep it that way at all costs.

13

Three hundred fifty miles away, in downtown San Francisco, Steve Roman's cell phone rang. The screen identified the caller as "AG."

He felt himself smile. The directive that Steve move to the Bay Area was a sure sign that he was trusted, but he missed seeing Martin Collins in person. Maybe the church would ask him to return to Los Angeles. Or perhaps Martin would be coming north for another big revival.

"Steve Roman," he answered. Steve, like Steve McQueen. Roman, like a gladiator.

"You're well?" Martin never identified himself during phone calls. It wasn't necessary. Anyone who had witnessed one of Martin's sermons knew the distinctive sound of his voice. Steve had first heard Martin's voice when a friend brought him to a revival in the basement of a Westwood tattoo parlor fifteen years earlier. Since then, he'd listened to Martin's preaching for hours—in person, on cassette tapes and then CDs, and now via streaming audio from the Internet.

Over the years, Steve had worked his way closer and closer to the inner circle. Advocates for God used a circle metaphor for a member's relationship to the church. It wasn't a hierarchy. Martin wasn't the top; he was the *center*. And through the center, the word of God could be heard.

"Yes," Steve responded. "Thank you, as ever, for the opportunity."

When Martin decided to expand AG's reach beyond his Southern California megachurch, he had dispatched Steve here. Even though Steve preferred the sunny glow and glitz of Southern California to the gloomy, windy Bay Area, he always expressed gratitude to AG for the opportunity. The church had found a studio apartment for him above Market Street and secured a job for him with a home-alarm company, Keepsafe.

Mostly, he was thankful for his new identity. He no longer used drugs. He didn't hurt people anymore. With the help of Martin Collins and AG, he was on a path to find himself by serving the Lord and the poor. He had even transformed himself physically. Before he ventured into the basement of that tattoo parlor, he had been skinny, with long straggly hair, often unwashed. Now he did a hundred sit-ups and push-ups every single day. He ate healthfully. He kept his hair shaved close to the scalp. He was hard, lean, and clean.

"Do you need something?" Steve offered.

Steve thought of himself as Advocates for God's own private investigator. He gathered dirt on former church members who tried to sully AG's reputation, often by slipping in and out of the homes of Keepsafe's customers unnoticed. When Martin got wind that a federal prosecutor was looking into the church's finances, it was Steve who had conducted the surveillance to prove the lawyer was cheating on his wife. Steve was never certain how Martin handled the crisis, but once he gave Martin photographic proof of the affair, the murmurs of an investigation disappeared.

His work for AG wasn't always strictly legal, but Martin—and Steve—saw it as a necessary evil to keep tabs on people who tried to suppress the church and its good works.

"Yes. I need you to keep an eye on someone. And to send a message when the time is right."

There was something about the way that Martin said "send a

message" that made Steve's skin prickle. Steve closed his eyes and thought to himself, Please, no, not that.

He accepted this life, in a noise-filled studio overlooking a traffic-filled street, in a city where he knew no one, because he was a better person here than he had ever been when he made his own choices. It had been years since he'd inflicted physical pain upon another living being. What if he tried it again and liked it too much? But then he reminded himself not to question the supreme Advocate for God.

"Whatever you need."

14

According to Nicole Melling's GPS, the drive to Palo Alto was supposed to take less than an hour once she hit the Golden Gate Bridge. Clearly her car's computer system hadn't taken traffic into account. She was stuck in yet another stretch of gridlock, this time through Daly City.

She looked up at the endless rows of nondescript houses packed on the hillside above I-280. What was that song someone—Pete Seeger, perhaps?—had written about this suburb? Little boxes, on the hillside, all the same, all made of "ticky tacky."

Nicole had a sudden memory of herself at barely seventeen years old. Thanks to her skipping fifth grade, she had been a full year younger than the other seniors ready to graduate, but still years beyond them academically. She had gotten into every school she applied to: Harvard, Princeton, Stanford, all of them. But her parents had been trapped in an income bubble—too rich for financial aid, too poor for private tuition. The plan had been for Nicole to attend UC Berkeley, but then the letter came in the mail: on-campus housing was full. She would need to find an apartment.

She remembered pleading with her father, the letter from Berkeley unfolded in front of him like a pink slip on the kitchen table. "I can do it, Dad. I'll spend all my time in classes and the library anyway, so it's only a matter of walking to and from campus once a day.

Just a few blocks. They even have safety monitors to walk you home after dark."

He had avoided eye contact with her as he endlessly twirled spaghetti around his fork. "You're too young, Nicky. You're just a girl. And it's *Berkeley*." He said it like it was a war-torn country on the opposite side of the world, instead of a six-hour drive from their home in Irvine.

"Mom, please. Tell him. I've never gotten into any trouble. Ask any teachers at school. I do everything I'm supposed to do, all the time. I follow every rule. I can be trusted."

Her mother was banging dishes around in the sink, but even in profile, Nicole could see her pursed lips. "We know all that, Nicky. But we won't be there. Your teachers won't be there. No one will be there to set the rules for you."

It was only when Nicole started to cry that her mother finally turned off the running water, joined them at the table, and grasped both of Nicole's hands in hers. "We know you, Nicole. I know you better than I even know myself, because you're my baby. We can't let you get *lost*."

Nicole remembered looking to her father for some explanation, but he just nodded once at the certitude of her mother's statement and continued to twirl his pasta.

Nicole had no idea what her parents meant at the time, but it would soon become apparent that her parents had indeed known their only daughter. Just like her family's income bubble, young Nicole had been in a bubble of her own—her intelligence robust, but her personality still . . . inchoate. They had feared that she would be lost in the crowd. Unfortunately, her fate was worse.

The sound of a car horn brought her back to the present. Noticing the short stretch of open road in front of her, she gave a friendly wave to the honking driver behind her and pulled forward.

According to the GPS, she had twenty-nine more miles to go. Nicole hadn't seen Dwight Cook since college, but she had read about him in the newspaper. Everyone in America had.

A full hour later, Nicole pulled into the crowded parking lot of an office park. The sleek glass buildings were surrounded by grass so green it looked spray painted. Above the entrance of the main building, giant purple letters spelled out the company name: REACH.

The young woman behind the high-gloss white desk in the lobby had piercings on the left side of her nose and through her right eyebrow. Nicole resisted the temptation to ask if her face felt crooked.

"Nicole Hunter, here to see Mr. Cook. I have an appointment." For the first time in nearly eighteen years, she had used her maiden name when she had called. Even then, she hadn't been certain that Dwight would remember her.

Nicole knew other people who still kept up with their college friends. Her neighbor Jenny had gone to school in New York but organized Bay Area mini-reunions once a year. And she knew from other friends that their Facebook pages were filled with shared photographs and remember-whens.

Of course, Nicole couldn't even have a Facebook page. It would undermine the very purpose of having a clean slate with a new last name in a new city.

But even without her special circumstances, Nicole wouldn't have stayed in touch with her college crowd. She never really had friends at UCLA, other than Susan. How lucky she had been to get paired with someone like her—someone who looked after her. She had won the roommate lottery.

It had been just the two of them freshman year. Then sophomore year, Susan had brought in Madison—a fellow actress from the theater department—because they could get a better suite if they took a triple.

It was also through Susan that Nicole had first met Dwight Cook,

who would go on to launch REACH the summer after his sophomore year in college.

"Nicole!"

She looked up at the sound of her name. The lobby was designed
as an atrium, open from the floor to the glass ceiling three floors up.
Dwight was looking down at her from the top of a circular staircase.

Once he had descended to the ground floor, he smiled awk-
wardly. "You look the same."

"As do you," she said, even though it stretched the truth. His face
was different—paler, fuller. His hairline was beginning to recede.

But his attire seemed like a retread of her memories: high-waisted
blue jeans and an ill-fitting Atari T-shirt that had already been retro
when they were college freshmen. Even more startlingly familiar
were his mannerisms. The jittery gaze and excessive blinking had
been noticeable in an awkward teenager but were even more so in a
grown man who was probably close to being a billionaire.

He led the way past the pierced receptionist, down a long hallway of offices. Most of the workers appeared to be in their twenties,
many of them perched on top of giant fitness balls instead of traditional office chairs. At the end of the hall, he opened a door, and
they walked into a courtyard behind the building. Four people were
shooting hoops on a nearby court.

He didn't wait for her to sit before taking a spot on a cushioned
chaise. She did the same, knowing he hadn't meant to be rude.

"You said you wanted to talk about Susan."

Again, she wasn't offended by the lack of small talk. He might
have been considered a king of Silicon Valley, but she could already
tell he was still the same uncomfortable kid who had worked in the
campus computer-science lab with Susan.

He sat affectless as Nicole told him about the show, *Under Suspicion*, and the possibility that they would be featuring Susan's case.
"Did you get a letter from the producer?" she asked.

He shook his head. "Once Susan's murder became a story about Hollywood, no one seemed to care that she was also a brilliant programmer. I doubt the producer even realizes we knew each other."

Back in college, it had taken Nicole a few outings as a trio—her, Susan, Dwight—to realize that Susan had been hoping to play Cupid between her lab partner and freshman dorm-mate. On one level, the pairing made sense: both Dwight and Nicole were off the charts in raw intelligence. And now that Nicole saw it for what it was, they were both—let's face it—peculiar. They were both projects for Susan, who tried her best to coax them from their shells. Dwight found comfort in computers. Nicole eventually found it in—well, she didn't like to think about that part of her past.

But after only two dates, Nicole had realized the fundamental difference between Dwight and her. Her oddness was short-lived. She had been young, sheltered, and so busy succeeding that she'd never learned how to exercise independent thought. She just had to find her way. Dwight's "issues" ran deeper. Nowadays, they'd probably say he was somewhere "on the spectrum."

At the time, Nicole thought that made her the better catch. But she hadn't learned the hard way—not yet—how dangerous a young, brilliant woman's desire to find her own way could be.

"Well, that's why I came here, Dwight. I'd like to tell the show about your friendship with Susan. How she had another side to her."

Dwight was looking in the direction of her face, as he had probably learned people expected him to do during a conversation, but he wasn't really connecting to her. "Of course. Susan was always so kind to me. She looked after me. I was lucky we happened to work for the same professor, or I never would have met her."

In other words, he felt the way she did about winning the roommate lottery.

"So I can tell Laurie Moran you'll help with the show? Appear on camera?"

He nodded again. "Anything to help. Anything for Susan. Should I ask Hathaway, too?"

"Hathaway?"

"Richard Hathaway. Our professor. That's how Susan and I met."

"Oh, I hadn't thought of him. Is he still at UCLA? Have you kept in touch?"

"He's retired from the university, but we're definitely in touch. He works right here at REACH."

"How funny to have your former professor in your employ."

"More like a partner, really. He's helped me from day one. I'm sure he'd be willing to help with the show, too."

Nicole wondered whether Dwight found comfort in keeping his college mentor close, someone who knew him before he was a twenty-year-old millionaire on the cover of *Wired* magazine. "Sure," she said. "That would be great."

She almost felt guilty for pulling Dwight Cook into this. He was the head of REACH, a tech company that had become a household name in the 1990s by changing the way people searched for information on the Internet. She had no idea what they worked on now, but from the looks of these grounds, Dwight was still a major player in the tech world.

But that was exactly why Nicole had come to Palo Alto. Frank Parker had become a famous director, but Dwight was a kind of celebrity in his own right. The more high-profile people who were involved in the production, the less screen time the show would devote to the roommate who dropped out after her sophomore year, changed her name, and never went back to Los Angeles again.

Once Nicole was in her car, she pulled Laurie Moran's letter from her purse and dialed her office number on her cell phone.

"Ms. Moran, it's Nicole Melling. You contacted me about my college roommate, Susan Dempsey?"

"Yes." Nicole heard the rustling of a plastic bag in the background and wondered if she had caught the producer midlunch. "Please, call me Laurie. I'm so happy to hear from you. Are you familiar with *Under Suspicion?*"

"I am," Nicole confirmed.

"As you probably know, the name of our show indicates that we go back and talk to the people who have remained literally under suspicion in cold cases. Obviously you don't fit that bill, but you and Susan's mother will remind viewers that Susan was a real person. She wasn't just the pretty girl with an aspiring actress's headshot. She wasn't Cinderella."

Nicole understood why Susan's mother put so much stock into this producer.

"If you think your show can help bring attention back to Susan's case, I'm happy to help."

"That's fantastic."

"And I hope you don't mind, but I took the liberty of contacting another college friend of Susan." She briefly described Dwight Cook's working relationship with Susan in the computer lab, followed by the news that Dwight was willing to participate in the show. The producer sounded thrilled, just as Nicole expected.

As Nicole pulled out of the office park's lot, she looked in the rearview mirror and felt incredibly proud of Dwight Cook. Susan's death had presented a gigantic challenge to the lives of everyone she knew. Both Nicole and Keith Ratner had quit college. Rosemary had told her she barely left her bed for a full year.

But somehow Dwight had managed to create something transformative in the aftermath. She wondered if whatever made him different from other people had enabled him to channel his grief in a way the rest of them could not.

She was so wrapped up in her own thoughts that she never saw the off-white pickup truck pull out of the parking lot behind her.

15

Dwight Cook closed and locked the door to his office, located far from most of REACH's employees. That was the way he liked it.

Dwight constantly felt all these kids looking at him, wanting to know the tall, lanky billionaire who still dressed like a teenage nerd but was nevertheless pursued by several well-known supermodels. His employees assumed that Dwight's office was isolated because he did not want to be disturbed. The truth was that Dwight could not possibly run this business the way it needed to be run if he made too many connections to the people who worked for him.

Dwight had realized in middle school that he wasn't like other people. It wasn't that his own behavior was so unusual, at least not that he could determine. Instead, he was different in his *reactions* to other people. It was as if he heard voices more loudly, perceived movements to be bigger and faster, and felt every single handshake and hug more intensely. Some people—too many of them—were simply too *much* for him.

For one year, in ninth grade, his school placed him on a "special" education track, suspecting that he suffered from some form of "autism-related disorder," despite the absence of an official diagnosis. He remained in regular classes and still dominated the grading curves. But the teachers treated him differently. They stood a little farther from him, spoke more slowly. He had been labeled.

On the last day of school, he told his parents that he would run away unless he could start tenth grade in a new school. No special treatment, no labels. Because although Dwight was different from other people, he'd read enough books about autism, Asperger's, ADD, and ADHD to know that those labels didn't apply to him. Each of those conditions was supposedly accompanied by a lack of emotional connection. Dwight, in his view, was the opposite. He had the ability to feel so connected to a person that the sensation was overwhelming.

Take today's reunion with Nicole, for example. He had forced himself to sit still in his seat across from her, to not touch her. He had a hard time maintaining eye contact because to hold her gaze too long would have brought him to tears. She was a living, breathing, vivid memory of Susan. He couldn't look at her without remembering the searing pain he had felt at Susan's kindhearted attempts to play matchmaker between him and Nicole. How could Susan have been blind to the fact that he loved her?

He hit the space bar of his computer's keyboard to wake up the screen. Every once in a while, misperceptions about him came in handy. Right now, for instance, the physical separation between him and his employees would ensure that nothing interrupted his activities.

He opened the Internet browser and Googled "Cinderella Murder Susan Dempsey." He suppressed a bite of anger at the fact that even *he* used Google most of the time as his search engine. REACH was a pioneer in changing the way people searched for information on the Internet. But then Google came along, extended the idea a step or two, and added some cool graphics and a name that was fun to say. The rest was high-tech history.

Still, Dwight couldn't complain about his success. He'd made enough money to live comfortably for ten lifetimes.

He clicked through the search results. He found nothing new

since the last time—probably a year ago—that he had checked for any developments about his friend's unsolved murder.

He remembered sitting at his computer twenty years earlier, knowing that he was probably among the top twenty people in the world when it came to maneuvering his way around the quickly changing online world. Back then, people still used telephones and in-person conversations to convey information. The police department produced hard copies of reports and faxed them to prosecutors. He had wanted to know the truth about the investigation into Susan's death so desperately—who knew what? What did the police know?—but his skills could only get him so far at the time. The information simply wasn't digitized.

Now every private thought had a way of casting a technological footprint that he could track. But he was the founder, chairman, and CEO of a Fortune 500 company, and hacking into private servers and e-mail accounts was a serious crime.

He closed his eyes and pictured Susan. How many times had he sat outside her dorm, hoping to catch a glimpse of her as she led an entirely separate life from the one they had together at the lab? This television show would be a onetime opportunity—every suspect on camera, questioned anew. Frank Parker, the man who seemed to care more about the success of his movie than Susan's death. Madison Meyer, who always seemed resentful of Nicole and Susan. Keith Ratner, who never realized how lucky he was to have a girl like Susan.

Being on this television show would be a small price to pay. He would know far more than even the show's producers. Dwight spun his office chair in a circle and cracked his knuckles.

It was time to get to work.

16

Laurie checked the time on her computer screen once again. Two forty-five P.M. Surely Brett Young was back from lunch by now. She had called him yesterday from Los Angeles and left a voice mail with an update. This morning, she had e-mailed him a more complete summary of the Susan Dempsey case. Still no response.

She closed her office door and allowed herself to kick off her pumps and lie down on the white sofa beneath her windows. Flying out to Los Angeles, just to catch Madison Meyer unguarded, had taken its toll. The coast-to-coast red-eye was unbearable, but not so much as being away from Timmy any longer than necessary. She was feeling the sleep deprivation now. She shut her eyes and took a deep breath. She just needed a little rest.

Before she knew it, she was no longer in her office above Rockefeller Center. She was in another place, in a different time. She recognized the playground on Fifteenth Street, back when they still lived downtown.

Timmy is so tiny, only three years old. His legs are straight in front of him, like pins, as he squeals from the swing. "Whheeeee! Higher, Daddy, higher!"

She knows precisely what day this is. She knows what will happen next, even though she was not there to see it with her own eyes. She has replayed this scene countless times.

As Greg pushes his son once more on the swing, he lets out a grunt, feigning physical exertion, even as he is careful not to let his toddler sail too high. As an emergency room doctor, he has seen more than his fair share of children injured during overly exuberant play. "This is the last one," he announces. "Time to go home and see Mommy. One-minute warning."

"Doctor!" a voice calls out.

In the last of countless selfless demonstrations of his love for his son, Greg sees the gun and steps away from Timmy in an attempt to pull this stranger's attention from the boy.

A gunshot.

"DADDY!!!"

Laurie bolted upright at the sound of her son's scream.

Grace was staring at her from the doorway, her hand still on the office doorknob.

"I'm sorry. I didn't mean to surprise you. I knocked but you didn't answer."

"It's okay," Laurie assured her, even though she knew she wasn't really okay. Would the nightmares ever end? "I must have dozed off. That red-eye was a killer." She felt a pang in her chest as the last word left her mouth.

"Really? I slept the whole way and feel fine," she said.

Laurie resisted the temptation to throw a pillow at Grace's sky-high upsweep. "And that's the difference between being twenty-six and thirty-seven. Anyway, what's up?"

"Brett called. He wants to see you in his office."

Laurie ran her fingers through her hair. Nothing like seeing your boss for an important meeting straight from a nap.

"You look fine," Grace said. "Good luck, Laurie. I know how much you want this."

17

Brett's secretary, Jennifer, waved Laurie past her guard station into the inner sanctum. But when Laurie opened Brett's office door, she didn't find Brett alone. A second man was in one of his guest chairs, his back to the door.

"Excellent timing," Brett declared, rising from his desk. "Look who we have here."

The second man also stood, and then turned to greet her. It was Alex Buckley. A former college basketball player, he rose at least four inches taller than Brett. She hadn't seen him for at least a month, but he was as gorgeous as she remembered. No wonder juries and television cameras loved him. She took in his dark, wavy hair; firm chin; and blue-green eyes behind black-rimmed glasses. Everything about his appearance made him seem strong and trustworthy.

She was glad that Brett was now positioned behind Alex so her boss could not see the way Alex was looking at her. It was the way he always looked at her when she walked into a room. Though he was clearly happy to see her, there was a tinge of sadness—almost longing—in his eyes. That look made her feel like she needed to apologize—both to Greg for somehow making another man feel that way about her, and to Alex for not being able to return the feelings he so obviously had for her (at least, not yet).

She looked away before either Alex or Brett could sense her thoughts. "What a nice surprise," she said with a smile. She held out her hand for a shake, and he leaned in for a quick hug.

She pulled her pencil skirt to her knees before taking the unoccupied chair across from Brett's desk.

"I know I've kept you on pins and needles all day, Laurie. But I wanted to make sure I had all the facts on your pitch for the Cinderella Murder. Your summary was helpful. But it also made it clear that your budget's going to skyrocket."

"Our costs are low compared to what we can bring in in ad revenue—"

Brett held up a palm to silence her. "I don't need you to explain the economics of television to me. You're planning to interview people who are sprawled all over the state of California, one of the most expensive places to film, by the way. Not to mention that last-minute trip you already made yesterday, just to get Madison Meyer on board."

She opened her mouth to speak, but up went his palm again.

"I get it. The trick worked, so good job. My point is that this isn't like talking to a dead guy's wife, mistress, and business partner, who all live in Westchester. You're going to be hopping from UCLA to the Hollywood Hills to Silicon Valley to who knows where. You're not going to keep some guy like Frank Parker on board if you're shooting from some dingy hotel conference room with tuna fish sandwiches from room service. You'll need a nice place to film, complete with the kinds of luxuries the Hollywood crowd is used to. You're going to be spending some serious dough."

This time, he held up the palm before she even got her mouth open.

"And that's why I wanted to talk to Alex. Every critic, every focus group said his hosting was the key to our first special."

"I understand that, Brett. But Alex has a law practice to run. He might not have that kind of time."

"The *he* you're speaking about in the third person," Brett said impatiently, "is sitting right next to you, and—great news!—he already agreed."

Alex cleared his throat. "Well, yes. But *he* was told that you specifically asked for me."

Typical Brett. Anything to get what he wanted.

"It's perfect timing," Brett announced. "He was just explaining that he had a major case that was supposed to be a one-month trial suddenly disappear. How did you explain it again?"

She could tell that Alex wanted to speak to her privately, but there was no way to extract themselves from Brett's office. "I convinced the prosecutor my guy had a legitimate alibi. I found security camera footage placing him in the VIP lounge at a club in Chelsea when he was supposedly shooting a rival gang member in Brooklyn. Not to mention the cell phone pings that placed their supposed eyewitness on the Lower East Side when the crime was happening."

"There you have it," Brett said, slapping his desk for emphasis. "No wonder this guy gets the big bucks. I can't *wait* to see him lay into Frank Parker. I'm hoping he's the one who did it. I can already see the ratings. You could end up with a Pulitzer!"

Laurie was pretty sure that no one gave Pulitzer Prizes to reality television shows.

Alex started to rise from his chair again. "I think I should let you two talk about this. If Laurie would prefer someone else—"

"Don't be ridiculous," Brett said, waving Alex back into his chair. "Laurie's *thrilled*."

"Of course," she added. "I'm absolutely thrilled."

And she was. He truly was a skilled interrogator. She knew her father would be happy too, for his own reasons. He was always trying to get her to spend more time with Alex.

"Very good then," Brett said. "Now, take the rest of the day off to celebrate the good news while Alex and I continue with our March Madness talk. We were having a heated debate about who'll make the Final Four. And, no offense, but you might want to brush your hair or something. That trip out to Los Angeles took a toll on you."

Right. No offense.

18

Steve Roman knew that Martin preferred to receive any bad news quickly, the proverbial bandage being pulled from the wound. After parking his pickup truck at the discount monthly parking space he paid for south of Market, he pulled up AG's number.

"Yes?" That high-pitched yet assertive voice.

"Nothing essential to report," Steve began. Yesterday's check-in had been easy: the target had left the house only for trips to Costco, a fish market, and a strip mall for something called Pilates. Now he had to keep Martin calm. "But she did hit the road, a straight shot from her home to a company in Palo Alto. Something called REACH. It looks . . . I don't know, modern."

"It's a computer company," Martin said. "Good to know. Keep watching her."

Steve felt a churning heat working its way up from his stomach. "Before, when you called me, you said something about sending a message? When the time was right. Is that something I should be doing now?" No, Steve thought to himself, please don't make me hurt anyone. I might not be able to stop.

"Nothing yet. Just watch her. And, as you did today, tell me where she goes. And, this is important—find out to whom she speaks."

Steve was always impressed by Martin's proper grammar. He swallowed, knowing how much Martin despised being questioned. For every loyal follower, the church seemed to have ten critics doubting AG's mission of advocating for God's goodness through service to the poor. While Steve had been so inspired by AG, cynics assumed the worst about the church's fund-raising efforts. As a result of all the scrutiny, Martin could be secretive. And just as *he* had fully devoted himself to the word of God, Martin expected his followers to devote themselves to him.

"Is she someone I should be worried about?" Steve finally asked. He had practiced the wording of his query.

"No," Martin said definitively. "She was—in the past. Just between me and you . . ."

Steve now felt a different kind of warmth encompassing him. Martin was letting him further into the AG circle.

"Between me and you," Martin continued, "I was younger then. I trusted Nicole too quickly, before I should have. But now she's an impediment to our advocacy of God's goodness, to say the least."

"Got it," Steve said.

It wasn't a complete explanation for why he was driving all over the Bay Area, but it was more knowledge than he had before. Steve merged onto I-280, reinvigorated.

19

Laurie was just packing up her briefcase when she heard a triple tap on her office door, followed by the appearance of Grace's head.

"Do you have time for a visitor?" Grace's voice was tremulous as she asked the question.

A visitor was the last thing Laurie needed. Though she could have done without Brett's comment about her appearance, her boss had a point when he suggested that she leave early. She'd been working nonstop since Rosemary Dempsey agreed to participate in the show. All she needed to do today was call Rosemary to tell her the good news about the studio's official approval, and then she was hoping to get home in time to greet Timmy when he and Dad got home from school.

"I'm sorry, Grace. Do I have an appointment I forgot about?"

She heard a man's voice behind Grace. "I can come back another time."

Alex.

"Of course." Trying to keep her tone even, Laurie said, "Please, come in, Alex."

When Alex safely passed Grace to enter the office, Grace batted her eyelashes and pretended to fan her face with her hands. It was her *What a hunk* expression, and she made it a lot around Alex Buckley. During the filming of the first installment of *Under Suspi-*

cion, when Blue Eyes had been killed by a policeman before he was able to kill Laurie, Alex had run immediately to her and Timmy and swept them into his arms. Grace and everyone else may have seen the moment as a brave man's natural reaction to a dangerous situation, but Laurie had felt his desire to connect to her, like heat from a lightbulb, ever since.

She waited for Grace to close the office door before speaking. "I swear, Grace's IQ drops fifteen points when you're around."

"If only I could replicate that effect with jurors."

She gestured for him to sit in the gray swivel chair facing the windows and then positioned herself on the sofa across from him. "How have you been?" she asked.

"Good. Busy. I've tried calling a couple of times."

She nodded and smiled. "I'm sorry. Time gets away from me. Between work and Timmy . . ." Her voice trailed off. "You wouldn't believe this kid's activities. I feel like I need an appointment to see my own son. He's taking karate lessons now. Plus, of course, soccer. And now he says he wants to take up the trumpet, ever since he accompanied his grandpa to a police benevolent association party and saw a brass band in action. Now Dad has him watching YouTube videos of Louis Armstrong, Miles Davis, Wynton Marsalis, and Dizzy Gillespie. Timmy just stares at the screen, mimics the movements with his hands, and puffs out his cheeks like a blowfish. Who knew there was such thing as air trumpet?"

She was rambling, and they both knew it.

"Leo told me about the trumpet obsession. Rangers game last week."

"Right, of course."

Her father had reminded her afterward to return the messages Alex had left her about trying to get together for dinner.

"So," he said, clasping his hands together, "that Brett Young's a little crafty, isn't he? He told me before you came into the office that you were the one saying the Susan Dempsey case would only work if I agreed to be the host."

" 'Crafty' is a word that suits him well. But, to his credit, you *are* the right person for the job. I don't think Frank Parker will exactly be forthcoming."

"I saw your expression when you saw me in Brett's office. He sprang this on you. The last thing I want is to be around if you don't want me there."

"No, I—" She forced herself to slow down and choose her words carefully. "I had been waiting to hear from Brett all day. So if I looked surprised when I walked in, it was only because I expected to find him alone. But of course I'm delighted you're available. I care about this case. Susan Dempsey was only nineteen years old when she was murdered. And now her mother has gone twenty years without any resolution. Can you imagine what that must be like for her? Her only child? Two full decades?"

It would be an even bigger hell than the five years Laurie had experienced without knowing who killed her husband. The loss of a child would devastate her.

"How can you do it, Laurie?" Alex asked. "You are drawn to these horrible, haunting stories. Aren't you ever tempted to—I don't know—produce a fluffy show about dating or models?"

"I guess some women know romance and fashion. I know people like Rosemary Dempsey." She gave him a sad smile. "I honestly feel like this show can help people, Alex. Sometimes I wonder what would have happened if—" She stopped herself from completing the thought.

"If someone had done for you what *Under Suspicion* has done for others."

She nodded.

"And you're really okay with me helping?"

"I want you to," she said. For Rosemary, she thought to herself.

She had originally asked for Alex as a host for the launch of *Under Suspicion* because of his uncanny ability to get witnesses in the courtroom to blurt out information they had vowed to keep secret. He was a present-day Perry Mason, but much better looking.

"Then I'll do it. Tell me what I need to know."

Susan could have handed him the files and gone home. Instead, she gave him the rundown on every person she'd lined up for the show and answered his follow-up questions the best she could. How certain were police about the time of Susan's death? Could anyone confirm Frank Parker's whereabouts besides Madison Meyer? How solid was Keith Ratner's alibi?

She was impressed all over again by the laserlike precision of his questions. It was this kind of interaction that had led to the attraction between them in the first place when they reinvestigated the case of "The Graduation Gala."

Without the show to work on together, they had fallen into a comfort zone where they might share an occasional meal, or Alex might take her family to sports events. But now he'd be back in her life on a daily basis, and together they'd pore over motivations like love, envy, and rage.

She took a deep breath to keep her thoughts from racing forward. "Well, now that it's all official, it's time to get ready for pre-production. I think I blacked out how much work it is. How did Brett get you to sign on again?"

"You know Brett. His main focus was explaining why I was so much better than anyone he could possibly imagine. The man must think the way to my heart is through my ego."

"We were successful enough last time that the studio has upped my budget. The aesthetics of the show will be a little better, but I've put most of the money into information gathering. Instead of putting each person in front of a camera, we're doing more research beforehand. We're trying to do preliminary interviews with everyone, mostly off-camera. Hopefully the process will get them comfortable. Maybe even produce leads."

"The way lawyers sometimes use depositions. Do your fishing expedition outside of the courtroom. Go in for the kill in front of the jury."

She smiled, flattered, and then looked at her watch. "I've got to get home to Timmy. And as Brett said, that red-eye took its toll on me. I feel like a wreck."

"Well, you don't look it."

She forced herself to break eye contact and then rose from the sofa to walk him out. Her focus right now was on her family and on telling Susan Dempsey's story. There was no room for anything—or anyone—else. Not yet.

20

"What are you going to have?" Lydia asked, perusing the menu. "Probably something healthy, I bet. I still can't get over that wholesome selection of groceries you brought home the other day."

Rosemary wished her neighbor hadn't brought up the contents of her shopping bags. It reminded her how annoyed she had been at the woman's nosiness. She pushed away the moment of irritation and reminded herself why she was having lunch with Lydia in the first place: because she was a neighbor, and her act of assistance that day had been generous, and Rosemary had not made any new friends since she had moved to Castle Crossings nearly a year and a half ago.

Rosemary's first attempt to return the gesture had come yesterday morning, when she'd brought Lydia a jar of jelly beans, which she had mentioned as her favorite vice. Now they were having their first real outing together, a lunch at Rustic Tavern. It was a gorgeous day, so they had agreed on a quiet table on the restaurant's garden patio.

"I'm not nearly as virtuous as my groceries would suggest," Rosemary said, closing her menu. "And to prove it, I'll have a bacon cheeseburger with french fries."

"Oh, that sounds delicious. I'm doing it, too. And a salad to start, just so we can say we ate a vegetable?"

"Sounds like a plan."

They had finished their salads and ordered refills on their glasses of cabernet when Rosemary asked Lydia how she had ended up living in their shared neighborhood.

"Don was the one who wanted the extra security," she explained. "It seemed weird to me, since the kids were out of the house by then. But we take the grandkids one weekend a month, and you see all these horrible stories about kids snatched when the adults aren't watching. Oh, Rosemary, I'm so sorry. I didn't mean—"

Rosemary shook her head. "No, please, go on."

"Anyway, Don said it would be safer for the kids in a gated community. Like he says, he can't crack heads like he used to."

Rosemary was silent, wondering if she'd misheard, but Lydia obviously saw the confusion register on her face.

"Right, no reason why that would make any sense to you. Don— that's my husband—his background is in security management. The hands-on variety. He ran body service, as they call it, for all kinds of professional athletes and musicians. That's how we met."

"You had a secret life as a professional athlete?"

"Oh, no. Sorry. My kids tell me all the time, I'm a horrible storyteller. I'm not *linear*, is what they say. *Drip, drip, drip with the information*, according to them. No, I met Don in 1968 when we were still young'ns. Well, he was a young'n: only twenty years old, working security on Jimmy O'Hare's first world tour." Rosemary vaguely recalled the name as that of a southern rock singer from around that era. "I was twenty-five but lied and told everyone I was twenty-one. Musicians back then didn't like us much older than that."

"So you were a—backup singer or something?"

"Oh, gosh no. I can't carry a note to save my life. We had a karaoke contest at the home association party a few years ago, and my friends threatened to evict me from Castle Crossings if I ever sang in front of them again. Trust me, you don't want to hear me sing. No, I lied about my age because I was a road companion. A *groupie* is the more common vernacular."

Rosemary nearly spit out her wine across the table. Never judge a book by its cover, especially when the book is a person, was the lesson.

The ice—and Rosemary's expectations—fully broken, their conversation fell into an easy rhythm. They had lived very different lives but found unpredictable parallels between Lydia's life on the road and young Rosemary's own adventure of leaving Wisconsin for California.

"And how did you decide to move across the street?" Lydia asked. "You didn't want to stay in your old house?"

Rosemary found herself picking at her french fries.

"I'm sorry. Did I say something wrong again?"

"No, of course not. It's just—well, the answer is complicated. I raised Susan in that house. I mourned her there. I lived more years in that house with Jack than anywhere or with anyone else. But when he passed, the place was just too big for me to live in alone. It was hard to walk away from all those memories, but it was time."

"Oh, Rosemary. I didn't mean to bring up something so upsetting."

"It's okay. Really."

Lydia reached over and patted her wrist. The moment was interrupted by the buzz of Rosemary's phone against the table.

"Sorry," she said, inspecting the screen. "I need to take this."

"Rosemary," the voice on the phone said, "it's Laurie Moran. I have good news."

Rosemary was muttering the requisite acknowledgments—"Yes, I see, uh-huh"—but was having a hard time ignoring Lydia's expectant looks.

When she finally hung up, Lydia said, "Whatever that was about, you seemed very happy about it."

"Yes, you could say that. That was a television producer in New York. The show *Under Suspicion* has picked my daughter's case for their next feature. The producer can't make any promises, but I have to pray that something new comes out of this. It's been twenty years."

"I can't imagine."

Rosemary realized that it was the first time she had spoken about Susan to anyone who hadn't known her or been investigating her death. She had officially made a new friend.

21

Dwight Cook wished he could gut the interior of REACH's head-quarters and start over. The design concept had sounded great when the architect first pitched it. The three-level building had plenty of open space, some of it with forty-foot ceilings, but was also filled with nooks and brightly painted crannies with couches and bistro tables for people to gather in small groups. The idea, according to the architect, was to create the illusion of one large, continuous, "mazelike" space.

Well, the maze effect had worked.

Was it only he who craved monochromatic symmetry?

He blocked out all the horrible visual distractions and thought about the work that was taking place within these ridiculously shaped walls. REACH had been around for nearly twenty years and still managed to hire some of the brightest, most innovative tech workers in the country.

He reached the end of the hall and turned right toward Hatha-way's office. His former professor had been at REACH from the beginning in every possible way. But regardless of their work together, he would always think of Hathaway as his professor, the man responsible for building REACH into an empire.

Hathaway's door was open, as was the norm in REACH's "corporate culture."

Richard Hathaway was well into his fifties by now but still looked essentially the same as when UCLA coeds had dubbed him the school's "most crush-worthy" teacher. He was of average height with an athletic build. He had thick, wavy brown hair and a year-round tan, and always dressed like he was about to tee off at a golf course. As Dwight approached, he could see that Hathaway was reading a magazine article called "Work Out Smarter, Not Longer."

Dwight took a seat across from Hathaway, unsure how to raise the subject that brought him there. He decided to ease into it, the way he had noticed people did when they were trying to avoid a topic. "Sometimes when I walk around the building, it reminds me of your lab back at UCLA."

"Except we were working with computers the size of economy cars. And the furniture wasn't as nice, either." Hathaway was always quick with a good line. How many times had he saved the day by "tagging along" to a meeting with a potential investor? Dwight had surpassed Hathaway in programming talent, but without Hathaway, Dwight would have always worked for someone else.

"The walls were straight, though," Dwight said, making his own attempt at the same kind of humor.

Hathaway smiled, but Dwight could tell that his self-deprecating one-liner had fallen flat.

"What I meant," Dwight continued, "was that we have all these kids—smart, idealistic, probably a little weird." Now Hathaway laughed. "They all believe they can change the world with the right piece of code. I remember your lab feeling like that."

"You sound like a proud parent."

"Yes, I suppose I am proud." Dwight tried so hard not to feel his emotions that he had never learned to describe them.

"It's fine to be proud," Hathaway said, "but REACH has investors with expectations. It would be nice to be relevant again."

"We're more than relevant, Hathaway." Dwight had called him

"Dr. Hathaway" long after they both left UCLA. Despite the professor's insistence that Dwight refer to him as Richard, Dwight just couldn't do it. "Hathaway" had been the compromise.

"I mean front-page-of-the-*Journal* relevant. Our stock price is holding steady, Dwight, but others' are going up."

Even as a professor, Hathaway was never the tweed-jacket-and-practical-shoes type. He made it clear to his students that technology could not only help people and change the world, it could also make you rich. The first time an investment banker wrote them a seven-figure check, enabling REACH to set up shop in Palo Alto, Hathaway had gone directly to the car dealer for a new Maserati.

"But you're not here to relive the old days," Hathaway said.

Dwight trusted Hathaway. They'd had a special connection from the moment Hathaway had asked Dwight, after freshman midterms, to work in the lab. Dwight had always felt like his own father was trying to either change him or avoid him. But Hathaway had all the same interests as Dwight and never tried to tell him to act like anyone other than himself. When they worked together, combining Dwight's code-writing skills with Hathaway's business savvy, it was a perfect match.

So why couldn't he tell his friend and mentor of twenty years that he was hacking the e-mail accounts of everyone who might be connected to Susan's murder?

Oh, how desperately he wanted to tell him what he'd learned. He knew, for example, that Frank Parker's wife, Talia, wrote her sister to say she was "dead set against Frank ever speaking that girl's name again." Was Talia opposed to the show because she suspected her husband was involved?

And then there was Madison Meyer's e-mail to her agent, insisting that once she was in a room alone with Frank Parker again, she was "sure to land a true *comeback* role." That one definitely made it sound like Madison had something to hang over Frank's head.

And yet, Dwight could not bring himself to tell Hathaway what he'd been up to. He knew Hathaway would worry about the corporate implications if Dwight were caught hacking into private accounts. No one would ever trust REACH with information again. Their stock price would plummet. This would have to be one secret he kept from his oldest friend.

But Hathaway was looking at him expectantly. "What's up, Dwight?"

"I think I actually forgot. That walk down the maze must have made me dizzy." He was pleased when Hathaway smiled. The line had worked.

"I do that all the time," Hathaway said. "But, hey, since you're here: I got a call from a Laurie Moran? A TV special about Susan Dempsey? They said you gave them my name. I thought everyone sort of knew Frank Parker did it but the police could never prove it."

Dwight wanted to scream, *But I might be able to!* Instead, he said, "I just want people to know that Susan was more than her headshot. She wasn't some wannabe actress. She was . . . truly phenomenal." Dwight heard his own voice crack like a middle schooler's. Once he was on camera, would everyone watching know how obsessed he had been with his fellow lab assistant? "And, let's face it," he added, "you'd be better on TV than me."

"Are you sure this is a good idea? They'll be asking about the work in the lab. You know I don't like anything that calls attention to how this company got launched."

It had been nearly twenty years since they started REACH. Sometimes Dwight actually forgot how the idea had originated, but Hathaway never did.

"It won't be like that," Dwight insisted. "Shows don't get ratings by delving into the details of web-search optimization. They just want to hear about Susan."

"Very well, then. If you're in, I'm in."

As Dwight returned to REACH's colorful labyrinth, he felt completely alone. He couldn't remember any time when he'd kept information from Hathaway. But he realized the real reason he had not shared his activities with his professor. He didn't want Hathaway to be disappointed in him.

He had to find out more, though. The reason I want to do the show, he thought, is because once I have physical proximity to the others, I can clone their phones and finally prove who killed Susan. But, no, he couldn't say any of that.

He had to do this. For Susan.

22

W ithout the rearview camera on the dash of her Volvo, Rosemary Dempsey might have clipped the edge of the newspaper recycling bin that had been thrown a bit too haphazardly to her curb after weekly pickup.

She loved the new technology that surrounded her every day, but it always made her wonder what Susan and Jack would have said about it.

As she shifted out of reverse, she caught sight of Lydia in her peripheral vision, watering her hydrangeas with a gardening hose. She wore bright orange rubber shoes and matching gloves, one of which waved in Susan's direction. Rosemary returned the wave and added a friendly beep of the car horn. She made it a point to watch her speedometer as she rolled down the street. Knowing Lydia, any excessive speed could threaten their budding friendship.

Rosemary smiled as she navigated the turns through Castle Crossings, trying to imagine Lydia Levitt forty years ago, with bell-bottoms and platform shoes instead of gardening gear.

She was still smiling when the GPS told her that her destination was on the right. The navigation system's estimate of the drive time had been nearly perfect: forty-two minutes to San Anselmo.

As Rosemary passed driveways filled with Porsches, Mercedes, even a Bentley, she started to wonder if her Volvo would be the worst car on the block. She saw one cream-colored pickup truck two houses down from Nicole's, in front of a McMansion that overfilled its lot, but that car obviously belonged to a landscaper.

"You have arrived at your destination," her car announced.

Rosemary had been to Nicole's home before but still took a moment to register its beauty. A perfectly restored five-bedroom Tudor in San Anselmo with sweeping views of Ross Valley, it was, in Rosemary's view, far too large for a couple with no children. But as Rosemary understood it, Nicole's husband, Gavin, could afford it, plus he frequently worked at home rather than commute to San Francisco's financial district.

The forty-minute drive was a small price to pay to deliver this news in person.

Nicole greeted her at the door before she had a chance to ring the bell. She gave Rosemary a quick hug before saying, "Is everything okay? You were so secretive on the phone."

"Everything is just fine. I didn't mean to alarm you." Rosemary was so aware of her own loss as a mother, sometimes she forgot how Susan's death must have affected others. When one of your best friends dies when you are only a teenager, do you spend the rest of your life on high alert?

"Oh, thank goodness," Nicole said. "Come on in. Can I get you anything?"

The house was silent.

"Is Gavin home?" Rosemary asked.

"No, he has a dinner meeting with clients tonight, so he's working at the office today."

Rosemary had grown up one of five children and had always wanted to have a large family. But it was more than ten years before joyfully, happily, Susan had come along.

She was a social bee, always attracting the neighbor kids and then her schoolmates. Even when she'd gone to college, the house wasn't silent. It still somehow buzzed from her energy—her phone calls, miscellaneous pieces of laundry left strewn around the house, her CDs blasting from the stereo when Rosemary flipped the switch.

Rosemary had never asked Nicole why she and Gavin had opted for a silent house, but she couldn't help but feel sorry for them over the choice.

She followed Nicole into a den lined floor-to-ceiling with books. One wall was dominated by business books and historical nonfiction. The other wall popped with every kind of novel—romance, suspense, sci-fi, what some people called more "literary" fare. She felt a pang as she remembered Susan's calling her from UCLA two days after the big move: "You'd love my roommate. She has amazing taste in books." The novels had to be Nicole's.

Once they were seated, Nicole looked at her expectantly.

"So you haven't heard yet?" Rosemary asked.

"No," Nicole said. "At least, I don't think so. I have no idea what you're talking about, and the anticipation is going to give me a premature heart attack."

"It's really happening. Laurie Moran called me. The head of the studio approved Susan's case as *Under Suspicion*'s next feature. And everyone has signed on: me, you, Madison, Frank Parker, and— color me shocked—Keith Ratner. She even got people who knew Susan from the computer lab."

"That is wonderful news," Nicole said, reaching over and briefly clasping Rosemary's hands in hers.

"Yes, I think so, too. I feel like I pressured you into it, so I wanted to thank you personally."

"No, no pressure at all. I couldn't be happier."

Rosemary had been on an emotional roller coaster ever since she opened Laurie Moran's letter, but she still felt like Nicole was responding strangely.

"Laurie said they'll do pre-production interviews with all of us. No cameras, for the most part. Just hearing our side of things so they know what to ask us once they yell 'action.'"

"Sure, no problem."

Did Rosemary imagine it, or had Nicole's eyes just moved toward the staircase of her empty house? "You're happy about this, aren't you, Nicole? I mean, you and Madison were the only people my daughter ever lived with besides her parents. And, well, Madison was always sort of the add-on. Whether you wanted to be or not, you were the closest thing to a sister that Susan ever knew."

Whatever distance Rosemary sensed in Nicole immediately vanished as her eyes began to water. "And for me, too. She was my friend, and she was . . . amazing. I promise you, Rosemary. I will help. Me, you, this show. If there's any way to find out what happened to Susan, we're going to do it."

Now Rosemary was crying, too, but she smiled through the tears. "We'll show Frank Parker and Keith Ratner what a couple of determined women can do. It has to be one of them, right?"

When Rosemary was ready to leave, Nicole led the way to the front door, and then wrapped her arm around Rosemary's shoulder as she escorted her down the steep walkway from her front porch to the street.

Rosemary paused to take in the breathtaking view of the valley, all green trees backed by blue hills. "I don't know whether I've ever told you this, Nicole, but I was so worried about you when you decided to leave school. I wondered whether you were, in some way, another victim of what happened to Susan. I'm so happy that things have worked out well for you."

Nicole gave her a big hug and then patted her on the back. "You drive safe, okay? We have big things to look forward to."

As Rosemary climbed into the driver's seat, strapped on her seat belt, and pulled away from the curb, neither woman noticed the person watching them from the cream-colored pickup truck, two houses down.

The truck pulled away from the curb and followed Rosemary south.

23

Martin Collins worked his way down the aisles of his mega-church, conveniently located right off I-110 in the heart of South Los Angeles, shaking hands and offering quick hellos and blessings. He had delivered a rousing sermon to a packed house of four thousand, on their feet, their hands raised to God—and to him. Most could barely make rent or put food on the table, but he saw bills flying when the baskets were passed.

The early days of recruiting new members in tattoo parlors, bike shops, and sketchy bars and painstakingly converting them, reinventing them, were long over.

To see thousands of worshippers enthralled by his every word was exhilarating, but he enjoyed this moment—after the sermons, after the crowd dwindled—even more. This was his chance to speak in person to the church members who were so devoted to him personally that they would wait, sometimes hours, to shake his hand.

He circled back around to the front of the church, saving for last a woman who waited in the front pew. Her name was Shelly. She had first arrived here eighteen months ago, a walk-in who had found a flyer for Advocates for God in the bus station. She was a single mother. Her daughter, Amanda, sat next to her, twelve years old with milky skin and light brown eyes fit for an angel.

Martin reached out to hug Shelly. She rose from the pew and

clung to him. "Thank you so much for your words of worship," she said. "And for the apartment," she whispered. "We finally have a home of our own."

Martin barely listened to Shelly's words. Sweet little Amanda was looking up at him in awe.

Martin had found a way to bring substantial funds into Advocates for God. Because they were now a government-recognized religion, donations were tax-free. And the dollar bills thrown from wallets in a post-sermon fervor were nothing compared to the big money. Martin had mastered a feel-good blend of religious and charitable language that was like a magic recipe for scoring high-dollar philanthropic contributions. He'd found a way to make religion cool, even in Hollywood. Not to mention the huge federal grants he landed with the help of a few like-minded congressmen.

The money allowed the group to back its mission of advocating God's goodness by helping the poor, including supporting members who needed a safety net. Shelly had whispered her gratitude for a reason. Martin could not provide a roof for every struggling follower—just the special ones, like Shelly and Amanda.

"Still no contact with your sister?" Martin confirmed.

"Absolutely none."

It had been two months since Martin had convinced Shelly that her sister—the last member of her biological family with whom she had contact, the one who told her she was spending too much time at this new church—was preventing her from having a personal relationship with God.

"And how about you?" he asked little Amanda. "Are you are enjoying the toys we sent over?"

The child nodded shyly, then smiled. Oh, how he loved that expression—filled with trust and joy. "Can I get a hug from you, too?" Another nod, followed by a hug. She was still nervous with him. That was okay. These things took time. Now that she and her mother were in an apartment that he paid for, he would increase the amount of time he spent with both mother and daughter.

Martin knew how to lure people in. He had been a psychology major in college. One course had an entire section of the syllabus devoted to battered woman syndrome: the isolation, the power and control, the belief that the batterer is all-powerful and all-knowing.

Martin had earned an A+ on that part of the course. He didn't need the textbooks and expert explanations. He had seen those characteristics in his own mother, so incapable of stopping his father from hurting her . . . and young Martin. He had understood the connection between fear and dependency so well that at the age of ten, he had vowed that when he was older, he would be the controller. He would never *be* controlled.

And then one day he was flipping channels in the middle of the night and saw a minister of a megachurch on television, a 900 number scrolling at the bottom of the screen for donations. He made everything sound so black-and-white. Ignore the word of the Lord and burn, or listen—and donate money—to the nice-looking man on the television and earn a place with God. Talk about power.

He started watching that preacher every night, practicing the words and the cadence. He researched the IRS rules for religions. He learned about faith-based grants, which allowed churches to get government money by administering charitable programs. He whitened his teeth, joined a tanning center, and printed glossy brochures promising people closeness to God by helping the poor.

The only problem had been the police. They didn't have any proof yet, but Martin's predilections had come to the attention of Nebraska law enforcement, and he was tired of their slowing down when they passed his house or saw him near a playground. Off he went to Southern California, filled with lots of sunshine, money, and people searching for a way to feel good about themselves. Advocates for God was born.

And though he clothed himself in religiosity, he knew that the keys to his power had been learned in his own household, watching the way his father controlled his mother.

Ingredient number one: fear. This part was easy. Martin didn't have to hurt anyone. A nondenominational yet fervently religious church like Advocates for God tended to attract people who were already afraid of the world as they knew it. They wanted easy answers, and he would happily oblige.

Number two: power and control. Martin was the "supreme" Advocate for God, a direct vessel for the voice of God. He, in short, was their god. When he spoke, they listened. That aspect of the church had earned AG more than its share of detractors, but Martin didn't need everyone in the world to believe. He had sixteen thousand church members and counting, and a track record of raising more than four hundred dollars per year per follower. The math worked.

Number three: isolation. No friends, family members, or other people to interfere with AG's hold. Early on, this had been Martin's biggest challenge, and he had learned his lesson with Nicole. Now he was more selective, forcing church members to earn their way into AG's inner circle with years of loyalty. Until they knew too much about AG's finances, he could afford to let people walk away.

His cell phone buzzed in his front pocket. He retrieved it and looked at the screen. It was Steve reporting from up north.

"I have to get this," he explained to Shelly. "But I'll check in on you tomorrow."

"That would be nice," the woman said, giving him another hug. Martin patted little Amanda on the head. Her hair was soft and warm. If he timed his visit right the next day, she would be home from school, before Shelly left the janitorial job he had found for her at an office building.

He answered as he made his way to the room's rear exit. "Yes?"

"Nicole had a visitor to her house today, the first in the time I've been watching. A woman, must have been seventysomething, driving a Volvo. I followed her to a neighborhood called Castle Crossings, outside of Oakland. Looks pretty nice. Maybe it's her mother?"

"No, her mother died in Irvine a few years ago." Martin slipped through a fire door into the stairwell for privacy. "Did you get a name?"

"Not yet. It's a gated community. Not to worry—Keepsafe has plenty of alarms here, so I can get past the entrance. I know the car and the license plate. I'll find her house tomorrow and get an ID."

Sometimes Martin thought about how easy it would be to collect dirt on his potential enemies if he had a police officer or two in his inner circle. A cop could run the plate in seconds. But cops weren't wired to succumb to Martin's formula. He had considered simply bribing someone to be on his payroll, but he figured any cop who would take a bribe would sell him out in a heartbeat.

Once *Under Suspicion* started filming, Martin could rely on Keith Ratner to find out what, if anything, Nicole planned to say about Advocates for God. But until then, all Martin could do was wait and take whatever drops of information Steve could gather.

"Very well," he said. "Thank you, Steve."

Once Steve hung up, Martin threw his phone so hard that the sound of the screen shattering echoed through the vacant stairwell.

24

When Laurie's eyes blinked open the next morning, she took a moment to realize that she was back in her own bed, not on a plane or catnapping in her office. The digital clock read 5:58. She couldn't remember the last time she woke up before the sound of her alarm. Crashing at 8:30 the previous night had certainly helped.

As she turned the alarm to OFF, she heard the clinking sounds of dishes in the kitchen. Timmy, as usual, was already awake. He was so much like his father that way, up and at 'em first thing in the morning. She recognized the smell of toast. She still couldn't believe her little boy could make his own breakfast.

A crack of light broke the darkness of her bedroom, and she saw Timmy backlit in the doorway, holding a tray. "Mommy," he whispered. "Are you awake?"

"Indeed, I am." She turned on the lamp on her nightstand.

"Look what I have for you." He walked slowly, his gaze fixed on the rim of a glass filled with orange juice, then rested the tray gently on the bed. The toast was crispy, just as she liked it, already slathered with butter and strawberry jam. The tray was one of two that had been her fifth-anniversary gift to Greg—made of wood, as tradition called for. They never had the chance to use them together.

She patted the empty spot on the bed next to her, and Timmy

crawled in. She pulled him in tight for a hug. "What did I do to deserve breakfast in bed?"

"I could tell you were sleepy last night. You were hardly awake when you tucked me in."

"I can't get much past you, can I?" She took a bite of toast, and he giggled as she used her tongue to catch a wayward drip of jam.

"Mommy?"

"Hmm-hmm?"

"Are you going to keep flying to California for work?"

She felt her heart sink. The first *Under Suspicion* had featured a case in Westchester County. She'd been home every night. But this show required a change in geography. She hadn't even thought about explaining all of this to the son who was apparently already feeling the impact of her travel.

She returned her toast to her plate and pulled Timmy close again. "You know my show tries to help people who've lost loved ones, like we lost your daddy, right?"

He nodded. "So bad guys like Blue Eyes might get caught. Like how Grandpa used to be a police officer."

"Well, I'm not quite as heroic as that, but we do our best. This time, we are helping a woman in California. Someone took her daughter, Susan, from her twenty years ago. Susan is the focus of our next show. And, yes, I'll need to be in California for a little while."

"Twenty years is a long time ago. More than twice as old as me." He was looking at his toes, wriggling out from beneath the sheets.

"Grandpa will be here with you full-time."

"Except Grandpa said you couldn't even call the other night because of time zones. And then when you got home, you were so sleepy, you almost fell asleep at dinner."

She'd spent all these years since Greg's death terrified for their safety, convinced that Blue Eyes would carry out his threat against them. Her son's anxiety over having his mother spend time away from the house for her career wasn't even on her radar. She had lived so long in warrior-widow mode that she'd never processed the guilt of being a regular working, single mother. She felt tears pooling in her eyes but blinked them away before he could see them.

"I always take care of us, don't I?"

"You, me, and Grandpa. We take care of each other," Timmy answered matter-of-factly.

"Then trust me. I'm going to figure this out. I can work and be your mom, all at one time, okay? And you always come first. No matter what." This time, she couldn't stop the tears. She laughed and kissed him on the cheek. "Look what happens when this sweet boy makes breakfast in bed. Mom gets all sappy."

He laughed and handed her the glass of juice. "Time to brush my teeth," he announced. "Can't be late."

He sounded like her now. All the pieces of the Cinderella Murder show were in place and she couldn't help thinking about what her father said about putting herself in the company of a killer. An involuntary shudder went through her. A working mother's guilt was the least of her worries.

25

The host at Le Bernardin greeted Laurie with a warm handshake. "Ms. Moran. I saw your name in the book. What a pleasure to welcome you again."

There was a time when this had been a regular stop for her and Greg on their weekly babysitter nights. Now that she was the sole breadwinner and her usual date for dinner was a fourth grader, the Morans were more likely to opt for hamburgers or pizza than three-star Michelin fare.

But today's decadent meal was meant to celebrate Brett Young's official approval for the Susan Dempsey production. And Grace and Jerry were Laurie's honored lunch guests.

"Three of you today?" the host confirmed.

"Yes, thank you very much."

"Oh, and here I was hoping I'd get a chance to see that adorable Alex Buckley," Grace said. "Jerry told me that he agreed to host again."

"Yes, but just the three of us for lunch, I'm afraid."

Jerry fit right into their elegant surroundings with his coiffed hair and dark blue suit. But as they were getting seated, Laurie noticed a woman at the next table glaring judgmentally at Grace. It could have been for the poofed-up hair, the heavy makeup, the three pounds of costume jewelry, the micromini hemline, or the five-inch stilettos. Regardless of the reasons, Laurie didn't like it. She stared straight at the woman until she looked away.

"In any event," Laurie teased, "don't you think Alex is a little old for you, Grace? He's got a dozen years on you."

"And from what I can tell," Grace said, "each one has made him better-looking."

Jerry smiled and shook his head, used to Grace's boy-crazy talk. "We have bigger fish to fry than your fascination with our host," he said. "I know you call the shots, Laurie, but I don't know how plausible it is for us to be flying back and forth to California constantly."

She thought about Timmy's wide eyes that morning in bed as he asked her how often she would be going to California. Now that she had convinced Brett Young to approve the Cinderella Murder, there was no turning back.

"I'm with you," she said. "If you could think of a way to produce the entire show from New York, you'd be my hero for life."

Grace registered her opinion with a *tsk*. "Sun. The ocean. Hollywood. Feel free to send me out to do as much work as you need."

"I've started a punch list." Jerry was the most organized person Laurie had ever met. The key to success, he liked to say, was to plan your work and work your plan. "We can hire an actress who looks like Susan to re-create—probably blurred—the foot chase in the Hollywood Hills."

"If we do that, we need to be careful not to add any ideas or inferences to what we absolutely *know* to a certainty," Laurie said.

"Of course," Jerry said. "Like, obviously, we wouldn't show the actress running out of Frank Parker's house. But we know her body was found, strangled, in Laurel Canyon Park. And based on the discovery of her missing shoe, abrasions to her foot, and the path of flattened grass leading to her body, police believed her killer chased her from the roadway of the park entrance into the park's interior. That was the part I thought we could re-create, the sprint from the park sign to the place her body was found."

She nodded her approval.

"The real question," Grace said, "is how she got to that roadway. Her car was parked on campus."

"We'll highlight that, too," Jerry said. "Photographs from the investigation will suffice, I think. And I've already got a forensic pathologist lined up to talk about the physical evidence. A woman named Janice Lane, on the medical school faculty at Stanford. She's a frequent expert witness and presents well on camera."

"Excellent," Laurie said. "Make sure she knows that we don't include any prurient details. Susan Dempsey's mother doesn't need grisly descriptions of her daughter's death on national television. Dr. Lane's primary role should be a discussion of the timeline. It was the estimate of the time of death that helped Frank Parker establish an alibi."

Jerry began to explain. "Based on temperature, lividity, and rigor mortis—"

"Someone's been brushing up on his science," Grace said.

"Trust me," he said, "it's all Dr. Lane. She makes this stuff sound easy. Anyway, based on the science, the medical examiner estimated that Susan was killed between seven and eleven P.M. on that Saturday night. She was scheduled to arrive at Frank Parker's house at seven thirty. When she hadn't arrived by seven forty-five, he called Madison Meyer, who jumped in her car and arrived at the house around eight thirty. According to both Parker and Meyer, she stayed until close to midnight."

"What were they doing all that time?" Grace asked. From the look of her arched brow, she had her theories.

"I'm not sure that's our business," Jerry said, "unless it has something to do with Susan Dempsey's death."

"You're no fun."

Laurie made a time-out sign with her hands. "Focus on the facts, guys. According to Frank and Madison, he made the decision to cast her within an hour. He was so excited about it that he wanted to show her the short film that was the basis for *Beauty Land* and talk more about the project. He hadn't eaten yet so he ordered takeout; a pizza delivery record from nine thirty P.M. backed that up."

Grace whispered a thank-you to the waiter who refilled her water glass. "But if Susan could have died any time between seven and eleven, and Madison didn't get to Frank's until eight thirty, she's not really a full alibi. Where was he between seven and eight thirty?"

"Except you've got to take all the evidence into account," Jerry reminded her. "Susan was due to arrive at Frank's at seven thirty. The idea is that there's no way Frank could have gotten into a chase with Susan, killed her, taken Susan's car back to the UCLA campus, and returned to his house, all before Madison arrived an hour later. Not to mention, placing a phone call to Susan's cell and then to Madison at the dorm room in the middle of it all. If Madison's telling the truth, Frank's in the clear."

"Still," Laurie said, "the whole alibi seems fishy to me: it seems hard to believe that Frank called another actress fifteen minutes after Susan was supposed to arrive, and that she just hopped in her car immediately."

"Ah, but it does make sense," Jerry said, "when Frank Parker is notoriously obsessed with punctuality. He has fired people for showing up five minutes late. And we saw how obsessed Madison is with being famous. If someone dangled a studio film in front of her and said jump, she'd ask how high."

Grace still wasn't fully sold on the theory. "But you also saw how she fixed her lipstick just to answer the door at her ratty house. I can only imagine the work she'd put into looking good for Frank Parker."

"See?" Laurie said. "These are all the things we have to establish in our initial interviews with them. We go first for a gentle retelling of whatever version of the story they gave back then. See if we can catch them in an inconsistency."

"When do we bring Alex in?" Grace asked, smiling.

"You are singular in your focus today, aren't you?" Laurie asked. "Brett Young has approved a budget to cover screening interviews with every participant, followed by what we'll call our summit session: back-to-back interviews, all in the same location. That's when Alex swoops in for the tough questions, after we've done our groundwork."

"For that part," Jerry said, "I thought we'd rent a house near campus, something big enough for the whole production team. That will save us money on lodging, and then we can use the house as the location for the interviews with Alex."

Laurie wasn't sure how she felt about living with all her coworkers, but from a financial perspective, she couldn't argue with Jerry's logic. "Sounds like a plan," she said. "If nothing else, I'd say we've already earned this delicious lunch."

As the waiter recited elaborate food descriptions from memory, Laurie nodded along politely, but her thoughts were spinning as she envisioned all the work they had in front of them. She had guaranteed Brett Young the best *Under Suspicion* possible. And, just this morning, she had given her word to her nine-year-old son that she would do it all while being a full-time mother.

How could she possibly keep both promises?

26

Lydia Levitt sat cross-legged on the sofa in her living room, her laptop perched across her knees. She typed a final period and then proofread her online review of Rustic Tavern, the restaurant she and Rosemary had selected for lunch the previous day. She deleted the last period and replaced it with an exclamation point. *I will definitely be back—five stars!* She hit the ENTER key, satisfied.

The website thanked her for her review. It was her seventy-eighth entry. Lydia believed in giving businesses feedback, for good or for bad. How else could they know what consumers valued and be able to improve? Not to mention, writing the reviews gave her something to do. Lydia loved to stay busy.

It wasn't just the delicious food and beautiful patio that had made yesterday so enjoyable. She was excited to have found a new friend in Rosemary Dempsey. Lydia had lived at Castle Crossings for twelve years now, and the entire time, she had been older than almost everyone else in the neighborhood. These kinds of planned communities tended to attract young couples, eager for a safe, predictable, homogeneous place to raise their children.

For the most part, Lydia had found company among the self-named "Castle Crossings grandparents," the parents of the young couples, living nearby to either help with child care or facilitate grandparent time.

But Lydia hadn't met anyone quite like Rosemary at Castle Crossings. Rosemary struck her as adventurous. Interesting. And, maybe because of the terrible loss she'd suffered, she seemed a bit haunted.

Even so, Lydia could tell that Rosemary had been shocked at lunch when Lydia mentioned her wild-child days in the late sixties. If their meal had not been cut short by the phone call Rosemary had received from that television producer, Lydia might have found a way to fully explain the connection between that part of her life and her current identity as the rule-follower of Castle Crossings. Lydia had seen what life was like when everybody did whatever he or she felt like doing, willy-nilly. After she saw friends overdose, or lose their families to alcoholism, or get their hearts broken because one person's idea of live-and-let-live is another person's definition of betrayal, she saw the value in playing by the rules.

Lydia set her laptop on the coffee table and walked to the front window, parting the gray linen drapes with her fingertips. Rosemary's driveway was empty. Shoot. She was looking forward to another visit.

She was just about to let the drapes close when she noticed a cream-colored pickup truck parked in front of the house next door to Rosemary's. The driver exited, wearing cargo pants and a black windbreaker. He was probably close to forty years old, with a shaved head. He looked tough and lean, like a boxer.

He was walking toward Rosemary's yard.

She let the drapes fall but kept a tiny slit open to peer out. Oh, how Don teased her when she did this. They both knew that everyone called her "the nosy neighbor."

"What else am I supposed to do with myself all day?" she would ask Don. "I'm bored, bored, bored." Spying on the Castle Crossings crowd, like posting online reviews of restaurants, kept her busy. She found such pleasure in conjuring up imaginary tales from the humdrum comings and goings around these quiet cul-de-sacs. In her alternate version of this neighborhood, Trevor Wolf's band of teen-age after-school buddies was plotting a series of bank robberies. Mr. and Mrs. Miller were cooking methamphetamine in the basement. Ally Simpson's new rescue dog was actually a trained drug K9, working undercover to expose the Millers' nefarious activities. And, of course, affairs abounded.

"You've got such an imagination," Don liked to say. "You should write a mystery novel one day."

Well, Don was at the health club, so he wasn't around to catch her spying today.

She peered through the crack in the drapes as the pickup-truck man first knocked on Rosemary's door, then leaned over to check out the view through her living room window. When he turned away and began retracing his steps through the yard, she assumed he was returning to his car. Instead, he turned left, facing away from her, and headed toward the side of Rosemary's house.

Now, that was interesting. She began conjuring explanations: a burglar who had somehow slipped past security at the front gate; someone affiliated with that television show Rosemary had mentioned yesterday; a door-to-door proselytizer, out to introduce Rosemary to a new religion.

That's it! Her church. She remembered Rosemary mentioning an upcoming flea market at Saint Patrick's. She said she was grateful that she didn't have to lug all of her giveaways to the church herself. A volunteer was supposed to come by to haul them for her. A pickup truck would be just the right vehicle for the job. Maybe Rosemary had arranged to leave the donations behind her house in the event she wasn't home to meet him.

Lydia pulled on a fleece from the coatrack by the front door. She could help load the truck, or at least say hello on Rosemary's behalf.

She crossed the street and then followed the same path the man had taken, walking to the right side of Rosemary's house to her backyard. She found him trying the sliding glass door, unsuccessfully. She remembered how Rosemary had unlocked her front door when Lydia helped her with the groceries earlier that week.

"I told her she really doesn't need to keep her doors locked," Lydia called out. "That's basically the reason most people live here."

When the man turned, his face was expressionless.

"I'm Lydia," she said, waving as she approached. "The neighbor across the street. You're from Rosemary's church?"

No change in expression. Only silence. Maybe he was deaf?

She stepped closer and noticed now that he was wearing black gloves. It didn't seem quite that cold to her, but she always seemed to run a little warmer than other people. He finally spoke, only one word. "Church?"

"Yes, I thought you were from Saint Patrick's. For the flea market? Did she tell you where she left everything? I got the impression she had a bunch."

"A bunch of what?" he asked.

Now that she was right next to him, she noticed the insignia on the breast of his windbreaker.

"Oh, you're from Keepsafe?" She knew about the company from Don's days in the security industry. They were one of the most common providers of home alarms in the country.

At the mention of the company, the man appeared to wake from his daze. His smile was somehow even stranger than his previously blank expression. "Yes, I'm from Keepsafe. Your neighbor's alarm sent an alert to our local station. She hasn't cleared it and didn't answer when we called. We automatically do a home visit to be sure. Probably just a misunderstanding—a dog knocking over a vase, that kind of thing."

"Rosemary doesn't have a dog."

Another weird smile. "I meant that as an example," he said. "These things happen all the time. Nothing to worry about."

"Are you sure you even have the right house? Rosemary doesn't have an alarm system." That was the kind of thing Lydia would have immediately noticed when she walked into Rosemary's house.

The man said nothing, but the smile was still there. For the first time in her life, Lydia believed that the danger she sensed was anything but imaginary.

27

After a ritualistic postdinner game of Clue and a nighttime snack of peanut butter on apple slices, Laurie tucked Timmy into bed to the sounds of running water and clanking dishes from the kitchen.

She found her father loading the dishwasher.

"Dad, you don't need to do that. You already do so much for Timmy when I'm at work."

"Used to be that cleaning up after dinner was an hour-long chore. I think I can handle throwing away takeout containers and tossing a few plates into a machine. I know how hard you've been working."

She took a sponge from the sink and began to wipe down the granite counters. "Unfortunately, I'm not even done for the day."

"It's nine o'clock, Laurie. You're going to burn yourself out."

"I'm fine, Dad. Just one more phone call." Producing the show in California was going to be a bear, but at least the time zone differences made it easier for her to contact the West Coast long after normal people would have stopped working. "Jerry is scheduling interviews with the other participants, but I owe it to Susan's mother to contact her personally."

Rosemary Dempsey picked up after two rings. "Ms. Moran?"

"Hi again. And, please, call me Laurie. I was calling to confirm some dates. We'd like to come next week for some one-on-one time with you. And then the following week, we'd like to have each person do a sit-down with Alex Buckley. That will be down in Southern California. Is that going to be possible for you?"

"Um, sure. Whatever you need."

Rosemary's voice sounded different—soft and hesitant. "Is everything all right?" Laurie asked. "If you're having second thoughts—"

"No, not at all. It's just . . ."

Laurie thought she heard a sniffle on the other end of the line. "I think I've caught you at a bad time. It can wait until tomorrow."

Rosemary cleared her throat. "Now is fine. I could use the distraction. Something awful has happened here. One of my neighbors was found murdered. Police think she was beaten to death."

Laurie didn't know what to say. "Oh, Rosemary. That's terrible. I'm so sorry." She realized the words were as unhelpful as any that were spoken to her when people learned about Greg's death.

"Her name was Lydia. She was very nice. She was—well, she was my friend. And they found her in my backyard."

"In *your* yard?"

"Yes. I don't know why she would have been there. They think it's possible she interrupted someone trying to break in."

"That's absolutely terrifying. This just happened today?"

"A few hours ago," Rosemary confirmed. "Police only just now let me back in my house, but my yard is still off-limits."

"So it was in broad daylight?" *Just like Greg*, she couldn't help thinking.

"The whole neighborhood is in shock. Things like this never happen here. So, honestly, getting out of the house for the show will be good for me."

It did not take them long to mark off a full day to film in the Bay Area, and for Rosemary to clear the three days they had planned to gather everyone in Southern California. Laurie promised to be in touch about location details for the latter once Jerry had located a rental house for what they were calling the "summit session."

"Again, I'm so sorry about your friend," Laurie said once more before wishing her good night. When she hung up, her father was lingering in the doorway.

"Something bad happened?" he asked.

"I'd certainly say so. One of Rosemary's friends, a neighbor, was killed in Rosemary's backyard. Police think she may have interrupted a burglar."

"Was Rosemary's house broken into? Anything missing?"

"I don't know," Laurie said. "The police had just let her back in. It sounded like she was still processing it all."

Her father was working his hands, thumbs against index fingers, the way he always did when something was bothering him. "Someone tries to break into her house and kills her neighbor, just as you're looking into her daughter's murder?"

"Dad, that's a stretch. You know as well as anyone that good people get hurt for all kinds of absurd reasons that only a sociopath could understand. And the victim here wasn't Rosemary Dempsey. It was a neighbor. This isn't even the same neighborhood that Susan grew up in. There's no connection."

"I don't like coincidences."

"Please don't worry about this, okay?"

She walked him to the front door as he pulled on his coat. He gave her a hug and kiss before leaving, but as she watched him walk to the elevator, she could still see him deep in thought, working those hands.

28

Leo's short walk to his apartment, a mere block from Laurie's, was filled with troubled thoughts. First he saw a woman hunched in the open door of a Mercedes—her back to the sidewalk, keys dangling from the driver's-side lock, completely focused on reaching for something in the passenger seat. One quick shove—maybe a blow to the back of the shoulder—and a carjacker could make off with her car before she could yell for help. Twenty feet later was a bag of garbage at the curb, a discarded bank statement clearly visible through the thin plastic. A half-decent identity thief could clean out the account before morning.

Then, right in front of his own building, a man was picking up scattered pills from the sidewalk and placing them into a prescription pill container. The guy was probably twenty-five years old. A tattoo on the back of his shaved head read FEARLESS.

Anyone else would assume the man had been a little clumsy, but not Leo. He'd bet the contents of his own wallet that the pills were aspirin, and that Mr. Tattoo Head had just scammed some poor pedestrian and was now reloading for the next round.

It was one of the oldest sidewalk shakedowns around. Sometimes the "dropped" item was an already-broken bottle. Sometimes a pair of preshattered sunglasses. Tonight, it was an open prescription container filled with baby aspirin. The con was to bump into a patsy, "drop" the item to the sidewalk, and then pretend it was the other person's fault. *I can't afford to replace it.* Generous people offered compensation.

Where other people would look down this block and see a woman at her car, a bag of garbage, and a guy picking up his dropped package, Leo saw the potential for crime. The response was completely involuntary, like seeing letters on a page and reading them automatically. Like hearing two plus two and thinking four. He thought like a cop at a basic cellular level.

Inside his apartment, he fired up the computer in the room that doubled as a home office and bedroom for Timmy. It wasn't as fast or sleek as the equipment Laurie had, but it was good enough for Leo.

He started by Googling Rosemary Dempsey. He skimmed the blog entry that had originally drawn his daughter to the Cinderella Murder case. Laurie had shown it to him when she was first considering the case. The author mentioned that Rosemary had moved out of the home where she'd lived with Susan and her husband before their deaths. Rosemary now lived in a gated community outside of Oakland. Bingo.

He Googled "Oakland murder gated community" and then limited his search to the last twenty-four hours. He found two news entries, both posted in the last hour by local media outlets in Northern California. Lydia Levitt, seventy-one years old, killed that afternoon in her neighborhood of Castle Crossings.

He searched for Castle Crossings and located the zip code for the area, and then entered it into the website CrimeReports. Only thirteen reported incidents in the last thirty days, almost all of them shoplifting. In the map function, he zoomed into the area directly around the gated community where the victim had lived. Zero incidents. He expanded the search to the last year. Ten incidents, nothing violent. Only one residential burglary in an entire year.

And yet today, just as *Under Suspicion* was getting ready to feature Susan Dempsey's murder, a seventy-one-year-old woman was murdered outside the home of Susan Dempsey's mother.

Leo knew that he had a tendency to worry about his daughter, not just as any father would, but as a cop. And the buzzing he felt right now was coming from the cop part of his brain. It was as primal as a lizard on an algae-covered rock, sensing the impending crack of a sledgehammer.

Leo wasn't being a paranoid parent. He was certain that Lydia Levitt's murder had something to do with *Under Suspicion*.

When sunlight broke through his bedroom blinds the next morning, Leo realized that he had not slept, but he had made a decision. He reached for the phone on his nightstand and called Laurie.

"Dad? Is everything okay?"

It was always the first thing she asked if he called too late at night, too early in the morning, or too many times in a row.

"You said you were worried about Timmy given the production schedule in California."

"Of course I'm worried. I'll figure something out, though. I always do. I can fly home on weekends. Maybe we can set up a Skype schedule, though I know that videoconferencing isn't the same as really being together."

He could tell he was not the only one who had spent the night worrying.

"That won't be necessary," he said. "We'll go with you. Timmy and me, both."

"Dad—"

"Don't argue with me on this. We're a family. I'll talk to his school. It's only a couple of weeks. We'll hire a tutor if necessary. He needs to be close to his mother."

"Okay," Laurie said after a small pause. Leo could hear the gratitude in his daughter's voice. "That's amazing. Thank you, Dad."

He felt a pang of guilt for not mentioning an ulterior motive for tagging along to California, but there was nothing to gain from discussing his worries. Laurie was not going to pull the plug on the Cinderella Murder at this point. At least he would be there to protect her if something went wrong.

He prayed that, for once, the cop part of his brain was misfiring.

29

Laurie and Grace pulled into the lot in front of REACH's Palo Alto headquarters shortly after ten A.M. The drive from their hotel in San Francisco had made New York City traffic seem hypersonic by comparison. They had only arrived in California yesterday, but Laurie was already homesick.

Today's interview with Susan's former classmate at the UCLA computer lab was the first of the preparatory interviews prior to next week's summit session in Los Angeles. It had made sense for them to start in the Bay Area, gathering background information before moving closer to both the scene of the crime and the likely suspects. While Laurie and Grace were meeting with Dwight Cook, Jerry would be scouting locations in Susan's old neighborhood. The plan was to open the episode with a montage of photographs of Susan, interspersed with footage of her high school and childhood home.

Laurie shivered as she stepped from the passenger seat of their rental car. She was wearing a lightweight cashmere sweater and black pants, with no jacket. "I always forget how chilly the Bay Area can be."

"How do you think I feel?" Grace wore a jade-green silk blouse with a deep V-neck and a black skirt that was short even for her. "I was picturing Los Angeles sunshine and mojitos when I packed."

"We're only here three days. Then you'll get your time in Hollywood."

Dwight Cook greeted them in the lobby, dressed in an expensive suit and solid red tie. Based on the photographs Laurie had seen, she had expected his uniform of jeans, T-shirts, zip-up hoodies, and canvas sneakers. She might ask Jerry to suggest that he wear whatever made him "most comfortable" to the summit taping. Looking at him today, he came across as an older version of a child in his first suit at confirmation.

Dwight led the way through the building, a labyrinth of brightly colored hallways and oddly shaped nooks and crannies. When they finally reached his office, it was absolutely serene by comparison, with cool gray walls, slate floors, and clean, modern furniture. The only personal touch in the office was a single photograph of him in a wet suit and flippers, preparing to scuba dive from the edge of a yacht into sparkling turquoise water.

"You're a diver?" she asked.

"It's probably the only thing I enjoy more than work," he said. "Can I offer you something to drink? Water? Coffee?"

She declined, but Grace took him up on the offer of water. Laurie was surprised when Dwight retrieved a bottle from a minifridge with a Nespresso coffeemaker on top of it.

"I half expected a remote-controlled robot to roll in," Laurie said with a smile.

"You have no idea how many times my own mother asked me to invent Rosie the Maid from *The Jetsons*. These days, Silicon Valley's all about phones and tablets. We've got data-compression projects, social networking apps, location interfacing technology, you name it—if it interacts with a gadget, I've probably got someone in this building working on it. The least I can do is grab my own water and coffee. Nicole tells me that your show has been successful in solving cold cases."

The abrupt change in subject was jarring, but Laurie could understand that someone as successful as Dwight Cook operated at maximum efficiency at all times.

"No guarantees," she said cautiously, "but *Under Suspicion*'s primary purpose is to revive investigations, shedding new light on old facts."

"Laurie's being too modest," Grace said, flipping a long lock of black hair behind her shoulder. "Our first episode led to the case being solved while we were still filming."

Laurie interrupted Grace's hard sell. "I think what Grace is saying is that we're devoted to doing our very best for Susan's case."

"Is it hard for you, Laurie, to work on these cases given that you lost your own husband to a violent crime?"

Laurie found herself blinking. Nicole had warned her that Dwight could be socially "awkward." However, she could not recall anyone ever asking her so directly about the personal impact of Greg's murder.

"No," she finally said. "If anything, I hope my experience makes me the right person to tell these stories. I think of our show as a voice for victims who would otherwise be forgotten."

He looked away from her direct gaze. "I'm sorry. I've been told that I can be overly blunt."

"If we're being blunt, Dwight, I may as well tell you that there are rumors that you and Susan were rivals at the lab. You were competitors for Professor Hathaway's approval."

"Someone suggested that I would have hurt Susan? Because of Hathaway?"

She saw no need to tell him that it was Keith Ratner who mentioned the theory during a phone call in which he also condemned Susan's mother for her long-standing suspicion of him and named everyone Susan had ever met as an equally viable suspect, including Dwight Cook. While Ratner's theories had all sounded pretty desperate to Laurie, these initial interviews were her opportunity to float every possible theory when cameras weren't rolling. It was good practice for when Alex Buckley grilled them more closely.

"It wasn't just about your mentor," she explained, "but your actual work. You were working at the school's lab and then formed REACH just two months after Susan died, quickly raising millions of dollars in investment capital to support your search-capacity innovation. That kind of money could be a powerful motive to get her out of the picture."

"You don't understand at all," Dwight said wistfully. Laurie had expected him to be defensive, to lash out at her with facts to demonstrate his superiority in programming skills over Susan. But instead, he sounded genuinely hurt. "I, of all people, would never have hurt Susan. I would never hurt anyone over money or anything else, but certainly not Susan. She was . . . she was my friend."

Laurie could hear the change in Dwight's voice every time he spoke Susan's name. "It seems like you were fond of her."

"Very."

"Did you know her boyfriend, Keith Ratner?"

"Unfortunately," he said. "He never took much of an interest in me, but he'd drop by the lab to meet Susan—when he wasn't late or standing her up. Let me guess: he was the one who suggested that I stole REACH from Susan?"

"I can't say."

"You don't need to. It's further proof that he never paid attention to Susan's work. He was clueless as to what she was doing at the lab. Susan never worked on search functioning, which is all REACH was when it started. She was developing voice-to-text software."

It took Laurie a moment to understand the phrase. "Like automated dictation?" she asked. "I use that on my phone to dictate e-mails."

"Exactly. If you have any doubts, we can clear them up right now." He picked up his telephone and dialed a number. "The *Under Suspicion* folks are here. Can you pop up?"

A minute later, a handsome man in his late fifties walked into Dwight's office. He was dressed casually in a lightweight madras shirt and khaki pants, but the look suited him well, with his tan and a full head of dark waves. He introduced himself as Richard Hathaway.

"We were just talking about Susan's work with you at UCLA," Laurie said.

"Such a waste. That sounds cold, I know. Any loss of a young life is a waste. But Susan was bright. She wasn't twenty-four/seven at the keyboard, the way some programmers are." He gave Dwight a smile. "But she was creative. Her ability to connect socially—in a way some of us computer types struggle with—helped her connect technology to real life."

"I'll step out for a moment," Dwight offered. "Mrs. Moran has something she needs to ask you."

Once she was alone with the former professor, Laurie asked if Susan had been working on a particular project.

"It might help to understand how I ran my lab. Computer work can be solitary, so my research assistants acted primarily as teaching assistants for my intro classes. They might also help on isolated portions of my own work, which at the time was in software pipelining—a technique for overlapping loop iterations. And of course you have no idea what any of that means, right?"

"Nope."

"Nor should you. It's a method of program optimization, interesting only to people who write code. Anyway, I selected students whose own independent projects during freshman year showed promise. Susan's was speech-to-text, what most of us would call dictation. It was all pretty rudimentary in the nineties, but Steve Jobs could never have given us Siri without basic speech-recognition function. If she had lived—well, who knows?"

"Did she work with Dwight on REACH?"

"REACH didn't exist yet. But she and Dwight worked in proximity to each other, if that's what you mean. But Dwight's work was quite different. As you probably know, REACH launched a new way to locate information on the Internet, back when people were still calling it the World Wide Web. No, that wasn't anything like Susan's area of interest."

"Professor—"

"Please, 'Richard' is fine. I retired from the academy long ago, and even then, I didn't particularly care for the titles."

"You seem young to be retired."

"And I've been retired a long time. I left UCLA to help Dwight build REACH. Imagine being a sophomore in college and having captains of industry fighting to get a meeting with you. I recognize brilliance when I see it, and I was willing to support him full-time while he insisted on finishing up at UCLA—to make his parents proud, if you can believe it. I thought it would be a pit stop for me as I transitioned to the private sector, and yet here I am, twenty years later."

"That's nice that the two of you are so close."

"It may sound corny, but I don't have any kids of my own. Dwight—well, yes, we are indeed close."

"I get the impression that Dwight might be more comfortable speaking with our host, Alex Buckley, if he has an old friend like you around." What she meant was that Hathaway would present far better on television than the unpolished Dwight Cook. "Is it possible you could join us for filming in Los Angeles? The current plan is to locate a house somewhere near the university."

"Absolutely," he said. "Whatever you need."

Keith Ratner's accusation of a professional rivalry between Susan and Dwight seemed far-fetched when first offered. Now both Dwight and Professor Hathaway had debunked it. Laurie would confirm with Rosemary and Nicole that Susan had never had run-ins with Dwight, because it was essential that she follow every possible lead.

But every fiber of Laurie's being told her that the real answers to Susan's death could only be found in Los Angeles.

30

Dwight was alone again in his office once Hathaway offered to escort the TV people out of their maze of a building.

He could tell from the look Hathaway gave him as he walked out that he wasn't pleased with the producer's questions about REACH, but at least they hadn't wandered into thorny territory. The notion that Susan had anything to do with the technology was completely off base.

Still, he wished he could rewind the clock and start the morning over again. He planned to bring up the subject of Laurie's late husband as a way to make his contact with her more personal. But the overture had gone over like a ton of bricks. When Dwight and Hathaway first started meeting with venture capitalists, Hathaway had told him, *You're just so* blunt! *I'm talking blunt like a ten-pound mallet. That's fine when you're talking to me, but when it comes to money, you've got to learn some nuance.*

Their relationship was blunt by design. Dwight's mind wandered to that Friday night of his sophomore year when Hathaway had stumbled upon him in the lab, catching Dwight hacking into the registrar's office's database. Though he wasn't cheating or changing grades, Dwight wanted to prove to himself that he could slip through the virtual walls of his own university. It was illegal, and a violation of the school's code of conduct, plus Dwight had been stupid enough to do it on the computer lab's equipment, which the university often monitored. Hathaway said he believed that Dwight had no ill motives and would defend him to the university, but he felt obligated to notify the administration to protect his own lab.

Dwight was so upset about disappointing his mentor that he came to the lab late the following night, intending to clean out his workstation and leave a letter of resignation. Instead of finding the lab empty, Dwight found a female student he recognized from the Intro to Computer Science class for which he was a teaching assistant. She was leaving Hathaway's office. Dwight couldn't help but think of the campus whispers about the most "crush-worthy" teacher.

He might have slipped out of the lab, resigning as intended, if the soles of his tennis shoes hadn't squeaked against the tile floors. Hathaway emerged from his office and explained that he saw no reason to report Dwight's hacking to the university after all. The administration would only blow the activities out of proportion, failing to understand the natural curiosity of someone with Dwight's blossoming talents. He forced Dwight to promise, however, that he would channel those skills into legitimate work—the kind that could earn a young man a fortune in Silicon Valley.

That conversation eventually gave rise to a strange kind of friendship. The student-teacher, mentor-mentee relationship became more peer-to-peer, marked by utter mutual honesty. Hathaway was the first adult to ever treat Dwight like a real person, not like a broken child who needed to be fixed or isolated. In return, Dwight accepted Hathaway, even if he was a little shady. How else would REACH have ever started if he and Hathaway had not trusted each other completely?

If only Dwight had Hathaway's knack for schmoozing. Maybe he could have mentioned Laurie's husband without sticking his foot in his mouth. He hoped he hadn't offended her so much that she would cut him from the production.

Once everyone was gathered in Los Angeles, all he'd need was a few seconds of access to each person's cell phone, and all their texts, e-mails, and phone calls would be downloaded automatically to Dwight's computer. The problem was, he didn't know whether they'd all show up for filming at once or if their appointments would be back-to-back.

Thinking about the Los Angeles shoot gave him an idea. He pulled up the last e-mail he had received from Jerry, the assistant producer who Laurie mentioned was scouting locations near campus. He opened a new message and began to type.

After hitting the SEND key, he leaned back in his chair and looked at the photograph next to his computer. Hathaway had snapped it three years ago on a dive trip during REACH's annual corporate retreat to Anguilla. The company had flown every single employee— down to the student interns—for a four-day stay at the luxurious Viceroy. Everyone had gushed over the sprawling resort property and the pillow-soft white sand of Meads Bay, but for Dwight, those trips were always about traveling beneath the water. The picture on his desk was from a wall dive at the keys of Dog Island with a sheer one-hundred-foot drop. He swam with tuna, turtles, yellowtail snapper, even a reef shark and two southern stingrays. Deep in the sea is where his thoughts found calm.

He stared into the water in the photograph, wishing he could jump through the frame. He needed calm right now. This television show had him feeling all the pain of losing Susan again. And when he wasn't reliving the pain, he was wired with anticipation about the possibility of finally learning who had killed the only woman he had ever loved.

31

Rosemary Dempsey ran her fingertips along the dark gray granite countertop as she paced the length of the kitchen. "It feels so strange to be back here. I cooked in this room almost every day for nearly forty years."

Rosemary had put together a collection of her daughter's childhood photographs and mementos—a blue ribbon won in a science fair, the banner she'd worn as her high school's homecoming queen. She had even given Laurie and her crew the guest book from Susan's memorial service.

Now they were inside the Dempsey family's former home, where Jerry had arranged for them to shoot today's interview. This was the kitchen where Rosemary first learned that her daughter's body had been found in Laurel Canyon Park.

"I thought it would be traumatic to come back here," Rosemary said. "But after what happened in my backyard last week, it's nice to get away from my 'new' neighborhood."

"Have the police made any progress in your friend's investigation?"

"Apparently not. You might have found another case for your show," she said with a sad smile.

Laurie could tell that Rosemary needed to ease into a conversation about that horrible morning when she learned of Susan's death.

Laurie shot a look to Jerry, who was lingering next to the camera-men stationed near the sliding glass doors at the edge of the kitchen. He gave her an *okay* sign. Though they were keeping their distance, they could capture what they needed to get on video.

"Has the house changed much since you lived here?" Laurie asked.

Rosemary stopped pacing and looked around her. "No, not in any obvious way. But it feels completely different. Their furniture— it's much more modern than ours. And our art is gone. The photo-graphs. All of the things that made this house our home are either with me at the new place or in storage."

"If it wouldn't be too painful," Laurie said, "maybe you can point out a few details in the house that were significant to your daughter. Perhaps we can start with her room?"

Laurie wouldn't need footage from other parts of the house, but a tour through the home was a way to get Rosemary to loosen up and start talking about Susan. The show only worked when they could portray the victim not as a piece of evidence in a mystery to be solved but as a living human being.

Rosemary led the way up the mission-style staircase to a bedroom at the end of the upstairs hallway. Her hand trembled as she turned the doorknob. The room was set up now as a nursery, with lavender-colored walls hand-stenciled with yellow tulips.

She walked to the window and fingered the latch. "See how the overhang above the front porch is just beneath the window here? I used to check this lock every single night because I had a fear that someone would sneak in and grab my baby."

Next she walked to the closet and ran her fingers along the inside of the door frame. "This is where we used to chart her growth, draw-ing a new line for every birthday. They've painted it over since then, but I swear, you can still seem them. See? Faint little lines."

Laurie looked over Rosemary's shoulder and smiled, even though all she saw was clean white paint.

When they were back in the kitchen and in front of the cameras, Laurie felt like Rosemary was ready. "Please," Laurie encouraged gently, "tell us how you learned about your daughter's murder."

Rosemary nodded slowly. "It was the weekend of Jack's sixtieth birthday. We had a big party here on Saturday, outside. It was a beautiful night. Everything was so perfect, except Susan couldn't be there. She called that afternoon to wish Jack a happy birthday, but he was at the club for a round of golf. He worked *so* hard. Always. She was in good spirits, excited about school, and very excited about the audition she had that night."

"The one with Frank Parker?"

"Yes. She told me his name, but I hadn't heard of him. She said he was a real up-and-comer. She said . . . she said she felt 'lucky,' like it was 'too good to be true.'" Her voice caught as she repeated her daughter's words. "Then we got the call from the police the next morning. The funny thing is, I had a terrible feeling all day that something was wrong, like this vague but terrifying foreboding."

"About Susan?"

"No, not initially. More this floating anxiety. But that all changed once the police called. It was the LAPD. They had found a body. You know the rest—one of her shoes had fallen off, presumably as she was chased through Laurel Canyon Park. Her cell phone was nearby too. Her lucky necklace had been pulled from her throat. They wanted to know why she might have been at the park. I told them she was meeting that night with Frank Parker. It was only later that we learned that his house was only a mile or so from the location where they found her body."

Laurie could see the grief gripping Rosemary, all these years later. She knew full well it would never disappear. "Going back to Frank Parker, did that strike you as peculiar, for him to meet with Susan at night?" Laurie asked gently.

"No, but she didn't tell me she was going to his house. And I assumed that her agent would be there. Trust me, if I could turn back time, I'd stop her from ever going to that audition."

"Why? Because you think Frank Parker is the one who hurt your daughter?"

Rosemary looked down at her hands and shook her head. "No. I wish I could have stopped her from going up to the Hollywood Hills that night, because at least she would have been closer to campus, where she knew her way around. She wouldn't have been wearing silver shoes that she couldn't run in. At the very least, even if she couldn't escape, she wouldn't have been called Cinderella, as if my daughter were some pretty little girl trying to win a prince for the night. That nickname and the Hollywood setting wouldn't have been such a painful distraction."

"A distraction from what, Rosemary?"

Rosemary paused, pressing her lips together as she chose her next words. When she finally spoke, any nerves she'd had about the cameras were gone. She looked directly into the lens like a trained TV star. "A distraction from the truth, which is that the most dangerous person in Susan's life was much closer to home: her boyfriend, Keith Ratner. He was a cheater and a liar, and he knew my Susan was going places he could only dream of. I will go to my grave believing he is the one who killed my baby."

32

The next morning, Laurie hopped out of the van in front of Nicole Melling's house. It was ten degrees warmer on this side of the Golden Gate Bridge than it had been when they'd left their hotel in downtown San Francisco half an hour earlier.

Jerry let out a whistle as he took in the view. "I may never go back to New York City."

The house was situated at the top of a ridge above town, at the edge of Sorich Ranch Park. They were looking out across Ross Valley to two tree-covered mountains in the distance, the green of the leaves broken only by the early blooming of dogwoods.

Laurie heard the van's rear door slide open and watched as Grace managed to climb out in form-fitting leggings and thigh-high leather stiletto boots. "Wow," she said, following the direction of their gaze. "That's almost enough to make me appreciate nature."

"It's hard to believe we're only twenty miles away from the city," Laurie said.

Jerry nudged Grace, who was fiddling with her iPhone. "Your love of nature didn't last long," he joked.

"Not true. I was doing research," she said indignantly. She held up the screen and showed an image close to the view in front of them. "Those are Bald Hill and Mount Tamalpais," she said, stumbling over the pronunciation. "And in case you're wondering, according to Zillow, this house is worth—"

Jerry admonished her with a scolding index finger. "No! It's bad enough that you cyberstalk everyone you meet, but I do *not* want to be a part of it. Yesterday, Laurie, she found a website called Who's Dated Who. The grammar's wrong, first of all. It should be Who's Dated *Whom*. But thanks to that nonsense, I spent the entire delay at baggage claim hearing about the various ingénues linked to Frank Parker before he finally got married."

"Oh, Jerry, if you only knew. That list was so long, it could have kept us occupied through hotel check-in."

Jerry wasn't done complaining. "And speaking of baggage claim, do you think you brought enough luggage, Grace? I managed to make the trip with only a carry-on."

"Don't blame the bags on me!" Grace protested. "It was your father, Laurie. He insisted on packing heat. Transporting a gun from New York to California means checking luggage. So, yes, Jerry, I figured if I had to go through the process, I might as well bring all my favorite shoes."

Laurie shook her head and laughed. Jerry and Grace worked incredibly well together, but sometimes she felt like they warranted their own reality show with their Mutt-and-Jeff personality differences.

"My father doesn't *pack heat*, Grace. But once a cop, always a cop: the man can't sleep if he doesn't have that gun in his nightstand. Now, let's focus on Susan's former roommate. And what she might be hiding."

The interior of Nicole Melling's home was as picture-perfect as its surroundings. Nicole greeted them in a light-filled foyer lined with brightly colored contemporary art. Laurie had done some cyber research of her own and had been unable to find a single photograph of Nicole online. All she had were a couple of high school yearbook photos Jerry had tracked down from Nicole's hometown of Irvine, and her freshman class photo at UCLA. Even in her college photograph, Nicole hadn't looked much older than fourteen.

The woman standing in front of Laurie today looked nothing like Laurie had expected. It's not that Nicole had aged poorly. The adult version was far more attractive than the plain-looking, freckle-faced girl from those photographs. But she had changed her appearance drastically. The strawberry-blond hair that had hung well past her shoulders was now dyed and cropped into a dark brown, chin-length bob. Perhaps it was only for the cameras, but at least for today, she wore dramatic makeup, her eyes lined with charcoal. Perhaps more striking than any identifiable physical change, there was a confidence in the way she carried herself that had been lacking in those early photographs.

"Nicole," Laurie said, offering a handshake, "thank you so much for being a part of *Under Suspicion*. Rosemary told me how close you and Susan became in college."

"She was very caring toward me," Nicole said quietly. She led them through the foyer into a large living room with open views of the valley outside.

They were interrupted by the appearance of a man wearing a loose oxford-cloth shirt and khakis. He had a bit of a paunch and was beginning to bald but had an inviting smile. Laurie thought she detected the faint smell of soap.

"Hey there. I thought I should at least say hello. I'm the husband, Gavin."

Laurie rose from her chair to shake his hand. "You certainly didn't have to take the day off for us," she said.

"Oh, I didn't. I work upstairs." He pointed to the staircase off the foyer.

"Gavin's in finance," Nicole explained. "His firm is in the city, but he works here unless he has meetings."

"Lucky you," Laurie said. "Did you also go to UCLA? Is that how you met?"

"Oh no. I was out of Harvard and working at a start-up in San Francisco—one of the first companies that let regular people buy and sell stock online without a broker. I met Nicole in a bar."

His wife rolled her eyes in frustration. "I hate it when you tell people that. It makes me sound cheap."

"What's worse is that she fell for my completely cheesy pickup line. I asked her if she had a Band-Aid, because I skinned my knee falling for her."

Laurie feigned a groan. "Oh, that is *awful*."

"True," Gavin said, "but it was intentionally awful. There's a difference."

"To be clear," Nicole said, "that's just how we *met*. I felt sorry enough to give him my phone number, but we began to date properly after that."

"And what brought you up to San Francisco after UCLA?" Laurie asked. She knew that Nicole quit school after her sophomore year and assumed it was because of what happened to Susan. She was always amazed to learn how the death of one person rippled out to change the course of so many other lives.

"I had originally wanted to go to Stanford or Berkeley, so I guess I felt a pull from Northern California. I mean, look at that view."

The story sounded polite but superficial. "So, did you continue school up here?" Laurie asked.

"Nope." Nicole shook her head and said nothing more.

"It's just, I couldn't help but notice that many of the people closest to Susan seem to have left school. You, Madison Meyer, Keith Ratner."

"You'd have to ask them. I assume it's not uncommon for actors to leave school if they start getting regular work. And of course Madison got that role in *Beauty Land*. As for me, I think Susan's death made me realize life was short."

"Are you still in touch with Madison or Keith?"

Nicole shook her head.

Laurie got the impression that this subject was making Nicole uncomfortable and decided to approach the questioning from a different angle. "So, when Mr. Pickup Man here threw you his clever line, you were still new to the area?"

Gavin was the one who laughed. "Like, just-off-the-train new. And nervous. She admitted giving me her number, but what she didn't tell you was that she gave me a fake name."

"No, really?" Laurie asked. "Why in the world?"

Nicole shifted in her seat. "Wow, I did *not* think we'd be talking about this. Truth be told, I was in that bar with a fake ID. I didn't want the bartender to hear me using a name that didn't match the license I'd just shown him. Besides, I can't be the first woman who made up a fake name with a stranger trying to talk her up at a bar."

"Certainly not," Laurie said. But usually the fake name would come with a fake number, too. How many times had a younger Laurie, borrowing the lyrics of an old pop song, scribbled *Jenny, 867-5309*, on the inside of some drunk playboy's matchbook?

"Anyway," Gavin said, "it was love at almost-first-sight. We got married exactly six months after we met."

Nicole smiled and patted her husband's forearm. "Like I said, life is short."

"I never realized that Susan was the reason you were willing to jump in so fast," Gavin said. "In fact, Nicole never even talked about being Susan's roommate until we happened to bump into Susan's mother, Rosemary, at one of those huge dim sum places in Chinatown. Remember that, honey?"

Nicole raised her eyebrows but said nothing.

"You remember," her husband prompted. "Over all that noise from the tables and the food carts, I heard some woman yelling, 'Nicole. Nicole Hunter?' That's her maiden name. And then Rosemary runs over and gives my wife this huge hug. So, of course, I ask her, 'Who's that?' And then she tells me she was roommates with the Cinderella Murder victim."

"It wasn't something I liked to talk about," Nicole said. "Even now."

"Anyway, I was the one who went back to Rosemary's table and insisted that she give us a call."

Laurie had gotten the impression from Rosemary that Susan and Nicole had been best friends, but now she was learning that Nicole initially did not mention Susan's murder to her own husband and had no relationship with Susan's mother until Gavin suggested it.

She had been warned by Rosemary that Nicole could be shy and might even come off as aloof. But sitting here in Nicole's living room, watching the woman continue that polite smile, Laurie was certain that Susan's supposed best friend was lying to her.

33

J erry snapped his seat belt closed and started the engine of the van. "Take one more look at that amazing view," he said, "because I think that was the only reason to drive up here."

"No kidding," Grace said, leaning forward from the backseat. "That was a total bust. Talk about a cold fish."

So Laurie was not the only one who had noticed that Nicole hadn't exactly been forthcoming with her memories of Susan Dempsey.

Jerry used his turn signal, despite the absence of any oncoming traffic, and pulled away from the curb. "It's like she wasn't even there."

"I agree," Laurie said. "She did seem a bit distracted."

"No, I mean, like she wasn't even there at UCLA," Jerry said. "She didn't stay in touch with her friends. She didn't offer any stories about Susan other than how nice she was to her. All she wanted to do was talk about everyone else: how strange it was that Frank Parker wanted to meet Susan at his home, how hungry Madison was for fame, how Susan had caught her boyfriend flirting with other girls multiple times. It's like she wanted us to focus on everyone else except her."

Laurie was trying to figure out why Nicole might have held back with them when her thoughts were interrupted by her cell phone. It was her father.

"Is everything okay, Dad?"

"All good. I think we've got Timmy on a decent schedule after the flight west. He slept until seven thirty, had a big breakfast at the hotel restaurant, then we went down to Fisherman's Wharf for lunch and had a whole platter of fish and chips."

"You know you're not supposed to eat that stuff." Only last year, her father had been rushed to Mount Sinai Hospital with cardiac fibrillation. Two stents in his right ventricle later, he was now supposed to keep a heart-healthy diet.

"No worries, Dr. Laurie. I got grilled halibut and salad. And—in full disclosure—four french fries."

"I suppose we can let that slide. We're on our way back to the hotel now. Dinner at Mama Torini's?" Laurie had visited San Francisco with her parents when she was considering applying to Stanford twenty years ago. Her best memories of the trip were of Leo locking Laurie's mother in a cell at Alcatraz and dinner at Mama Torini's, with its red-and-white-checked tablecloths and heaping portions of fettuccine Alfredo prepared tableside. "I think Timmy would love it."

"Great minds think alike. That's why I was calling. I made a reservation at seven. Figured that was as late as we could push it with Timmy but knew you were working."

Even with Timmy and her father here, she was having a hard time juggling her schedule to see them. She assured her father she'd be back to the hotel within the hour and hung up.

Grace was leaning forward from the backseat again, fiddling with her phone. "Remember that site Who's Dated Who?" she asked.

"*Whom*," Jerry corrected. "Who's Dated *Whom*. I'm going to write them an e-mail, demanding that they add an 'm.'"

"Well, I looked up Susan's high school sweetheart, Keith Ratner. Get a load of this." She began rattling off a long list of names of women who had been linked to the B-list actor over the years.

"I think I've only heard of two of those people," Laurie said. They were both actresses a good ten years younger than Keith.

"Oh, he's in no position to land anyone famous anymore," Grace said. "But my point is that the list is long. Rosemary and Nicole both said he cheated on Susan. Guess a player's always a player."

"But cheating's not the same as killing someone," Jerry said.

"No," Grace said, "but if she caught him? I could picture it. Keith could've been driving her up to the audition either hoping to get a part for himself or making sure Frank didn't try to get handsy with his girl. If Susan confronted him about cheating, they could have gotten into a fight. She gets mad and storms out of the car. I know I've done it. He starts chasing her. They fight, and things get out of control."

It wasn't a bad theory. It would explain how Susan had wound up near Laurel Canyon Park while her car was found on campus.

Jerry stopped at a red light. "Too bad Keith has an alibi, and we don't have any evidence."

"It's like that old game Clue," Laurie said, thinking about playing the game with her son at home. "We look at every possible theory and try to poke holes in each one. When there's only one theory standing, we might actually have some answers."

"And that's where our dreamy host, Alex Buckley, comes in," Grace said. "Speaking of which, let's type his name in here and see what we find. Ooh, he's no Keith Ratner, but he's not exactly a monk." Grace began reading names from Who's Dated Who. Laurie recognized more than a few: a model, an actress, an opera singer, a morning news anchor.

The light turned green, and Jerry took a right turn. Laurie was so distracted by Grace's babble that she did not notice that the cream-colored pickup truck that had been parked on Nicole's street was now taking the same turn behind them.

34

Martin Collins rested in a rattan lounger on the back deck of his 8,700-square-foot Sunset Strip home. He looked out beyond his infinity pool to the sun beginning to set on the city below. He had purchased this house four years ago for more money than he had ever dreamed of earning. It was a far cry from the fleabag apartment where he'd grown up in Nebraska. He was born to live here.

He returned his attention to the folder of documents on his lap. They were mock-ups of the latest brochures for Advocates for God, complete with photographs of smiling church members handing out canned goods to the needy, family picnics, and Martin throwing a Frisbee for a yellow Labrador retriever. Market research showed that, more than any breed, people associated Labradors with strength and trust. Martin nodded approvingly. These were the kinds of images that new followers could pass on to friends and family members to expand Advocates for God's numbers. More members meant more contributions.

The moment of optimism was cut short as he remembered that he needed to call Steve Roman for an update on Nicole. He pulled up the number on his cell and hit ENTER.

"Good timing," Steve said by way of a greeting. "I just left Nicole's house. The TV crew was there."

"Any chance you know what she told them?"

He felt his frustration rise when Steve answered in the negative. For the past week, Steve's reports had been abnormally terse. It might be time to send another minion to replace him.

"Is there something you're not telling me?" Martin asked.

"Of course not," Steve assured him.

Martin was aware of Steve's violent past—the robberies, the bar fights, the unpredictable attacks of anger he used to have before finding the church. Still, Steve had never given him cause for worry. More than perhaps any other devotee of Advocates for God, Steve had truly changed. And he was loyal.

"I stayed in the truck while the crew went in the house," Steve was saying. "It's a big place. She must have done pretty well for herself—money-wise, I mean."

"So that's all you have?"

"For now, but I'm tailing the TV crew. They just dropped off two guys and a bunch of equipment at a warehouse and are weaving through downtown San Francisco now. I figure if I stay on them, I might be able to overhear something. What specifically should I be listening for?"

"You know how we talk about people who don't understand Advocates for God? Who try to say the worst about our good works? Well, Nicole might be the worst enemy this church has. Given a platform on a national TV show, she may be tempted to attack our beliefs. To make up lies about either AG or me personally. I need to know what, if anything, Nicole reveals about her time at UCLA."

Though Martin typically gave away no secrets, it had been impossible to rely on Steve as his eyes and ears without trusting him with at least some background information. So Steve knew that Nicole had been an early member of Advocates for God who left on bad terms. He knew that Nicole's college roommate Susan Dempsey had been murdered, and that her death was the focus of this television show that had Martin concerned about unfavorable news coverage.

Martin had no plans to reveal anything more. After all, that had been his mistake with Nicole—letting her know a side of him that she was not ready to see. At first, when she quit school and left town, he kept waiting for the other shoe to drop, questioning whether he had done enough to ensure her silence. But then months became years, and years became close to two decades.

And now this stupid show. He had watched the first special and knew how thorough they were in their reporting. Would Nicole be able to get through this without her association with AG coming to light?

"But the show is about Nicole's roommate," Steve said. "What does Susan Dempsey's murder have to do with AG?"

"You are asking more questions than you should, Steve."

Martin spoke with his usual chilly confidence.

"My apologies," Steve said cautiously. "I'll keep watching. Wait, they're stopping now at some high-rise hotel. Yeah, they're getting out. I can tell which one's in charge by the way she's giving orders— a woman in the front passenger seat. I'll park and get a bead on her on foot. See what I can find out."

"You do that, Steve."

35

It was barely seven o'clock in the evening, but Nicole was already at her bathroom vanity, washing off the heavy layer of makeup she'd worn for the cameras today. Gone, too, was her tailored black sheath dress, replaced with her usual ensemble of yoga pants and a hoodie.

When she was done patting her face dry, she opened her eyes to find Gavin's image behind hers in the mirror.

"That's my wife," he said, wrapping his arms around her waist and giving her a kiss on her freshly scrubbed cheek. "You looked beautiful today, but I always prefer you like this."

She turned to face him and returned his embrace. "I've never been beautiful. The makeup certainly helps, but I don't understand how anyone can put up with all of that work every day."

"You've always been beautiful to me."

"Please, when you met me, I still looked like a dorky teenager. I guess I should be grateful now that I've always looked young for my age."

Gavin was smiling to himself.

"What's so funny?" she asked.

"Telling that TV producer about how we met. It's been a long time since I thought about that. We owe our marriage to that fake ID of yours."

"I had that ID because of Madison. She got them for Susan and me so we could go celebrity-watching on the club scene."

"I can't even picture you doing that."

That, Nicole thought, is because you never knew me when I was a follower. A lemming. The girl whose own parents knew she would get "lost" on her own. The one who started spending more time with the crooks at Advocates for God than with her own best friend.

"Are you done with your work?" she asked.

"Just a couple e-mails, and I'll be yours for the night."

"Sounds good. I'll start dinner. Lasagna sound good?"

"Delicious," he said, giving her another buss on the cheek.

He padded down the hall to his office, while she made her way downstairs to the kitchen. As she chopped some fresh basil for the pasta sauce, she replayed her conversation today with the television crew. Nicole thought that she'd done a good job talking about Madison, Keith, and Frank Parker, the three people who were truly under suspicion. But before they'd even spoken about the investigation, Laurie had launched all those questions about why Nicole had left college and moved to the Bay Area. She even seemed a little too curious about the fact that Nicole had given Gavin a fake name when they first met.

Did she know that Nicole had been using that fake identification for more than wine purchases after she fled Los Angeles? Did she already know about Advocates for God?

No, it was impossible. Nicole had never even spoken the words "Advocates for God" or "Martin Collins" since she left L.A. She was too terrified.

Maybe Keith Ratner had told the producers about Nicole's association with AG. After all, she was the one who first introduced him to the racket. No one in Advocates for God would refer to it as a racket, of course. They called it a religion. They said they were committed to "good works."

That was so long ago that sometimes Nicole had a hard time remembering when exactly Susan had started to feel so much animosity about Advocates for God. At first, Susan was supportive. Just like Susan had her theater activities and computer work without Nicole, Nicole was finding a new network of friends in what she had initially described to Susan as a "volunteer group" focused on "serving the poor." But when Nicole began to advance farther into the circle — and began soliciting donations from wealthier students like Susan — Susan questioned the church's ongoing demands for money.

It was the very beginning of spring semester, sophomore year, when Nicole told Susan that she had started seeing Martin Collins over the holiday break, not just as part of the group, but as his girl-friend. She expected Susan to be worried about the age difference: Nicole, having graduated early from high school, was only eighteen, and Martin was twenty-nine. But Susan's concerns ran deeper. She said Advocates for God was a fraud. That Martin was lining his pock-ets with money meant for the poor. That he was enlisting vulnerable people to treat him like God. She said she felt like Nicole was slip-ping into "another world." That she was "brainwashed." She asked why a twenty-nine-year-old man would be interested in a college sophomore in the first place.

"How can you know anything about Martin when you've never met him? How can you judge AG when you refuse to learn anything about it? No wonder Martin says you're trying to corrupt me!" Ni-cole had yelled. It was their very first argument.

But it wasn't until Nicole invited Keith to join Martin and her at a revival that Susan truly became angry. Nicole had never seen her like that. Susan was always so calm, smiling like she was tell-ing herself a secret joke or listening to her own private soundtrack. But that day, she was screaming at Nicole with such fervor that her pale face turned bright red, makeup streaking her cheeks. *Keith needs attention from every girl he meets. First it was Madison. Now it's you. But you're worse than Madison. She's a harmless flirt, but you had to take my boyfriend to your ridiculous Bible-thumping cult! What is* happening *to you, Nicole? It's like I don't even know you anymore.*

Even now, Nicole could not actually remember picking up her political science textbook and throwing it at Susan's head. She just saw Susan freeze, her mouth open in shock. She remembered trying to apologize, but Susan wouldn't calm down. "That's it, Nicole," she had screamed from the doorway. "I love you, but you either quit that cult or you're moving out!"

It was the last conversation they ever had.

Nicole had fled the dorm, too, walking to Martin's house, and then into his bedroom unannounced. He wasn't alone. In that moment, Nicole realized why Martin had liked her in the first place. She had always looked younger than her age. But as it turned out, she was not quite young enough for Martin Collins.

36

Mama Torini's looked exactly as Leo remembered it: red-and-white-checked tablecloths, dark wood molding, bright yellow walls barely visible beneath decades of Italian movie posters and signed celebrity photographs. He couldn't believe it had been twenty-two years since he was here with Laurie and Eileen. He wished his wife were here to share the experience with her grandson, but he had lost her ten years earlier to a heart attack, before she'd even had a chance to meet Timmy. He wished Laurie's husband, Greg, were here, too. But like the song said, you can't always get what you want. He was lucky to have Timmy and Laurie in his life.

Leo noticed a well-dressed man at the next table admiring Laurie's appearance as she took her seat. As usual, his daughter was completely unaware of the attention. Her focus was entirely on Timmy as she pointed out an autographed picture of Wynton Marsalis with two of the restaurant's waiters.

"So what did you and Grandpa do today?" she asked once they were settled in.

"We walked and walked," Timmy said, "like probably a hundred miles. We walked even more than we do in New York. And you can feel it more because of all the hills. I was like . . ." He stopped talking long enough to pant like a tired dog. "I told Grandpa when we got back to the hotel room that if we took one more step, my feet would fall off."

She feigned a look beneath the table. "We just walked here, and you've still got your feet. Did you actually see anything while you did all this walking and panting?"

"It was awesome! We saw everything," he said excitedly. "Chinatown; the piers; a place called Exploratorium, which was totally cool. And, Grandpa, what was that super-steep, twisty street?"

"Lombard. And the kid here walked it bottom to top like a champ."

"That certainly does sound like a busy day," Laurie said.

Timmy's rendition made it sound as if sightseeing had consumed their entire day. But Leo had found time to do some work on his own. His primary job here was to watch his grandson while Laurie was working, but if he was truly going to keep them both safe, he couldn't turn off the part of his brain that had brought him to California—the cop part.

NYPD inspector Leo Farley had spent twenty minutes of Timmy's television time on the phone with Detective Alan O'Brien, the lead investigator in the murder of Lydia Levitt. Somebody else calling the Alameda County sheriff's department about an unsolved homicide the previous week might have gotten the brush-off, but more than thirty years on the job came in handy, despite retirement and being on a different coast.

He knew from Detective O'Brien that the police had no suspects in Lydia's murder, even unofficially. The sad reality was that domestic violence was usually to blame when women were killed. But police had found absolutely no evidence to suggest any discord, let alone physical violence, in the Levitt marriage. By all accounts, Lydia's husband, Don, was a stand-up citizen with an ironclad alibi at the time of his wife's murder, thanks to surveillance cameras at his gym.

The next theory was some kind of secret life that might have put Lydia in danger. But a thorough search of the family's home and computers had turned up no reason to believe that Lydia was any-thing other than she appeared to be: a seventy-one-year-old wife, mother, and grandmother who liked to garden, eat out at restaurants, and talk to her neighbors.

According to Detective O'Brien, the most likely explanation was that Lydia interrupted a burglary attempt at Rosemary's house. The police were chasing down the local thieves in hopes of a tip.

"Did Rosemary tell you that her daughter was murdered twenty years ago?" Leo had asked the detective.

"She did," Detective O'Brien had said. "She was understand-ably upset about her neighbor and then mentioned it brought back memories of Susan. The Cinderella Murder. Gotta wonder whether that one will ever be solved."

"That's actually why I'm in California." Leo explained Laurie's decision to feature Susan Dempsey's case in *Under Suspicion*. "I've got to admit that I didn't feel too right when I heard there was a mur-der at the home of one of the show participants right when produc-tion was starting."

"You think Lydia Levitt's murder is somehow related to *Under Suspicion?*"

"I thought I should at least throw the possibility out there. And if you happen to pick up on anything that indicates a connection, I'd sure appreciate a call."

Leo had to hope Detective O'Brien would keep his word. He sounded trustworthy over the phone. Until Leo could prove to Lau-rie that Rosemary's neighbor was killed because of the show, he would never be able to convince her she was in danger.

There'd been one other phone call during Timmy's nap, from Alex Buckley. That one he could share with his daughter.

"Alex called today," he said.

"He called me too but didn't leave a message. What's he up to?"

Leo could never tell whether Laurie was actually interested in

Leo's Alex updates or was just following along, as she would with any other story.

"He's looking forward to the trip out."

"Great. Once we get to the summit session, he can go into cross-examination mode."

"That's why he was calling. He's heading to Los Angeles tomorrow."

Leo saw the confusion on his daughter's face.

"I think you misheard, Dad. We're laying the groundwork for now, getting some first-person narratives. Alex isn't needed until the summit."

"I know that was the plan. But I guess Brett decided he wanted Alex to have as much contact as possible with the suspects, or the players, or whatever you call them. Alex said something about Brett having sprung news on you before, so he was trying to make sure you knew he was flying out early."

Timmy's summary of the day's activities had finally gotten Laurie out of work mode, but now Leo could see the tension immediately return to his daughter's face. "No, I didn't know that. Typical Brett."

"Are you upset? Alex is our friend. He's a good man."

"I want him to come. Of course I do. But I had intended to get my own fix on the people he'll be interviewing first."

"It sounds like you are trying to come up with reasons to keep him away—"

"Dad. Please."

Leo knew it was time to change the subject. "So you met Susan's roommate today? Nicole?"

She nodded. "She was nothing like I expected. I got a very peculiar vibe off of her. I know it sounds crazy, but I've got to wonder if the police even looked into her as a suspect. They may have had their hands too full with the others to have even asked where Susan's supposed best friend was."

"Sometimes I really do think you inherited my cop brain."

"This is more my reporter brain. *Under Suspicion* may be reality TV, but I haven't forgotten my journalistic roots. Just as we don't want to skew the facts to make people look guilty if they are not, I don't want to present Nicole as the angelic best friend if there's another side to the story."

"So what are you going to do?"

"I'm going to find out the truth about who Nicole Melling really was back at UCLA—back when she was known as Nicole Hunter."

Steve Roman's thoughts were halted by the appearance of the bartender, his dark hair slicked back into a ponytail, his tight black T-shirt accentuating his biceps.

"Another club soda, sir?"

Steve snuck a glance at the woman, older gentleman, and child. The woman was signaling for the check. "I'm good," he said. "Thanks."

Steve tried to avoid any temptation to imbibe alcohol, but tonight, his presence at the bar in Mama Torini's was unavoidable. This stool, just fifteen feet from the television woman's table, allowed him to overhear her conversation with ease.

From what he could gather, Nicole Melling, née Hunter, was keeping her mouth shut about whatever beef she had with Advocates for God. If that were the only news to report, Martin would be relieved. Maybe he would even cut Steve loose from this assignment, and Steve could return to his former routine.

But now Steve had learned they had a new problem. From this bar stool, he had Googled "production of Under Suspicion." He had immediately found a photograph of the woman he'd identified as the boss of the production team. Her name was Laurie Moran. She was the show's creator and producer. He had also learned that Laurie was a crime victim herself, and the daughter of a cop. One more search had confirmed that the older man at the dinner table was her father.

And now the woman had announced that her curiosity about Nicole was piqued and that she'd be taking a close look at her background. *I'm going to find out the truth about who Nicole Melling really was.*

Martin would not be happy.

37

Alex Buckley looked down at the suitcase and garment bag, packed up and still open on his bed. He had traveled long distances before for cases, and he was accustomed to appearing on television, but this was the first time he had combined the two. He had managed to accommodate six suits and a variety of more casual options in his luggage.

When Brett Young had called him this afternoon to ask him to move up his plans to fly to Los Angeles, Alex had wanted to check with Laurie. He had seen the way Young had surprised Laurie by calling without telling her. So he bought himself time by telling Brett he needed to check his trial schedule. In reality, he had used the borrowed moments to call Laurie, but she hadn't answered. He had phoned Leo instead, who assured Alex that Laurie would value his early input. But now that his bags were packed, he had to wonder whether Leo might have his own reasons for wanting to bring Alex to California. When he got there, would he cramp Laurie's rhythm with her production team? This would be the first time they'd worked together since developing a friendship outside of the show.

When he was invited to host *Under Suspicion*'s inaugural episode about the Graduation Gala Murder, he couldn't resist. He had followed the case closely when he was a sophomore at Fordham and had always been convinced that one of the guests celebrating at the gala was the killer. As it turned out, his suspicions were incorrect. The lasting mark of his participation in the show wasn't the discovery of the true killer's identity but his devotion to Laurie Moran.

"Do you need a car service for tomorrow, Mr. Alex?"

"How many times do I need to tell you to drop the 'Mr.,' Ramon? Alex is fine. Heck, you can even call me Al, as the song says."

"That is not how Ramon rolls, sir."

Alex shook his head and laughed. Occasionally he looked at his own life and could not believe it. Ramon was sixty years old, born in the Philippines. Divorced, with one adult daughter in Syracuse, he was Alex's "assistant." Alex preferred that term to "butler," which had been Ramon's title in his previous employment for a family that had relocated to the West Coast. The decorator who had ensured that Alex's apartment was finished tastefully had recommended hiring Ramon when she saw that Alex was so busy at work that he frequently bought new undershirts because the laundry was backed up.

Alex's apartment on Beekman Place, with views of the East River, had six rooms, plus servant's quarters, much too large for a bachelor. But it had enough space for a dining room to entertain friends, a home office, Ramon, and Alex's younger brother, Andrew, a corporate lawyer who visited frequently from Washington, D.C. In Alex's mind, his home reflected his commitment to friends, family, and loyalty. And yet, he understood how it all probably looked to someone who didn't truly know him.

What he really meant was how it probably looked to Laurie.

Last December, he thought it was all going to be easy. The man Timmy called Blue Eyes had tried to kill the boy and his mother. On instinct, Alex ran in and swept both Laurie and Timmy into his arms. For that brief moment, they almost felt like a family.

But, just as quickly, Leo had appeared, and Laurie and Timmy had pulled away from Alex's embrace. Leo, Laurie, and Timmy were the family. Alex was a friend. A coworker. A buddy. Not family. Not, most important, Greg.

At first, Alex reasoned that Laurie simply wasn't ready for another relationship. Certainly he could understand the possible reasons. She had a demanding career and a child to juggle. She had lost her husband. She wasn't over Greg yet. Maybe she never would be.

But now, the night before he was supposed to fly to Los Angeles to work with Laurie again, he wondered if her reluctance was specific to him personally. In addition to an apartment that might have seemed too large and a butlerlike assistant who called him "Mr. Alex," he had somehow been saddled with a public persona fit for the tabloids.

How many times had he seen his own photograph in the society pages with a woman on his arm, the caption hinting at a growing romance? But because his part-time job as a trial commentator had made him something of a pseudocelebrity, these pairings always seemed to be blown out of proportion. Andrew had even told him about a website that purported to list every single person Alex had ever supposedly dated. Most were names Alex didn't recognize.

Why would a woman as smart and confident as Laurie trust someone like him? She had a career and child to worry about. There was no room for some six-foot-four, airbrushed, blow-dried lothario. Could she allow Timmy to become attached to another man who, as she perceived it, might fall out of his life?

Alex looked down once again at his bags and then replaced a flashy purple paisley tie with conservative navy stripes, knowing the swap wouldn't make one bit of difference.

38

"Wow, Mom. This is almost like that big breakfast they had at the hotel when we went to Aruba."

The Aruba vacation last winter had celebrated the success of the first episode of *Under Suspicion*. Laurie felt like she'd been working nonstop ever since.

Laurie placed a hand on Timmy's shoulder as she took in the breakfast options spread across the gigantic island in the middle of the kitchen. Laurie had been skeptical about the idea of their all camping out under one roof in Los Angeles, but with Brett already complaining about the show's budget, she'd been in no position to challenge Jerry's logic about using one house for both lodging and the summit-session filming.

Of course, she hadn't anticipated the house in Bel Air would look like a Normandy estate. Nor that each of them—Jerry, Grace, Laurie, Timmy, Leo, and Alex—would have a separate room, complete with en suite bathroom and king bed topped with the smoothest sheets Laurie had ever felt. Now she and Timmy had woken up to find a fully catered meal waiting for them in the kitchen, courtesy of Jerry's careful planning.

"Can I have a bagel?" Timmy said, starting to flip through the assortment on the tray.

"Please don't touch every single one, okay?" Nine-year-old boys had no concept of germs. "And of course you *may* have one."

"And *may* I have butter and cream cheese and lox and fruit salad?"

"You may. Just make sure you leave enough of everything for everyone else."

"You mean, no hogging."

"Exactly." Where did he learn this stuff?

She was watching Timmy smear cream cheese on a poppy-seed bagel when Jerry walked in. He was dressed as casually as she'd ever seen him, in a yellow polo shirt and navy chinos. His hair was still damp from the shower. "Oh, excellent. Craft services has already been here."

"You know we're not filming here today, right?" Laurie clarified. "We're doing our preinterview with Keith Ratner."

"I know. But having them provide the food is really not much more expensive than going out to eat, plus it saves time. They'll be here for all three meals with cleanup at night unless I call them off. And I figured, why not indulge on our first morning? Besides, we saved so much money on this house that we could afford to have the extra catering."

She gestured for him to look at their surroundings. Next to the open kitchen was an enormous living room, complete with a fireplace and three separate seating areas. The dining room could easily accommodate sixteen people. Outside, a swimming pool fit for a resort sparkled in the sun.

"I find it hard to believe that this house fits within a budget set by Brett Young."

"It does for us," Jerry said, beaming with pride, "because we got it for free."

"Excuse me?"

"That's right. When I called Dwight Cook to set an interview schedule, I told him that the location for the summit session was to-be-announced and that we'd be finding a house near campus. Turns out he bought this place for his parents when REACH first hit it big. His parents decided a couple of years ago that they needed a smaller place, all on one floor. I guess he won't sell it because of capital gains taxes or something I'm not rich enough to understand. He has a property manager handle it as a high-end rental for movie shoots and whatnot. But we got it for free. Are you mad?"

"That the house came from Susan's coworker at the computer lab?"

He nodded. "I probably should have run it by you, but I figured you were busy enough without having to micromanage those kinds of details."

She had been swamped, but it would have been nice to know that they were receiving a subsidy from Dwight Cook. It certainly was not the first time they had received assistance from someone involved in a case. For "The Graduation Gala," they filmed the entire show at the home of the victim's husband. He had even paid participants additional compensation out of his own pocket to guarantee their presence. Still, the journalist in her cringed a little.

Jerry helped Timmy pour a glass of orange juice. "I figured it was okay since Dwight's not even a suspect. He was a friend of Susan, and let's face it, he's so successful that crashing in his empty house isn't exactly a deep reach into his wallet. Plus in the Graduation Gala case—"

"It's okay, Jerry. You don't need to explain. I would have made the same decision. We just need to disclose it during the show."

Laurie's own job would be easier if she started trusting Jerry more to make autonomous decisions.

"The house is really pretty," Timmy said, setting down his orange juice glass. "Thank you for finding this place for us, Jerry."

"My goodness. If you could bottle up that sweetness and sell it in a can, Dwight Cook wouldn't be the only one who was rich."

Laurie turned at the sound of footsteps and saw her father and Alex Buckley walking into the kitchen.

"What's all this?" Leo boomed.

"Jerry got us breakfast!" Timmy exclaimed.

"Even better," Jerry said. "Jerry hired someone to get us breakfast."

Alex gave her a quick good-morning peck on the cheek and headed straight for the coffee. He had an iPad in hand, which she knew he would use to peruse the *New York Times*. He had arrived so late the previous evening that they'd barely had a chance to say hello to each other.

She watched as Timmy leapt out of his seat to give Alex and his grandfather an overview of the buffet. Looking at the three of them, she realized she was smiling and still felt the warmth of Alex's kiss on her cheek.

She deliberately glanced away at the empty place setting at the table. "So we're all here except for Grace," she said. "She's probably still working on her hair and makeup."

"Actually," Jerry said, "I told her she could sleep in."

"We're supposed to see Keith Ratner today." She looked at her watch. They should be leaving before too long. "We can review strategy on the ride there. Rosemary has always been convinced Keith was involved."

"I know, the boyfriend's important. But he's almost as celebrity-conscious as Madison Meyer. That's why I thought you should bring Alex instead of me and Grace. Assuming, of course, that's okay with you, Alex."

Alex looked up from his coffee. "I wouldn't say I'm a celebrity, but I'm happy to do whatever Laurie would like."

Another point for Jerry. He was right. Alex would likely snow Keith Ratner—she might as well take advantage of his expertise. "Alex, if Keith has been holding on to information about Susan's murder all these years, I can't imagine anyone who might have a better chance of getting him to talk."

"I don't know, Jerry," Leo said cheerfully. "It sounds to me like you're playing Alex and Laurie to get yourself a day off."

"Absolutely not, Mr. Farley," he said, waving his punch list. "Grace and I have a long to-do list ahead of the summit session next week."

Laurie smiled. "Dad, I can assure you that Jerry is always working. Speaking of work, Alex, you and I should be heading out. And, Jerry, you can scratch one phone call off your list. We'll make sure Keith knows where to come next week for the big shoot."

39

Three hundred sixty miles north, Dwight Cook was just waking up in his Palo Alto mansion. Though the home had more than nine thousand square feet, he spent most of his time in this enormous master suite with sweeping views of the foothills. But this morning, he was more interested in another one of his real estate holdings. He immediately reached for the laptop on his nightstand and opened the viewer for the surveillance cameras in the Bel Air house.

The first camera to appear overlooked the entryway. Laurie Moran was walking toward the front door. He recognized the man behind her as Alex Buckley, the show's host.

Dwight used the right-arrow key to flip through the cameras situated around the house.

The assistant, Grace, was coming out of one of the bedrooms on the second floor, singing an old disco song. The others were all finishing breakfast in the kitchen, the child asking whether they'd have time for a trip to Disneyland. The surveillance equipment—built into the walls, completely undetectable—was working flawlessly. Dwight had had the system installed in all his properties for extra security, but now it would be serving another role.

Dwight wouldn't be going to Los Angeles until this weekend, but for all practical purposes, he was right there with the production team. And once the summit sessions began, he'd be able to see and hear everything.

40

Laurie led the way to the their black SUV. In addition to the Land Cruiser, they had also rented a full-size van for production use, and a separate sedan for Leo and Timmy to tool around in. She dangled the keys as she walked. "Would you care to drive, or should I?"

"Your choice."

"I've never driven in Los Angeles before. I suppose I should at least try it. If I feel like I'm putting our lives in danger, I'll pull over and we can switch."

"Sounds like a plan," Alex said, "though I'd be more worried about the life of any driver stupid enough to upset you."

"I'll admit, I can be a tough customer," Laurie laughed. "I'll try to avoid any road-rage incidents."

She had already entered their destination into the GPS. Once they were both belted in, she started the engine for the short drive to Westwood.

"I'm surprised you don't have a driver," Alex said.

"Says the man with the butler," she said wryly. "Seriously, have you not *met* Brett Young? He has been all over me about the budget for this episode. It's not cheap to shoot in California. I think we can manage our own driving."

"That house certainly doesn't look like budget-friendly lodging."

"Funny you should mention that. Jerry just told me this morning that it belongs to Dwight Cook. We're using it free of charge."

"You sound irritated."

"It's fine. I just know that Jerry had a hundred opportunities to mention that detail a little earlier."

"But then you might have said no, and he'd be back to trying to find a space big enough to house us all, and suitable for filming, all on the studio budget. As they say, better to ask for forgiveness than permission."

"You're right. I think it's hard for me sometimes to see Jerry as someone other than the skinny intern who used to fetch coffee."

"It's not my business, but from what I've seen, he's a far cry from that. He's very good at his job."

"I know. Sending you to meet with Keith today is a perfect example. He and Madison are status conscious. They live in a world where their worth is measured daily by how fast the valet at the Ivy fetches their car. He's not exactly A-list, but he'd run right over Jerry and Grace."

"No one runs over Grace," Alex said.

"True."

"Where are we meeting him?"

"A little bookstore in Westwood. From what I read online, it seems like an alternative kind of place—counterculture stuff."

"Why there? I thought he said he was at some church thing the night Susan was murdered."

She should have known that Alex would have fully reviewed all the case materials. "Yes, at least *allegedly*. But the church wasn't exactly a church yet. It was fledgling. A bit fringy, if you ask me. At the time, Keith told police he was at a discussion group at the bookstore. Once the police investigated further, they learned that it was a meeting for some group called Advocates for God."

Several group members vouched for Keith's whereabouts at the time of Susan's murder, but, based on what Laurie knew about the church, she wondered if they might be so insular as to cover for one another.

"They've come a long way since holding recruiting meetings at indie bookstores," Alex said. "Isn't it a big West Coast megachurch now?"

"And how do you think they got there?" she asked. "Money. They say they 'advocate for God's goodness'"—she added air quotes for good measure—"but they're all about raising money. Supposedly it all goes to serving the poor, but you've got to wonder. Meanwhile, the church's members seem to follow along blindly."

"And that's why you said Keith *allegedly* has an alibi for Susan's murder."

"Exactly. Admittedly, at the time, Ratner was a starving actor and was only just beginning with AG. If he was involved in Susan's murder, I don't see why the church would stick its neck out to cover for him."

"In the lawyering world, we call what you're doing arguing with yourself."

"I know. I can look at every suspect and think they're completely innocent, then, in the blink of an eye, picture them chasing poor Susan into that park. Even her friend Nicole was acting completely out of sorts when we spoke to her, like she was hiding something. I can see why the police were never able to solve the case."

"Hey, don't get frustrated yet. We're just getting started."

The tiny store was crammed floor to ceiling with books, many of them used. A whiteboard behind the cash register listed upcoming events. That night, an author would be signing copies of his book *Legalize Everything*.

The sole employee sported a bushy beard that made it difficult to estimate his age. "You guys looking for a coffee shop or something?"

So she wasn't alone in thinking that she and Alex looked out of place here. Fortunately, the jingle of the bell on the front door inter-rupted the moment. Laurie could tell from Keith Ratner's expres-sion that he immediately recognized Alex from television.

"I didn't think we were shooting today." He ran his fingers through his tousled dark hair.

"We're not," she explained. "But Alex wanted the opportunity to meet you before the cameras are on."

Alex offered a handshake. "Hey, Keith, good to meet you. I was a huge fan of *Judgment Calls*." Keith Ratner had played a young pros-ecutor in the short-lived courtroom drama.

"Thanks for meeting us," Laurie said. "And before I forget, we have the location for next week's summit session. It's a house not too far from here." She handed him a piece of paper with the Bel Air address on it.

"No problem," he said, slipping the address into the front pocket of his jeans. "Wow. This store hasn't changed at all. Talk about a blast from the past."

"You haven't been here for a while?" Laurie asked.

"I only came here twice, I think, both for events."

"Advocates for God events, you mean."

"Sure. Does that matter?"

"Only if your church members were backing you up because you share the same religion."

"So much for a little friendly conversation." He looked to Alex for help, but Alex pretended to browse a shelf labeled HAIKU AND TANKA. "The only reason I was ever *under suspicion* in the first place was be-cause Rosemary never liked me. I had six different people confirm to the police I was with them all night—first here at the store, then we went out for coffee. But because we were part of a new church people didn't understand, it's like our word didn't count."

"Sorry, Keith, this isn't about oppressing you for your belief sys-tem. You have to admit, when we spoke on the phone, you tried to deflect attention onto anyone but you."

"Human nature." Keith looked to Alex again. "The criminal defense lawyer here must understand that. Someone killed Susan, and it wasn't me—so, yeah, I guess you could say I suspect everyone else. People seem to forget that she was my girlfriend. For four years. I loved that girl."

"Yet you cheated on her," Alex said. He wasn't going to play good cop.

"I never said I was perfect. Why do you think I went looking for a religion? Something to believe in? I was a bad boyfriend, but that doesn't make me a murderer. Did you even look into the stuff I told you about Dwight Cook? Pretty convenient that he happened to *invent* something so valuable within months of Susan's murder."

"Actually," Laurie said, "I did look into your theory. And what I learned was that you knew so little about your own girlfriend that you had no idea what she was working on. Her professor even confirmed that Susan's research had nothing to do with the idea that became REACH."

"Professors don't know anything about who their students *really* are. Dwight followed Susan around like a lapdog. It seemed like every time I'd come by her dorm, he'd be lingering nearby. I don't care how much money he's made. I'm telling you: something was off about that kid."

"You sound desperate, Keith."

He shook his head. "Check it out if you don't believe me. You know, when I said I'd do this, you told me you'd be objective, that you were a reporter at heart. But it's obvious that Rosemary's infected your brain about me. I'm out of here."

"We're just asking questions," she said. "And you signed a contract."

"Then sue me."

The jingle of the bell as he exited felt like a buzzer ending a boxing round that Laurie knew she had lost.

41

Keith could feel his cell phone shake in his hand. It had been years since he'd lost control. He certainly could not recall ever speaking to Martin Collins so firmly. "I can't do it. You should have heard the way they were running down AG. I couldn't control my anger. I had to leave to keep myself from saying more than I should."

"Of all people, Keith, don't you think I know what it is like to have our beliefs belittled by people who can never understand our good works?"

Keith should have known that Martin would not accept his decision, but Martin didn't understand his frustration. Keith had heard the ridicule in Laurie Moran's voice when she mentioned Advocates for God. She could never begin to understand how AG had saved him after Susan died.

Service to others and guidance from Martin as to the certainty of God's goodness had kept Keith from taking out his grief through booze and girls. And then there were the group sessions. Keith began to examine his guilt at treating Susan poorly when she was alive. He realized that all his betrayals were little acts of revenge. As much as he loved Susan, she made him feel small. He remembered how other couples in high school would talk about being treated like honorary family by one another's parents. His friend Brian even got birthday and Christmas presents from his girlfriend Becky's family.

But Keith had never gotten the slightest sign of approval—let alone affection—from Rosemary or Jack Dempsey. Jack worked so hard, he probably wouldn't have been able to pick Keith from a lineup. And Rosemary? She treated Keith like dirt, with her constant sighs of disappointment and barbed comments insulting his dream of being a star.

Susan always told him to ignore it. She said her mother was just protective and would have had the same response if Susan were to date a prince who was also a Rhodes scholar. But, after Susan's murder, Keith realized that he had absorbed the criticism. Hurting Susan—having power over her—had been a way to keep her from hurting him.

Now Keith felt like Rosemary Dempsey was calling the shots all over again. He tried once more to explain it all to Martin.

"The way that television producer spoke to me brought back all my old insecurities. And the way they talked about AG reminded me of how Susan would call it a scam when Nicole first became involved."

"You didn't give them any indication that it was Nicole who introduced you to the church, did you?"

"Of course not."

"Remember, if they ask, you were handed a flyer on campus and were curious. With all the pamphleting I did back then, it's perfectly believable. Do not say *anything* to link Nicole with AG."

"I won't be saying anything at all. I don't want to be part of that show."

"You know better than this. Sometimes it's not about you, Keith. How are you best positioned to serve the work of God?"

"How can it be God's work to be in a house full of people who make fun of everything our church stands for?"

"A house?"

"Yes, they have a house for filming. They're also going to be staying there." He retrieved the address from his pocket and read it to Martin.

"Listen to me: you will call the producer and confirm your participation. Advocates for God is a *group* serving God, and Nicole's participation in this show is a direct threat to that group. I have reason to believe that Nicole isn't saying anything about us for now, but the television show may be digging into Nicole's background."

" 'Reason to believe'?"

"I'm relying on you to update me about her involvement and to steer the investigation away from anything that might lead to AG. Do you understand?"

Sometimes Keith wondered whether he should be more questioning of Martin's commands. But without Advocates for God, what would he have?

42

Determined to stick to her family's postdinner board game ritual, Laurie gathered the crew in the den of the Bel Air house to play Bananagrams, which was like Scrabble on speed. Timmy's favorite moments of the game were the banana-related puns: "split" to start playing and "peel" to pull new tiles. Grace had won the last three games in a row, each time telling Timmy that she might not have been the smartest person in the room, but that she was the most competitive person in the entire world, "and that matters more in the long run."

Laurie could tell that both Timmy and Leo approved.

Everyone was playing except for Jerry, who was hunkered in a chair by the fireplace, working on plans for next week's summit sessions.

"Take a little break," Leo said. "Your eyes are going to cross."

"Can't take a break when you live with your boss." Jerry looked up from his notes and winked at Timmy, who laughed at the joke.

Laurie thought that if anyone should have been working late tonight, it was her. She had blown the meeting with Keith Ratner today. The man was arrogant, but he had a point. Rosemary was so convinced that Keith was involved in Susan's death, but was her suspicion based in fact or on her belief that Susan never would have gone to Los Angeles in the first place if not for her boyfriend? And would anyone have even questioned his alibi if it had come from six members of a book club or established group, instead of Advocates for God?

She was supposed to be spelling out words with her tiles, but she kept hearing Keith's voice: *You told me you'd be objective.* Objective reporting meant checking his alibi.

She excused herself to make a phone call. She looked up the phone number for the church of Advocates for God and received a message system. "This is Laurie Moran, calling for Reverend Collins." She had read that Martin Collins was the founder and minister of Advocates for God. Though the alibi witnesses who had spoken to police were all individual church members, she had to believe that Collins would have been aware of the situation given the group's relatively small size at the time and the high-profile nature of the investigation. "It's about a church member named Keith Ratner and a police investigation from 1994. If he could return my call, I'd appreciate it."

Laurie was heading back to the makeshift game room when Jerry waved her over to his corner.

"You really should hang it up for the night," she said. "I'm starting to feel guilty."

"Then you have no idea how late I usually work in New York. Besides, this is fun. I was just going through old copies of the UCLA newspaper that I downloaded onto my computer. I thought it might be worth exploring the aftermath of Susan's killing on the campus. Were students afraid? Did the university add security? That kind of thing."

"Good thinking."

"Thanks. And then I saw this."

He rotated his laptop so she could see the screen. The headline read TECH PROFESSOR LEAVES FOR PRIVATE SECTOR, FIRST JOB IS FOR UCLA STUDENT.

The article was published in September 1994, the first edition in the school year following Susan's death, reporting the university's loss of Richard Hathaway, a popular and prolific computer science professor, to a booming, Internet-fueled private sector job.

According to the article, a university policy requiring ownership of all faculty research and development could have played a role in Hathaway's departure. The author hinted that the policy could make it difficult to hire and retain professors in the most innovative and profitable fields. It also reported that Professor Hathaway's first private-sector gig was as a consultant to UCLA junior Dwight Cook, who was currently seeking financing for his Internet-search technology.

The caption beneath Professor Hathaway's photograph read, "Professor could earn his annual UCLA income in a day's work for a successful start-up."

But it was the last paragraph of the article that Jerry highlighted for Laurie on his screen:

Professor Hathaway may be familiar to students beyond the computer science department as the male professor named "most crush-worthy" by this publication for three of the last five years. Though that award is one of many tongue-in-cheek honors bestowed by the paper's editorial board, not everyone always saw the humor. Last year, a student filed a complaint with the university, repeating campus rumors that Professor Hathaway had dated female students and alleging that he showed favor to attractive female students on that basis. The student withdrew the complaint when she was unwilling to provide the names of any students who may have been involved with the popular teacher, and no other students came forward to confirm her allegation.

Jerry looked at Laurie to make sure she had finished reading. "We know Susan was one of his favorite students. And she was definitely attractive."

Laurie looked again at the photograph accompanying the article. Hathaway would have been in his late thirties at the time. When she met him in Dwight Cook's office, she had noticed he was handsome, but his face was fuller and his hair thinner than in this photograph. As she looked at the younger version, it dawned on her that Hathaway's features were similar to Keith Ratner's. Dark hair, strong cheekbones, and a killer smile. She could imagine that a woman might be attracted to them both.

Susan and her professor? It was a theory that the police had never even considered.

"I'll check with her roommates, see if there were any signals that Susan and Professor Hathaway might have been an item. If they were, Dwight Cook certainly didn't know about it. I could tell when I first spoke to him that he'd been carrying a torch for Susan himself, and then Keith made it sound like Dwight was pretty obsessed with her. No way would he have kept Hathaway as his righthand man at REACH if the teacher crossed that line with Susan. But the article calls him a consultant. We know that Hathaway was instrumental to REACH from the very beginning. That means he got stock options and big money. I know you told me that Hathaway confirmed that the idea for REACH was Dwight's and not Susan's, but—"

"You're thinking Dwight Cook might have murdered Susan?"

"I don't know, Jerry. If I've learned anything, it's that it's often the least likely suspect."

She thought of her husband's murder. Because Greg was an emergency room doctor, the police thought he might have crossed paths with a deranged patient who became fixated on him. It never dawned on anyone that Greg was targeted by a sociopath consumed by hatred of her own father, NYPD inspector Leo Farley.

Laurie was reminded of her conversation with Alex that morning; Jerry really had moved on since his intern days. He was now close to a partner for her on the show, and she needed to treat him that way. "I'll call Rosemary again so we aren't just taking Hathaway and Dwight's word for it about Susan's lab work. She'll know what Susan was working on."

Laurie had hoped to narrow the field of people under suspicion before the summit session, but her list of suspects seemed to be growing.

43

By the time Dwight Cook slipped his key into the lock of his Westwood bungalow, it was nearly midnight. He and Hathaway had taken REACH's jet to Los Angeles, but the flight had been delayed by fog in the Bay Area.

Hathaway teased him for hanging on to this modest little house, which Dwight had bought at the end of his junior year, once REACH appeared solid enough as a start-up for him to get a small mortgage. In fact, Hathaway teased him for returning to college at all. Hathaway was so confident in REACH's potential to pull in major cash that he'd retired from his tenured position.

But Hathaway had always been more financially motivated than Dwight. It sounded overly simple, but Dwight really did enjoy college—not the parties or hanging out in the quad, but the learning. So even after REACH launched, he found a way to finish college. Besides, he had Hathaway to oversee the corporation.

As soon as he locked the door behind him, he opened his laptop and logged in to the surveillance cameras at the Bel Air house. He had not been able to check updates while he was with Hathaway.

He fast-forwarded through hours of tape for a quick overview. The house was empty most of the day. The little boy and his grandpa came home first, followed by some television for the boy and phone calls for Grandpa. Then Jerry and Grace, followed by Laurie and

Alex Buckley. It looked like they were wrapping up the night with some kind of game in the den.

He hit PAUSE. Jerry was in the corner by himself while everyone else was playing the game. Laurie seemed to stop and talk to Jerry alone. He rewound to the beginning of their conversation and hit PLAY.

By the time he watched Laurie resume her seat at the game table, Dwight wanted to throw his laptop across the room. When he set out to monitor the activity at the house, he thought it would give him some semblance of control, but this was maddening. What he really wanted was to be in the room with them. If they would only ask him the right questions, he could set them straight.

Susan and Hathaway? The thought made him physically ill. It was also ridiculous. Susan was too blinded by her devotion to that abominable Keith Ratner to notice anyone else.

And the idea that Susan had been the one to develop REACH? The technology that had launched REACH wasn't Susan's idea; it wasn't even Dwight's—not really. As Hathaway had pointed out, he and Dwight were two halves of a whole. On his own, Dwight might never have conceived such a grand idea. But without Dwight's programming talent, Hathaway might have gotten bogged down and someone else would have caught up and surpassed him before REACH was off the ground.

It had nothing to do with Susan.

He wanted Susan's murder solved, but now the people at *Under Suspicion* were on the completely wrong track, and he couldn't correct their misconceptions without revealing the fact that he was monitoring their conversations. He was stuck. All he could do was watch and listen and hope. Oh, Susan, he thought wistfully.

He switched his screen over to the We Dive SoCal website. He hoped someone might have tips about new sites for him to explore while he was in Los Angeles, but it looked like he was going to stick with his usual dives: Farnsworth Bank, on the windward side of Catalina, and the oil rigs off of Long Beach.

It was probably good he'd completed these tens of times before. Dwight was at his best when he kept a routine. Eight A.M. wake-up. Coffee. Three-mile jog. Cereal with fruit. Work. The occasional dinner with Hathaway. Reading. Sleep. Repeat.

Ever since Nicole had appeared at REACH with the news that *Under Suspicion* would be featuring Susan's case, that routine had been disrupted. Once he found out who killed Susan, his life could return to normal.

And in the meantime, he needed a reprieve in the water. Just three more days before he could dive.

44

Madison Meyer pushed open the door marked 2F. "I can*not* . . . believe . . . that this dorm is still here. It was new at the time, but, wow, is it dated now."

The building was three stories of blond brick, divided into efficient suites. Every campus in America had similar dormitories from the same era. This was the triple room that Susan, Nicole, and Madison had shared sophomore year.

"Hey, guy in the black baseball cap." Madison was pointing to one of the cameramen. "I'm turned this way for a reason. Please don't move around to my right side. I told you it's not a good angle for me."

"We have *all* your requests from your agent," Grace said flatly.

Laurie could tell that Grace wanted to put Madison the diva in her place, New York City style. Jerry would have had more patience but had stayed at the house in Bel Air to stage the upcoming summit sessions. "I think what Grace is trying to say," Laurie gently offered, "is that we take care of all of that during editing. Besides, most of your camera time will be at the summit session."

"And, yes," Grace added, "we'll have someone there for hair and makeup. And vegetarian options for all meals. And the brand of bottled water you requested."

Alex Buckley placed a hand gently on Grace's shoulder. "And

now I think Grace is trying to say that your agent did a very good job by you."

Grace and Madison both laughed at the line. Laurie would never stop marveling at the way attention from a good-looking man could make some women forget everything else.

Temporarily assuaged, Madison continued with her tour of the dorm room. Laurie would have preferred to have both Nicole and Madison here, but Nicole had been reluctant to extend her trip down to Los Angeles before the summit session. The one upside to Nicole's absence was that they might be able to get Madison to open up about what Nicole had been like when they were dormmates. Laurie was determined to uncover whatever Nicole had been holding back.

Once they were finished with the walk-through, Laurie asked Madison how she came to live with Susan and Nicole as sophomores, after the two others were assigned as roommates freshman year.

"Let's just say they were luckier on the freshman-roommate draw than I had been. The woman I roomed with first year was a real piece of work. Her own family called her Taz. As in, the Tasmanian Devil. All she had to do was walk in a room, and it was as if a tornado had blown in. She was loud and obnoxious and would borrow my clothes without asking. A nightmare in every way. So, no, we were not going to be one of those pairs, like Susan and Nicole, who would stick together like glue going forward. When the housing lottery opened for the next year, I let everyone who would listen know that I wanted to pair up. Susan asked if I wanted in with her and Nicole."

"How did you know Susan?" Laurie asked.

"From the theater department."

"I've heard that the two of you were rivals of sorts. You ended up competing for the same parts, given your physical resemblance."

"You know what they say. Sometimes you need a competitor to bring out your best."

"Was that odd for you, to live with your rival? Plus, I assume by then they had their own rhythm as a twosome. Did you ever feel like a third wheel?"

"Forgive me if this sounds cocky," Madison said, looking directly at Alex, "but I have never felt redundant. It's just not how I'm programmed. But, sure, if you're asking if sometimes I felt like I was the odd woman out, there were certainly times. Little things, like teasing me about being too flirtatious. We all have a little mean girl in us, and Susan and Nicole weren't above giving me the occasional cold shoulder."

Laurie could sense resentment beneath Madison's otherwise cautious words, but the petty feuds that arose among friends weren't usually grounds for murder. It was time to move on to issues that had been raised during other interviews.

"Do you happen to recall what Susan was working on in the computer lab?" Laurie asked.

Madison answered without a pause. "A dictation program. She got the idea because her father would often work at home on the weekend, using a dictation machine to draft motions and briefs. But then he'd have to wait until Monday for a secretary to do the typing."

In addition to Dwight and Professor Hathaway, Nicole and Rosemary had also confirmed the nature of Susan's work. It was clear that Dwight Cook had not stolen the idea for REACH from Susan, as Keith Ratner had suggested.

But then there were also the rumors about Professor Hathaway being romantically involved with students. Laurie had spent last night trawling the Internet for more information about Hathaway. From what she could tell, even though he initially left UCLA to pursue opportunities in the private sector, his only work since then had been for REACH and had been extremely lucrative. She had even found some trade journals speculating that Hathaway was the real brains behind the operation, while Dwight provided the kind of young, quirky persona that investors were looking for in the early dot-com years. But she had found nothing more about allegations of on-campus dalliances.

"How about Susan's relationship with her boyfriend?" Laurie asked.

"Oh yeah," Madison said offhandedly, "that guy. What was his name again?"

"Keith Ratner." It struck Laurie as peculiar that Madison wouldn't remember Keith, especially since both of them had gone on to have some success as actors.

"Right. The two of them were high school sweethearts. Totally devoted to each other."

"Really?" Alex said. "Because we've been told that Keith may have had an eye for other girls."

"Not that I ever noticed."

"Do you think it's possible that Susan could have been seeing someone else besides Keith?" Laurie asked.

On this point, Madison was more emphatic. "Absolutely not. She wasn't like that. Besides, she just wasn't that into dating. I mean, she had a boyfriend, but even Keith wasn't really a top priority. She was into school and her work and theater. It's like Keith was her fourth priority, like they were some old married couple."

Laurie noticed that Madison was looking directly at Alex again. Why didn't she come right out and say it: *I would never be boring. I make men my priority.* She was so obvious.

"And what about Nicole?" Laurie asked.

"What about her?"

"Rosemary tells me what a good friend Nicole was to her daughter, but sometimes mothers don't know every detail of a child's life while she's away for college. Like you said, we all have a little mean girl in us. Were Nicole and Susan ever mean with each other?"

"Funny. I can't remember anyone asking about Nicole after

Susan was killed. The whole focus was on Frank and me. I'll be hon-est. I didn't like Nicole very much, and I assume the feeling was mutual. But if she was going to kill someone, it would've been me, not her beloved Susan. That was a joke, by the way. She wouldn't kill anyone. And neither would I, and neither would Frank Parker."

"So who does that leave as a suspect?" Alex asked.

"I've always thought the key to finding her killer was figuring out how she got up to Laurel Canyon. Her car was still on campus." She looked out the window and pointed to a parking lot behind the dorm. "Just back there."

Alex paused to follow her gaze out the window but already had the follow-up question locked and loaded. "People have suggested—"

"That Frank did it, I covered up for him, and one or both of us drove her car back to campus afterward. But I am one of two people in the very unique position to know that didn't happen. Susan's car had been giving her trouble, so I've always wondered if she accepted a ride with somebody to avoid the risk of a breakdown."

Laurie didn't remember seeing anything in the police reports about car problems. "Was her car not working?"

"It was—what was the word she'd use? One of those SAT words for being moody. 'Mercurial'! She loved that word."

As Laurie thought through the possibilities, she realized that this tiny detail about Susan's car could be significant. The reconstruction of Susan's timeline on the day of her death had been built around the assumption that she would have driven herself from campus to Frank Parker's for the audition. Based on that assumption, the likely killer was either Frank or someone she might have been with prior to her audition. But what if she had gotten into someone else's car on her way to Frank's?

As if reading her mind, Alex asked, "Do you think Susan would take a ride from a stranger?"

Madison shrugged. "I can't see it, unless she was late and really desperate. But sometimes we don't think of strangers as strangers, you know? Maybe someone she recognized from campus offered her a lift? And then she didn't realize he was a creep until it was too late."

Or, Laurie thought, the *someone* was her boyfriend, Keith Ratner, just as her mother thought from the very beginning.

Alex was shifting gears to another topic. "You mentioned being one of only two people who knew for certain where you and Frank Parker were that night," he said. "How has it felt for you all of these years, to have people question your credibility?"

"Obviously, it's horrible, and frustrating, and infuriating. It's not that complicated: I got a call from a critically acclaimed director saying that another UCLA student stood him up and would I be willing to read on short notice. I knew the other student was Susan and figured she must have chickened out or something. So I thought, Her loss, my gain. I hopped in my car and went straight there. I stayed until close to midnight. You know the police checked his phone records, right? And we had pizza delivered around nine thirty, and that was confirmed too. And yet people who have never met me are essentially calling me a liar, based on absolutely no evidence."

It was true that the police investigation confirmed the pizza delivery, but the delivery boy had no idea whether the man who paid for the pizza at the door was alone or with company. Phone records also confirmed the fact that Frank placed a call to the phone in Madison's dorm room, but, as Madison had noted, only the two of them knew what was said during the call or what transpired afterward.

"You just happened to be home on a Saturday night?" Laurie interjected. She had thought from the very beginning that something was odd about Madison's account of the evening. Just last week, Madison had made them wait on her porch while she freshened her lipstick. Would she really hop into her car on no notice for an audition?

But now that Laurie had a better sense of who Madison was, she saw the wrinkle that had bothered her. "I got the impression you had a busy social life back then. It's hard to imagine that you'd be in your dorm, standing around, when the phone rang at seven forty-five on a Saturday night."

"I wasn't feeling well that night."

"And yet you were well enough to get in your car for an audition? I can't imagine you went to Frank Parker's house wearing sweats and no makeup."

Madison smiled, again directly at Alex even though Laurie was firing the questions. "Of course not. And I was never sitting around my dorm on Friday and Saturday nights. That particular Saturday? I was supposed to go to a Sigma Alpha Epsilon party, so, yes, I was looking my best. But then I wasn't feeling well—as I said—so I thought I might stay home. Then Frank called, and I just happened to be dolled up and ready to go. I hopped in my car and got a fantastic role. I mean, I won a Spirit Award, but people still want to believe I only got that role because I vouched for Frank. But I *earned* it."

"But the role might have gone to Susan if she hadn't been killed."

"You don't think that put a huge cloud over the entire experience for me? Susan and I were competitors, but we were also friends. Everyone seems to forget that. How many times do I have to say this? I got Frank's call at seven forty-five, I went straight to his place, I was with him from eight thirty to midnight, we got pizza around nine thirty, and then I came home. I had nothing to do with Susan's death."

45

Laurie let Grace do the driving back to Bel Air. She never got the chance to drive in New York City and was enjoying the experience, despite the hideous Los Angeles traffic.

"So what do you think?" Laurie asked once they were on the road. Alex had climbed into the SUV's backseat before Laurie could protest.

Grace was the first to offer an opinion. "Uh-uh, I'm not buying it. That line about her and Susan being friends? Maybe so, but just as quickly, she was all, *I won a Spirit Award, and I earned it.* I'm sorry, but that's cold." She was waving one finger around in the air for emphasis, and Laurie felt the car swerve within the lane.

"Grace, two hands on the wheel, please."

"Sorry, I just get a little worked up by that woman. And that timeline? Whoa, did that sound rehearsed. *Seven forty-five, eight thirty, nine thirty, midnight,* like a little wind-up doll."

Laurie agreed on both points. Madison had stood by her alibi of Frank Parker, but it was almost too good. Every detail of her recollection of that night was absolutely consistent with the version she had given police twenty years ago. That was not how real memories worked. They evolved over time, some pieces deteriorating while others crystallized. Details got muddled and mutated. But Madison had nailed every line, as if she were acting.

"The one inconsistency I did catch," Laurie noted, "was at first she said she was home because she was sick. Then when I asked how she could have left so quickly for the audition, she said she was going to a frat party but then thought she was sick, and then Frank happened to call when she was still prettied up. It sounds convoluted to me."

"And a frat party?" Grace said skeptically. "Please. I may not have known Madison Meyer twenty years ago, but I can't picture her hanging out with the campus Greeks. Something's not right."

Laurie's thoughts were interrupted by her phone buzzing. Two new voice messages had come in while her cell was turned off during the shoot.

"Hi, this is Tammy from Advocates for God. You left a message last night for Reverend Collins about an old police investigation? The reverend apologizes that his schedule did not permit him to return your call personally, but he asked me to call you. He says police interviewed several of our members at the time, and in his recollection, they verified the whereabouts of the individual you mentioned in your message. He has nothing further to add but suggested that you could contact the police for details."

Laurie skipped to the next message. "Ms. Moran, this is Keith Ratner. I wanted to apologize for losing it yesterday. It's frustrating, to say the least, that people still question me after all these years. But I do want to help if the show will still have me. Give me a call when you have a chance."

She hit the RETURN CALL button, and Keith picked up immediately. "You got my message?" he asked.

"I did, and I feel like I also need to apologize. My tone was sharper than I intended yesterday. And I want to assure you that our show will remain objective. In fact, since we saw you at the bookstore, I looked into your alibi for that night, and we've also been exploring every possible theory with the same amount of depth. For what it's worth, I thought you might want to know that Susan's mother and both of her roommates all said that Susan was much too devoted to have been involved with anyone but you."

She saw no point in telling him that Rosemary's response to the question had been, "Oh, I would have been *thrilled* if Susan had stepped out on that jerk."

Keith confirmed the address for the summit session in Bel Air and then said good-bye just as they were pulling into the driveway.

"Pretty boy is back on board?" Grace asked.

"Careful," Alex said. "I'm starting to think you call everyone pretty. My feelings are hurt."

"Yes," Laurie reported, "Keith Ratner—a.k.a. Pretty Boy Number Two—is back. But I'm starting to wonder whether he has a point about Rosemary suspecting him for no reason. His alibi is at least as good as Frank's. He's got multiple people vouching for him, not just one person who had a lot to gain in sticking by a critically acclaimed director."

Alex unstrapped his seat belt as the SUV rolled to a stop. "I don't think you can ignore the fact that the multiple people belonged to what some have called a brainwashing religion. Advocates for God doesn't exactly have a squeaky-clean reputation."

The sun felt good on Laurie's face as she stepped down from the front seat. Maybe she could get used to California. The neighborhood was absolutely silent except for the distant sound of a lawn mower and Grace's voice.

"And you heard what Madison said about Susan's car being fickle," Grace was saying. "If she was worried about a breakdown on her way to the audition, who would she ask for a ride? Her boyfriend, that's who. Her agent was on the road, driving down to Arizona. So she called Keith. I still say they got into a fight on the way up there, she hopped out of the car, and it got out of control."

Once again, Laurie felt like she was swimming through mud.

The entire purpose of these early interviews was to crystallize the case so Alex could move in for the kill during the summit session. But they were supposed to start shooting in two days, and she still had no clearer picture of who killed Susan than when she'd first spotted the Cinderella Murder case online. Brett Young would never trust her again with this kind of budget. And more importantly, it was possible that this episode would fail by the only measure that really mattered to her—revealing something new about the investigation.

She was so distracted that she slipped her key into the front door without checking the knob first, accidentally locking them out instead of letting them in. She turned the key in the other direction and pushed the door open. It parted a few inches before she felt something blocking the way.

"Hello?" she called out. Jerry must have moved a piece of furniture into the foyer during his staging. "Jerry? We can't get in! Hello?"

"Let me try." Grace jumped in front of Laurie, crouched low, and placed both of her palms against the door, shoving with all her weight like a football player pushing a blocking sled across a field. She grunted from the effort and the door opened enough for her to step sideways through it.

"No!" Grace cried out. Through the crack in the door, Laurie saw her assistant fall to her knees on the hallway floor.

"Grace?"

Alex reached out to grab her arm, but it was too late. Laurie stepped inside and saw Grace crouched next to the obstacle that had been blocking the door. It was Jerry. His face was barely recognizable through the injuries. Streaks of red marked his journey from the den to this spot on the floor, his cell phone extended in his right hand. Laurie felt her breath leave her chest and leaned back against the door for support. She felt something damp and sticky on the wood behind her.

She heard Alex's fist banging against the door but could not bring herself to move.

Jerry had been here alone. He had tried to call for help and had tried to crawl outside, but despite all of that effort, he was still all alone. And he was covered in blood.

46

Talia Parker tapped on the door to her husband's den. He had been in there for the last three hours, supposedly watching screeners of the ever-growing number of films campaigning for Academy Award nominations. Getting no response, she slowly pushed the door open.

There he was, reclined on the Eames sofa, his stockinged feet crossed at the ankles, his hands clasped just beneath the remote control resting on his barrel chest. On the wide-screen television, an A-list actress had been paused midsentence. A low, steady snore was the only sound in the room.

She gently lifted the remote control, turned off the entertainment system, and draped a light blanket over him. He slept better when he was warm.

Back in their bedroom, she reviewed the wardrobe choices she had made for tomorrow's meeting with the TV people: an open-collar dress shirt, gray slacks, and navy blazer for him; a white sheath dress and neutral pumps for her. Casual, but put-together and respectable. Frank was known for being a demanding and meticulous filmmaker, but she knew him to be a solid person. A good, caring man. To her, he looked most like himself in conservative clothing.

When she had first overheard Frank agree to do this show, she'd worried it could be trouble. And now, as production was approaching, she knew she had been right. For days, Frank had seemed distracted and nervous. It wasn't like him. She was used to seeing her husband confident and decisive.

He had been staying up late and then mumbling through the night once he finally fell asleep. And he wasn't murmuring about negotiations with production companies or screenwriters, as he sometimes did. She'd heard the words "police" and "Madison" more than once.

She had finally mustered up the courage to ask him about it this morning. He insisted he had no recollection of whatever dream had provoked the mysterious words, but in the Parker marriage, she was the actor, not him.

Their marriage had lasted ten years in a town where Botox outlasted the length of the average relationship, and that was because they always fought for what was best for each other. And sometimes that meant Frank doing things she didn't immediately agree with. It was Frank, after all, who'd killed Talia's first and only offer of a starring role in a feature film. He had said the director was "frighteningly unscrupulous, even by Hollywood standards." She had been so tempted to leave, accusing him of not wanting to share the spotlight with her. But then, sure enough, when the film was released, it barely earned an R rating because of explicit nudity that the lead actress insisted was unauthorized. Frank was too decent to say *I told you so*, but Talia had learned a valuable lesson about the give-and-take of a marriage.

Ever since they met—she had a bit part in Frank's seventh movie—he had taken such good care of her, even when it meant upsetting her.

Now it was time for her to return the favor.

47

Laurie hated hospitals, and not for the usual reasons: the chaos, the smells, the reminders at every turn of our fragility and the ticking of the clock. Laurie hated hospitals because they reminded her of Greg. She could not stand beneath those fluorescent lights, surrounded by the odor of disinfectant, without picturing Greg coming down the hall in sea-green scrubs, a stethoscope draped around his neck.

The doctor who walked into the lobby at the Cedars-Sinai emergency room looked nothing like Greg. She was a woman, probably not much older than Laurie, with blond hair pulled into a ponytail. "Jerry Klein?"

Grace's jump from the seat next to her woke Timmy, whose head was resting in Laurie's lap. Timmy rubbed the sleep from his eyes. "Is Jerry okay?"

Laurie had called her father as soon as the EMTs whisked Jerry away in the ambulance. Leo immediately cut short their visit to the La Brea Tar Pits, dropping Timmy off at the hospital so he could stay with Laurie while Leo tried to get more information about Jerry's attack from the police.

Laurie hugged Timmy close to her chest and patted his head. She did not want him to hear any more bad news.

Alex appeared next to the doctor, two cups of fresh coffee in hand, which he delivered to Grace and Laurie. Laurie was truly impressed at how well Grace was keeping herself together. She was desperately worried about her friend Jerry but had been helping to comfort Timmy and had even thought to call Dwight Cook and inform him of the break-in at his house.

"I'll take Timmy," Alex offered, seeming to read her mind.

The doctor introduced herself once Timmy was out of earshot. "I'm Dr. Shreve. Your friend is stable, but the assault was quite serious, multiple blows from a blunt instrument. The injuries to his head are the most significant. The bleeding impaired his breathing as well, which has led to a comalike state. He's showing signs of improvement already and seems to be neurologically normal or near normal, but we won't know for certain until he regains consciousness."

Grace choked back a sob. "Can we see him?" she asked.

"Sure," the doctor said with a patient smile, "but don't expect too much, okay? It's unlikely he can hear you, and he certainly won't respond."

Despite the doctor's warning, Laurie gasped at the sight of Jerry in bed. His head was swathed in bandages and twice its usual size. Beneath the oxygen mask, his face was swollen like a balloon and beginning to bruise. An IV drip was taped to the crook of his left arm. The room was silent except for the constant hum and rhythmic beep of a machine next to the bed.

Grace reached for Laurie's hand, then rested her free hand on Jerry's shoulder and began to pray. They had just said "amen" when Leo walked in. "I didn't want to interrupt, but I said my own words from the hallway."

Laurie gave him a quick hug. "Is Timmy okay?"

"Yep, he's in the lobby with Alex. He's a tough kid."

After his father's murder and the mayhem at the end of filming "The Graduation Gala," Timmy had seen more violence than any person, let alone a child, should experience.

"Any word from the police?"

"I just came from the house. The entire block's covered. The lead detective, a guy called Sean Reilly, seems like a good cop. They're canvassing for witnesses, but I've got to tell you, I'm not optimistic. The lots in that area are so huge, you can't even see your next-door neighbor."

"I don't understand it," Grace said, sniffling. "How could anyone want to hurt Jerry, of all people?"

"I've got a theory on that," Leo said. "The house was tossed. Drawers opened, luggage rifled through. Laurie, you had your laptop with you, but the rest of the computer equipment is missing."

"A robbery?" Laurie asked.

"Except they left behind everything else. They didn't even touch some very expensive speakers that would have been easy to grab. And unless you took the case files with you, I think those are missing, too."

She shook her head. They had stored the files in two large banker boxes. The last time she'd seen them, they were in the den. "So this is related to the show?"

Leo nodded. "It's the show."

"The summit session. We told them all the address for filming." She was thinking out loud now. "Someone was worried about what we might know. They took the files and the computers to find out what everyone else was saying."

"Or they wanted to scare you into stopping production altogether."

Laurie knew her father could be overprotective at times, seeing danger around every corner. But no one would break into a house that luxurious and leave with only documents and a few inexpensive laptops unless they were interested in *Under Suspicion*.

"Dad, you were worried when Rosemary's neighbor was killed that it was somehow related to the show."

"And I still believe that."

"Can you reach out to the police up there? Make sure that both departments know there's a possible connection between Lydia's death and the attack on Jerry?"

"Absolutely."

She leaned over Jerry, carefully avoiding the tubes and wires, and gave him a light kiss on the cheek. She had spent so much time telling her father not to worry about her while she worked on the show, but she never stopped to think that her production might be putting others in this kind of danger.

She had to find out who did this to him.

48

At nine o'clock, Leo turned off the light in Timmy's room. Timmy had taken the next volume of the Harry Potter books with him to bed, but as Leo had expected, he had fallen asleep on the first page after their long and strenuous day.

He made his way to the hall, leaving the door cracked open in case Timmy cried out in the night.

If there was any sliver of light to be found in the brutal assault on Laurie's colleague, it was that she was finally willing to concede that someone might be targeting people connected to her show. After all, the murder of Rosemary Dempsey's neighbor had been Leo's primary reason for coming to California.

Still, Leo was not happy about Laurie's decision to stay at the Bel Air house. Detective Reilly had cleared them for reentry after the crime-scene unit had finished its work, but the bigger question was whether they'd be safe. "It's obvious the guy was after one thing," Reilly had said, "your computer and research on the show. You say there was nothing pertaining to the show that he didn't take. So presumably he got what he wanted and won't be coming back."

Leo didn't agree with Reilly's logic, but the fact was that they were a large group, and the police planned to drive past the house every twenty minutes to be safe. And, Leo thought, my gun is at the ready in a worst-case scenario.

The police hadn't located any witnesses yet in their neighborhood canvass. Some of the homes had surveillance cameras, but detectives still needed to wade through the footage. If they were extremely lucky, they might be able to locate images of cars or people coming and going from the street.

In his bedroom, he shut the door and pulled up a recently dialed phone number on his cell. It was the number for Detective O'Brien at the Alameda County sheriff's department.

"Detective, it's Leo Farley. We spoke earlier this week about your investigation into the murder of Lydia Levitt."

"Of course I remember. In fact, I happened to touch base yesterday with one of my friends in the NYPD. Name of J. J. Rogan."

"Talk about a blast from the past. I was his lieutenant when he first moved to detective squad."

"That's what he told me. He confirms you're 'good people,' in his words."

In light of what Leo was about to ask of Detective O'Brien, he was grateful for the recommendation on his behalf.

"You mentioned that you had some camera footage from the roads going in and out of Castle Crossings."

"We do, but it's a major thoroughfare. A whole mess of cars that could be heading in any direction. We've got no clear idea who exactly went into the gated community. I've got an officer capturing stills of license plates, matching each car up to a driver, but we're talking about a lot of people to track down. I've been prioritizing the burglary angle, working my sources, but if this was a botched break-in, the person who did it hasn't spoken a word of it on the street."

Leo told O'Brien about the assault on Jerry and his belief that both that attack and Lydia Levitt's murder could be connected to *Under Suspicion*.

"We'll certainly pursue that theory," O'Brien said. "We're looking at every possible lead."

"The gated community doesn't have cameras right at the entry?" Leo asked.

"You'd think, but those places really don't have any major crime. The walls themselves act as their own kind of deterrent, and the guards at the gate have a dog and pony show, but they also wave a lot of people through if they seem to belong."

Leo had been hoping that O'Brien would have gotten further in his investigation since they last spoke, but he knew how slowly things could move when no clear suspects have emerged. "So what you're saying is that your footage from the road outside could be a search for a needle in a haystack."

"You got it."

"Any chance you could use the assistance of a retired cop from New York to wade through that list of drivers?"

"Could I *use* it? I'll pay you back in whiskey at the first opportunity."

"Sounds like a deal."

After a quick discussion that Leo didn't entirely understand involving digitization, file size, and data compression, Detective O'Brien estimated that he could get everything to him by e-mail tomorrow morning.

"I'll probably have to get my grandson to help me open them," he said before hanging up.

Sifting through images of cars on a busy street would indeed be searching for a needle in a haystack, but if Leo happened to find the same needle in two different haystacks on opposite ends of the state, he might just have himself a lead.

49

Four and a half miles away in Westwood, Dwight Cook was pacing at the foot of his bed.

He flashed back to a long-forgotten memory of his father screaming at him in what must have been the eighth grade. *Stop pacing. Just stop. You're driving me crazy. And it's weird. Maggie, tell your son how nervous he makes people when he acts that way.*

His mother grabbed his father's arm and whispered: *Stop yelling, David. You know loud noises make Dwight jumpy. He paces when he's jumpy. And* don't *call your son weird.*

Dwight had trained himself to control the obsessive pacing in high school by sitting on his hands instead. He learned that remaining still, focusing on the feeling of his weight on the back of his hands, didn't make people nervous the way his pacing had. But he was alone in his bungalow now, so he didn't need to worry about affecting anyone else. And he had tried and tried to sit on his hands, but the racing in his head—the *jumpiness*—wouldn't stop.

He momentarily paused at the center of his bed to hit REWIND and then PLAY once again on his laptop.

Dwight had been speed-watching footage of the empty house when the man first appeared on the screen, walking directly through the unlocked front door with a ski mask over his face. Twenty-three minutes. That was the amount of time Jerry had been gone, returning to the house with a bag from In-N-Out Burger. Had he eaten his fast food in the kitchen, maybe the masked man would have snuck out through the front door undetected.

But Jerry hadn't taken his lunch to the kitchen. He walked directly into the den, where the masked man was rifling through the documents Jerry had left scattered across the coffee table.

Dwight continued to pace, clenching his eyes shut as each blow found its target. The weapon was the engraved crystal plaque Dwight had received from UCLA when he donated his first hundred thousand dollars upon graduation.

Dwight watched as the assault ended and the masked man turned to run out of the den, his arms filled with two banker boxes.

He had to make a decision.

If Dwight did not turn over this video, the people investigating the attack would not have it as evidence. If he did, he would reveal the fact that he'd been monitoring the activities of *Under Suspicion*. He could be ruined professionally, not to mention the possibility of criminal charges. More important, he would lose all access to the production team and be cut out of the case.

It was a cost-benefit analysis, a matter of statistics. What had a higher likelihood of being helpful: the videotape of this assault or his continued surveillance of the Bel Air house?

He hit REWIND and then paused on the clearest still image of the masked man. Dwight stared once again at the insignia on the left side of the man's white polo shirt. Even with Dwight's ability to manipulate computer images and search for information on the Internet, the quality of the video simply wasn't detailed enough to make out the logo. The attacker was lean, muscular, obviously very strong, but there was no way to identify him.

This video was useless. But if he kept monitoring the television show's production, he still had a chance of figuring out who killed Susan.

He flipped the laptop closed and stopped pacing. He had made his decision. Now he had to make sure that the gamble paid off.

50

Laurie was finally ready to call it a night when she noticed light glowing beneath her father's bedroom door. She tapped gently on the door and cracked it open.

He was beneath his covers, reading a copy of *Sports Illustrated*.

"Sorry, I saw the light."

He set the magazine down and waved her in. "You holding up okay, baby girl?"

If she had any doubt that she looked like she'd aged a decade in a day, his question sealed the deal. She plopped herself horizontally at the foot of the king bed, her head resting on his blanketed shins. She couldn't think of a more comfortable place at that moment. "I used to hate it when you called me that. And then somewhere down the road, it became music to my ears."

"Sometimes dads do know best."

"Not always. Remember when you tried to push Petey Vander-mon on me?"

"I'm not sure I'd agree with that wording, but I'll concede that my matchmaking effort was what Timmy would call a *fail*."

"Petey was the *worst*," Laurie continued with a laugh. "You convinced me to go to that stupid carnival out in Long Island with him. He got terrified in a mirror maze and ran out screaming. He left me bumping around in there for twenty minutes in search of a way out."

Leo chuckled at the memory. "You stormed into the living room, swearing you would never speak to me again if I ever tried to play Cupid. Then I got another lecture from your mother that night before I could go to sleep."

"You had good intentions, though."

"If I recall correctly, Petey was supposed to distract you from that Scott whoever-he-was."

"Mr. Future President. Intern to a congressman. Carried a briefcase to high school."

"I didn't like him. He was . . . weaselly."

"I don't think I ever told you this. He became a lawyer and got indicted for embezzling client funds."

Her father flipped back the covers with excitement. "See? Daddy does know what's best."

"Sometimes I think no one knows best. Look at how I met Greg." The word "met" was an overstatement given that she'd been unconscious at the time. She'd been hit by a cab on Park Avenue, and Greg was the ER doctor on duty. At the time, Laurie's parents—and eventually Laurie—had been grateful for the reassuring treatment, but she wound up engaged to him three months later. Then Laurie's mother had died a year after that, and Greg had been there for everyone.

Her father sat up and stroked her hair. "You only reminisce like this when something's troubling you. I know you're worried about Jerry. He's going to be fine."

Laurie took a deep breath. She couldn't cry again today. "Not to mention, I just got off the phone with Brett. I swear that man might be a vampire—I don't think he sleeps at night. I was the one who had to beg him to cover the Cinderella Murder, and now that someone's coming after the show, he's dead set against canceling it. Part of me is relieved I don't have to make the decision, but he won't even delay the production schedule. He gave me a big song and dance about how Jerry would want us to keep working, but I know it's all about the bottom line."

"I was wondering whether that bottom line had something to do with your decision to stay in this house. If so, I'm going to strangle that man."

"It's just a few more days, Dad, and we're all on high alert now. And you heard what Detective Reilly said about the police keeping an eye on us."

"You do what's right for you, Laurie. You know I've always got your back."

"Thanks, Dad. It's okay. If anything, this attack on Jerry has me convinced that whoever killed Susan is one of our participants. That makes it all the more important to me that we follow through on this."

"I called the police up in Alameda County. They're going to send some surveillance pictures of cars that were near Rosemary's house around the time her neighbor was killed. I'll go through them. Maybe we'll catch a break."

"You don't sound too optimistic."

His shrug said enough. She stood and gave him a hug. "I better call it a night. We meet with Frank Parker tomorrow."

"Tomorrow? You weren't kidding when you said Brett didn't want to disrupt the schedule."

"Hey, we saved the big celebrity interview for last. Then it's on to the big summit session, and then back home to New York."

"You do know you can't set a timeline like that, Laurie. Don't get your hopes up about solving this thing. All I want right now is to keep everyone safe. And don't you dare—not for one second—blame yourself for what happened to Jerry."

"Of course I do. I can't help it."

"If it's anyone's fault, it's mine. We realized after you and the others left to meet Madison that we didn't have enough house keys to go around. Jerry gave me the last copy, assuming it would be fine to leave the door unlocked if he had to run out for a few minutes here and there."

"Dad—"

"My point is that you can drive yourself crazy asking whether things would have been different if a, or b, or x, y, and z."

He didn't need to say any more. How many times had they both wondered if they could have done something to save Greg? She saw the light click off beneath the door as she closed it but knew neither of them would find sleep any time soon.

51

Laurie hadn't expected to be at her best the next morning, but she felt like she was still half-asleep. She had spent the night waking up every twenty minutes, picturing Jerry being lifted onto the gurney by EMTs.

Alex must have had a rough night too. In the back of the van, parked at the curb in front of Frank Parker's former home, a makeup artist was touching up his eyes. He had rightly said to Laurie, "I look like I was on a bender."

For today, it was just the two of them and the camera crew from the *Under Suspicion* staff. Jerry, of course, was in the hospital, still in what the doctors politely called "a comalike state." Grace had stayed at the house to keep Timmy busy while Leo pored through the surveillance footage coming in from Alameda County. If they could somehow connect the murder of Lydia Levitt to the break-in at the Bel Air house, they might figure out who assaulted Jerry. Laurie was nearly certain that person would also turn out to be Susan's killer.

Right now, the immediate goal was to lock Frank Parker down on his timeline for the night of Susan's murder. He and Madison had been consistent in sticking to their stories, but Madison's mention of Susan's car acting up before her death had added a new layer to the mix.

Laurie watched as a cameraman on a wheeled cart backed up to film Alex and Frank walking side by side. They were there now: a turn in the road entering Laurel Canyon Park, just off Mulholland Drive, the exact spot where Susan's body had been found. For Laurie, it was a poignant moment. She couldn't help but think of the playground where Greg had been killed. As she began to tear up, she forced herself to look toward the sky, focusing on the individual branches of a huge sycamore tree towering above them.

Her composure regained, Laurie kept up with the cameraman as he continued to film Alex and Frank walking out of the park and toward Frank Parker's former home. The purported purpose of this stroll had been to get footage of the iconic setting for the show, but she and Alex had another goal in mind: to establish the short distance between the body and Parker's house. It was less than half a mile.

As planned, Alex and Frank made their way past the home's front gate to an interior courtyard, where, with the permission of the present owner, they had staged two chairs next to the front garden. Once they were seated, Alex stole a casual glance at his watch. "Our walk from the scene of Susan's death was only ten minutes, and I think it's safe to say that we weren't exactly hurrying."

Frank gave a warm smile. In the short time Alex had spent with the director, he had already managed to find a camaraderie that was apparent on camera. "You may not believe me, Alex, but I could have told you the number of minutes without even looking at a watch. I have an inner clock that never stops ticking, and I really can pinpoint the time of day—within one to three minutes—at any given moment. It's a useless party trick, but I have a feeling that's not why you brought up the time."

"Susan Dempsey lived on the UCLA campus, more than eight miles from the spot where she was killed. Yet your house is only a ten-minute walk from that spot. Or perhaps five minutes if someone were running from your house in terror. And Susan was scheduled to be at your house the very night of her murder. You must understand why people suspected you."

"Of course I understand. If I had thought the police were un-reasonable in initially questioning me, I might have hired a team of lawyers and refused to have anything to do with the investigation. But that's not what I did, is it? Ask any of the detectives who were involved. They'll confirm I was cooperative. Because I had no cause *not* to be. I was shocked, of course, when they told me Susan's body had been found. And *where* it was found. I provided a thorough ac-count of my whereabouts for the night. They confirmed that ac-count, and that really should have been the end of the story."

"But it wasn't the end of the story. Instead, your name is forever associated with the Cinderella Murder case."

"Look, it would be easier if I could take some magic truth serum so people would finally believe me, but I get it. A young, bright, talented woman lost her life—and her family has never gotten the closure they richly deserve. So I have never expected anyone to feel sorry for me. She was the victim, not me."

"Well, let's go over that account you gave the police."

"Susan was supposed to be here at seven thirty, and she wasn't. Her agent surely would have told her that I am absolutely intoler-ant of lateness by anyone working or potentially working for me. If time is money, it's never truer than in the film business. Once she was fifteen minutes late, I called Madison, who had been my second choice, to see if she was interested. She must have come straight here, because she arrived by eight thirty. She left shortly before mid-night. In fact, I even recall her saying, "I can't believe it's almost midnight." His version matched Madison's, minute for minute.

"And you ordered pizza," Alex prompted.

"Yes, the pizza. My order was logged at nine twenty-seven, deliv-ered at nine fifty-eight. Check the records. You know Tottino's still has a copy of the takeout receipt framed on their front wall? They at least had the good judgment to black out my address."

"And how did Madison look when she arrived?" Alex asked. This was a question they had planned in light of Madison's waffling about whether she'd been feeling sick the night of Susan's murder.

"How did she *look*? Like a million dollars. That role called for an absolute beauty, and she fit the part."

Laurie smiled to herself but was impressed that Alex kept his expression neutral.

"The coroner estimated Susan's time of death as between seven and eleven P.M. She was expected here at seven thirty. You and Madison said Madison arrived here at eight thirty. The assumption has always been that you could not possibly have killed Susan, called Madison, returned Susan's car to campus, and then returned home by the time Madison arrived."

"No, I have not yet found a way to navigate Los Angeles traffic at hyper speed."

"But our research has revealed a new wrinkle to the timeline," Alex said. "We have learned that Susan had been having car trouble prior to her death, so she may have gotten a ride to her audition from someone else. That means you could have had a violent interaction with her upon her arrival and have been home before Madison arrived."

"If I went to a movie studio and pitched a story where a culprit sets an appointment to meet with someone at seven thirty, then phones her dorm room at seven forty-five, and then for some reason chases her into a park and murders her by eight thirty or so, I would get laughed out of the room. Alex, you're one of the best criminal defense lawyers in the country. Does that really sound plausible to you?"

Laurie watched Frank smile on the screen. She knew how this would play on television. The director was cocky, but he had a point. Unless they broke his alibi, Frank was in the clear. And so far, every part of the evidence supported his alibi: the phone records, Madison's statements, the pizza receipt. But Laurie still felt in her gut that the evidence was almost too perfect. What was she missing?

52

Talia lingered at the edge of the yard, in her carefully selected white sheath dress, wondering why she had bothered. By the time she met Frank, this was the starter house he would ask their driver to cruise by after he'd had too many drinks, eager to reminisce about his younger, less privileged days. It was probably worth two million dollars by now, but by comparison to their current homes—five total—this place was a shack.

Why had she thought for a second that the producers of *Under Suspicion* would ask her opinion? She wasn't a part of the narrative. When the press wrote about Frank, at best an article might mention that the previously hard-to-get bachelor had now been married for a decade. But they never bothered to name his wife, or to mention that she was the valedictorian of her class at Indiana University, was an accomplished pianist and singer, and had had a semi-promising acting career before she'd fallen in love with Frank.

Though she'd never played out the full arc of her career, she knew enough about show business to recognize that her husband wasn't hitting a home run on the screen right now, answering Alex Buckley's questions. Yes, he had scored a single—maybe even a double—pointing out the ridiculousness of Alex's theory: how could he have decided to kill Susan, executed the deed, and been back in time to answer his door in less than an hour's time? Yet, at the same time, he sounded a bit too much like those guilty guys in bad movies who sneered while taunting, "Too bad you don't have any evidence."

In short, Frank had noted the lack of evidence of his guilt but hadn't offered any alternative theory of his innocence. He had told his version of the story but hadn't helped the show with theirs.

Talia watched the crew pack up the cameras into their overstuffed van. This clearly was not a high-budget operation. Why, oh why, had Frank even bothered participating? It would have been so easy for him to say he was too busy to help.

Their equipment was loaded, and the crew was ready to leave. Alex Buckley and the producer, Laurie, were thanking Frank again for his participation. They'd be heading to their cars soon.

She was about to miss her opportunity. How was she going to catch them without Frank's seeing her?

Just as Alex and Laurie were walking down the driveway toward the black Land Cruiser parked on the street, Frank's assistant, Clarence, stepped out of the production trailer, one hand covering the microphone of his cell. "Frank, I've got Mitchell Langley from *Variety*. He's been trying to reach you all day. I told him there's no truth to the rumors about Bradley pulling out of the project, but he wants to hear it straight from you."

She overheard Frank offer a final good-bye before he followed Clarence into the trailer. She caught up to Laurie and Alex at the end of the driveway.

"My husband is being overly cautious."

When they turned toward the sound of her voice, it was as if they were seeing Talia for the first time. At forty-two years old, Talia knew she was still beautiful, with high cheekbones, catlike green eyes, and shoulder-length waves of dark blond hair.

Laurie said cautiously, "I'm sorry, Mrs. Parker. We really didn't get much of a chance to talk. You have something to add to your husband's replay of the night?"

"Not directly. I didn't even know Frank then. But I'm tired of this cloud hanging over him. I get it—her body was found a hop and skip from this house, and she was killed when she was supposed to be right here, alone with my husband. But, despite that, Frank truly has never understood why his alibi for that night hasn't put him in the clear. In that respect, my husband can be a bit naive. Until someone comes up with a better theory, he will always be suspected. But, I'm telling you, you're on the wrong track with the movie connection."

"I understand your frustration—"

Talia cut Laurie off before she chickened out. "Susan Dempsey had a huge fight with her roommate just hours before her murder."

"With Madison?"

"No, the other one; the third girl, Nicole. At least, according to Madison. You know how after Frank couldn't reach Susan on her cell phone, he called the dorm room? Well, when Madison answered, she said that Susan had a knock-down, drag-out fight that afternoon with their other roommate, and maybe that's why she was late."

"This is the first we've ever heard of this," Alex said. "Are you sure?"

"I wasn't there, but I know for a fact that's what Madison told Frank. It was so bad that Nicole even threw something at Susan. Then Susan called Nicole insane and said she was going to get her kicked out of the dorm, maybe even school, if she didn't change her ways. Back when the police were clearly targeting Frank, he hired investigators to look into it. It turns out that Nicole suddenly quit school after Susan was killed. And she didn't just take a semester or school year off. She left Los Angeles entirely and started all over again. Cut off ties with everyone. She was even using a fake name when she first moved. Then she changed her last name when she got married. Look into it: it's like Nicole Hunter died right along with Susan."

"Why didn't your husband ever tell anyone this before?" Laurie asked.

"His lawyers admonished him not to," Talia explained, clearly frustrated. "They were planning to use Nicole as the alternative suspect if he was ever formally charged."

Talia watched Laurie look to Alex for guidance. "It's probably what I would have advised too," he said. "Better to say as little as possible and spring it on the prosecution at trial."

"But there was never a trial," Talia said. "And yet twenty years later, here we are. Formal accusations aren't the only kind of punishment. Maybe now that you know the truth, you can ask the question the police never did: what happened between Susan and that other roommate?"

While Alex was starting the engine of the SUV, Laurie snapped her seat belt in place. "Good timing," she said. "Not even noon, and we're already wrapped up with Frank Parker."

Alex turned to her and smiled. "That means there's no need to rush back. Your dad is at the house with Grace and Timmy, so we know they're all safe. I have a suggestion. Let's drive up the coast for an hour and find a place on the water for lunch. I don't know about you, but my brain is scrambled. It's as though every time we talk to one of the witnesses, a new suspect emerges."

Laurie started to protest that they needed to get back to the house, but Alex was right. It would be good for the two of them to quietly discuss what they had been hearing from the potential suspects these past few days.

And a little time alone with him would be a nice bonus.

53

The next morning, Laurie was on her knees by the front door, buttoning Timmy's jean jacket.

"Mom, are you sure you and Alex can't come to the zoo with us?"

She had the fleeting thought that Timmy had begun to call her Mom instead of Mommy. He was growing up so fast.

"Sorry, sweetie, but we talked about this. Alex and I have to work, just like if I was in New York, but we get the bonus of being out here in California. I'll see you tonight, though. *Dad,*" she called out. "*Are you about ready to hit the road?*"

She looped the last jacket button and glanced at her watch. This was the start of the summit sessions, and today's participants would be here any minute. Up first was Susan's social group: Keith Ratner, Nicole Melling, and Madison Meyer. Rosemary was coming, too, because she wanted to watch. Tomorrow they'd talk separately to the computer crowd, Dwight Cook and Professor Richard Hathaway.

She heard rushed footsteps down the stairs. "Sorry, sorry," her father said. "I'm coming. I got that e-mail I was waiting for from the Alameda police: a list of license plates that were near Rosemary's neighborhood the day her neighbor was killed."

"Dad," Laurie whispered protectively.

"Aw, don't worry about Timmy. Kid's tough as nails, aren't you?" He tousled Timmy's brown wavy hair.

"Nails made of kryptonite," Timmy shot back.

"When we're done with the zoo, I might swing by the local precinct here for a little help running some criminal records. How does that sound, Timmy?"

"That sounds *cool*. And can we go see Jerry too? I want to get him a stuffed animal from the zoo and bring it to his room to keep him company until he wakes up again."

When they had agreed to bring Timmy out to California for an adventure, this wasn't what Laurie had in mind.

"You guys have a good day," she said. "And, Dad, try to take it easy on certain subjects, all right?"

Alex and Grace came out of the kitchen in time to say good-bye. Just as the rental car pulled out of the driveway, a red Porsche convertible replaced it. Keith Ratner was here. They were greeting him at the door when a black Escalade arrived, carrying Rosemary, Madison, Nicole, and Nicole's husband, Gavin.

Laurie leaned toward Grace to whisper a question. "Madison's staying at the hotel with the out-of-towners? Her house is, like, twenty minutes from here."

"Tell me about it. But girlfriend's agent insisted."

As Keith, Nicole, and Madison exchanged polite hugs and exclamations of *It's been so long* and *You look just the same,* Laurie escorted Rosemary and Gavin into the house to settle in as the day's observers. "Craft services brings in a ton of food throughout the day, so please, help yourself. It's all set up in the kitchen. Gavin, I didn't realize you were making the trip down to L.A."

"It was the least I could do, given how nervous Nicole has been. You're probably used to camera shyness, but I've never seen her like this."

After the bombshell Talia had dropped about Nicole and Susan fighting just hours before Susan's murder, Laurie had to wonder if the cameras were the only reason for Nicole's nerves.

With Jerry still in the hospital, Grace was doubling as production assistant, escorting Keith, Nicole, and Madison to the bedroom they were using for hair and makeup. Once they were camera ready, they'd have a group conversation with Alex in the living room.

"You ready to roll?" Laurie asked Alex. Their lunch excursion to the coast the previous afternoon had been fruitful. They had rehearsed the plan ad nauseam, but now Laurie found herself hoping that their suspicions about Nicole were wrong.

54

As they had planned, Keith was on the far end of the sofa, farthest from Alex's chair, followed by Madison and Nicole.

"I thought we'd start," Alex said, "by having each of you walk through where you were the night of the murder. Keith, would you like to begin?"

Keith explained that he was at a bookstore with several people who had vouched for his whereabouts, and then volunteered that the gathering was an Advocates for God event. "People can form their own opinions about Advocates for God, but I've always been very open about my relationship with AG. I was still learning about the church's mission at the time, but once Susan died, I poured myself into it. I found that I was a happier person when I was providing service through the church. I became less selfish. But, anyway, that's where I was—the whole night."

Alex nodded, satisfied for the moment. "And what about you, Madison?"

"I suspect many of your viewers already know my version, because I'm probably most famous for being Frank Parker's alibi for that night." Laurie was impressed by how quickly Madison changed her affect for the cameras. Gone was the diva striving for a celebrity comeback. Speaking in the serious, measured tone of a news anchor, she repeated her memorized timeline.

"And according to Frank Parker," Alex noted, "you arrived for the audition looking like 'a million dollars.'"

"Well, I'd like to think so. But it was my audition that got me the role."

Alex nodded again. So far, so good.

Next up was the speaker Laurie was most interested in, Nicole.

"That night? I never really think about where I was. When I think of that May seven, I always remember it as the night Susan died."

"I understand. But surely when a close friend—your room-mate—is killed, you must go through a process of saying, *What if I had been there? What if I could have stopped it?*"

Nicole was nodding along. "Absolutely." This was how Alex oper-ated on cross-examination. Give the witness easy statements to agree with, and then use those statements to lead the witness in the de-sired direction.

"So," Alex continued, "you must recall where you were."

"Yes," Nicole said quietly. "To be honest, I'm heartsick and ashamed about that night. I went to O'Malley's, a local bar. I ended up drinking way too much." Without being asked, she added, "I was desperately nervous about a biology exam."

It had only been a matter of seconds, and Nicole already sounded defensive.

"You weren't too upset about your argument with Susan to focus on your studies?" Alex asked sternly.

Even beneath the makeup, Nicole's skin tone faded three shades. "Excuse me?"

"Our investigation has revealed that just that afternoon, shortly be-fore Susan was killed, the two of you had a very significant argument."

"Susan was my best friend. We had the occasional squabble, but nothing I'd call a *significant argument*."

"Really? Because according to our source, the dispute was so heated that you threw something at Susan. She then threatened to drop you as a roommate if you didn't change."

Nicole was stammering, pulling at the mic looped through the buttonhole of her silk blouse, trying to remove it. Next to her, Madison tried to suppress a smile. She was eating this up.

"Madison," Alex said, shifting his attention, "you seem to enjoy seeing Nicole's feet to the fire."

"I wouldn't say I enjoy it. But, yes, after all these years of being under suspicion, as you call it, I find it a bit ironic that the so-called *nice* roommate was actually throwing things at Susan."

"Some might say it's ironic," Alex said, "that *you* were the one who overheard the fight. So the question I have for you, Madison, is why you never told the police what you heard."

"There was no reason. I was coming down the dormitory hall and heard them shout at each other. I didn't want to get involved. When the door opened, I stepped into the bathroom to avoid the whole scene. Susan left first, then Nicole. That was right around six o'clock. Once I knew the drama had left the building, I went to our room. Then Frank called, and the rest is history."

"You say you resent being under suspicion, but evidence of a bitter dispute between Susan and Nicole might have helped deflect that attention. And yet you never mentioned the fight to anyone." There was a note of astonishment in Alex's voice.

The entire room was silent. Laurie found herself leaning forward, waiting for the next words. She hoped viewers would do the same.

When Madison did not answer, Alex continued to press. "How about this as a theory, Madison? Drawing attention to Nicole as a suspect would have meant deflecting it from Frank. And then your alibi for Frank wouldn't have been quite so valuable."

"The reason I never said anything is because I never thought for a second that Nicole could ever kill Susan."

"*And* you liked being needed by Frank Parker. Isn't that right, Madison?"

55

Laurie could feel the tension in the room. Moments like this were the reason they invited multiple suspects on camera at once. Each person acted as a check on the others, making it harder to sneak in a lie that could easily be disproven by someone else.

Alex continued to press Madison. "Some people have questioned why Frank Parker—a mere fifteen minutes after Susan's expected time of arrival—would invite another actress, who just *happened* to be Susan's roommate, to audition. Tell the truth: When Frank called your dorm room that night, the call wasn't really for you, was it? Isn't it true that Frank was calling for Susan, to see where she was?"

"Fine," Madison conceded. "He didn't actually invite me to audition. But when I realized Susan had no-showed, I saw an opportunity. Susan had told me where Frank lived, so I drove up there. I had *no idea* at the time that she was in danger. When Frank said she didn't show up, I figured she was off crying on Keith's shoulder about the fight."

"And just like you seized the opportunity by auditioning, when you realized that Susan had been killed, you seized the opportunity to be Frank's alibi."

"I *was* his alibi. I was at his house."

"But not by eight thirty. He called at seven forty-five inquiring about your roommate, and it's at least a thirty-minute drive. You'd have to be awfully conniving for your first instinct to be to steal her role."

"I didn't *steal*—"

"But some time must have passed before you *saw the opportunity*, as you described it. To have arrived at Frank Parker's house looking like—quote—'a million dollars,' I imagine you would have spent some time on your hair and makeup."

"No, in fact, I was already dolled up."

"Right. During our preinterview, you first said you were sick at home when the phone rang. Then you corrected yourself to say you had gotten dressed for a Sigma Alpha Epsilon party and then changed your mind because you weren't feeling up to it."

"That's what happened."

"A fraternity party? Really? Nicole and Keith, you knew Madison in college. Was she the type to show up for a frat party?"

They both shook their heads. "Absolutely not," Nicole added for emphasis. "She hated them."

"Oh my gosh," Madison snapped. "Can you stop already? Talk about minutiae. Fine, if you absolutely must know why I was home that night, ready to walk out the door, it's because I had been expecting a gentleman caller, so to speak."

"A boyfriend?" Alex asked.

"No, nothing serious—but someone I thought was interested. I had sent him a flirty little note, suggesting it would be worth his time to pick me up at the dorm at seven thirty. I got myself dolled up, expecting him to take the bait. Apparently he wasn't interested, because there I was when Frank called at seven forty-five. Not the kind of thing I wanted to advertise at the time, but not a big deal in retrospect. I got a career-defining role instead. The point is: I was home, the phone rang, and the call records back it up. I saw my opportunity, drove immediately to Frank's house, *begged* for a chance to audition, and then acted my little butt off. I was there from eight thirty to midnight, just like I said."

"And yet you and Frank have always maintained that he *invited* you to audition. Why the lie?"

"A *white* lie."

"Perhaps, but why stretch the truth at all?" Alex asked.

"Because it sounded better, okay? Susan never came home that night. I thought she was still mad at Nicole and crashing somewhere else. The next morning Rosemary called, completely panicked. She said a body had been found in Laurel Canyon Park and the police thought it was Susan. She was hoping we'd tell her it was all a mistake, that Susan was safe in her room."

"But she wasn't," Alex said. "You'd been to Frank's house. You would have known how close the park was. You must have suspected him."

Madison was shaking her head and starting to cry. She was no longer putting on a performance. "No, absolutely not. I had been at his house, just like I said. And I knew he'd called the dorm at seven forty-five. So I knew for sure it wasn't him. But I also knew I was the only person who could prove that."

"And so?" Alex asked.

"So I went to Frank's. I told him there was nothing to worry about—that I knew he wasn't involved and that I'd back him up to the police."

"But you set contingencies, didn't you? You threatened him. You told him that you'd only support his alibi if he cast you in *Beauty Land*."

After a long pause, all she could say was, "I *earned* that role."

If this had been a courtroom, Alex would have resumed his seat at counsel table now. His job with respect to Madison was done. She was so conniving that even after she knew Susan was dead, her first priority was becoming a star.

But this wasn't a courtroom, and Madison wasn't the only witness. Alex paused and looked again to Nicole. "Nicole, you must see now that the argument you had that day could be the key to solving her murder. She fled the apartment at six o'clock with every intention of getting to that audition. But she was also having car trouble. We have no idea where she was between that moment and her death. What did you fight about?"

"I remember now that we had some kind of spat, and I went to O'Malley's and started drinking. It was a college hangout, and I got pretty wasted. I'm sure you could find people who'd remember. As for the reason we argued? I have no idea. Something stupid, I'm sure."

"Keith, you've been very quiet during this. Wouldn't Susan have confided in you that she was quarreling with one of her closest friends?"

He shrugged as if this was the first he'd heard of any tension between the two friends. His seeming indifference struck Laurie as odd.

Alex made one more effort. "I want to ask you all, now that the importance of the question is clear. For the first time, we have revealed that Susan stormed out of her dorm room. It is likely because of her car problems that she did not drive herself to Frank Parker's for the audition. That means she may have encountered someone the police never questioned. Where should we be looking? Where would she have gone?"

Madison appeared genuinely perplexed, but Laurie noticed Nicole and Keith exchange a wary glance.

From the first time Laurie had met Nicole in person, she'd believed Nicole was being intentionally vague about her reasons for leaving UCLA. They hadn't yet solved the case, but one thing was clear: Nicole's departure from Los Angeles had something to do with her fight with Susan, and Keith was covering for her.

56

Leo Farley sat back on the sofa to rest his eyes. Detective O'Brien, the lead detective, had e-mailed Leo a list of license plates from camera footage near Castle Crossings, the gated community where Lydia Levitt had been killed. Today, after taking Timmy to the zoo, he had stopped by the LAPD and gotten driver's license photos for most of the cars' owners, as well as their criminal history reports.

He had excused himself from the dinner table early, eager to pore through the materials. This house was luxurious, but at the moment, he missed the bulletin boards and laminate furniture of a police precinct. The documents and pictures were spread around him in layers across the sofa cushions, glass coffee table, and plush carpet.

Two hours later, he had finished his second perusal of every single piece of paper. He had been hoping for an obvious lead: a name associated with the Susan Dempsey case, something to connect the murder in Rosemary's backyard to the murder of Rosemary's daughter twenty years earlier. He had to believe that Laurie's decision to feature the Cinderella Murder case had led to the attacks on both Rosemary's neighbor and Jerry.

But nothing was jumping out.

Timmy came bounding out of the kitchen toward him. "Grandpa! Have you found anything yet?"

224   Mary Higgins Clark

"Careful," Leo warned as Timmy tipped over a stack of printouts on his way to Leo's side. "I know this stuff looks like a mess, but I've actually got a system going here."

"Sorry, Grandpa." Timmy reached next to him and began straightening the pile that had been toppled. "What are these?"

"Those are photographs of drivers who were near Castle Crossings on the day I'm interested in but who have prior addresses in Los Angeles."

"And you're interested in that particular day because that's when Mrs. Dempsey's neighbor got killed?"

Leo looked toward the kitchen, where he could hear the others finishing up their dinner. Laurie didn't like him talking so openly about crime with Timmy, but the boy had witnessed his own father's murder and spent years under the killer's threat to come for Timmy as well. As far as Leo was concerned, the child was going to have a natural curiosity about crime.

"Yes, that's why we're interested. And if the person who hurt Lydia has something to do with your mother's case—"

Timmy completed the thought. "Then he might have lived down here when Susan was in college." He was sneaking peeks at the driver's license photos he was supposedly straightening.

"That's right," Leo said. "I tell ya, Timmy. You can do anything you want when you grow up, but you've got the chops to be a better cop than I was."

Timmy suddenly stopped fiddling with the pictures and pulled one from the pile. "I know him!"

"Timmy, we're not playing police right now. I've got to get back to work here."

"No, I mean it, for real. I saw him in the restaurant in San Francisco, the one with the huge meatballs and all the pictures of celebrities on the walls."

"At Mama Torini's?"

"Yes. This man was there. He was sitting at the bar, right above our table. Whenever I looked at him, he turned around really fast."

Leo took the photograph from his grandson. According to the driver's license, the man was Steve Roman. His current address in San Francisco had been changed with the DMV two years earlier. Before that, he had been a longtime resident of Los Angeles.

"You're saying you saw this man, in person, when we were in San Francisco?"

"Yes. He had big muscles and pale skin. And his head was shaved. Not like bald when the hair falls out, but it was shaved, like when you say you have five o'clock shadow, Grandpa. And I remember thinking it was funny he'd shave his head while other grown-ups complain all the time about their hair falling out. Plus the bartender had long dark hair but kept it in a ponytail, so in a way he was hiding his hair too."

"Timmy, are you sure?" But Leo could tell Timmy *was* sure. As much as he credited Timmy's ability to deal with hardship, the threat of Blue Eyes had trained the boy to constantly monitor any man in his vicinity.

Leo believed that Timmy had indeed seen Steve Roman. Still, he'd like to have something more to connect this man to the case.

"Do me a favor, kiddo. Can you fetch me your iPad from the kitchen?"

Seconds later, Timmy was back with his gadget in tow. "Are we playing a game?"

"Not quite yet." Leo opened the browser, typed in "Steve Roman," and hit ENTER.

He found listings for a Boston Realtor, a New York City investment banker, the author of a book about rain forests. He scrolled to the next page of results.

Timmy touched his index finger to the screen. "Look, Grandpa. Click on that one. Weren't Mommy and Alex talking about that today?"

Leo knew immediately from the name of the website that he had found the correct Steve Roman. He finally had the connection he was looking for between Lydia Levitt's murder and *Under Suspicion*.

"Laurie!" he called out. "You need to see this!"

57

"Alex, that was delicious." Laurie could still smell the aroma of cooked red wine and mushrooms as she filled the cast-iron pot with sudsy water to soak overnight.

"I'll pass the compliment on to Ramon. He's the one who taught me everything I know about coq au vin." It had been Alex's idea to send craft services away early so they could have one home-cooked meal in this gourmet kitchen.

"A five-star dinner," Laurie said, "and then in the morning, little elves will appear to carry away the dirty dishes. I could get used to this."

She had just stacked the final plate in the sink when she heard the sound of her father's voice from the living room. "Laurie!" Was it her imagination, or did he sound excited? "You need to see this!"

She turned off the faucet and ran to the living room. Her father and son were next to each other on the sofa.

"We've got something, Laurie. It was actually Timmy who made the connection."

"Dad, I told you I didn't want him exposed to all this."

Now Timmy was on his feet, extending a printout of a driver's license. "I recognized this man right away, Mommy. His name is Steve Roman. His car was photographed right outside Mrs. Dempsey's neighborhood the day Lydia Levitt got killed in her yard." Laurie could not believe she was hearing her nine-year-old son talk this way about a homicide. "And I also saw him right next to us at the restaurant in San Francisco, at Mama . . ."

He looked to his grandfather for help with the name. "At Mama Torini's," Leo said. "Timmy got a good enough look at him to recognize this picture. The man's name is Steve Roman. He lives in San Francisco, but until two years ago, he was in Los Angeles. And get this."

Her father handed her the iPad. Part of her didn't want to look. She didn't want to believe that Timmy had been sitting right next to someone involved in Lydia Levitt's murder. She didn't want to believe that the woman's death had anything to do with her decision to reinvestigate the Cinderella Murder.

She saw the name "Steve Roman" multiple times on the screen. The website was for Advocates for God. Someone named Steve Roman was a frequent poster to the community forum.

She shuffled a pile of documents off a chair so she could sit and process the information.

A member of Keith Ratner's church had been watching them in San Francisco and had been spotted near the murder of Rosemary Dempsey's neighbor? This couldn't be a coincidence.

She thought back to that moment at the end of filming today. When Alex had pressed Nicole about her fight with Susan, Keith Ratner appeared to know more than he was saying. Did the fight have something to do with AG?

Laurie stood from the sofa and steered her son into the kitchen. "Grace? Do you mind keeping an eye on Timmy? I have a few more questions for Nicole."

58

When Laurie knocked on Nicole's hotel door, Alex was at her side. He and Leo had insisted that she not leave the house alone. They finally agreed that Leo would stay home with Timmy and Grace while Alex accompanied Laurie to the hotel.

When the door cracked open, it was Nicole's husband, Gavin, who answered.

"Laurie, hi. It's after nine o'clock. Were we expecting you?"

"We need to talk to Nicole."

"I hope this is important. My wife is in bed."

He stepped aside, allowing them to enter. Laurie was surprised to find a large living area, with a separate dining room to the side. Clearly Gavin had used his own money to upgrade them beyond the standard suite provided by the show. "She's not in any danger, is she?" Gavin asked. "She's been so darn nervous ever since Rosemary called her about this show."

Laurie heard Alex intentionally clear his throat. He was reminding her not to slip into her normal mode of trying to comfort her witnesses. "Actually, yes, there's a real possibility she's in danger, Gavin."

"That's impossible," he snapped. "Nicole, you need to get out here."

When she emerged from the separate bedroom, Nicole was

wearing a pajama set topped by a robe. "Sorry, I was getting ready for bed."

She did not sound sorry.

"They said you're in danger."

"I said you *might* be in danger," Laurie emphasized. "Have you ever seen this man?" Laurie handed her a printout of Steve Roman's driver's license photograph, monitoring Nicole's face for a reaction.

Her expression was blank. "No, I don't think so."

"His name is Steve Roman. We believe he's the man who killed Rosemary's neighbor, Lydia Levitt."

"How would I know a burglar?"

"We think Lydia interrupted this man snooping behind Rosemary's house, but he wasn't a burglar. He was trying to learn more about the people involved in *Under Suspicion*. In fact, just days after Lydia's death, he was following my family and me in San Francisco. He was probably watching you as well. He could also be the person who attacked my assistant producer, Jerry."

"I'm afraid I'm not following your logic," Nicole said.

"Steve Roman is a longtime member of Advocates for God."

Laurie had been prepared to lay out AG's connections to Keith Ratner and her theory that Keith may have sent one of his church friends, Steve Roman, to sabotage the show and stop production. But the expression on Nicole's face at the mention of Advocates for God made it clear that Nicole already knew something about them.

"Today during the shoot, you said you didn't remember what you argued about with Susan. And when I first met you, you were vague about your reasons for leaving Los Angeles. It has something to do with this church, doesn't it?"

"I don't—I don't know anything about it."

Alex handed her the file folder they had prepared before leaving the house. Laurie slipped the first photograph from the file, an eight-by-ten of nineteen-year-old Susan, smiling up at the camera.

Laurie quickly followed it up with a second picture, this one of Lydia Levitt.

"These two women are dead. This is no longer about whatever personal history you want to keep private," Laurie said. "People are being hurt. My friend Jerry is in the hospital right now. And it has something to do with Advocates for God."

Gavin wrapped a protective arm around his wife's shoulder. "Nicole, if you know something—"

"I never meant to hide anything from you, Gavin. I was trying to protect myself. To protect *us*." Nicole took Gavin's hand in hers and faced Laurie directly. "I'll tell you. But only to help. No cameras."

Laurie nodded. At this point, the truth mattered more than the show.

59

Dwight stepped carefully from the dock onto the stern of his boat, a forty-two-foot cruiser perfect for short trips. He immediately felt a calmness enter his body as he rocked with the sway of the boat on the water. The waves slapping gently against the fiberglass were like a lullaby. Once his scuba partner arrived, he'd be out in Shaw's Cove, diving into the darkness. He loved nothing more than the solitude of night diving.

He would not truly be able to enjoy the scuba dive until he first completed one task. He climbed down into the cabin, retrieved his laptop from his messenger bag, flipped it open, and clicked on the surveillance video of the Bel Air house. It had been two days since Dwight had decided not to go to the police with the video of the horrible attack on Jerry. He had to hope that his continued monitoring might lead him to some answers about Susan's death, and possibly Jerry's attacker.

He sped through the video, slowing down only when something interested him. When he reached the end of the tape, he rewound to the scene that fascinated him most, the joint interview with Madison Meyer, Nicole Hunter, and Keith Ratner.

Alex Buckley had caught Madison in a couple of inconsistencies, but they were small ones. She was still vouching for Frank Parker. The bigger revelation was that Susan had a fight with Nicole and had stormed out of the dorm that evening.

Dwight knew how excited Susan had been about that audition. She wouldn't have missed it voluntarily.

He rewound the video once again, replaying Alex Buckley's final question over and over again: *Where would she have gone?*

He closed his eyes and pictured Susan on the night when he decided that he truly loved her. They had worked so late at the lab that they realized that dawn was only an hour away. They decided to drive to Griffith Observatory, reportedly the best place to watch the sun rise. As they sat in the grass, in the dark, she had filled the silence, talking about how petty girls could be to each other. How the theater department was filled with actresses who had the same amount of talent as she did but twice the ambition. How too many of her friends prioritized their boyfriends over their girlfriends. The way, even with Keith, she always felt she had to boost his confidence. She said there was only one place where she could let another side of her personality take over.

Where would she have gone?

Dwight was pretty sure he knew.

He used his computer to pull up an online calendar from 1994 to refresh his memory. By May 7, it had been weeks since Hathaway had caught Dwight hacking into the university computer system. Dwight remembered the timing because he was counting down the days until the end of the semester. He wanted to go to La Jolla for another scuba trip.

All this time, he had suppressed the connection between the date of Susan's death and another event that had changed his life.

He closed his eyes again and recalled Susan's excitement about her audition with Frank Parker. She always said she liked to feel calm and focused before a performance, trying to channel her character. If a fight with Nicole had forced her from her dorm room at six, that gave her at least forty-five minutes to calm herself down. If she had needed another place to feel calm and safe, Dwight knew exactly where Susan would have gone. And he knew exactly what she would have heard when she got there.

His skin felt hot. He stood up and started pacing in the boat's cabin. He was having a hard time controlling his own breathing. He needed his own safe place now. He needed to be in the water.

But he also wanted to get his thoughts out. His plan had worked: he finally believed he knew who had killed Susan.

He pulled up Laurie's number on his cell and hit ENTER. *"You've reached Laurie Moran . . ."*

"Call me ASAP," he said at the tone. "I need to talk to you."

He was so focused on leaving a message that he did not hear the footsteps on the deck.

60

Gavin led his wife to the sofa and held her hand protectively. "I'm here for you," he whispered. "Always. No matter what. If there's anybody you're afraid of, I'll protect you."

Nicole spoke quickly, focusing on some random spot in the distance. "The fight with Susan was about Advocates for God. I'd been a member of the church for months, and Susan didn't approve. She said they were crooks, that they used religion to bilk people of their money. She said I was getting brainwashed. And it didn't help that I was . . . in a relationship with Martin Collins. I thought he was the most generous, inspiring person. I thought I was in love with him, but I was so young and impressionable."

The moment was disrupted by the buzz of Laurie's phone. Laurie fumbled in her purse and glanced at the screen. It was Dwight Cook. She did not want to interrupt Nicole, so she hit the REJECT CALL button. "If you'd been with the church for months," Laurie said, "why did you fight about it that day?"

"The argument was about Susan's boyfriend, Keith. I took him to a new-member party. Susan was furious, saying I was out to convert him. The fight was as bad as Alex described earlier—even worse. I felt attacked. I threw a book at her. I can't believe that's the last time we saw each other." She dropped her head into her hands.

"You realize, Nicole, that some people might not believe that. If Susan was threatening to kick you out of the dorm—"

"No, she never would have done that. It was an ugly fight, but honestly, I think she only snapped at me because of the culmination of everything at once: the audition and her agent leaving for Arizona because of his mom's heart attack, and she was harried, rummaging through her drawers in a mad search for her lucky necklace. I walked in, and she lashed out at me about taking Keith to an AG event. I think it was just the icing on the cake. We would have been fine. And I would certainly *never* have hurt Susan."

Something about Nicole's version of the argument was bothering Laurie. "You say you wound up at O'Malley's drinking too much. If it wasn't truly a blowout, why were you so upset?"

"After Susan stormed out, I walked to Martin's to vent about our argument. Whenever I was with Martin, he had this way of making it all seem okay." She whispered to Gavin, *"I'm so sorry I never told you, please forgive me,"* before continuing. "When I got to his house, the lights were on, and his car was in the driveway. He didn't answer the door, so I just walked in, assuming he couldn't hear me knocking. When I got to his bedroom—"

Her voice broke, and she started to shake. Gavin pulled her close and told her that everything was going to be all right. "These secrets are torturing you, Nicole."

"When I walked into his bedroom, he was with a little girl. My gosh, she couldn't have been more than ten. They were . . . in the bed. I ran from the house, but he caught up to me in the driveway. He told me if I ever breathed a word of what I'd seen, he would kill me. And not just me. The girl, too. He threatened to kill anyone I loved—my parents, my friends. He said he could find me forty years later and kill my children and grandchildren. And I could tell he meant it. I think he would have killed me on the spot if that little girl hadn't been there to witness it."

"And you never said a word to anyone?" Laurie asked.

Nicole shook her head and then looked down, sobbing into her hands. "You have no idea how much guilt I've carried. Every time I see him on television, I feel nauseous, wondering how many others he has victimized. I was tempted so many times to tell you, Gavin, but I was ashamed. And afraid for both of us. And I had no idea who the child was, and no proof. Martin is powerful. At the very least, he would get other church members to say I was crazy. And I didn't doubt for a second his ability to carry out his threats. It's why I was always afraid to have children, Gavin. I didn't want to spend every moment terrified about Martin coming after them."

Laurie knew the fear of knowing that someone wanted to hurt your child. "Do you think Martin had something to do with Susan's death?" Laurie asked.

"I'm sure he's capable of murder," Nicole said. "But he had no reason to harm Susan, and I saw him at his house that night with my own eyes."

"But if Martin found out you were doing our show," Laurie said, "he'd worry that you might end up saying too much about the past."

Nicole wiped away a tear. "Yes, that's how he operates. He's insular and deeply paranoid. That's why I've kept such a low profile all these years. The thought of me on television, talking about my days at UCLA? He would have gone nuclear. That man in the picture is probably one of Martin's henchmen, sent to shut down your show."

Laurie was having a hard time processing the new information. She had been so certain that if they found the person who attacked Lydia and Jerry, they'd also find Susan's killer. And there was still something nagging at Laurie about Nicole's description of her argument with Susan that afternoon.

Alex had been quietly allowing Nicole to answer Laurie's questions. Now he spoke up. "Let's talk about Keith Ratner. We know he's still active in the church. He knew who the other show participants were. He probably told Martin that Nicole had signed on to appear. Then Martin could have asked Steve Roman to keep an eye on her, which could have led Roman to Rosemary's neighborhood. You two see each other, right?"

"Yes," Nicole said excitedly, "that's it! Rosemary came to my house the day before Lydia was killed. This man could have followed her from there."

"Our best shot at finding anything on Martin would be to go through Keith Ratner," Laurie said.

Dwight Cook and Richard Hathaway were supposed to be coming to the house for their interviews in the morning, but their scenes would be short. Laurie pulled her phone from her purse. Ignoring the alert of the missed call from Dwight, she composed a text to Keith, reading aloud as she typed with her thumbs. *Thanks for all the help today. I hate to tell you this, but a technical glitch swallowed up some of the footage. Any chance you can reshoot the part about your bookstore alibi in the morning? I promise it won't take long. —Laurie*

She hit the ENTER key and breathed a sigh of relief when he immediately texted back: *No problem. Just tell me the time.*

Great, thanks. Be sure to wear the same shirt.

"Add a smiley face for good measure," Alex suggested, reading over her shoulder.

"Got him," she said.

"We should have Leo fill in the LAPD on what we've got," Alex said. "Nicole, we can keep what you've told us confidential, at least for now. If the police agree, they can monitor the questioning of Keith while disguised as camera crew."

"Maybe Rosemary was right about Keith all along," Laurie said. "He could have sent one of his church buddies to shut down production on the show."

"You guys are the experts," Nicole said. "But if any of this is related to Advocates for God, I wouldn't bother worrying about Keith

Ratner. Martin Collins is the truly dangerous one. If this Steve Roman works for Collins, he'd be the kind of person willing to do anything for him. Trust me, I know."

On her way to the car, Laurie was replaying Nicole's description of Susan in a frantic search for her necklace, stressed out about her audition and lashing out at Nicole for introducing Keith to her fringe church. There was something about the scene that was bothering her.

Her thoughts were distracted by a new voice mail alert on her phone. It was Dwight. *"Call me ASAP. I need to talk to you."* He would have to wait until morning. They needed to find an LAPD detective willing to help them corner Keith Ratner.

61

The next morning, Laurie stood in the driveway of the Bel Air house, watching for cars. She checked her watch. It was 9:58 A.M. Dwight Cook and Richard Hathaway were scheduled to arrive at ten, so she had asked Keith Ratner to come at eleven thirty. She figured he would be less likely to be suspicious about being called back in if he were one of multiple witnesses at the house.

She snuck a glance through the door into the living room. LAPD detective Sean Reilly blended in with the camera crew, wearing blue jeans, a baseball cap, and the black *Under Suspicion* T-shirt Laurie had provided. He was the detective assigned to the assault on Jerry. He was young, probably early thirties, the only lines on his face the kind that came whenever a cop took his job seriously.

It had taken a long late-night phone call to explain the connection from Lydia Levitt to Steve Roman to Advocates for God to *Under Suspicion* to Jerry, but Reilly finally agreed to come to the set to hear what Keith Ratner had to say about the church's involvement in all of this.

Nicole Melling was already waiting in the house. Laurie had to hope that when the time came, all the pieces to the plan would fall into place.

A white Lexus SUV pulled into the driveway at 10:02. Hathaway was driving. No one else was in the car.

"I thought you and Dwight would come together," she said as he opened his door.

"My place is in Toluca Lake." Hathaway must have registered her blank expression because he added, "It's in Burbank. Great place. Private lake. One of the best golf clubs in the state. Anyway, Dwight still has his student crash pad in Westwood. Driving out of your way during the L.A. commute? No one's that good of a friend."

"We'll get you in and out quickly, just a little background about Susan's technology interests. Her father was a successful intellectual property lawyer, and they shared an excitement for the tech world. You can talk about that side of her in a way our other witnesses can't."

Dwight still hadn't arrived by the time Hathaway had been miked and powdered by the makeup technician. It was 10:20. Laurie listened as Hathaway left yet another voice mail message for Dwight: "Hey, man. Laurie and I have both been calling you. Hope you're on your way."

"I don't get it," Hathaway said, slipping his phone in his sports coat pocket. "He's usually so prompt."

Laurie was kicking herself for not finding the time to return his "ASAP" call last night. She now had a feeling that he had been calling to cancel. "I wonder if the idea of the cameras scared him off on the eve of the shoot," she said.

Hathaway shrugged. "Maybe. But he had been so eager to help with the show."

Laurie had planned to get Dwight and Hathaway out of here shortly after Keith arrived. Otherwise, Keith might lose patience and leave.

She made a quick decision to proceed with Hathaway alone. He was telegenic. He had cachet, having earned his tenure in his early thirties and then moved on to help a protégé form a ground-breaking company. If she could rope Dwight back in later, Alex could question him separately. It was more important not to ruin their plans for Keith Ratner.

As she had expected, Richard Hathaway was a natural on camera. "I had a lot of talented students at UCLA," he told Alex, "but Susan was among the best. When she died, there was so much talk about her promising acting career, but I've always believed she could have gone on to be a star in the tech world. She could have been another Dwight Cook. Such a tragedy."

His handsome face furrowed in thought, his voice resonating with the authority of a man who had been a professor, with step-by-step reasoning, he continued to talk about Susan and then, under Alex's questioning, the night of her death.

"I remember the absolute shock of hearing on Sunday that her body had been found. Dwight was only nineteen years old then, the brain of a wizard but still adolescent in his relationships. It was impossible not to realize how he felt about Susan. Whenever they were in the lab together, his eyes were shining and he was smiling. When he got the awful news, he tracked me down at my home and cried in my arms."

"Do you happen to know where Dwight was on the night Susan died?" Alex asked quietly.

"With me, actually. Dwight was in the throes of writing code for his project, and I knew he wanted to talk to me about it. I didn't have any plans for the evening, so I called Dwight and asked him if he wanted to join me for a burger."

"What time was this?" Alex asked.

"I called him around seven. Met him just after that at Hamburger Haven."

"One more thing," Alex added. "I wouldn't be doing my job if I didn't mention the fact that you were very popular among female students and had a bit of a reputation as a Don Juan."

Hathaway laughed. "Ah, yes. Most crush-worthy professor, according to the campus paper. All rumor and innuendo, I assure you. I'm convinced it's inevitable when you're a young, single academic."

"So anyone who suggested you may have taken a more-than-professional interest in Susan . . . ?"

"Would be deeply mistaken. Not to mention, Susan was very clearly taken by her boyfriend. It broke my heart watching poor Dwight pine for her."

Hathaway had been perfect, providing the touch of personality she'd been looking for. Dwight Cook was the face of REACH, but Hathaway was a hundred times better on camera than Dwight would have been.

She had just yelled *"Cut!"* when she heard the purr of a sports car outside the house, followed by the sound of a car door slamming. Keith Ratner was here. She could send Hathaway home. Perfect timing.

62

Laurie placed Keith in the same spot on the sofa where he'd been the previous day, wearing the same shirt, as requested.

"Again, I'm so sorry," she apologized. "We lost the footage of you telling us where you were the night of Susan's murder. If you can just repeat that, we'll shoot you close in. It will look just like you're sitting next to Madison and Nicole."

"Sure, no problem."

She double-checked that Detective Reilly was positioned with the camera crew, then gave the signal to start filming.

Alex started with the identical line he'd used the previous morning. "I thought we'd start," Alex said, "by having each of you walk through where you were the night of the murder. Keith, would you like to begin?"

Keith repeated the same story he'd given many times over the years: he'd been at a bookstore with fellow AG members.

"Now, speaking of Advocates for God," Alex said, "do you know this man?" He placed a photograph of Steve Roman on the coffee table in front of Keith.

Keith shot Alex, and then Laurie, a confused look. He picked up the picture for closer inspection. "Never seen him."

"He's a member of your church, and we believe he is determined to shut down this show's production—using violence when necessary."

Keith reached for the mic clipped to his shirt collar. They'd assumed he would try to leave once he realized they were departing from yesterday's script, but at least they had him here. The LAPD was here. All they had to do was get him to say something that would give Detective Reilly probable cause to detain him.

"Keith, it's important," she said. "There are things about the church you don't know."

Keith's gaze suddenly darted away from Laurie. She turned to see Nicole stepping from the kitchen. Nicole was terrified of retribution from Martin, but Laurie, Leo, and Gavin had convinced her the previous night to be present at the house, listening from the next room, in case she decided to help confront Keith.

"I told them about my fight with Susan," she said. "They know I was the one who introduced you to Martin and AG. You know I left the church. Los Angeles, too. But I never told you my reasons."

"You left because Susan was killed. She was your best friend."

As Nicole took a seat next to Keith on the sofa, Laurie noticed Detective Reilly take a step forward. He was paying close attention.

"No, that wasn't it. Keith, Reverend Collins is not the man you think he is."

63

Keith Ratner could not believe the words that were coming out of Nicole's mouth.

First Nicole claimed to have had a secret relationship with Martin, and now she was saying he abused a little girl?

"Nicole, these are crazy accusations. No wonder Martin was so worried about you being a part of this show."

"I saw him with my own eyes, Keith. And you would not believe he was a good man if you heard the threats he made against me. Some part of you must see the truth. Look at his lifestyle. All that money he raises isn't going to good works. It's lining his pockets. And think about those families he chooses to help—always with young girls, always with vulnerable parents. I didn't see the pattern either until that night. But I couldn't prove anything. Who knows how many other victims he's had? You can help. You're in his inner circle."

Keith covered his face with his hands. This was absolutely insane. "I haven't seen you in twenty years, Nicole. Why should I believe you?"

"Ask yourself: How did Martin feel about your doing this show? Did he want you talking about AG?"

"Yes, in fact. I didn't even want to do it. Martin's the one who *pushed* me to accept." But as Keith finished the sentence, he felt a tug of doubt. He recalled the moment he first mentioned *Under Suspicion* to Martin. Keith had wanted no part of the show. He hated the idea of having his name dragged through the mud again. Martin had been the one to steer him here. Martin had wanted to know what Nicole was up to. His exact words had been, *You let me worry about my own enemies.*

But child abuse? Was it possible that Keith had devoted his entire adult life to a church led by a man who would do something so heinous? It was unimaginable.

He cleared his throat, as if it could somehow clear his thoughts. "What do you people want from me?"

A cameraman in a baseball hat lunged forward, a badge in his hand. When were the surprises going to stop?

"Mr. Ratner, my name is Detective Sean Reilly with the Los Angeles Police Department. Let me be straight with you. I've got Ms. Melling's twenty-year-old recollection of an unconfirmed observation. I don't have the name of whatever child she saw with your reverend. It's not even close to the evidence we'd need for a prosecution. But I think you'll agree that a person of good conscience can't ignore this. You asked what we want from you? Under California law, police can monitor a telephone conversation with the consent of one party."

"You're asking me to turn on Martin."

"You're not *turning* on anyone. Just tell him two things." Reilly ticked off his points on his thumb and index finger. "The police asked you about this man Steve Roman. And they raised the possibility of child abuse in the church. If he's innocent, we'll find that out. But if he's not?"

Keith thought of all the hours he had spent at Martin's side, delivering food to needy families. Without the church, Keith would still have been the shallow, insecure kid he used to be. Then he pictured all the young girls he'd seen in the families Martin helped. He hadn't seen Nicole for twenty years, but she was right about the type of family Martin preferred. And he couldn't imagine Nicole lying about something so awful.

"Okay, let's do it." He said a silent prayer that this was all a misunderstanding.

While Detective Reilly prepared Keith for his phone call to Martin Collins, Laurie walked Nicole to the driveway, giving her a brief hug before turning her over to the care of her husband, Gavin. Two weeks ago, when Laurie first met the couple in their gourmet kitchen, Nicole had seemed distant and cold, still trying to cover secrets that were two decades old. Now Nicole couldn't stop sobbing, and Laurie wondered whether the woman would ever regain control over her emotions.

But Laurie forced herself to focus on the hard facts. Even twenty years ago, Nicole had been mature enough to begin a relationship with Martin, an adult man. She had ignored Susan's warnings about Martin and his so-called church. Even after she caught Martin inflicting perhaps the worst harm imaginable, she had buckled under his threats, running away and leaving the child behind.

Laurie could empathize with Nicole, but she couldn't sympathize.

64

Laurie was surprised at how simple it was for Detective Reilly to record Keith's call to Martin Collins, with a simple cord from Keith's cell phone into a laptop's microphone port. After considerable negotiation, Reilly agreed to let Leo and Laurie listen in on the call, but with no cameras or recording on their part. If the call panned out, Laurie could find another way to report the facts for the show. Right now, she just wanted to hear what Martin Collins had to say.

With the help of an audio splitter, Leo, Laurie, and Detective Reilly were all plugged in with their own earphones. She gave Keith a thumbs-up as he hit the dial button. The man was far from perfect, but today he was doing the right thing.

"Hey, Martin, it's Keith," he said when the call connected. "You got a sec? I had a weird visit from the police."

"The police?"

"Yeah, asking about a Steve Roman. Bald, muscled, maybe in his forties. They said he belonged to Advocates for God, but I told them I didn't know him. Does the name ring a bell?"

"Sure," Martin said nonchalantly.

Laurie arched an eyebrow in her father's direction. They had just connected the head of AG to a man spotted near Lydia Levitt's murder, a man who was monitoring their movements just days prior to the attack on Jerry. Was it really going to be this easy?

Through her headphones, she listened as Martin continued. "I told you I wanted to know what Nicole was saying to those TV people? I asked Steve to lend a hand. He's helpful that way."

"Helpful? The police think he killed a woman in the Bay Area while he was snooping on one of the show's participants. And three days ago, someone broke into the show's set, stole a bunch of equipment, and nearly killed a member of the production team."

There was a long pause on the other end of the line. "Steve used to be a violent person. But that was a long time ago. I don't know anything about a woman in the Bay Area, but, yes, he did tell me about the unfortunate situation at the house in Bel Air."

Laurie clenched a fist in celebration. *Yes*, they had identified Jerry's attacker.

"*An unfortunate situation?*"

"He crossed a line. He said he found a door unlocked. He went in. Then someone came home and found him there. He told me he panicked, but he didn't tell me how bad it was until I read about the assault in the paper. I've been counseling him, but it may be time for me to call the police before he hurts someone else."

As Keith had explained it to them, Advocates for God encouraged all members to open up fully to the church but did not observe the traditional priest-penitent privilege. Instead, it was for the church to decide when disclosure of the information was necessary to "advocate for God's goodness." It sounded like Martin was getting ready to use what he knew about Steve Roman to distance himself from the man's crimes, depicting Roman as an out-of-control lone wolf.

"Martin, it gets worse. The police also asked me whether—I feel gross even saying it. They asked if I had ever seen you be *inappropriate* with children."

The line fell silent.

"Martin? Are you there?" Keith asked.

"Yes. This has to be coming from Nicole. She's crazy. She fabricated something like this when she was in college. That's why I wanted to keep an eye on her during the TV show. Obviously it's not true, so don't repeat that to anyone. Now, I better track down Steve. He's clearly become a problem."

When Martin hung up, the kitchen immediately broke into cacophony as they all spoke at once, rehashing every last word of the conversation. Detective Reilly formed his hands into a capital T to quiet them. "Good work, Keith. We've got what we need for an arrest warrant for Steve Roman. I'll follow up with Martin Collins to get him locked down on the details of whatever Roman told him about the assault on Jerry."

"Wait," Laurie said. "You're not arresting Collins?"

"I've got no probable cause. It's not against the law to ask someone to keep an eye on a situation. If it were, there'd be no private investigators."

"But Steve Roman's not a PI. He's hurting people. He probably *killed* Lydia."

"And that's why we're going to arrest him. But until we can prove Martin Collins solicited Steve Roman to commit these crimes, he's an innocent man."

Laurie started to argue, but Leo interrupted. "He's right on the law, Laurie. But a running start is just the beginning, right, Reilly?"

"Absolutely." Reilly's brow momentarily unfurrowed. "Once we get our hands on this Steve Roman character, he might have a different story to tell. Happens all the time. We'll get the phone records, search his apartment, the works. I'll get the arrest warrant out pronto. We can apply over the phone now. Trust me, we'll get to the bottom of all of it."

Laurie tried not to be disappointed. After all, they had probably solved Lydia's murder and the attack on Jerry. But they still had no idea how any of this connected to Susan's murder.

Reilly had just finished packing up his recording equipment when Grace came running into the kitchen. "Turn on the television!" she yelled, reaching for the remote control on the counter.

Laurie placed her hand gently on Grace's forearm. "Hold on a just a minute, Grace. I'm about to walk Detective Reilly out."

"No, it can't wait." She fumbled with the buttons and began flipping channels until she reached her destination. "Look!"

On the screen was a helicopter's aerial footage over bright blue water. An anchor's voice said something about a "thirty-nine-year-old genius" and the "revolutionizing of the Internet." It wasn't until Laurie read the text at the bottom of the screen that she understood what she was watching: *REACH founder and CEO Dwight Cook's body recovered from a scuba accident, sources say.*

No, not Dwight. Please don't let it be him, Laurie thought.

65

Laurie didn't want to believe that Dwight was dead. Three hours after Detective Reilly's departure, she wanted to hear that this was all some misunderstanding. When Dwight had called last night, she was so wrapped up in tracking down Steve Roman and his connection to AG, she hadn't even found the time to return his phone call. Now that sweet man—that sweet, overgrown boy—was dead, and she was convinced that his death had to be connected to her investigation into Susan's murder. And she was wondering if she could have stopped it.

Timmy was upstairs playing video games, but the adults all huddled in the den to watch the television coverage. Between Keith's phone call to Martin Collins and the news reports of Dwight's death, they were on edge. The LAPD had obtained a warrant for Steve Roman's arrest, but he was still at large. Was he still in Los Angeles, on his way back to San Francisco, or on the run toward the Mexico border? Could he return to target the team again?

At the sound of the doorbell, Grace let out a yelp, then placed a hand to her chest. "Oh my Lord. I'm like some girl in the middle of a horror movie."

Leo went to the front door, gun in hand, and gazed through the peephole. "It's Detective Reilly," he announced.

Laurie could feel their collective relief.

"Sorry to disturb you," Reilly said, entering the den with a laptop already in hand. "First I'm afraid I have some bad news. Dwight Cook's body has been positively identified. I'll spare you the physical details, but there's no question that it's him."

Laurie blinked back the tears that were starting to form.

Alex leaned toward her and whispered, "Are you okay? We can take a break."

She shook her head. "No, I'm okay. Please, Detective Reilly, tell us the rest."

"I didn't realize this when I was here earlier, but apparently this house is owned by Dwight Cook?"

"Yes," Laurie said. "He lent us the house to help us out."

"*Help you out*, huh? See, one of my fellow detectives was going through Mr. Cook's computers as part of their investigation. Apparently Reverend Collins wasn't the only person keeping an eye on your production. Cook had every inch of this place wired for surveillance."

"Like, spying on us?" Grace asked. "Not to speak ill of the dead, but that's straight-up perverted."

"Not your showers or anything like that," Reilly clarified. "But pretty much everything that has happened in this house since your arrival is on video."

"The house is usually vacant," Laurie said. "It would make sense he'd have a state-of-the-art security system in a high-end property like this."

"It's not only a matter of the equipment," Reilly explained. "Given how the video files are set up, we can tell that Dwight actually viewed them. We can also tell when he was watching and what footage he watched. Apparently he stopped watching last night at nine twenty-three P.M."

Laurie checked the voice mail log on her own cell phone. "He called me just a few minutes later. He said he needed to talk ASAP."

"And . . . ?"

"We were in the middle of trying to figure out Steve Roman's connection to our case. I didn't have time to call. Obviously if I had known . . ."

She felt her stomach drop as Reilly rolled his eyes, clearly frustrated by the dead end.

"Well, here's the thing." Reilly flipped open his laptop on the coffee table and began tapping away. "Dwight watched a couple of clips repeatedly."

He turned the screen so they could all see it. "One clip was the attack on your friend," Reilly said. Laurie felt sick as they watched the brutal assault on Jerry. Reilly paused the tape just as Jerry's masked assailant rose from his bloodied body. "See that insignia on his shirt? We've got a tech trying to sharpen the image, but at least the body type is consistent with Steve Roman."

"So Dwight must have called me because he had Jerry's assailant on video," Laurie said.

Reilly was shaking his head, fast-forwarding through the video. "I doubt it. He saw the assault for the first time three nights ago and has replayed it multiple times since. He would have called you earlier. But here." He slowed the tape. "This is the segment Dwight watched right before he called you."

Laurie immediately recognized the scene from yesterday: Keith, Madison, and Nicole, side by side on the living room sofa, discussing the day Susan was killed. Reilly played the interview to its end and then paused it. "It looks like he kept replaying the very end. Is there some reason he'd be interested in that scene?" Reilly asked.

"I have no idea," Laurie said. "He wasn't really friends with any of them apart from Susan. I've got to ask, Detective Reilly. If you have colleagues searching Dwight's computers, are they certain Dwight's death was an accident?"

"No. If anything, it looks like the scene was staged to seem accidental. They found traces of bleach throughout the entire interior of the boat, and according to the medical examiner's initial inspection, the nitrogen levels in his tissue are inconsistent with having scuba dived that night. The current theory is that he was already unconscious when his body hit the water."

"Could this be more of Steve Roman's crime spree?" Laurie was thinking aloud, wondering if Roman would have a reason to go after Dwight. "The alternative is that Dwight knew something about one of the other suspects."

"That's our theory," Reilly said, "especially if he figured it out as he was watching the end of this video. I thought you might realize its significance."

Laurie shook her head. What are we missing? she thought.

The buzz of Laurie's cell phone broke her concentration. She wanted to throw the thing across the room until she saw that the call was from Rosemary Dempsey.

"Hi, Rosemary. Can I call you right back—"

"Are you watching the news? They're saying that Dwight Cook is dead. And now there's a warrant out for some man named Steve Roman, and it has something to do with the attack on Jerry? Are we in danger? What in the world is going on?"

66

Steve Roman rocked back and forth, shirtless, on the motel bed.

His name was all over the news. The police would be monitoring his credit cards as they searched for him. The second he heard his name on the car radio, he made a quick cash purchase on the streets of South Central L.A., then found a fleabag dive willing to accept cash for a room, no ID necessary. He counted the remaining bills in his wallet. Twenty-three bucks. Not much he could do with that.

A used-car ad blared at him from the crummy television set on the dresser. He flipped the channel in search of more news about his arrest warrant. He halted at the sight of a familiar face. It was Martin Collins, standing in his front yard in a throng of reporters.

"It has come to my attention that the LAPD is searching for a man named Steve Roman. Some of you have already gleaned from the Internet that he is a member of Advocates for God. I founded this church a quarter century ago. In that time, Advocates for God has gone from a car full of good people willing to help the downtrodden, to thousands of believers who sacrifice every day to help their fellow man. I do know Steve Roman and truly believed he had reformed himself through the healing power of God's goodness. But I've been speaking with the police, and, unfortunately, it seems that a disturbed individual found his way into our flock. But that shouldn't reflect on our group as a whole. Our church is doing everything within our power to apprehend this criminal."

"*Reverend Collins,*" a reporter called out. "*We have sources who say the arrest warrant for Steve Roman is related to the attack this week on a producer for the show* Under Suspicion. *They are in town covering the Cinderella Murder. What is the connection between your church and the unsolved murder of Susan Dempsey?*"

Martin placed his hands on his hips, as if this were the first time he had really contemplated the question. "*It's not my place to speculate about the motivations of a sick mind. But our best guess is this person—obviously ill at some level—was making a misguided attempt to protect Keith Ratner, another AG member who has been unfairly under suspicion all these years in the death of his former girlfriend. That's all I have for now, folks.*" He gave a friendly wave and retreated into his mansion.

Steve pulled on a white undershirt, warming himself as the air-conditioning unit rattled in the wall beneath the motel window. *A disturbed individual? Criminal? Ill? Misguided?*

Steve had always done whatever Martin asked of him. Yet now Martin was selling him out, feeding into the worst stereotypes of their church, for his own benefit.

Steve clenched his fists. He felt old impulses rising in his blood, the way he felt when that neighbor found him in Rosemary Dempsey's yard, when the production assistant had surprised him in the house in Bel Air. He needed a punching bag. He needed to run.

He left the motel room, checking first that no one was watching. He made his way through the parking lot to his pickup truck and then popped the glove box.

He retrieved his newly purchased nine-millimeter. It was small for his hands, but it had been cheap. He tucked the gun in the back of his waistband.

He had made some mistakes in recent weeks, but that was because Martin Collins had treated him as an errand boy. He was feeling levelheaded now. He was in charge.

67

Laurie's first instinct was to rush to the hotel after Rosemary's panicked phone call. This woman, whom she'd convinced to trust her with her daughter's case, had learned the news of both Dwight Cook's death and an arrest warrant being issued for Jerry's attacker from the television. Laurie owed her an in-person update.

Alex insisted on coming with her, while Leo stayed at the house with Timmy and Grace. "Alex, thank you for keeping an eye on me," Laurie said once they were in the hotel lobby. "But I think I should speak with Rosemary one-on-one."

"No problem," Alex said. "I'll check in with hotel security to make sure they're on the lookout for Steve Roman."

Outside Rosemary's hotel room, Laurie heard the muted sounds of a television. She took a deep breath and knocked on the door. Rosemary answered immediately.

"Laurie, thank you for coming. I'm so afraid. I don't understand what's happening. Yesterday it was that whole scene at the house with Susan's friends. I can't believe Nicole, after all these years, never told me about that fight. And now Dwight Cook is dead? And the police think this man who attacked Jerry, who's on the loose, is connected to Advocates for God? Now I'm wondering if I was right all along: maybe Keith Ratner is behind everything—Susan's murder, the attack on Jerry, now Dwight."

On the television screen behind Rosemary, Laurie spotted Martin Collins at an impromptu press conference in front of his house.

"Hold on," she said. "Can you turn up the volume?"

"It's not my place to speculate about the motivations of a sick mind," he was saying. *"But our best guess is this person—obviously ill at some level—was making a misguided attempt to protect Keith Ratner, another AG member who has been unfairly under suspicion all these years in the death of his former girlfriend. That's all I have for now, folks."*

Martin Collins was attractive and charismatic. He duped thousands of people into turning over their hard-earned money to him every year. Now he was using those skills to sweet-talk the viewers watching him on television.

Laurie muted the volume and led a ghostly pale Rosemary to a wing chair in the living area of the suite. Laurie sat on the couch facing her. "I wish I had all the answers," Laurie said. "But we don't know much more than you do, and new information is coming in fast. The reports about Dwight Cook are true, but police suspect foul play. We think this Steve Roman person is trying to shut down the production, but on whose behalf? We're not sure."

"Because of Susan? Is this the man who killed my daughter?"

Laurie reached out and held Rosemary's hand. "We honestly don't know. But the LAPD is on top of this. They're going to search Steve Roman's apartment tonight in San Francisco, and they've got out a high-priority arrest warrant throughout the state. Alex is downstairs right now speaking to security. We'll be sure there's security around the clock for you, Rosemary. And we'll all breathe a sigh of relief—and hopefully learn more—once Roman is caught."

As she made her way to the elevator, Laurie checked her phone. There was a text from Alex: *All set with security. Waiting in lobby.*

She almost missed the familiar face of the man exiting the room at the end of the hall. Richard Hathaway.

On instinct, she turned her back, continuing to check her phone, until she heard the *ding* of the elevator. What was Hathaway doing here? He had turned down the offer of a hotel room.

Laurie walked quietly to the end of the hall, pressing her ear gently to the door of the room he had left. She could hear music playing inside. Before she could even think about what she was doing, she was tapping on the door.

When it opened, Madison Meyer appeared in a white robe.

68

Madison tightened her robe's sash around her waist. "Laurie. Hi. What are you doing here?"

"Um, I was here to see Rosemary," she said, pointing down the hall. "I— Did I just see Richard Hathaway leave your room?"

Madison's face broke out into a wide smile, then she let out a girlish giggle. "Fine. I guess there's no harm in admitting it now that we're both grown-ups."

"You and Hathaway?"

"Yep. I mean, not this whole time, of course. But let's just say those rumors about the handsome young computer science professor were true. I heard he was down here for the production, so I figured I should say hi—see how my older crush turned out. I'm actually surprised myself, but we're . . . *rekindling*."

Laurie found herself with nothing to say. There was too much happening on the case right now to carry on with Madison about her love life. Madison wanted to know if the search for Steve Roman was going to affect the filming schedule. "Just so I can tell my agent," she added.

Laurie refrained from rolling her eyes. "We'll know more soon, Madison. Congratulations on your romance with Hathaway."

As Laurie pressed the elevator button, she realized that something was bothering her about discovering Hathaway in Madison's room. The facts themselves certainly weren't surprising. After all, Hathaway had a reputation as a ladies' man, Madison was an obvious flirt, and they were both extremely attractive.

But, still, something was nagging at her. She'd had this same feeling the previous night when she'd spoken to Nicole about her fight with Susan. Maybe this case had her second-guessing every conversation.

As she stepped onto the elevator, she noticed the eye of a security camera in the upper corner to her left. Surveillance was ubiquitous in the modern world, she thought, shuddering at the idea of Dwight's secretly monitoring them these past days.

Secretly. The cameras. Unlike this hotel security camera, Dwight's equipment had been hidden behind the walls.

Once she stepped from the elevator, she pulled up Detective Reilly's number on her cell and hit ENTER. Come on, she thought. Please answer.

"Reilly."

"Detective, it's Laurie Moran. I've got something for you—"

"Like I said, Ms. Moran. We're working every angle. It takes time. Just ask your dad."

"Dwight Cook had the house in Bel Air wired for surveillance."

"I know. I'm the one who told you, remember?"

"But the equipment was hidden behind the walls, and he only offered us the house last week. He didn't rebuild those walls on a week's notice. This has to be his regular MO."

"The boat," he said, following her logic.

"Yes. Be sure to check the boat for hidden cameras. If Dwight's death wasn't an accident—if he really was murdered—you might have it all on video."

"I'll call the team at the boat and have them check. And good work, Laurie. Thanks."

She had just hung up from Reilly when her cell rang. It was Alex.

"Where are you?" she asked. "I'm in the lobby but don't see you. You won't believe who I spotted Madison with—"

Alex interrupted. "I pulled the SUV around out front. You ready for some good news?"

"After the last couple days? Definitely."

"It's Jerry. He's conscious. And he's asking for visitors."

69

Steve Roman sat behind the wheel of his pickup truck outside the soup kitchen. He knew Martin Collins would be inside. He had photographers here every week to make sure they caught him on film, feeding the needy. Steve also knew that the millions of dollars Martin had raised for this center far exceeded what AG actually spent here feeding the homeless.

He had seen over the years the way Martin's excesses had grown. Early on, Martin would offer explanations for his seemingly small indulgences—a fine meal was the ultimate pleasure, a custom-cut suit would make him more presentable to donors, and so on. But over time, the indulgences became larger and more frequent—the mansion, trips to Europe, vacation homes—and Martin stopped making excuses for them.

But Steve had always truly believed that Martin's impact on the world—and guidance of Steve personally—made him a genuine leader. That's why he had always been willing to do everything the church had ever asked of him.

Steve felt his grip on the steering wheel tighten as he replayed Martin's words to the media that day. He had described Steve as a "disturbed individual" who had "found his way into" Advocates for God. He had assured the press that AG was doing everything in its power "to apprehend this criminal."

Steve knew he'd messed up—bad. He hit that man who interrupted his break-in at the *Under Suspicion* house harder, and more times, that he should have. And that neighbor lady back in Oakland—that had gone really wrong.

But if Steve was such a disturbed, ill criminal, shouldn't Martin Collins have to take some responsibility for his conduct? Martin, after all, had known Steve's struggles with his temper. And yet who had Martin turned to when he needed someone to get to the bottom of what Nicole Melling was saying about him to *Under Suspicion*? That's right: Steve. As far as Steve was concerned, his actions—right or wrong—belonged to Martin just as much as to him.

He felt the comfort of the nine-millimeter in the back of his waistband as he spotted Martin exiting the homeless shelter. Because Martin was a firm believer in what he called "the strengthening power of routine," Steve knew that Martin's next stop would be home. Steve also knew that Martin would spend several minutes shaking hands and posing for photographs before getting in his car.

That would give Steve plenty of time.

He started the engine and drove to the hills, parking one block away for safety, even though he'd stolen the blue pickup he was now driving. As he strolled on the sidewalk, he kept alert, checking for any police or security guards circling the neighborhood. If necessary, he could crouch in a nearby garden, posing as a landscaper. Steve knew how easy it was to hide in plain sight, simply by looking like someone who belonged in a setting. But the block was quiet. There was no need for camouflage.

Within seconds, he slipped right through the front door, using tools he'd wielded so many times on Martin's orders. All these years, he had looked to Martin for guidance about what was right and what was wrong. Now Martin had turned that entire world upside down.

It was time for both of them to be judged by the only voice that counted.

He made himself comfortable on the living room sofa, placing his gun on the coffee table in front of him. He could not recall ever being so self-assured inside Martin's home.

When he heard the mechanical rumble of the garage door, he rose and picked up his weapon. It was showtime.

Fifteen minutes later, a reporter named Jenny Hughes was jogging in the Hollywood Hills, admiring the homes as she passed. Her own digs were quite different, a converted warehouse in downtown Los Angeles. But on most days, Jenny's runs doubled as a chance to check out how the other half lived. She had a serious case of real estate envy.

She used the approaching hill as an interval opportunity, breaking into a full sprint. By the time she reached the top, she was gasping for breath, and her pulse had spiked to maximum capacity. She slowed to a casual walk, feeling the endorphins surge with each deep inhale. There was a reason she had a resting heart rate of fifty-one.

She found her pace slowing further as she neared the next house on the block, an all-white modern number, chock-full of floor-to-ceiling picture windows. Her particular interest in this house wasn't limited to the property itself. The home's sole resident was Reverend Martin Collins, founder of the Advocates for God megachurch. Before she'd left for her run, the newsroom had been abuzz with reports that one of the church's members was on a one-man crime spree.

She'd watched the reverend's impromptu press conference. According to Collins, the man wanted by the LAPD was a free agent—a rogue who had gone off the deep end. But some in the newsroom speculated that the man's arrest might be a chance for police to peer behind the church's carefully crafted façade. There had been rumors for years that the church and its charitable activities were all a front for financial shenanigans. What would this Steve Roman say about AG now that Collins had thrown him under the bus on live television?

Jenny felt her pulse dropping beneath cardio level. Time to get back at it.

She gave a final look at Collins's house as she picked up the pace. Just like her dream of owning a mansion was a distant fantasy, so too was a world in which she'd be trusted to write a front-page article exposing corruption at a megachurch. Jenny was a reporter in title, but so far her bylines were limited to human-interest stories, "personality" features, and other lightweight fare. If Collins had a dog who could ride a skateboard, that would be the kind of thing her editor might send her way.

Her thoughts were broken by the sound of two quick blasts, back to back. On instinct, she dove to the grass median next to her, seeking shelter behind a station wagon parked on the street. Were those *gunshots*?

The sounds were gone now. The distant hum of a lawn mower reminded her that she wasn't exactly in East L.A. She was rising to her feet, laughing at her own wild imagination, when she heard one more blast.

This time she was certain. It was gunfire. And unless her ears were playing tricks on her, it sounded like the shots had come from Martin Collins's house.

She entered 911 in her cell phone but then deleted the numbers for a quick call to her editor first. She finally had dibs on a major story.

70

Madison Meyer slid into the booth at one of her favorite Italian restaurants, Scarpetta, careful of her extra-short hemline. "Did you miss me, Professor?" she asked coyly. She had excused herself to the powder room to reapply her lipstick. Men had a tendency to stare at her lips when they were coated in cherry red.

Richard Hathaway smiled at her from across the table. "Terribly. And you missed the dessert tray. The waiter was a minute into his elaborate descriptions before I finally pointed out your absence. I think there might be an inverse correlation between basic common sense and the ability to go on and on about a tray of food. But I did ask him to come back once you returned."

"I love it that you use terms like 'inverse correlation' in everyday conversation."

When she first got the letter about *Under Suspicion*, she'd had a fleeting hope of reconnecting with Keith Ratner. At one point, they'd been so well matched. Both actors. Both driven. Both a little bit sneaky. Maybe she could finally get Keith to love her the way she had once loved him.

But now she wasn't the least bit interested in Keith. She'd always thought that his connection to AG was a gimmick, as if the do-gooder, Bible-thumping image would compensate for the he-might-have-killed-his-girlfriend stigma. But nope, apparently he really was a changed man. Good riddance.

Then it turned out that Keith wasn't the only former flame at this little UCLA reunion. The years had been kind to Richard Hathaway. If possible, he had even gotten better with age. Of course, the millions of dollars he'd earned certainly didn't hurt. He had the kind of money that made A-list actors feel broke. Plus he was smart. There was a reason all the female students had been so drawn to him in college.

She was trying not to get her hopes up, but she couldn't help it. He was planning to return to Silicon Valley in a couple of days. She just needed to plant the seed that she was available to go with him if he wanted company.

"I've been meaning to tell you," she said breezily, "my agent wants me to audition for a play in San Francisco. It's a small production, but a few movie stars are interested in the lead, so it will get plenty of attention." There was no play, of course, but she could always tell him later that the funding fell apart.

"Sounds like a good opportunity." His gaze wandered around the restaurant. "I'm starting to think that waiter's never coming back. The desserts really did look spectacular."

"I'll be going up next week," Madison continued. "You know, if you want to get together."

"Sure thing. Let me know what hotel you'll be at, and I'll find a restaurant nearby."

Well, dinner was better than nothing. Madison could swing a couple nights in a hotel if it meant a chance at landing a man like this one. "Oh, speaking of hotels, I almost forgot to tell you: Laurie Moran saw you leaving my room today. I guess the cat's out of the bag."

"Not much of a cat: we're two consenting adults."

"True, but it still feels a little naughty, doesn't it?" Madison took another sip of the red wine Hathaway had ordered without even looking at the list. It tasted expensive. "Anyway, you wouldn't believe how out of control her production has gotten. Did you see there's an arrest warrant out for that guy from Keith's church? Plus I heard some of the crew at the hotel saying that Dwight had that house in Bel Air seriously wired up for surveillance. Totally creepy, right?"

"Surveillance?"

"Yeah, and not just normal security cameras, either. Like hidden cameras and microphones in every room. I know he was your friend and everything, but that seems pretty stalkerish. Made me remember how he used to look at Susan all weird and dreamy in college. Did you know him to be the type to spy on people without telling them? Maybe it was his way of having control. Ah, here he is!"

The waiter was back, and as Richard promised, the choices looked delicious. She never ate dessert—sugar was a surefire way to bloat, which the camera magnified tenfold. But maybe she'd allow herself just one bite of that amazing-looking chocolate torte.

The waiter was midway through his tour of the tray when Richard suddenly dropped three hundred-dollar bills on the table. "I'm terribly sorry, but I'm afraid my stomach is having troubles."

"Sir, is everything okay?" the waiter asked. "I can call for medical assistance if it's serious."

"No." He was standing up already. "I just—I need to go. Can you please make sure she gets a cab?" He was stuffing fifties in the waiter's hand. "I'm terribly sorry, Maddie. I'll call you tomorrow. And, please, if it's not too forward, I'd like you to stay with me when you come up for your audition, okay? It's a ways from San Francisco proper, but we'll get you a driver."

He blew her a kiss, and then he was gone.

The waiter looked at her apologetically. "So, should I call you that cab?"

"Sure. But first, I'll have the chocolate torte. And a glass of your best champagne."

"Very good, ma'am."

Twenty years ago, Richard had stood her up for a date, and look what happened. She'd won a Spirit Award. He may have left tonight's dinner early, but he had invited her to his home. He had called her Maddie.

Before he knew what hit him, she'd have him wrapped around her little finger. Madison Meyer Hathaway. It had a nice ring to it.

71

The mood in Jerry's hospital room was as bright and celebratory as the last visit had been terrifying and dreary. He still looked weak and his head was still bandaged, but the oxygen mask was gone. The bruises were deep purple but beginning to fade ever so slightly.

Laurie and Alex had driven straight here from the hotel, arriving at the hospital's parking garage just behind Leo, Grace, and Timmy. They'd only been in Jerry's room a few minutes, and already the nurse had popped in twice to remind them not to get "the patient" too excited.

Jerry pressed an index finger to his lips. "Keep it down," he said groggily, "or Nurse Ratched will send me to sleep without a martini." He glanced toward a tiny stuffed panda bear resting on a nearby tray. "Timmy?"

Laurie nodded.

"I thought so. One of the nurse's aides said the 'sweetest little boy' had brought it."

"He's just outside." Laurie sent a quick *OK* text message to Grace, who was waiting in the hall.

"You were afraid the bruised and battered mummy might scare a nine-year-old?" His voice was still weak but growing stronger by the minute.

"Possibly," she admitted.

Leo's cell phone rang at his waist. He silenced it as he took a seat in a chair in the corner. "I keep telling her the kid's probably tougher than she is."

"And I keep telling you he's only a nine-year-old."

"Speak of the devil," Jerry said as Grace and Timmy rushed in. Jerry managed to hold up his wired fist to Timmy, who "bumped" it with a grin. "I've got a bigger crowd here than I get for some of my parties."

"Yeah, right," Grace said, leaning in for a gentle hug. "I've seen your parties, honey. You'd need a larger dance floor."

"I have a feeling it will be a while before I'm doing any dancing." His tone suddenly became more serious. "I can't believe I was out for three whole days."

"How much do you remember about what happened?" Alex asked.

"I left the house to pick up some lunch. When I came home, a man with a ski mask was in the den. I had this second where I thought there was some explanation, because his shirt said 'Keepsafe' on it. Then I thought, Why would a guy from a security company wear a mask? I remember trying to run, then blackness. You know the worst part of it? Now you guys know I sneak greasy fast food when no one's looking."

Laurie was pleased to see Jerry hadn't lost his sense of humor in the assault.

Leo's cell was buzzing now. He glanced at the screen and then slipped out to take the call while Jerry continued to talk.

Laurie and Alex were still filling Jerry in on everything they had learned from Nicole about Steve Roman and Martin Collins when Leo returned to the room and asked Grace if she could take Timmy downstairs for some frozen yogurt in the hospital cafeteria.

Laurie was worried. If her father didn't want Timmy to hear, whatever he was about to say was going to be bad.

"But you said I was tough as nails," Timmy complained. "Why can't I listen?"

Grace responded matter-of-factly, "Because your grandpa said so."

"That's just what I was going to say," Laurie told him.

"And I'm backing them all up," Alex added.

"Hospital patients get to vote, too," Jerry said.

"Not fair," Timmy sighed. His feet dragging, he left the hospital room, shooed out by a determined Grace.

"What's up, Dad?" Laurie asked once her son was out of earshot.

"Those calls were from Detective Reilly. There was a shooting at Martin Collins's house. Steve Roman is dead—a self-inflicted gun-shot. He left a note confessing to both the attack on Jerry and the murder of Lydia Levitt. As we thought, he was spying for Collins, starting first with Nicole and then moving out from there to see what she had said to others."

"Was Collins there?" Laurie asked.

"Two gunshot wounds. Steve Roman was trying to kill him, but they think he'll live. The police found a videotape collection in Collins's bedroom. It looks like whatever child Nicole saw him with twenty years ago wasn't his only victim. Collins may survive, but he'll never get out of prison. And speaking of video, Reilly said to thank you, Laurie, for the tip about Dwight Cook's boat. Turns out it was packed with surveillance equipment too, just like the house. Once again, Under Suspicion is bringing some much-deserved justice."

"So does it show what happened the night Dwight died?"

"Not yet. It's all digital, so they've got a computer tech trying to find where the video files may have been uploaded. If you don't mind getting everyone back to the house in the SUV, I'll take the rental car to meet Reilly. I want to make triple sure there's no reason for us to fear some other crazy church member following in Steve Roman's footsteps."

Laurie assured him they'd be fine in one car. He hugged her good-bye, whispering, "I'm proud of you, baby girl."

When she turned back to Jerry, his eyes were closed. It was time for them to go, too. She gave him a gentle kiss on the forehead before following Alex into the hall.

Laurie was quiet as they rode the hospital elevator to the lobby level. She was elated that they'd nailed Collins, a fraud and, worse, a pedophile. But when this all started, she had made a promise to Rosemary to do her best to find Susan's killer.

Laurie couldn't imagine losing a child. Twenty years later, and Rosemary still went to bed with haunting images of her only daughter running through a park with one bare foot, her necklace being torn from her throat in a violent struggle for her life.

The realization came with the *ding* that sounded as the elevator doors parted. "The necklace," she said aloud.

72

"What about a necklace?" Alex asked as they stepped out of the elevator.

"I don't know. Not yet, anyway."

"Come on, Laurie. I know you. I can tell when you're working on a theory. It's that kind of hunch that Leo calls your cop instinct. Is this about Susan's necklace? The one found near her body?"

"Just give me two minutes to work it out in my head, okay?" She could barely hang on to the various threads of thought starting to knit together in her mind. She didn't want to lose her momentum by trying to spell it all out prematurely. "Can you round up Grace and Timmy from the cafeteria? I'll get the car from the garage and swing around front."

"Aye-aye, Captain. But I'm dragging that hunch out of you once we hit the road. You know my interrogation skills," he added with a smile.

As she walked to the parking garage, she pulled up Nicole's number on her phone and dialed, holding her breath, hoping that she would answer.

She did. "Laurie, did you hear the news? Martin Collins was shot."

"I know, but I need to talk to you about something else." Laurie got right to the point. "You said that Susan was rummaging for her lucky necklace when you argued about Keith and the church. Did she find it?"

There was a pause on the other end of the line. "I really don't remember after all these years. So much else happened later that day."

"Think, Nicole. It's important."

"Um, she was running around, opening drawers and searching in her bedsheets and behind the sofa cushions. That's right: she was digging through the couch in our common area when I got so mad I threw my book at her. Then she stormed out. So I'm just about sure she didn't find it."

"Thanks, Nicole. That's a big help."

Susan had fled her dorm room without her necklace but had been wearing it by the time she was killed. *Where would she have gone?* That had been the question that Alex had pressed with Keith, Nicole, and Madison. And that had been the question that Dwight Cook kept replaying on the surveillance video before his death.

Laurie thought about her own habit of taking off her jewelry when she was busy at her desk. She believed she knew where Susan had found her lucky necklace.

She pulled up another name on her phone and hit ENTER.

Alex answered after two rings. "Hey, I just found Grace and Timmy. We'll meet you out front."

"Okay, I'm walking into the garage and am about to lose my signal. Can you do me a favor and call Madison? Remember how she said she sent a sexy note to some love interest to pick her up at the dorm but he never showed? Can you ask her who the guy was?"

"This is for your theory, right? Just tell me, Laurie."

"Call Madison first. It's the last piece of the puzzle, I promise. See you in a jiff."

As she beeped the Land Cruiser's locks open, she already knew in her gut what name Madison would give Alex.

Richard Hathaway.

73

Richard Hathaway stepped out of his SUV. He could not believe his good luck.

He had dashed from the restaurant after Madison mentioned the hidden cameras at the Bel Air house. Two years ago, Dwight had installed the same technology at the REACH offices and his Palo Alto home. Now it turned out that he'd also wired his parents' house in L.A. Had he gone so far as to wire his boats?

Yes, Hathaway thought, it would be exactly like Dwight to order the job for all his property at once, and he cared about his boats at least as much as that empty house in Bel Air.

And if the boat Dwight had used last night was equipped with hidden cameras, had they been on when Hathaway stepped onto the cruiser for his scheduled dive with Dwight? Had the cameras recorded Dwight as he angrily accused Hathaway of killing Susan, insisting nonsensically that he'd figured it out by watching "the video"? Had they filmed Hathaway as he smothered Dwight with a life vest and then staged his body to appear in the water as a scuba accident? Had the police found the footage yet?

These were the questions that had swirled through his head as he drove from the restaurant, circling aimlessly through Hollywood, too panicked to go home or even to REACH's jet in case the police were waiting for him.

Instead, he'd gone to the storage unit he'd been renting for two decades to grab his "go bag," containing false identification, fifty thousand dollars, and a gun. He had identical bags in separate storage facilities in five different California cities, waiting in the event this day ever came.

But now that the moment he had been dreading was actually here, he realized he did not want to run. He had enjoyed the success of the last twenty years, and it was all about to improve further, as he was poised to become the new CEO of REACH. If he had even a shred of a chance to stay in this life, he was going to seize it.

At least he now understood Dwight's reference to a video. Something Dwight saw on the surveillance footage of that stupid TV production had alerted him to Hathaway's role in Susan's death.

He had to figure out what Laurie Moran knew and then silence her—and anyone else necessary—for good.

Parked on the street outside the Bel Air house, he saw an older man, a little boy, and the woman named Grace pile into a car. It was simple enough to follow them.

Once in the parking garage outside the hospital, Hathaway watched as Laurie and Alex pulled in a few minutes later in a black Land Cruiser. Since then, he'd been waiting, planning his next move.

Now Hathaway had caught two lucky breaks. The first was when Laurie's father, an ex-cop who was probably armed, had driven away from the hospital alone. At the sight of his leaving, Hathaway had experienced the same sense of relief he'd felt the moment Susan strapped on her seat belt on the night she died.

It had been May 7, a Saturday. Hathaway had asked Dwight to meet him in the lab because no one else would be there that night.

He wanted to talk to Dwight alone about REACH. Hathaway had

created a search technology with the potential to revolutionize the way people found information on the Internet. It was worth thirty times more than a professor could make in a lifetime of teaching. But technically, even though Hathaway had invented REACH, the idea didn't belong to him. He was owned by UCLA, which in turn owned anything he created during his employment there.

But students were in a different position. Students, unlike faculty who were paid a salary, owned their own intellectual property. And given Dwight Cook's invaluable assistance with the code, who was to say that REACH wasn't the sole invention of the young genius?

Hathaway had been so focused on making his pitch to Dwight— convincing him that this technology could change the world and that it would be wasted in the hands of UCLA—that he almost didn't notice Susan watching them in his peripheral vision. But then he turned to see her standing by her desk near the door, looking as he'd never seen her before—her hair and makeup perfect, in a yellow halter dress. He had known immediately from the way she was rushing out of the lab that she had overheard their conversation.

Why had she been there on a Saturday? Why did she have to walk in unexpectedly at that very moment?

Hathaway knew he needed to stop her. He needed to provide a context for what she'd overheard. He said, "Dwight, stay here where it's quiet and think about it. I'll call you later." Hathaway then ran after Susan, catching up to her as she was walking toward Bruin Plaza.

"Susan, can I have a word with you?"

When she turned, she had a necklace in her hand. "I have an audition. I have to go."

"Please, I just want to explain. You don't understand."

"Of course I do. Everyone I know is disappointing me today. It's like I don't really know anyone. I can't deal with this now. I have to be in the Hollywood Hills in an hour. And my jinx of a car is back at the dorm and probably won't even start."

"Let me drive you. Please. We can talk on the ride there. Or not. Whatever you want."

"How will I even get home?"

"I'll wait. Or you can call a cab. Whatever you'd like."

He thought back to that two-second pause as she pondered her options. He just needed her to get in the car, and he was certain he could convince her that what he was doing was the right thing.

"Okay," she agreed. "We can talk. And honestly, I just need a ride."

When Susan strapped on her seat belt and began putting on her necklace, he was certain he'd avoided a potential crisis.

But that moment of relief had been fleeting. Once he started to drive, he laid out the same argument for her that he'd offered to Dwight Cook. The bureaucrats in the UCLA administration could never begin to understand the potential of this technology. It would be tied up for years awaiting layers of approval, while competitors in the private sector worked at a rapid-fire pace. Besides, crediting Dwight with the technology was only a thin stretch of the truth, given how much programming work he'd put into the project.

He was certain Susan would go along, either out of dedication to technological development or to support Dwight. If worst came to worst, he would offer her a cut of the action. But Susan was too principled and, more important, too smart. Her father was an intellectual property lawyer. She knew from his work how important the creator of technology was to its development. In her eyes, Hathaway's plan was not only stealing from the university but from potential investors.

"With dot-coms," she had argued, "the face of the company is half of the product. You're leading people to think that a creative genius like Dwight—someone who doesn't care in the least about money, someone who looks at the world and sees only the best—was the seed for all this. That he'll be calling the shots. That's fundamentally a different company from one run by you. It's *fraud*."

He began to slow at the curves, buying time to build his case. "But a company run by me would be worth more," he had insisted. "I have more experience. I'm a tenured professor. I don't have Dwight's personality quirks."

"The tech market loves quirks," she had said. "Besides, it's not simply a matter of dollar value. It's just dishonest. Aren't we getting close now? Why are you slowing down?"

When they were half a mile from her audition, he pulled the car to the side of the road. "Susan, you can't tell anyone what you heard. It will ruin my career."

"Then you shouldn't have done it. You offered to drive me to my audition. I've heard you out. Now I need to get to my appointment."

"Not until you understand—"

Just like that, she was out of the car, determined to make the rest of the trip on foot. He had to go after her. She ran faster in those heels than he would have thought possible. By the time he caught up with her in the park, one of her shoes had fallen off.

His first move had been to grab her by the arm. "You're being naive." He was still trying to persuade her. Why couldn't she be as gullible as Dwight?

And before he knew it, she was beneath him, hitting him, kicking at him. Sometimes he even convinced himself he couldn't remember what happened afterward.

But of course he did.

Once it was over, he made a quick decision that his best option was to leave her body. All her friends knew she was coming up here for an audition, so hopefully that would distract the investigation.

He called Dwight immediately, not long past seven o'clock, asking him to meet at Hamburger Haven to explore his suggestion further. If anyone ever asked, Dwight could vouch for his whereabouts for all but this short window of time.

Just as he hoped, the investigation had focused on Frank Parker, with Susan's boyfriend, Keith, the alternative suspect. For twenty years, he was convinced he'd gotten away with it, until he arrived at Dwight's boat last night. Now here he was, wondering how much Laurie Moran knew.

And that was the second piece of good luck to come in Hathaway's direction. First, the ex-cop had driven away. And now here was Laurie Moran, keys in hand, all by herself.

74

As Laurie walked through the parking garage toward the Land Cruiser, she realized that the clues pointing to Hathaway had been there all along. Susan had fled her dorm room after her fight with Nicole, eager to find her lucky necklace before her audition. Where would she have gone? To her desk at the lab.

And what would she have seen when she got there?

Laurie wasn't certain about this part yet, but if Susan went into the lab on a Saturday, she could have walked in on a moment that Hathaway assumed would be private. Maybe she'd caught him in one of those rumored liaisons with a female student or in the midst of some kind of academic impropriety. Hathaway could have talked Susan into getting into his car to discuss whatever she'd seen, especially since her own car had been acting up and she was set on getting to her audition.

Hathaway claimed to have been with Dwight the night Susan was killed, but the timeline was hazy, and now Dwight was dead. There was no way to know with certainty where Hathaway was that evening, but that's where the phone call to Madison came in.

Laurie realized what had been nagging her about her conversation with Madison after Laurie spotted Hathaway leaving Madison's hotel room. Madison had said that she had nothing to hide *now* that they were both grown-ups. She said they were *rekindling*. This wasn't a new relationship for them.

Laurie was certain that once Alex called Madison, she would confirm that Hathaway was the love interest who never showed up to her dorm room the night Susan was murdered. He never showed up because he was killing Susan in Laurel Canyon Park.

She opened the car door and paused to glance at her cell phone. No signal, as she suspected. Oh well, she thought, once I pull around to the hospital entrance, Alex can tell me if he reached Madison.

She had just slipped her cell phone in the pocket of the driver's-side door when she felt a hard object pressed against her back. In the side-view mirror, she saw the reflection of Hathaway standing behind her.

"Get in," he ordered, shoving her behind the wheel. Keeping the gun on her, he climbed over her into the passenger seat. "Now drive!"

75

Alex knew there was no stopping Laurie once her mind was on a mission. So when she asked him to call Madison about the identity of the love interest who turned down her invitation the night of Susan's murder, he did, even though he did not understand the significance.

"Madison," Alex said once he had her on the phone, "you sent a note to someone inviting him to see you the night Susan was killed. We'd like to know who that was, if you don't mind."

Alex was shocked when she responded, "Professor Hathaway. We'd had some flirtatious interactions already, so I thought we might spend a Saturday night together. But he was a complete and total no-show. No phone call, no nada. It's the kind of slight I take seriously—I blew him off after that and never spoke to him again. Until two days ago."

"Thanks, Madison," Alex said. "That's helpful."

Alex could see now the theory Laurie had been mulling over. From what they'd heard about Hathaway, he wasn't the type to have ignored a beautiful young woman's overture.

Then Alex realized why Laurie had mentioned the necklace. Susan had been searching for her lucky necklace during the argument with Nicole. From there, she might have gone to Hathaway's lab to look for it.

He found himself fiddling anxiously as he waited for Laurie to pull the car around so they could connect all the dots.

"Mom just turned the wrong way," Timmy said.

They were standing just inside the double doors of the hospital exit.

"You saw your mother?" Grace asked.

"She's over there," he said while pointing to an SUV heading to the hospital exit. "Is that Grandpa in the car with her?"

Alex pulled up Leo's number on his phone and hit ENTER. "Leo, it's Alex. Are you with Laurie?"

"No, I'm just pulling into the police station to catch up with Detective Reilly. Is everything okay?"

"I have a horrible feeling," Alex said. "Laurie figured out who killed Susan. And now he has her. Richard Hathaway has our Laurie."

76

Laurie felt a surprising sense of relief when Hathaway ordered her to turn left out of the parking garage, away from the hospital. No matter what happened, at least Timmy, Alex, and Grace, who were waiting for her, would be safe.

"Up here," Hathaway barked. "Take a left at the next light."

This was not the same cool, confident man she'd seen over the past week. He was ranting to himself under his breath. She could almost smell his desperation.

"You must have access to cash and a plane," she said. "Just let me out. You take the car."

"And give up everything I've worked for my whole life? No, thank you. Take a right up here, after we pass Santa Monica Boulevard."

She did as instructed.

"Tell me about the video, Laurie. What exactly did Dwight see? And don't play stupid or this will be worse for you than it needs to be. Tell me what Dwight knew."

"I'll never be certain," she said. "He left a message but died before I could speak to him. But I think he was calling me about you," she added. "To tell me that Susan went to your lab before her audition."

"And the boat?"

"What boat?"

"Were there cameras on Dwight's boat?" Hathaway yelled. "And don't forget, I can go back for your son if you need an incentive to talk."

Not Timmy, she thought. "Yes," she blurted, "Dwight had hidden cameras on his yacht."

"What do they show?"

"I have no idea. The police haven't found the digital upload yet."

"Take the next left."

As she hit her blinker, she could feel him calming down in the passenger seat. He mumbled something about his ability to find the data files before the police.

She slipped a hand into the pocket of the door to awaken her phone. She risked a glance at the screen and saw a list of recent calls.

As she took the turn, she let her hand drop into the door pocket one more time. She tapped the screen to redial her most recent caller.

Please, God, she thought, *please let this work*.

77

Alex had never heard Leo sound so panicked. "What do you mean, Hathaway has Laurie?" Leo demanded.

"She thinks Hathaway killed Susan Dempsey, and Timmy just saw her drive out of the garage with someone in the passenger seat. She was only alone for a minute—"

Alex heard the beep of an incoming call. He checked the screen and saw one name: *Laurie*.

"Wait, that's her now," Alex said. "I'll call you right back." He clicked over to the incoming call. "Laurie, where are you?"

But he didn't hear Laurie's voice in response. He heard silence, then eventually the sound of a man's voice. It was Hathaway. "Slow down," he ordered, "and stop swerving. I know what you're doing. If you get pulled over by a cop, I'll shoot you both, and that's a promise."

"Where are you taking me?" Alex heard Laurie say. "Are we going to your house? Why are we heading into the Hollywood Hills?"

Alex hit the mute button on his phone to block his end of the line. "Grace," he said, waving her over to the alcove. "Call Leo back and have him put Detective Reilly on the line. Laurie's giving us clues about their location."

Within seconds, Grace handed Alex her phone.

"Reilly," Alex said, "I'm certain of it now: Hathaway has Laurie and is taking her to the Hollywood Hills."

If something happened to Laurie, he would never forgive himself.

78

Laurie didn't dare steal another glance at her phone. She just had to hope that the call had connected and that Alex was able to hear her.

"Just do what I say, and no one else will be hurt," Hathaway said. "Your son and your father will be fine."

But not me, she thought. You have other plans for me.

Maybe if she kept him talking, she could buy herself more time. "Why did you do it? What did Susan see in the lab that afternoon to make her such a threat to you?"

"It didn't need to be such a big deal. Dwight had already done so much of the code work. Whether REACH was his idea or mine was just a matter of semantics. She overheard us and completely overreacted. It was worth millions. Did she really expect me to turn it over to a bunch of academic know-nothings?"

Hathaway was almost talking to himself at this point, but Laurie was able to piece the story together. She remembered the article published in the campus newspaper when Hathaway retired. It mentioned that, as a faculty member, Hathaway did not own any of his own research. She pictured Susan walking into the lab as Hathaway enlisted his favorite student to take the credit for his work so they could both profit from it.

Hathaway suddenly stopped muttering and told her to take another turn. His expression was cold and determined.

"Don't do this, Hathaway." She made it a point to say his name. If nothing else, maybe Alex would know who did this. "You'll never get away with it."

"I may live my life under suspicion, as you call it," Hathaway said, "but I won't be convicted. There's no real proof I killed Susan. As for Dwight, I can find the video files from his boat faster than any low-level hack working for the LAPD. And once I'm done with you, my next stop will be to Keith Ratner. He'll kill himself, leaving behind a distraught note confessing to the murders of both you and Susan. This entire thing will go down in the history books as being wrapped up with Advocates for God."

Laurie remembered taking this exact route when they'd driven to the spot where Susan Dempsey's body was found.

"You're taking me to Laurel Canyon Park, aren't you? We're going to the place where you killed Susan."

"Of course that's where we are going," Hathaway said. "It's exactly what Keith Ratner would do in a meltdown over the downfall of his beloved church leader—a demise that *you* brought about."

Laurie thought about the terror Susan must have felt when she realized Hathaway was trying to kill her. It was about to happen to her, too.

She had to find a way to save herself.

79

Alex felt helpless as he continued to listen to the open line. Hathaway was forcing Laurie to drive to the spot where he killed Susan Dempsey.

Good, Laurie, he whispered. *Just keep talking.*

She had already gotten Hathaway to admit to killing Susan Dempsey, and now he had a plan to kill Laurie and pin all his crimes on Keith Ratner.

"He's taking her to Laurel Canyon Park," Alex said to Reilly, who was doing his best to overhear through Grace's phone. "You have to send police cars there now, Reilly. You have to find Laurie."

Laurie could see the park entrance approaching. They were just seconds from what Hathaway intended to be her final destination.

Just as she knew he would, Hathaway instructed her, "Take the left turn up here, into the park."

She turned slowly, hoping to see a cavalry of police cars waiting for them, but the park was empty, dark as pitch.

This was it—her one chance. She remembered the exact location of the sycamore tree she'd noticed when they were filming here with Frank Parker.

She thought about making a quick move to latch her seat belt before impact. But she did not want to risk alerting Hathaway to her plan. If she was unable to buckle the seat belt, she wanted to have two hands on the wheel when they hit.

As they approached the sycamore she gunned the gas as hard as she could. Hathaway began to yell—"What are you—?" She swerved left and piloted the front side of the SUV squarely into the tree.

Laurie cringed when she heard the loud bang, at first believing that Hathaway had shot her. The bang was not a gunshot but the sound of the airbag deploying. Laurie felt a jolt in every part of her body as the airbag flung her back against her seat. For a moment she wasn't sure where she was.

As Laurie's head began to clear she looked over at Hathaway. He too had been stunned by the impact but was beginning to stir. She looked in his hands and on the floor for the gun but couldn't find it. Should she try to fight him now? No, if he woke up quickly, he would easily be able to overpower her. There was only one thing to do: run!

Detective Reilly spoke quickly as Alex pressed his ear to the cell phone. "We dispatched all local units to Laurel Canyon Park. One unit is in the park interior. I've been tracking the movements of Laurie's cell phone. It stopped moving about one minute ago. Either the phone is no longer in the vehicle or the vehicle has stopped."

With her body protesting every move, Laurie managed to open her door. She slid out of the car's raised seat and briefly lost her balance as her feet hit the sandy soil. She heard a groan and saw Hathaway raising his hand and massaging his forehead. Reaching into the driver's door side pocket, her hands groped for the cell phone in the darkness. It was gone.

Laurie ran a few strides until she felt her feet on pavement. Disoriented, she looked up and down the road, which was faintly illuminated by the moonlight. She wasn't sure which direction would take her toward Frank Parker's former house or deeper into the park. Her time to decide ended when she heard the crunching squeal of metal from the car. The passenger-side door was beginning to open.

Laurie began running as fast as her bruised legs would allow. How many times had she wondered what her beloved Greg was thinking in the final moments of his life? In trying to understand Susan Dempsey she had imagined Susan's terror as she fled through Laurel Canyon in a desperate attempt to outrun her killer—Our killer, she thought—Richard Hathaway! She thought of Timmy. She could not let him go through the loss of another parent. She had promised him she would always be there for him. She then heard Richard Hathaway's footsteps growing ever closer.

Highway Patrolman Carl Simoni had been inside Laurel Canyon Park investigating a complaint about illegal campers when he received the emergency dispatch about a carjacking. It had taken him several minutes to hustle back to his cruiser from the elevated campground. He was now pushing his cruiser as fast as he dared through the winding roads that led to the entrance of the park.

Laurie wasn't sure if the burning feeling in her chest was the result of the jolt from the airbags or if her lungs were unable to accept more air as she approached exhaustion. The quiet of the canyon was no longer disturbed only by her. Interspacing the sound of Laurie's footsteps was the faint wail of a siren.

Patrolman Simoni rounded a winding curve as the latest dispatch cackled from this radio. The carjacking victim's cell phone signal had been traced to an area just inside the park. He would be there in less than a minute. He squinted as he believed he saw a silhouette moving on the park road.

As Laurie ran, she looked back over her shoulder. The hulking figure of Hathaway grew larger every time she turned. Without realizing it she stepped on the border of the road and the soft soil to the side sent her sprawling to the ground. She flipped over and tried to get up. Hathaway had stopped a few feet away. She watched as he extended his arm toward her. There was a glint of moonlight off the gun in his hand. "Laurie, would you prefer that I shoot you or do you want to die the way Susan Dempsey did? Either way, they'll find your body in the same spot they found hers."

Before Laurie could respond, a bright light briefly covered her body from behind. It then moved quickly over to Hathaway, who raised one hand to shield his eyes from the blinding glare. Over a megaphone she could hear a voice echoing across the canyon ordering him to put his gun down and drop to his knees.

The gun was still pointed at her head. He was laughing, a maniacal, defiant sound. With all the strength she could muster, she swung her leg up and managed to kick his hand. The gun went off, with the bullet exploding in the sand next to her. The patrol car was rocketing toward them. Before Hathaway could aim again, it had slammed into him, knocking him to the ground.

As a swarm of patrol cars thundered down the road, she struggled to her feet. The force with which she had kicked Hathaway's hand had caused her shoe to slip off. As she reached for it, she could only think of the shoe Susan Dempsey had lost when she was trying to escape her killer.

80

Laurie had assumed that her next visit to Cedars-Sinai hospital would be to escort Jerry from the ICU. But she was back in the lobby again, Alex at her side. Once the doctors pronounced Laurie in good health after the collision, Grace had taken Timmy back to the house. Now she was waiting to hear about Richard Hathaway's injuries.

"I was so afraid," Alex said, "and then when your cell phone stopped moving, it was unbearable."

"I didn't think I'd make it," Laurie said. "I counted on you to pick up the phone." She managed a laugh. "Thank God you didn't put me on hold!"

Leo appeared from the ICU, his expression ambiguous. "Hathaway's got two broken legs but he'll make a full recovery."

"You sound disappointed," she said.

"He killed two people in cold blood, then came after my only daughter tonight," Leo said. "I wouldn't have lost sleep if he'd broken every bone in his body."

"He's only fifty-seven years old," Laurie said. "There's plenty of time for karma."

"The prosecution has a slam-dunk case against him," Alex said. "Kidnapping and attempted murder for tonight. Plus he confessed to killing both Susan Dempsey and Dwight Cook."

"And," Leo added, "Reilly says his techs found the camera feed from Dwight Cook's scuba boat. When Hathaway showed up to dive with Dwight, Dwight confronted him about Susan's murder. He'd figured out that Susan went to the lab after arguing with Nicole and overheard them talking about REACH. Hathaway admitted catching up to her and driving her up to the hills, but he tried to make her death sound like an accident. When Dwight didn't believe him, Hathaway smothered him and then faked the supposed 'scuba accident.'"

"And the police have the whole thing on film?" Laurie asked.

"In living color."

Epilogue

Two months later, Alex Buckley looked out from the television screen in Laurie's living room. "She became known to the public as Cinderella," he said solemnly, "but to a mother, she was always Susan. And tonight, on May 7, exactly twenty years after her death, we hope you feel you know her as Susan, too. Her case is now officially closed."

A round of applause broke out as the program ended. They had all gathered here to watch together: Laurie, her father, Timmy, Alex, Grace, Jerry. Even Brett Young had joined them. He was so happy with the show that he had flown Rosemary, Nicole, and Gavin to New York for their viewing party.

"Congratulations," Leo declared, holding up his beer bottle for a toast. "To *Under Suspicion*."

They all clinked glasses—Timmy's filled with apple cider—and then someone yelled out, "We need a speech, Laurie."

"Speech, speech," they all began to cheer.

She rose from her spot on the sofa. "Talk about a demanding crowd," she joked. "First off, *Under Suspicion* has always been a group effort. The show wouldn't be the same without Alex, and probably wouldn't have been *made* if not for Jerry and Grace. And I think it's safe to say that Jerry took an extra *hit* for the team this go-round."

They groaned at the pun. Two months ago, she couldn't have imagined making light of the horrible assault. But Jerry had recovered fully, and the man who'd assaulted him, Steve Roman, was dead. Jerry himself jokingly referred to the beating as a reminder that he shouldn't sneak out for junk food.

"And Timmy and Leo," Laurie added, "I'd say the two of you should have pushed the studio to be listed in the credits."

"That would've been *cool*," Timmy announced gleefully.

"Hey, don't forget a shout-out for the guy who signs the checks," Brett jokingly chided. "And who made sure you aired on May seventh."

"Thank you for that gentle reminder, Brett. And I'm sure the fact that May seventh fell during sweeps was completely a coincidence. But most of all," Laurie said in a more serious tone, "I want to thank Rosemary."

They all gave another round of applause.

"You were our inspiration throughout the entire production— from the early research to Alex's closing line. I don't often talk about the loss we suffered in my own family." She smiled gently at Timmy and Leo. "Losing a loved one is hard enough, but not knowing who did it, or why, is its own kind of torment. For me, every day has gotten just a little better since we finally got our answers. I only hope the same will be true for you."

Rosemary wiped away a tear. "Thank you so much," she said quietly.

Laurie noticed Nicole pat Rosemary soothingly on the back. Rosemary had vowed to forgive Nicole for the long delay in discovering who had killed Susan, but Laurie knew true forgiveness would take time.

Grace, always quick to lighten the mood, jumped from her chair and began topping off glasses. "So am I the only one who caught Keith Ratner on *Morning Joe* today? Seems like he's had a conversion of a different kind."

Undoubtedly timed to coincide with the airing of *Under Suspicion*, Keith's tour on the talk-show circuit was billed as an "insider's view" of Advocates for God. Martin Collins was already facing multiple abuse charges stemming from the videos discovered at his home. According to Detective Reilly, federal prosecutors were also putting together a racketeering case, alleging that Collins had used the church as a corrupt enterprise to cover criminal activity ranging from theft to bribery to extortion to his own predatory acts against children. Keith was not only cooperating with police but also using his disenchantment with the church to get back in the spotlight.

"Well, his PR tour is working," Laurie said. "A publishing friend told me there's a bidding war for the memoir he's pitching. Madison and Frank Parker are using the case as publicity, too. *Variety* reported yesterday that Frank has given Madison a small but 'comeback-worthy' role in his next film. She'll be playing a ruthless businesswoman willing to do anything to get ahead."

"Talk about typecasting!" Leo said.

When Rosemary went to leave, she gave Laurie a long hug at the door. "I think you and Susan would have been such good friends. Please, stay in touch. It would mean so much to me."

"Absolutely," Laurie assured her. Rosemary's approval meant more to her than any ratings or awards her show might earn.

Alex was the last to leave. At the door he said, "Congratulations, Laurie. The show was spectacular." He started to kiss her cheek, then involuntarily reached out his arms, and she stepped into them. His lips found hers and, for a long minute, they clung to each other.

Then as they stepped apart, he said, "Laurie, get something straight. I'm not a man about town. I'm a guy who's desperately in love with you and willing to wait."

"I don't deserve that," Laurie said.

"Yes, you do. And you'll know when the time is right."

They smiled at each other. "Not too much time," Laurie whispered, "I promise."

They both became aware of a small figure in the hallway to the bedrooms. Timmy was smiling happily. "Awesome!"

Mary Higgins Clark & Alafair Burke

ALL DRESSED IN WHITE

The thrilling new novel in the *Under Suspicion* series

Five years ago Amanda Pierce was excitedly preparing to
marry her college sweetheart. She and Jeffrey had already
battled through sickness and health, although their lives
were certainly more richer than poorer as Amanda was set
to inherit her father's successful garment company.

Then Amanda disappeared the night
of her bachelorette party.

In present-day New York City, Laurie Moran realizes
a missing bride is the perfect cold case for her 'Under
Suspicion' television series to investigate. By recreating the
night of the disappearance at the wedding's Florida resort with
Amanda's friends and family, Laurie hopes to find the same
success solving the cases featured in the series' first episodes.

But Laurie and 'Under Suspicion' host Alex Buckley
quickly discover everyone has their own theory about
why Amanda disappeared into thin air . . .

Coming in November 2015

LIKE YOUR FICTION A LITTLE ON THE DARK SIDE?

Like to curl up in a darkened room all alone, with the doors bolted and the windows locked and slip into something cold and terrifying...half hoping something goes bump in the night?

Me too.

That's why you'll find me at The Dark Pages - the home of crooks and villains, mobsters and terrorists, spies and private eyes; where the plots are twistier than a knotted noose and the pacing tighter than Marlon Brando's braces.

Beneath the city's glitz, down a litter-strewn alley, behind venetian blinds where neon slices the smoke-filled gloom, reading the dark pages.

Join me: WWW.THEDARKPAGES.CO.UK

AGENT X

@dark_pages

Paul Spicer was born in London, spent his childhood in Kenya and Jerusalem, and attended Eton and Sandhurst in the 1940s. He served in the Coldstream Guards, followed by a long career with Shell and then Lonrho, where he spent many years travelling the world, rising to Deputy Chairman. Paul divides his time between Dorset and Kenya. This is his first biography.

'In Paul Spicer, the notorious American expatriate and radiant beauty Alice de Janzé has finally met her match. Like Byron, she was "mad, bad and dangerous to know", one of those Pilgrim Daughters who travelled abroad and enriched the European aristocracy, becoming a social celebrity in Paris during the early 1920s.

With the dedication and zest of a private detective, Paul Spicer pursues her into the ironically named "Happy Valley" of equatorial East Africa, where her melodramatic life ended in violence and tragedy. She appears like one of those extreme characters from the pages of Evelyn Waugh and Scott Fitzgerald. But, as Paul Spicer shows, truth is again stranger than fiction.'

Michael Holroyd
(Sir Michael De Courcy Frazer Holroyd CBE)

The Temptress

THE SCANDALOUS LIFE OF ALICE, COUNTESS DE JANZÉ

PAUL SPICER

SIMON &
SCHUSTER

London · New York · Sydney · Toronto

A CBS COMPANY

First published in Great Britain by Simon & Schuster UK Ltd, 2010
This paperback edition published by Simon & Schuster UK Ltd, 2011
A CBS COMPANY

1 3 5 7 9 10 8 6 4 2

Simon & Schuster UK Ltd
1st Floor
222 Gray's Inn Road
London WC1X 8HB

www.simonandschuster.co.uk

Simon & Schuster Australia
Sydney

A CIP catalogue record for this book
is available from the British Library.

ISBN: 978-1-84739-914-4

Typeset in Perpetua by M Rules
Printed in the UK by CPI Cox & Wyman, Reading, Berkshire RG1 8EX

To June Elizabeth Cadogan Spicer, my wife,
and our two children Rupert and Venetia.

And to our two grandchildren,
Alexander and Tara Watson.

Contents

Part Two

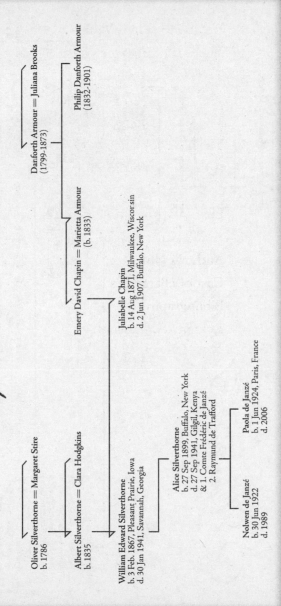

Relatives of Alice Silverthorne

Oliver Silverthorne = Margaret Stire
b. 1786

Danforth Armour = Juliana Brooks
(1799-1873)

Albert Silverthorne = Clara Hodgkins
b. 1835

Philip Danforth Armour
(1832-1901)

Emery David Chapin = Marietta Armour
(b. 1833)

William Edward Silverthorne
b. 3 Feb. 1867, Pleasant Prairie, Iowa
d. 30 Jan 1941, Savannah, Georgia

Juliabelle Chapin
b. 14 Aug 1871, Milwaukee, Wisconsin
d. 2 Jun 1907, Buffalo, New York

Alice Silverthorne
b. 27 Sep 1899, Buffalo, New York
d. 27 Sep 1941, Gilgil, Kenya
& 1. Comte Frédéric de Janzé
2. Raymund de Trafford

Nolwen de Janzé
b. 30 Jun 1922
d. 1989

Paola de Janzé
b. 1 Jun 1924, Paris, France
d. 2006

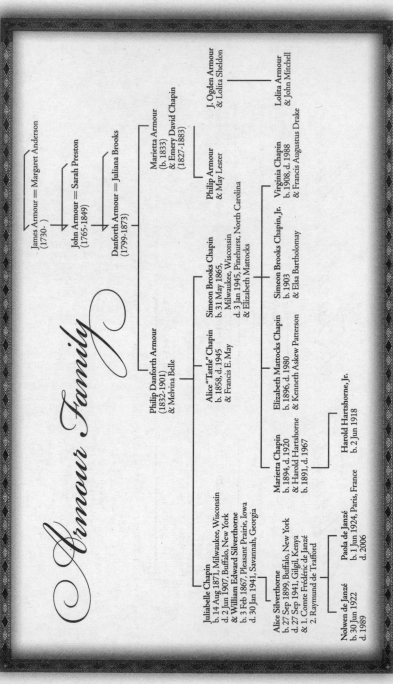

Armour Family

James Armour = Margaret Anderson
(1730-)

John Armour = Sarah Preston
(1765-1849)

Danforth Armour = Juliana Brooks
(1799-1873)

Marietta Armour
(b. 1833)
& Emery David Chapin
(1827-1883)

J. Ogden Armour
& Lolita Sheldon

Philip Armour
& May Lester

Lolita Armour
& John Mitchell

Philip Danforth Armour
(1832-1901)
& Melvina Belle

Simeon Brooks Chapin
b. 31 May 1865,
Milwaukee, Wisconsin
d. 3 Jan 1945, Pinehurst, North Carolina
& Elizabeth Mattocks

Virginia Chapin
b. 1908, d. 1988
& Francis Augustus Drake

Alice "Tattie" Chapin
b. 1858, d. 1945
& Francis E. May

Simeon Brooks Chapin, Jr.
b. 1903
& Elsa Bartholomay

Elizabeth Mattocks Chapin
b. 1896, d. 1980
& Kenneth Askew Patterson

Juliabelle Chapin
b. 14 Aug 1871, Milwaukee, Wisconsin
d. 2 Jun 1907, Buffalo, New York
& William Edward Silverthorne
b. 3 Feb 1867, Pleasant Prairie, Iowa
d. 30 Jan 1941, Savannah, Georgia

Marietta Chapin
b. 1894, d. 1920
& Harold Hartshorne
b. 1891, d. 1967

Harold Hartshorne, Jr.
b. 2 Jun 1918

Alice Silverthorne
b. 27 Sep 1899, Buffalo, New York
d. 27 Sep 1941, Gigil, Kenya
& 1. Comte Frédéric de Janzé
2. Raymund de Trafford

Nolwen de Janzé
b. 30 Jun 1922
d. 1989

Paola de Janzé
b. 1 Jun 1924, Paris, France
d. 2006

De Trafford Family Tree

Sir Humphrey de Trafford 2nd Bt = Lady Annette Mary Talbot
b. 1 May 1808
d. 4 May 1886
d. 1 Jul 1922

Mildred Mary Josephine de Trafford
b. 27 Mar 1856
d. 29 Dec 1934
& Sir Charles Bertram Bellew
3rd Baron Bellow Of Barmeath

Sir Humphrey de Trafford 3rd Bt
b. 3 Jul 1862
d. 10 Jan 1929
& Violet Alice Maud Franklin
d. 20 Jul 1925

Sicele Agnes de Trafford
b. 22 Feb 1867
d. 5 Feb 1948
& Charles William Clifford

Raymund Vincent de Trafford
b. 28 Jan 1900
d. 14 May 1971
& 1. Alice Silverthorne
& 2. Eve Drummond

Sir Humphrey Edmund de Trafford 4th Bt
b. 30 Nov 1891
d. 6 Oct 1971

Violet Mary de Trafford
b. 8 May 1893
d. 28 Feb 1968
& 1. Hon. Rupert Oswald Derek Keppel
& 2. Col. Keith Graham Menzies

Sir Rudolph Edgar Francis
de Trafford 5th Bt, OBE
b. 31 Aug 1894
d. 16 Aug 1983
& 1. June Isobel Chaplin MBE
2. Katherine Lo Savio Balke

Sir Dermot Humphrey de Trafford 6th Bt
b. 19 Jan 1925
d. 22 Jan 2010
& 1 Patricia Mary Beeley
& 2 Xandra Carandini Lee

Prologue

It was around 3 a.m. on 24 January 1941 when the body of Josslyn Hay, Earl of Erroll, was discovered lying curled up and face down on the floor of his Buick car in Kenya, East Africa. The car had come to a rest over a gravel pit by the side of the Ngong road, eight miles from the capital of Nairobi. Joss, as he was known to all, had been shot at close range, the fatal bullet entering by the side of his left ear. Even in death, his otherwise unmarked face remained that of a very handsome man. At thirty-nine years old, Josslyn Victor Hay – twenty-second incumbent of the Erroll earldom, the hereditary High Constable of Scotland – was a lynchpin of Kenya's colonial community. Blond, clever, an ace card and polo player, Joss devoted a good deal of his considerable energies to seducing women,

1

especially those who were already married. His very arrival in Africa in 1923 had taken place in scandalous circumstances – he had eloped with Lady Idina Gordon, an older divorcee and veteran of two marriages.

Much has been made of Joss and Idina and the famously decadent 'Happy Valley' crowd they gathered around them during the 1920s, although the truth is perhaps a little less exotic. The Errolls and their coterie were a small, tight-knit group of mainly British and aristocratic friends and farmers, attempting to forge a new existence in the Wanjohi Valley (a place that later acquired the epithet 'happy' due to the good spirits induced by its high altitude). Certainly, they found time to enjoy themselves there – house parties would begin at sundown and last until dawn, fuelled by alcohol and sexual intrigue. After his murder, it became clear that Joss – who had already been married, divorced, had remarried and was recently widowed at the time of his death – could have had any number of enemies. He had carried on numerous adulterous affairs throughout his life and had recently started a relationship with yet another married woman.

Although his death made newspaper headlines around the world, sympathy for the murdered earl did not always run deep. The American press, ever succinct, printed the immortal headline 'Passionate Peer Gets His'. There was, however, plenty of interest in who had committed the crime. After Joss's murder, the Kenyan Police, and the Attorney General in particular, decided the obvious culprit was Sir Henry 'Jock' Delves Broughton. Jock's new wife, the blonde and vivacious Diana, had become Joss's latest conquest, and the police reasoned that Jock had murdered Joss in revenge for stealing his bride. Jock was duly charged and then imprisoned. He went on trial on 26 May 1941, but was never convicted and after being acquitted on 1 July 1941, he was discharged. Although his name was cleared, Broughton never recovered from the ignominy of the trial, committing suicide the following year. To this date, the Erroll crime remains officially unsolved.

So who shot Lord Erroll? The question hangs in the air. Many possible answers have been given by a number of pre-eminent writers. The first to set his sights on the story was British journalist Cyril Connolly. A prominent contributor to the *New Statesman* in the 1930s, a critic for many years on the *Sunday Times* and literary editor of the *Observer* from 1942 to 1943, Connolly had been fascinated by the Erroll case from the beginning. In 1969, he joined forces with fellow journalist James Fox to undertake a complete investigation of the murder for the *Sunday Times* magazine. The result was published in that same year and was entitled 'Christmas at Karen', its content gleaned from dozens of interviews. With its accompanying photographs, including a picture of Erroll's head with its bullet wound, Connolly's article stopped short of naming a murderer, but even so, it reignited the controversy. Fox pursued the case even after Connolly's death, publishing his book about the murder, *White Mischief*, in 1982. It became a classic of crime reporting and was later made into a film starring Charles Dance and Greta Scacchi. In both book and film, a heavy shadow is cast over Broughton's self-proclaimed innocence: after all, Jock was the only person to stand trial for the murder. Many have taken his suicide to be tantamount to an admission of guilt.

Since the publication of *White Mischief*, there have been other authors who have either substantiated Fox's theory or disputed it. In 1997, Leda Farrant published her own version of events – *Diana, Lady Delamere and the Lord Erroll Murder* – in which she claimed that it was Diana herself who had committed the killing. According to Farrant, Diana was furious with Joss for refusing to marry her. In the 1999 memoir *Child of Happy Valley*, Juanita Carberry, who grew up in Kenya, relates that Broughton confessed his culpability to her three days after the murder when she was just fifteen years old. Most recently, the biographer Errol Trzebinski's biography of Lord Erroll, *The Life and Death of Lord Erroll* (2000), pins the blame on MI6 or another branch of British intelligence. The motive for assassinating Erroll, according to Trzebinski, was that Erroll had fascist leanings. The Oscar-winning screenwriter Julian Fellowes also revisited the facts of the case in his 2005 television special *A Most Mysterious Murder: The Case of the Earl of Erroll*, placing the blame squarely back on Broughton.

A peripheral character in all these narratives is Countess Alice de Janzé. Alice sustained an on-again-off-again affair with Joss for the best part of two decades and was probably still in love with him at the time of his murder. Born in Buffalo, New York in 1899, this transcendently beautiful American heiress became a French countess by marriage. After she arrived in Africa via Paris, attired in the latest French fashions, she quickly won over almost every man she encountered there, while still managing to befriend most of their wives. Alice was the very definition of a colourful character and, although hardly a well-known figure in our times, she achieved infamy during her own, making newspaper headlines around the world with her exploits. It is Alice's story that I will tell in this book.

For my part, I have been aware of Alice's name since childhood. Alice was a friend of my mother, Margaret Spicer. The two women met in Kenya when they were both newly arrived there in 1925 (my father, Roy Spicer, was serving as Commissioner of Kenya Police). At the time, Alice and her husband, Count Frédéric de Janzé, were staying with their friends Joss and Idina in the Wanjohi Valley. Margaret and Alice had much in common. Both were Americans abroad – Alice from Chicago, Illinois, and my mother born in Larkspur, Colorado. They were both fluent in French: Alice had arrived in Paris in 1920, chaperoned by her aunt; Margaret had been educated in Montreux, Switzerland. As new arrivals in Kenya they found themselves surrounded by a predominantly British expatriate crowd, so it is perhaps not surprising that they sought one another out. Alice and my mother were both musical, often entertaining the Happy Valley circle by singing popular American songs and spirituals from the Deep South, with Alice accompanying on the ukulele. My mother's friendship with Alice lasted until 1927, when she left Kenya to return to England.

Evidently, Alice exerted a considerable fascination for my mother – as she did for so many who knew her – because when my mother died in 1953, I came into the possession of her diaries and family papers and it was among these that I discovered numerous press cuttings and references to the glamorous countess. As well as the papers and cuttings, my mother left me her copy of *Vertical Land*, a book of sketches depicting life in Kenya in the mid-1920s written by Alice's husband, Frédéric. For most readers, the characters in Frédéric's *Vertical Land* appear to be fictional, since he changed the names of the real-life characters he described, but my mother had decoded these pen portraits, writing in pencil in the margins of her copy the true names of the characters.

In one story in *Vertical Land*, Alice appears as Delecia, a elegant American who is seen pulling up at Nairobi's exclusive Muthaiga Club in a low-slung Buick piled with luggage and a lion cub. Later in the book, in a portrait entitled 'Just Like a Gipsy' Frédéric describes another woman who can only be Alice, her ukulele transformed into a mandolin. The passage is characterized by the rather flowery Symbolist language fashionable in France at the time, and as such it gives us a highly stylized version of her person and presence:

Wide eyes, so calm, short thick hair, full red lips, a body to desire. The powerful hands clutch and wave along the mandolin and the crooning somnolent melody breaks; her throat trembles and her gleaming shoulders droop.

That weird soul of mixtures is at the door! her cruelty and lascivious thoughts clutched the thick lips on close white teeth.

She holds us with her song, and her body sways towards ours. No man will touch her exclusive soul, shadowy with memories, unstable and suicidal.

Like most depictions of Alice, the portrait raises more questions than it answers, but there is no doubt that Frédéric was correct in his assessment of Alice as 'unstable and suicidal'. She was a woman who suffered throughout her life from the demons of melancholy, and who tried to take her own life on a number of occasions. Alongside this dark streak, however, was a vein of impetuous and often reckless daring. As a young heiress, she quickly tired of the Chicago debutante scene and began to explore the Jazz-Age nightclubs of the city, starting up an affair with a local mobster. After being banished to Paris by her family, she took a job at a French fashion house by day, cutting a swathe through the city's clubs and cafes by night. It was in France that she won her independence from her family when she married Frédéric, the sensitive, intellectual count who took her to Africa to help cure her of her unhappiness. After only a few months in Kenya, she decided to build a home there, leaving her two young children in France, too fearful of being a bad mother to grace them with more than the occasional visit. In Africa, her marriage to Frédéric fell apart after she started affairs with the two men who would become her great loves, Joss and her second husband, Raymund de Trafford.

As I began to research her life, the Alice I discovered was a lesson in contradictions. She could be bold and eccentric – she would go out riding alone amongst wild animals, kept a Nile crocodile in her bathtub in Paris, and launched herself with abandon into affairs with a string of dubious lovers. But her letters and other writings often reveal a sense of wrenching need and at times overwhelming unhappiness. In 1941, only eight months after Joss Erroll's murder, she finally succeeded in taking her own life at home in Kenya. She was forty-two. In virtually every depiction of the Erroll murder to date, Alice is described, suspected and cleared of suspicion. She is written about without any depth or explanation of her origins, her moods, her strengths and weaknesses. Her stunning beauty and great wealth is noted and then, in each instance, the author moves on. In Michael Radford's 1987 film of Fox's book, Alice was played by Sarah Miles, who portrayed her as an irresponsible and dizzy drug addict. The truth in such matters is, of course, always more complex and usually more interesting. Such was the case with Alice. (In fact, Alice never took drugs other than barbiturates for sleeping, relying on absinthe-spiked vodka cocktails for her highs.)

The more I read and investigated, the more I came to see that within the Alice legend were dozens of compelling anecdotes, inconclusive leads and half-told stories. Through my research, I discovered a woman who was in fact central – rather than peripheral – to the Erroll case. She seemed to me a figure worthy of further scrutiny, someone who needed to be placed in her full context. How did an American such as Alice end up in British colonial Africa? What was the nature of her affair with Joss? What hard evidence has ever been produced about the murder? What psychology has been deployed? According to anonymous letters sent to Jock Delves Broughton's defence counsel during his trial, the assassin was in fact a discarded mistress.

Part One

1

The Heiress

Alice de Janzé was born Alice Silverthorne, at home in Buffalo, New York on 28 September 1899. Home was an appropriately extravagant and elaborate setting for the arrival of this little heiress who would one day grow up to become a countess. The year before her birth, Alice's father, the Buffalo millionaire William Silverthorne, had bought a brand-new three-storey red-brick Georgian Revival mansion on Delaware Avenue, also known as Millionaire's Row. It was here that Alice was born and spent her early years. The house – designed by the pre-eminent Buffalo architects Esenwein and Johnson – was ostentatious, even by the standards of Millionaire's Row. There were large Doric pillars around the main doorways, a maze of vast and elegant rooms inside, and stables and servants' quarters at the bottom of a five-acre garden. William had made his fortune in the lumber trade and was eager to be counted amongst the most powerful in newly thriving Buffalo. His wife, Juliabelle Chapin, was a Chicago society beauty from one of the richest families in America, and she had brought to her marriage a considerable dowry and pedigree. The house was a monument to William's successes, both financial and social.

Alice was christened at the local Presbyterian church two weeks after her birth. Her parents had been married and childless for more than seven years prior to Alice's birth and they were overjoyed by the arrival of their much longed-for child. Such doting, wealthy parents ensured that their daughter's very early years were marked by an extraordinary degree of privilege. From the beginning, the attentions of an army of nurses and nannies were lavished upon Alice. William and Juliabelle were determined that their daughter would never want for anything in life and set about providing her with the very best that money could buy. Baby clothes were made specially in expensive fabrics imported from Paris. Juliabelle would take regular shopping trips to Chicago, New York and Boston, where she would purchase vast quantities of gifts and toys for her little girl. As Alice grew from infant to child, her parents supervised her education at home, employing private governesses who instructed her in French, German, reading, writing and basic arithmetic. For her seventh birthday, Alice was given her own pony and trap: there is a delightful photograph in existence of a 7-year-old Alice dressed in a short jacket and smock with a straw boater, sitting proudly in the wicker trap and holding the reins of the small black pony. By all accounts, the very young Alice was a carefree and affectionate child who adored her parents and was devoted to her pets.

Even so, the union between Alice's parents was far from easy. Juliabelle and William had always been something of a mismatch. William was robust, energetic, and careless. Juliabelle was more fragile, physically and emotionally, and prone to prolonged periods of sadness. What's more, they were both from very different social backgrounds. William was born in Pleasant Prairie, Iowa on 3 February 1867, the third of seven children born to Albert David Silverthorne and Clara Frances Hodgkins, a solidly 'merchant class' couple. William's father had made his money in the lumber business in the period after Chicago's Great Fire of 1871 when construction materials were at a premium. William himself had gone into the family business at a young age, working his way up through the ranks from the most menial of positions to the highest of managerial levels. He quickly proved himself to be a natural and talented businessman with a powerful drive for financial gain in this most socially and professionally mobile of cities. He was good-looking and popular, made friends easily and enjoyed socializing, carousing, playing cards and chasing girls.

Born on 14 August 1871, Juliabelle was the youngest daughter of the union between two of the most powerful Chicago families of the nineteenth century, the Armours and the Chapins. Her mother, Marietta Armour, was the sister of the famous Chicagoan Philip Danforth Armour, who is still listed as one of the forty richest American men of all time. Thanks to her father, Emery David Chapin, Juliabelle was related to the Springfield Chapins, founders and benefactors of Springfield, Massachusetts. Her paternal grandfather had made his money from investing in the railroads in Springfield, but the Chicago faction of the Chapin family was also associated with the meat-packing industry, much like their friends and colleagues, the Armours. When Juliabelle's parents married, the Chapins and the Armours were united by wedlock, and not for the first time. In fact, there had already been several Armour–Chapin weddings in Chicago and by the late nineteenth century the two families had become the city's equivalent of royalty: society columns were full of gossip about the family and their appearances at weddings, social events and debutante parties.

From birth, Juliabelle had been groomed to marry a wealthy and influential husband. Needless to say when William Silverthorne began to pursue Juliabelle, the Armour–Chapins were far from impressed. Despite William's quite significant wealth and promising career as an entrepreneur, the Armour–Chapins considered him a highly inappropriate match for one of the most eligible heiresses in Chicago. Even though William could trace his ancestors back to their arrival in Virginia from England in 1656, the Silverthornes had become comfortably affluent through business endeavours such as making felt and selling lumber and were therefore deemed socially inferior. Furthermore, the Armour–Chapins wholeheartedly disapproved of William's reputation as a drinker, gambler and ladies' man. Undeterred, William courted Juliabelle relentlessly, pursuing her with the same zest, determination and enthusiasm that he usually reserved for his business deals. Eventually, his good looks, charm and persistence won the day and he quite simply swept Juliabelle off her well-heeled feet. The undivided disapproval of her family notwithstanding, Juliabelle and William were married in Chicago on 8 January 1892. It was a modest affair by Armour–Chapin standards, with only close family in attendance. Shortly afterwards, the couple left for Buffalo where William and his brother Asa had recently purchased their own lumber yard.

At the time, Buffalo was the eighth largest city in the United States. By the early 1900s, it had a population of close to 400,000. Its proximity to Niagara Falls made it a popular tourist destination and a railway hub. It was an appealing and efficient centre of commerce for the many entrepreneurs – William and Asa included – who flocked to the city in the 1890s in the hope of making their fortunes there. Juliabelle began setting up home but William was doggedly determined to build up his business and was often away for long periods at a time, travelling across the country as far afield as Arkansas and Missouri in order to open new sawmills and set up plants. The seven years in which the couple failed to conceive a child were a period of enormous loneliness for Juliabelle, who found herself living far away from her home and family and with a husband who was frequently absent. Although the eventual birth of her daughter brought her a degree of fulfilment, it could not mend her fractured marriage.

In the years after Alice's birth, Juliabelle and William were unable to conceive another child, and although Juliabelle adored her only daughter, she continued to feel dissatisfied with her life in Buffalo. To make matters worse, her health was failing: she was weak and permanently tired. Meanwhile, William continued his regime of working and heavy socializing. He was drinking, gambling and spending more and more time in Chicago. There were rumours that he was having affairs, possibly even one with Juliabelle's cousin Louise Mattocks (a member of the Chapin clan). By the early part of 1907, Juliabelle was beside herself with unhappiness. She was now convinced that her husband and cousin were having a relationship. Gathering up her courage, she confronted William. What followed was a vicious argument that culminated in William locking Juliabelle out of the house at night in the middle of the icy Buffalo winter. Juliabelle was not readmitted until the morning. Shortly afterwards she was diagnosed with vascular laryngitis. She died six months later on 2 June 1907 at the age of only thirty-five. William had his wife embalmed with surprising speed and she was buried two days later on 4 June 1907.

William now found himself living alone with a young and very unhappy daughter. Juliabelle's death was a crushing blow to Alice who was deeply attached to both parents but who had always spent so much time with her mother. To a 7-year-old girl who woke up one morning to find her mother gone, it was little compensation that Juliabelle had willed an enormous inheritance to her daughter, placed in trust until she reached the age of eighteen. The trustees of the will were Juliabelle's father, her mother's elder brother Simeon B. Chapin (Uncle Sim) and her mother's elder sister, Alice (Mrs Francis May, known as Aunt Tattie). Meanwhile, in an effort to ease Alice's confusion and moderate his feelings of guilt, William redoubled his efforts to spoil his only daughter completely. He fawned on Alice, taking her with him everywhere he went. After Juliabelle's death, they travelled to Chicago together and on a whirlwind tour of Europe, with William continually showering his daughter with gifts and indulgences. A dangerous expectation was being established between father and daughter – one that would forever complicate Alice's relationships with men in the future. Whenever she wanted something from William, she was immediately and elaborately appeased.

There can be little doubt that William adored Alice, but it has to be said that he recovered from Juliabelle's death with remarkable ease. Barely a year later, he remarried. As it turned out, Juliabelle had been correct in her suspicions that William and her cousin were having an affair. His bride was none other than her cousin, Louise Mattocks. The wedding ceremony took place at the American Church on the quai d'Orsay in Paris on 8 July 1908 with Alice and two witnesses in attendance. It is likely that William proposed to Louise before he left for Europe, but that the engagement was kept secret in order to stifle the growing rumble of rumours back in Chicago. After the wedding, Alice accompanied her father and new stepmother on their lavish honeymoon around Europe. The Silverthornes travelled in the luxurious compartments of first-class train cars. They ate at the finest restaurants and stayed in the most well appointed of hotels. If William had set out to distract Alice from the death of her mother and to win over the heart of his new bride, this trip was certainly very successful, if fantastically costly.

For her part, Alice was developing an early and extensive knowledge of the great European cities. Before she was twelve, Alice had visited London, Paris, Nice, Monte Carlo and Rome. She was a precocious child, and it seems she appreciated both the sights and the culture on offer. Throughout her life, she would continue to travel, always feeling more at home when abroad. During the honeymoon, Alice charmed her stepmother, and the pair developed a genuine soft spot for one another. In this difficult period after her mother's death, the relationship with Louise must have been a welcome and stabilizing one. But William's latest conquest only served to redouble his problems with the Armour–Chapins. He had married into their ranks for a second time, an unforgivable outrage. The two families also believed, possibly with some justification, that William was an inadequate father. By parading Alice around the best hotels and restaurants in the world, they believed, he would damage her development and reputation. They were horrified by William's excesses and feared he would ultimately diminish Alice's chances of being accepted in society.

William, of course, carried on after his own fashion. On returning from Europe with his daughter and new bride, he set about looking for a new home. William and Louise decided to leave provincial Buffalo for New York City where William bought a house at 40 East 60th Street in Manhattan and a weekend retreat in Sharon, Connecticut. Over the coming years, Louise had several children by William, only two of whom survived to adulthood: Bill, born in May 1912, and Patricia, born in July 1915. Despite these new arrivals, Alice remained her father's particular favourite. At the age of twelve, she crossed the Atlantic in his company from New York to Cherbourg on the *Aquitania*, the magnificent Cunard liner. Alice liked to dress beyond her years and William did not deter her. Even at twelve she could pass for seventeen and she relished wearing silk dresses and make-up. Everyone she met on the *Aquitania* treated her as an adult. Word reached the Armour–Chapins that William would deliberately fail to introduce Alice as his daughter, with the result that many aboard the ship assumed that this beautiful young woman was his companion. Although it is likely that the relationship between Alice and her father remained innocent, Alice's relatives on her mother's side found William's approach to parenting distasteful and even outright obscene.

By 1913 William's fast lifestyle and ever-increasing expenditures were beginning to catch up with him. Some of his investments were failing, but despite this he continued to spend beyond his means. He had a reputation for extravagance and was determined to live up to it. In 1913 he bought himself a top of the line Stoddard Dayton motorcar with a six-cylinder, 8.6-litre Knight engine, hiring a uniformed chauffeur to drive him around town in it (his daughter would later inherit his taste for luxury

American cars). No expense was spared to feed his appetite for ostentation; it is suspected – although not proven – that William was dipping into Alice's trust fund in order to help with his business debts and to keep himself in the manner to which he had become accustomed. He was also drinking heavily and was almost certainly an alcoholic.

Then, in 1913, some kind of traumatic incident (or possibly an accident) involving William took place. Although we do not know the exact nature of the 'incident' we do know that it galvanized the Armour–Chapins. They became determined to act. That year, Juliabelle's brother, Uncle Sim, decided to take action against William Silverthorne, applying for Alice to be made a ward of the court. Uncle Sim was a Wall Street broker and a Chapin to boot. He could use his considerable influence and money to put forward the notion that William was an unfit father, that he had a reputation as a drinker and gambler, that he was failing to educate Alice properly and that he was embezzling funds from her inheritance. The court in New York ruled in Uncle Sim's favour. William lost custody of his daughter. Legal guardianship of Alice was awarded to Alice's Aunt Tattie. Juliabelle's family had achieved their intended revenge: they had taken from William his most precious possession, his daughter.

For Alice, this must have been a period of extraordinary heartbreak and confusion. She was a thirteen-year-old, on the brink of puberty, accustomed to her father's affection and indulgences. She would have been oblivious to the questionable morality of her relationship with William.

She only knew she adored this man who had been the one constant in her life since the loss of her mother. Now Alice was sent to live with relatives whom she barely knew, in unfamiliar surroundings. Although William was far from an ideal parent, the effect of this severance on Alice was dramatic and damaging. Alice went from being the object of her father's constant attention and care to being a complete exile from his presence and love. It's no wonder that as an adult Alice could react with astonishing violence when the men in her life threatened to leave her.

It was left to Aunt Tattie, Alice's legal guardian, to look after her, to arrange for her to be educated and to prepare her for adulthood. Aunt Tattie had no children of her own and no experience of childrearing. Although she was a kindly and well-meaning woman, she hoped to fashion her young charge into an obedient debutante, someone who would slip easily into Chicago's elite circles. Alice had other ideas. She was entirely accustomed to a life lived on her own terms and did not adapt well to the limits imposed on her by her aunt's vision. Doubtless exasperated, Aunt Tattie thought it best to send Alice away to boarding school. Alice was uprooted again, sent this time to Mount Vernon Seminary, a school for girls in Washington DC. A non-sectarian private school, it had been founded in 1875 by Elizabeth Somers. (The school has since been absorbed into George Washington University.) Alice stayed at Mount Vernon for the next four years. As a student, she excelled at English, and began to develop an interest in writing, publishing short stories and verses in the school's magazine. One of her poems, which appeared in the Mount Vernon Seminary magazine in 1917 – the year that the United States entered the First World War – gives us an insight into her state of mind at this time:

The Storm
by Alice Silverthorne

A chill light shines in the sullen sky
With an angry sulphurous glow.
And a sharp wind sifts
Through the mountain rifts,
And whirls the leaves in eddying drifts,
To die on the earth below.

The grim-voiced winds are approaching fast,
Lean clouds slink out of the sky.
And a terror reigns
Amid the hurricanes
That whip the trees with the lash of rains
As the storm goes sweeping by.

So when you come, like the great red storm,
My cares, like the clouds, flee too.
And my heart leaps high,
With a happy cry,
Toward the turbulent blue of the wind-streaked sky,
– Swept free of the clouds by you!

The poetry, although obviously amateur in nature, reveals a troubled sensibility and an intense longing in

Alice. By the age of sixteen she had undergone the death of her mother, separation from her father, and displacement on a number of occasions. It is hard to imagine that such a headstrong personality, who was used to being constantly appeased, would have adapted easily to the structured environment of a traditional girls' boarding school. In her poem, when she longs for the clouds to be 'swept free', it is easy to interpret this as a cry for help to her father, whose leniency she must have sorely missed.

In fact, the turbulent weather Alice described in her poem had a direct correlation in her emotional life. Around the time of 'The Storm', she attempted suicide. Patsy Chilton – the former wife of Dr Roger Bowles, who served as a part-time doctor to Alice in Kenya and who knew Alice well between 1938 and 1941 – remembers being told by an American friend that Alice had tried to slash her wrists as a young girl at school. The attempt may have been simply a cry for help, inspired by the hope that her father would come to her rescue. There is no doubt that Alice was lonely and missing William during this period of her life, but it is also likely that she was already suffering from cyclothymia, a strain of bipolar disorder or manic depression that would afflict her for the rest of her life. It is extremely common for sufferers of the disease to first experience its symptoms during adolescence, at which point stress or trauma can easily trigger its alternating periods of lows and highs. Although Alice's attempt to kill herself failed, it had an immediate impact on her life. Shortly afterwards, she was taken out of the school and went to live with Aunt Tattie in Chicago.

Alice was now seventeen years old, extremely pretty and advanced for her years. At Aunt Tattie's, she quickly made a new friend, her cousin, the debutante Lolita Armour. Two years older than Alice and already a minor celebrity in Chicago, a young woman whose every appearance was reported in the newspaper gossip columns, Lolita was immediately attracted to her troubled but highly attractive younger cousin. Lolita's mother, Mrs J. Ogden Armour, was a patron of music and the arts and spent the war raising money and helping to boost the morale of the troops. Alice was enlisted to help with the war effort by selling programmes at charity events, knitting hats and scarves for the soldiers, and serving tea and coffee at church functions. Lolita also began introducing Alice to Chicago's debutante circles, filling her in on all the latest gossip and goings-on amongst the most fashionable families in the city. Despite Alice's recent difficulties, she found she socialized easily and, thanks to her good looks, was an appealing new presence on the Chicago scene. She was given her own 'coming out' ball, after which she was quickly invited to all the good parties and social occasions, attracting the attentions of many of the city's well-to-do young men in the process. Alice was now a fully fledged member of the Chicago elite. She served as bridesmaid at many of the Armour–Chapin family weddings during this time and appears in formal photographs, an especially attractive girl with a pout. She soon began to outshine all the other debutantes, even her cousin Lolita.

A newspaper illustration from her debutante years shows

Alice's early beauty to great effect. In the picture, her distinctive wide-set, almond-shaped eyes are enhanced with mascara, kohl and shadow. Her lips – painted and defined – form a perfect bow. Her hair is bobbed and waved, worn to one side, giving her the look of a silent film star, a Clara Bow or a Louise Brooks. Even at such a young age, her gaze in the illustration is assured rather than demure (if perhaps a little sullen). Now in her late teens, Alice had already learned to use her eyes in a highly seductive way and she had no trouble getting the young men of Chicago to notice her: she would bow her head and look up, without diverting her gaze from the object of her attentions, allowing her suitor to talk, and continuing to look at him while inclining her head from side to side, giving herself an air of wonderment. This technique was highly effective and became a trademark with Alice. She was also short-sighted, but rarely wore glasses, which gave her grey eyes an especially dreamy expression. Another distinctive feature was her voice, which, by late adolescence, was already lowering in tone. She had a ready and captivating laugh, and threw her head back as she exercised it. The only aspect of her physical appearance with which she struggled was her hair: it was thick, curly and hard to control. She changed her hairstyle numerous times during her youth and adulthood, sometimes parting it down the middle, sometimes plaiting it into buns on either side of her head. The most glamorous effect came from straightening it with the help of a maid or hairdresser so that it was either sleek against her head or loose around her shoulders.

Initially, Alice enjoyed the attention she received at parties and in the press, but as she became more accustomed to the Chicago social whirl, she quickly began to tire of it. She possessed an adventurous spirit and hated to be placed in a box. Evidently, she was frustrated by the restrictions and unspoken codes of the debutante lifestyle where she could barely move without being spotted and recognized. This was a somewhat shallow world ruled by somewhat shallow people who placed enormous value on the 'right' make-up and clothes, and who cared most of all about whom you were seen with and where you had gone for dinner the previous night. No end of effort was made to look attractive. Chicago debutantes were known to take the train to New York just to have their faces, hair, eyebrows and lips made up by Elizabeth Arden on Fifth Avenue, before dashing back to Chicago in time to get dressed for the next ball. Alice, a natural beauty, had no such compulsion. She began to find the rounds of debutante parties unspeakably dull. It was at this point in her life that Alice began to explore Chicago's seamier sides.

The novelist F. Scott Fitzgerald dubbed the decade to follow the 'Jazz Age' but Chicago was ahead of the game. In 1918 and 1919, when Alice began to frequent Chicago's nightclubs, jazz was helping to create a new atmosphere of post-war optimism and liberation that crossed racial and class boundaries. Partygoers were unhindered by the Prohibition that would begin in 1920 – Alice learned to take her drink and loved to dance until the early hours. She was moving away from her elite circle and beginning to explore her identity outside her family and their expectations for her. She was also meeting some decidedly shady characters. Organized crime was rife in Chicago. James 'Big Jim' Colosimo, the most powerful mobster in the city, ran 'The Outfit', as it was known. His gang of Irish, Italian, Jewish and Greek cohorts controlled the fourteen gangland districts of the city and all of the vice, gambling and labour racketeering. When Al Capone fled Brooklyn in 1919 and came to Chicago, it was to join Colosimo's ranks. Jazz clubs like the Green Mill, where Alice was a regular, were the places where the leading mobsters went to socialize and operate.

Around this time, rumours began to circulate that Alice was stepping out with a good-looking man of Italian descent with a doubtful reputation. The mobster in question has never been named but later in life Alice spoke of him to her friend Margaret Spicer. This unnamed character couldn't have been Al Capone, because he arrived for the first time in Chicago in 1919 (at which point he was newly married to an Irish girl baptized Mary, known as Mae) but there were plenty of other candidates. Whatever the exact identity of this new boyfriend, Uncle Sim and Aunt Tattie were quite naturally alarmed. It was feared that the gang member in question might begin to exert pressure on the wealthy Armour–Chapins. Worse, the sensitive Alice could be dragged into a mire of criminality. Alice was popular with all her relations who felt, quite rightly, that she was vulnerable. What's more, she had recently come into her inheritance and although the exact degree of her wealth is unknown, it is assumed she was worth several million dollars. In order to put some distance between

Alice and the growing scandal, Uncle Sim and Aunt Tattie thought the best course of action was to remove Alice from Chicago for a time. Aunt Tattie had an apartment in Paris so it was decided that Alice should be taken there immediately.

Alice arrived in Paris with Aunt Tattie early in 1920, a few months before her twenty-first birthday. The two women installed themselves in Aunt Tattie's apartment, close to the Bois de Boulogne, at 115 rue de la Pompe, from which Alice could explore the city. Paris had rebounded from the First World War in spectacular style. The cafes of Montparnasse were awash with artists, composers, poets and writers. In the city's bals musettes and nightclubs the strains of the same jazz music that Alice had loved in Chicago could be heard. Alice took to the city immediately. She was young and adventurous, keen to assert herself beyond the limited role established for her by her family. Aunt Tattie had friends who ran a small fashion house called Arnot in rue Saint-Florentin near the place de la Concorde. Alice had always loved dresses and was already showing an excellent eye for fashion, and so Monsieur Arnot employed her as his head manageress in the shop and enlisted her help on buying trips. This was Alice's first job and her first taste of an identity for herself as a woman with her own career and interests. The 1920s were an exciting time to be involved in dress design: these were the inter-war years, a time of regeneration and abundance, and those in the fashion industry were taking full advantage of the new and exuberant mood. Waistlines were dropping, hems were rising, and corsets were being cast off. Alice thoroughly enjoyed the time she spent working at Arnot. During the day she worked, but in the evenings she socialized, eating in the best restaurants, mixing with artists and local celebrities, visiting nightclubs and late-night bars, always dressed exquisitely.

Then, just as Alice began to take flight, she was brought quickly back down to earth. She was about to meet the man she was going to marry.

2

The Countess

In May of 1921, Alice Silverthorne was introduced to Count Frédéric de Janzé in a Paris antique shop. She was nearly twenty-two. Frédéric was twenty-five. The count was tall and good-looking with acutely blue eyes. A sensitive man and an intellectual, he read voraciously, wrote a daily journal, and later published autobiographical works in the guise of fiction. Alice's obvious sense of style and her American manners and accent immediately set her apart from the other women of Frédéric's acquaintance. It is possible that even from their first meeting he detected in her a rare combination of fragility and brazenness that appealed to his romantic nature.

Frédéric was born on 28 February 1896 in Paris, the eldest son of Count François Louis Léon de Janzé and Moya de Janzé, née Hennessy. The family's nobility originated in 1815 when the first Count de Janzé, a lawyer from Brittany, was given his title by Louis XVIII after he helped the Duke de Rohan safeguard his considerable power and wealth in the aftermath of the 1789 revolution. The title was passed down to Frédéric via his uncle, Count Albert de Janzé. Frédéric also had strong American connections on his maternal side. His mother, born Moya Hennessy, was from a well-connected Irish-American family in Connecticut — her own mother was Charlotte Mather, a descendant of Increase Mather, the early American Puritan minister and father of the influential author and minister Cotton Mather. The young Moya had met Count de Janzé on a trip to France and after their marriage the couple settled at the de Janzé ancestral estate, Château Parfondeval, in Normandy. Their two sons, Frédéric and Henri, both inherited the title of Viscount at birth, and after the death of their father in 1921, Frédéric, being the eldest, took on the title of Count.

Frédéric grew up in Paris but attended Cambridge University where he read English literature and discovered a proclivity for writing prose and poetry in English. Thanks to his time as a student, he spoke English with barely a hint of a French accent. He left Cambridge in the early part of the First World War to serve as an officer in the French Air Force. By 1917, he had been appointed aide-de-camp to Maréchal Lyautey in Morocco but after contracting malaria he was sent back to Paris to convalesce. On his return, Frédéric continued to pursue his interests. He frequented literary circles, and developed close friendships with Marcel Proust, Maurice Barrès and Anna de Noailles. He also became romantically involved with an American girl named Ruth Fiske. On 31 March 1918, the *New York Times* reported his engagement to this 23-year-old nurse from New Jersey whom he had met during his stay at the Astoria Hospital in Paris. After much pressure from his mother, who believed that a 'mere' nurse was an unsuitable bride for the viscount, he was persuaded to call off the engagement. Moya de Janzé had clear ambitions for her son. She wanted him to marry well, preferably a wealthy heiress who could help restore the de Janzés' crumbling estate and fortunes.

Moya liked Alice from their first meeting, not only for her money, but also for her style and liveliness. An immediate bond was formed between these two women who spoke the same language and came from the same part of the world. Moya vigorously encouraged Frédéric's courtship of Alice Silverthorne, although it was doubtful that he needed too much persuasion. Frédéric was already smitten with the beautiful American heiress. Alice's enthusiasm for the count was more muted, but she was intrigued. Frédéric was likeable, shy and unassuming but also clever and charming. The new couple complemented one another. She was the poor little rich girl from Chicago; he was the elegant, sophisticated aristocrat from Europe. He was timid, she was bold. She lacked constancy, he provided stability. Both parties were aware that the outside world deemed this to be a 'good match'. He would bring aristocratic credibility to the marriage, while she would provide him with her considerable wealth. But

although there was a degree of affinity between the two –
and certainly a good deal of eagerness on the part of
Frédéric – it seems passion was never a major feature in
their relationship. They were, from the beginning, excellent friends.

With Moya's encouragement, Frédéric pursued Alice in
earnest. He escorted her to restaurants and nightclubs. He
introduced her to members of his aristocratic and literary
French set and met her wealthy American expatriate
crowd in return. During the summer of 1921, Alice
accepted an invitation by her old friends from Chicago, the
Spauldings, to go on a motoring tour in the South of
France. By the time they had reached Biarritz a fortnight
later, Frédéric was waiting there with a marriage proposal.
Alice accepted and wired Aunt Tattie in Chicago with the
news. Alice's aunt was delighted. Like Moya, she agreed
that Frédéric and Alice were an excellent match, evidently
approving of the count's aristocratic credentials. The
engagement was announced on 10 August 1921 in the
Chicago Daily Tribune. 'Interest in the announcement is not
lessened by the fact that it has been expected daily,' it was
reported, 'rumours of the young Viscomte's attachment to
Miss Silverthorne having reached Chicago society some
time ago.'

Aunt Tattie hurried to arrange the wedding, which she
insisted should take place in Chicago. For her part, Alice
was stipulating that she wanted to be married by the end
of September, in only a few weeks' time. It appears that
Alice's haste to marry had less to do with her eagerness to
become Countess de Janzé and more to do with her fear

that she would change her mind. On the one hand she wanted to marry Frédéric as this was her chance to escape from Aunt Tattie and her family. On the other hand, she wasn't in love with Frédéric and she knew it. It is possible that Alice's reaction also had to do with fear of her wedding night. She was most probably a virgin: young girls of Alice's background and upbringing were allowed to be flirtatious and sexy to the point where kissing and heavy petting were permitted, but it went no further. Virginity was prized and essential for marriage, which meant that Alice was almost certainly completely inexperienced. The thought of going to bed with Frédéric may have been extremely alarming to her, especially as she did not find him particularly attractive. On two separate occasions she told Aunt Tattie that she wanted to pull out. Pat Silverthorne, Alice's half sister, remembers Alice's tantrums during this period and poor Aunt Tattie's exasperation as a result.

Alice's trepidation and ambivalence continued, but the engine of the wedding had been set in motion and could not be stopped. In order for Alice – who was Presbyterian – to marry in a Catholic church to a Catholic man, she had to be given Catholic instruction. Father Casey and Father Shannon of East Lakeview, a section of Chicago, carried this out in some haste. Father Casey informed Alice that any children of the union were to become Catholic and they must be baptized as Catholics. By now, the invitations and guest list had been agreed upon, the church was booked and Frédéric and his family were already in New York preparing for their journey to

Chicago. On their arrival, even the aristocratic de Janzés would have been impressed by the vast means of the Armour–Chapins, and by Aunt Tattie's lavishly well-appointed home.

The wedding took place as planned on 21 September 1921 at five in the afternoon at the Church of Our Lady of Mount Carmel in East Lakeview. It was a small but elegant affair. Guests included various Armour–Chapin family members as well as some notable society friends. Alice looked the picture of sophistication in a white satin gown with a court train and bouquet of lilies. Her floor-length veil was made from lace that had been her mother's and was held in place with a band of medieval pearls. The matron of honour was Alice's cousin Lolita Armour, who wore a simple beige gown of satin and a hat of brown velvet. Her two bridesmaids were her cousin Elizabeth Chapin and a friend, Mary Baker. Following the ceremony there was a small reception at Aunt Tattie's lakeside Chicago apartment on Sheridan Road. The event was reported in the *Chicago Daily Tribune* alongside a photograph of the newlyweds. Although Alice looks stunning in her long gown and veil, there is little evidence of the exuberance or radiance that is normally associated with a bride on her wedding day. In fact, Alice looks positively morose.

Although Alice's stepmother, Louise, travelled to Chicago for the occasion, William Silverthorne was not invited to his daughter's wedding. In her father's absence, it was left to Uncle Sim to give Alice away. Did Alice appeal to her Armour–Chapin relatives to allow William to attend? She had long since come of age, and was about to become a newly married women, therefore possessing a newfound degree of independence. She could have requested that he be invited. In fact, there is every possibility that she simply did not want William there. In the coming years, Alice did not attempt a reconciliation with her errant father and it seems that, for whatever reason, William was disinclined to play an active part in his daughter's life. Since his separation from Alice, he had continued with his business interests, experimenting in patenting various inventions including new pour-outs for bottles and ways of treating paper to make it waterproof; he was also instrumental in developing several mining prospects in Canada. Alice and William certainly corresponded during the ensuing years, but they would rarely meet. Their estrangement, if not complete, was effective.

After the wedding Alice and Frédéric spent two weeks at the Armour house on Long Island. There is a photograph of Alice from this time that can still be found in the de Janzé family albums at their ancestral estate, Château Parfondeval, in Normandy. She is sitting cross-legged on a rumpled bed at the house on Long Island wearing nothing but her nightdress, big windowpane reading glasses on her nose. On her face is a look of wry bemusement, an expression that seems to be saying, 'Is that all? What a big fuss over nothing!' If Alice had been at all nervous about marriage and the necessity of entering into a sexual relationship with Frédéric, then her timidity soon turned to disappointment. While Frédéric was clearly very attracted to Alice, his new wife could not return the compliment and in all likelihood, the consummation of their marriage was a tepid affair. Frédéric was an instinctive gentleman, only a little more experienced than his new wife, someone who would never be able to match the powerful masculinity and sexual chemistry Alice later enjoyed with subsequent lovers.

Nonetheless, the newlyweds were about to become very happy travelling companions. They set sail for France on 5 October 1921, en route to Morocco, where they would spend most of the winter. Frédéric had been stationed in North Africa during the war and was keen to show his new wife around. Since the cessation of hostilities, Morocco had begun to be a popular tourist destination and the de Janzés stayed in five-star hotels, visiting the cities of Agadir, Casablanca and Rabat, as well as smaller outlying townships. They wandered through the rabbit-warren streets of the Marrakesh souk, absorbing the sights and smells of saffron, orange flower, almonds, dates, olives, bargaining with the vendors for leather goods, carpets and ceramics. They marvelled at the colourful medieval city of Fez and the historical wonders of Tangiers. They visited the Sarhro Mountains and took a short drive through the Sahara Desert to see the sand dunes in Merzouga where Alice drank mint tea and ate some of the best olives, dates and nuts she had ever tasted. Significantly, Morocco provided Alice with her first experience of Africa: it was during her honeymoon that she first became intoxicated by this vast and diverse continent, its raw energy and the untamed spectacle of its landscapes. The Moroccan trip marked the beginning of a love affair with the continent, a place that was to play both blessed saviour and cruel destroyer in her life.

Upon their return to Paris, Alice discovered that she was pregnant. Both the de Janzés and the Armour–Chapins were delighted with this news, as was Frédéric. It is likely that Alice was more circumspect. She was a young woman with a penchant for freedom and it's highly possible just the idea of motherhood would have made her feel weighted down. There is no doubt that this woman who adored French fashions found the physical changes of pregnancy to be both unpleasant and unbecoming. What's more, she was someone whose own mother had died at an early age. The process of becoming a parent was fraught with unresolved emotion and feelings of loss for Alice. While her new husband and relatives happily made plans for the baby's arrival, Alice retreated, cutting herself off from those around her and from the inevitability of what was about to take place.

For the time being, at least she could distract herself with the matter of where she was going to live. Aunt Tattie had invited the newlyweds to move into her apartment in rue de la Pompe in the fashionable and elegant 16th district. Frédéric's mother, Moya Hennessy, urged them to come to Parfondeval, the de Janzés' country home in Normandy. But Alice and Frédéric were keen to maintain a modicum of autonomy. With Aunt Tattie's help, they opted to pool their resources and buy an apartment of their own in the rue Spontini, not far from the rue de la Pompe. For Alice, Paris was unquestionably the preferred option to Normandy. She had many friends in Paris, knew her way around, there were parties to attend, places to go shopping and a lifestyle to maintain. Despite the fact that she was expecting a baby, she was not yet ready to give up her urban existence for the isolation of the northern French countryside.

Alice's first child, Nolwen Louise Marie Alice, was born in Paris on 20 June 1922. Mother and baby both recovered quickly from the birth. A suitable nanny was found and after only a few weeks of respite, Alice went on with social life in much the same way as she had before Nolwen's arrival. From the beginning, Alice found it difficult to bond with her daughter. After the baby's birth, the dark moods that had first plagued Alice in adolescence returned and she may have blamed motherhood for their re-emergence. No wonder she was keen to step out of her new maternal role, continuing to define herself as a social and independent creature. For Frédéric's part, although he had long suspected that Alice might be somewhat unstable, he had secretly hoped that a child might cure her of her sadnesses. He loved Alice and was determined to support her in whatever she wanted to do, but he was also disappointed to discover that the birth of their first child had failed to revive her spirits. On the contrary, the arrival of Nolwen seemed to have made her more prone to withdrawal, and her estrangement from the baby disappointed him greatly.

As Alice instinctively moved away from the demands of her husband and child, she began spending a great deal of time with her new friend Paula Gellibrand. Born in London in 1898, Paula was a famous society model, described by many of her contemporaries as the most beautiful woman in Europe. Later, Paula became a favourite model for Cecil Beaton, who photographed her many times, emphasizing her Modigliani features and exquisitely slender hands. She was also a muse to the novelist Enid Bagnold, who used her as an inspiration for the eponymous heroine of her novel *Serena Blandish* (1924). Alice first met Paula in Paris in 1921, when Paula had recently become engaged to Cuban-Castilian count Pedro José Isidiro Manuel Ricardo Mones Maury, the Marquis de Casa Maury, otherwise known as Bobby or, less flatteringly, the Cuban Heel. This Bugatti-driving Grand Prix winner lost his fortune during the Wall Street crash, and then later remade it running the Curzon cinema in London. Although no one could quite understand why Paula was marrying the marquis – it seems he had few redeeming qualities – the newly engaged Paula was in Paris to visit friends and to organize her wedding, which ultimately took place in 1923 at St James's Church, Spanish Place, in London.

Paula and Alice quickly became close friends and allies, attending soirées, going to the opera and ballet together, frequenting the best art exhibitions and fashion shows. They were both fun-seekers, naturally adventurous, with a shared tendency for daring and a love of haute couture (Paula went on to become a fashion designer). Both were brunettes, extremely beautiful into the bargain, and their attraction to one another may also have had something to do with the fact that they sensed neither one would ever become jealous of the other. Of all the women in Alice's life, it was Paula who came closest to providing her with a soulmate. Alice attributed much of her recovery after the birth of her daughter to the fact that she could spend so much time with Paula, and so when Paula left Paris for London in January 1923, Alice was bereft.

There was nobody in her immediate group of friends who could replace Paula. For Alice, already ill-at-ease with the roles of countess and mother, Paula's departure triggered another bout of depression. Although the upper echelons of aristocratic Paris might have seemed glamorous at first, such society soon revealed itself to be stultifying in its elitism and formalities. Alice remained close to Frédéric's mother, Moya, but found the rest of her husband's extended family and friends to be cold, forbidding and snobbish. There were rules that had to be followed for the simplest of actions and every social interaction was a complex affair. Alice's French was good, but even so, she spoke with an American accent and was intelligent enough to know when she was being looked down upon. As she struggled to improve her language skills and her knowledge of 'comme il faut', she would have found it exhausting and tedious work.

It was under these circumstances that Frédéric was able to persuade Alice that a spell in the countryside at Parfondeval with her daughter might do her some good. Situated in the heart of Normandy, near the small town of Londinières, the château at Parfondeval had been in the de Janzé family since the mid-seventeenth century (in fact, the house is still in the possession of the de Janzé family). It is spacious and sprawling, with three separate living quarters. The central apartment, where Moya lived, consisted of a series of wide floors connected by a steep staircase. The right pavilion or east wing belonged to Frédéric's brother, and the left pavilion or west wing was Frédéric's birthright and where he kept a small library.

In Normandy Alice found herself at a healthy distance from her social life in Paris and in sympathetic company, at least for the most part. Aunt Tattie had arranged for Edward, her faithful African American butler from Chicago, to go to France and join the staff at Parfondeval. Alice had grown very fond of Edward when she lived with Aunt Tattie as a teenager. He had a quick sense of humour and was a talented magician who frequently performed little conjuring tricks to entertain her. He was also an accomplished photographer and was given his own darkroom at Parfondeval. In later years Edward proved to be a close friend to Alice's two children, both of whom gravitated to him.

Moya de Janzé, the mistress of the house, was a kindly woman who was proving to be an adoring grandmother to Nolwen. Alice had always felt comfortable in the company of her mother-in-law who understood Alice's struggles to adjust to France and the French way of life. As a fellow American who had become a French countess, Moya could help explain exactly what was expected of Alice when it came to etiquette and protocol. Even in this isolated corner of Normandy, manners and traditions were an integral part of daily life and to ignore them would only have caused consternation amongst the staff and neighbours. At Moya's urging, Alice agreed to stop riding her horse astride, as she had done in America, and to ride sidesaddle, on the left side, as was the local custom. Any other method was considered inelegant and unbecoming for a French woman of Alice's status. Alice had been trained from early girlhood to ride sidesaddle and had left and right sidesaddles in her trousseau. She was an able horsewoman and quickly accommodated to European tackle, bridles and riding style.

Riding and hunting were among Alice's greatest pleasures during her stay at Parfondeval. At her husband's estate she was surrounded by miles and miles of open countryside and forests, mostly full of deer and wild boar. When riding, Alice experienced the kind of freedom from her responsibilities that she craved. As a woman with a strong visual sense, she also appreciated the spectacle of the Parfondeval hunts: as many as six elegantly attired huntsmen would ride out equipped with large curling hunting horns and high domed hunting hats. Isolated for the most part from those around her, Alice often found a more natural and satisfying interaction with animals and nature. Throughout her life, she loved to ride and always kept pets. At Parfondeval, she surrounded herself with her four beloved Alsatian dogs. In a photo of the young countess taken in Normandy, she is gazing lovingly and intently at these large and wolf-like creatures. Even with her animals for solace, however, Alice soon grew restless in the countryside. After three years in France, Alice still spoke with a heavy accent and often complained to Moya and Frédéric that the servants at Parfondeval were laughing at her behind her back.

What's more, Alice had a new sister-in-law with whom to contend. Shortly after Nolwen's birth in June of 1922,

Frédéric's younger brother, Henri de Janzé, had married an English beauty called Phyllis Boyd. Unable to afford a place of their own in Paris or London, the newlyweds had since taken up residence at Parfondeval, occupying the east wing of the château, sharing the grounds with the other members of the household. Henri was twenty at the time of the wedding and Phyllis was twenty-eight. Born in London in 1894, Phyllis was the daughter of Lady Lilian Boyd and the granddaughter of the second Earl of Munster on her mother's side. Her father, W.A.E. Boyd, had been a captain in the Life Guards. Phyllis could also boast that she was the great-great-granddaughter of the beautiful Dorothea Bland (better known by her stage name Mrs Jordan), the long-time mistress of King William IV. In other words, Phyllis possessed the exact kind of aristocratic pedigree that Alice, as an American, lacked. There is no doubt that Alice perceived Phyllis's appearance at Parfondeval as a threat. Phyllis was five years older than Alice. She was intellectual and cultivated, having studied art at the Slade School in London, where she had shown impressive talent. The writer Osbert Sitwell later commented on Phyllis's 'artistic ability' and 'unusual personal charm and distinction'. The novelist Barbara Cartland, who witnessed her dancing at London's Embassy Club in the early 1920s, noted her 'mysterious, haunting beauty', her 'high cheekbones and pale aquamarine eyes' as well as her 'violent temper'. The artist Dora Carrington, who fell in love with Phyllis during her time at the Slade – and who visited her at Parfondeval towards the end of 1922 – found her 'dazzling', 'like a grand Persian whore with a scarlet mouth'.

In other words, Alice's place in the de Janzé family had been somewhat usurped by this impressive new arrival from England and inevitably there was some competition and tension between the sisters-in-law. Alice was ahead of the game slightly because she had produced a child by the middle of 1922, and this placed her in good stead with the family-conscious de Janzés. But in the background, there was a rumble of sniping from Phyllis's side. It seems that Phyllis found Alice to be intellectually bereft and childishly moody. It is true that Alice would rather be outdoors than in a library, but it is still worth noting that throughout her life she managed to hold her own with a string of intellectual men and women. As for her moods, these were by no means predictable, and so it is no surprise that Phyllis, who was from a more reserved English background, would have found them unseemly. Above all, Phyllis was bold, confident and upper class, therefore much more at home in the gentrified world of the de Janzés. Phyllis regularly sneered at Alice's 'gauche' and 'American' behaviour and frequently joined in mocking her French and her refusal to learn the codes of conduct befitting a countess. It was at this time that Phyllis and Henri began referring to Alice as 'La Negresse'. This strange tease may have had something to do with Alice's hair, which was naturally very curly. Or it may have originated from the haughty European assumption that all old white American families had once employed slaves and therefore were likely to have African ancestors somewhere along the line. The rumour that Alice had black blood – as propagated by Henri and Phyllis – was one that stuck. Years later, Alice's grandson,

Guillaume de Rougemont, remembers that Henri de Janzé's daughter Solange believed that Alice was a 'negresse', and that consequently her cousin Guillaume de Rougemont must have 'a touch of the tar brush'.

For some months during Alice's stay at Parfondeval, there was much backstabbing between the two women. Finally, a truce was reached after it became apparent that they shared a passion for haute couture. Alice and Phyllis even put aside their animosity for long enough to talk about the idea of going into business together. They spoke of starting a little boutique in Paris, recognizing in one another the qualities that would be needed for a successful business venture – Phyllis had the flair while Alice had the contacts and money to make it work. The boutique never materialized and so we can only imagine what owning a business might have done for Alice's sense of worth and independence during this period of her life. She had loved working for Arnot as a young woman in Paris and had benefited greatly from the feelings of usefulness and satisfaction an occupation can bring. Now, Alice found herself in Parfondeval, far from Paris, without direction, bored and unfulfilled. It was in this frame of mind that she allowed Frédéric to persuade her that a second child might be the answer to her problems.

Alice named the new baby Paola, after her friend Paula, whom she still missed terribly. Paola Marie Jeanne was born on 1 June 1924. Once again, Alice fell into an prolonged depression soon after the birth. This was not an easy time for Alice and there was little anybody could do to help. For his part, Frédéric had learned to forgive his wife's bouts of sadness and inertia, especially as these were followed by bursts of marked vivacity, giving him the impression that she had completely recovered. But then the dark moods would return again. It is likely that members of Frédéric's family regularly wished that Alice would simply snap out of her introspection, assuming she was simply lazy, selfish, or even heartless, particularly when she failed to bond with her daughters. Certainly, her relationship with Frédéric suffered as a result of her shifting moods. While Frédéric pursued his intellectual life, confining himself to his books, his library and his literary friends, Alice was lonely. Motherhood simply held no real interest for her. Instead of bringing her a degree of fulfilment, her duties to her two daughters only made her feel trapped in a role for which she felt unsuited.

The cyclothymia, which Alice almost certainly suffered from, is a strain of bipolar syndrome that can often develop into full-blown manic depression later in life. Her moods and frequently erratic behaviour reflected the classic symptoms of the disease: sufferers undergo periods of mild but often debilitating depression alternating with periods of high spirits and irritability. It is estimated that a quarter of those afflicted attempt suicide at some point in their lives, as Alice had done as a teenager. The term 'cyclothymia' was coined as early as 1877, but it was only much later, in the latter part of the twentieth century, that effective medications for stabilizing its symptoms were developed. It is highly likely that if Alice had lived in the present day, she would have been given the drugs she needed to alleviate her moods, thereby drastically altering the shape of her life. However, in 1925, no such treatments existed. To make matters worse, in the course of her time at Parfondeval, Alice had begun having frequent bronchial attacks brought on by lingering consumption, a condition with which her mother had also struggled.

Ever dutiful, Frédéric remained hopeful that another change of scene would help. He began to make plans to take Alice away, to Africa, a place that he hoped would lift her spirits completely.

3

Kenya

By the autumn of 1925, Alice was suffering from both physical and emotional problems: she was plagued by her bronchitis and what can best be described as an ingrained depression. In an effort to cure his wife of her difficulties, Frédéric decided to take Alice to Kenya in what was then British Colonial East Africa, where he hoped the balmy climate and high altitudes would help alleviate Alice's troubles. The African trip was to be a mutually beneficial arrangement. Frédéric was an avid traveller and hunter. In Kenya he would have ample opportunity to satisfy his interest in exotic locations and passion for shooting. Alice, meanwhile, could look forward to discovering another corner of the fascinating continent she had first encountered during her honeymoon in

Morocco. In Kenya, Frédéric reminded her, she would be able to ride for miles under wide-open skies, surrounded by herds of wild and exotic animals.

What's more, the de Janzés would be staying with friends who would provide the perfect antidote to the stuffy confines of French society. Frédéric and Alice had an invitation to visit Josslyn Hay, the future Lord Erroll, and his new wife Lady Idina, at their home in Kenya's Wanjohi Valley. Joss and Idina had first met the de Janzés in Paris in 1923, at which time both couples were only recently married. The Hays were a striking pair, two people whose reputations preceded them. Joss was an Etonian who had been expelled from the school, and whose diplomat father had taken him away to Berlin as an honorary attaché, in the hope that his son might still enter the Foreign Office. Although stationed in Berlin, Joss found London and Paris far more amusing and often neglected his duties in a continuing quest for fun and women. It was in Paris that he met Frédéric and Alice. Joss was tall and attractive with pale-blond hair and an air of swagger about him which came, in part, from an innate belief in his own superiority: his ancestors could be traced to the fourteenth century and, as the heir to the earldom of Erroll, he would also inherit the hereditary title of High Constable of Scotland. Despite his illustrious heritage, however, there was a wildness to Joss: he was a natural womanizer, without respect for rules, regulations, or husbands in particular.

When Joss first met Lady Idina (née Sackville) in London in 1922, she was still married to her second husband, Charles Gordon. The daughter of the eighth Earl de la Warr, she was something of a femme fatale, even by present-day standards. She had married her first husband, Euan Wallace, in 1913, an arrangement that didn't prevent her from carrying on numerous affairs. Attractive, witty and liberated – with the kind of slender frame that suited 1920s fashions for loose, sheath-like silk dresses – Idina was renowned for her skills at seducing (and then often abandoning) men. When Nancy Mitford came to write her satire of the British upper classes, *The Pursuit of Love* (1945), it was Lady Idina who served as the model for the heroine's mother, a woman who 'ran away so often, and with so many different people, that she became known to her family and friends as the Bolter'. Joss and Idina's union sparked a cause célèbre in London – the already disreputable Lady marrying a much younger soon-to-be Lord. In a photograph published on the cover of the *Tatler*, they are the picture of louche happiness, Idina in a flowing Grecian shift and barefoot, and Joss in snazzily patterned pyjamas.

Although there was doubtless a frisson of attraction between Alice and Joss upon first meeting, for the time being, it went no further. Alice was newly married and either pregnant or recovering from her pregnancies during the period of their first meetings. By early 1924, Joss and Idina recognized that they were on the verge of becoming society outcasts due to their scandalous union, so they decided to leave for Kenya, where Idina had lived for a time with husband number two. In the spring of 1924, they took up residence in the Wanjohi Valley, in the Kenyan highlands. Such a highly sociable couple might have felt isolated in the wilds of East Africa, but in fact the opposite was true. As soon as they arrived, they began sending out invitations to friends from Europe to come and visit. The de Janzés were high on the list of invitees.

In the early part of 1925, Frédéric started to make plans for the trip. He made enquiries as to how best to travel; on which boat line and by which route; he bought clothes, licences, weapons for shooting expeditions, and arranged for the necessary typhoid injections. The de Janzés decided to leave their daughters Nolwen and Paola in the safe hands of Frédéric's mother, Moya, ably assisted by Alice's Aunt Tattie. Paola was just fifteen months old; Nolwen was three years old. At such tender ages, they could not have understood that their mother was being taken away for the sake of her health or that both parents would be gone for such a long period of time. Alice and Frédéric planned to stay in Kenya for two months, with another two months factored in for travel there and back. If Alice was sad to bid farewell to her daughters, she also knew she had been given a reprieve. Here was her chance to escape from her responsibilities as a mother and as a countess. Together with Frédéric, she was eager to begin this new adventure.

In 1925, the journey from Paris to Mombasa took a little over a month. The de Janzés flew from Le Bourget airport in Paris to Marseilles in September 1925, having sent their cabin trunks ahead by rail. On the 17th of September, they set sail from Marseilles on the SS *Gascon*, a 28-year-old, single-funnelled vessel of the French Messageries Maritimes line. The ship housed seventy-eight first-class cabins, two of which were of a superior variety. The de Janzés had one of these; it was located on the preferred port (left) side, where passengers could gaze out on the coasts of France and then Italy. In her teenage years before the Great War, Alice had crossed the Atlantic from New York to Cherbourg on the *Aquitania*, the magnificent Cunard luxury liner popular with wealthy Americans making their way to France. By contrast, a working vessel like the SS *Gascon* must have come as something of a shock. Although the de Janzés dined at the captain's table, they would have felt they had little in common with their fellow passengers.

The ship passed Monaco, then San Remo at breakfast time. At Genoa there was time to go ashore for a drive before returning to dine on board. By the evening of the fifth day, the captain steered to the port side so that the more privileged passengers could see from their cabins the island of Stromboli, with its active volcano sending luminous red sparks of lava into the night skies. The *Gascon* navigated the Straits of Messina where temperatures began to rise. In the evenings, a small band played on board and Alice danced. Three days after leaving the Straits of Messina, they arrived at Port Said, where Egyptian 'Gully Gully' men, or conjurors, came on board to entertain the passengers. After the ship docked at Port Said, Alice and Frédéric went ashore to shop at Simon Artz, the famous department store, and to take tea at the Casino Hotel, re-embarking in time to leave at midnight en route for the Suez Canal. At Suez, the *Gascon* stopped for a half-day in order to off-load cargo. Alice and Frédéric would have looked down at the docks to see legions of completely naked ebony-skinned Sudanese labourers with massive halos of curly black hair ('Fuzzy Wuzzies' in the colonial lingo of the time). The passage through the canal took eight hours and was eerily calm after so many days at sea. Passengers aboard the *Gascon* would have appreciated the respite from the rolling of the ship as they contemplated Ferdinand de Lesseps's miracle of engineering. By now it was hot, with temperatures reaching 90 degrees Fahrenheit. In a time before air-conditioning, everyone cooled themselves with cabin fans. Games were organized on deck. Four days after Suez, the Gascon arrived at Aden. Most people preferred to stay on board since the only place to visit was the neighbouring port of Crater, a prospect which seemed daunting due to the heat. One more dress dinner and dance and five more days later they were through to the Indian Ocean.

The *Gascon* was bound for Mombasa. This lush island, connected to the mainland of Africa by a precarious-looking causeway, has its main port at Kilindini. As the ship approached its final destination, the view of Kilindini harbour would have been stunning: an ancient Portuguese fort, clusters of palm trees, hundreds of black porters, some in red fez hats, and Thomas Cook agents in sharp peaked caps thronging the harbour. After disembarking, Alice and Frédéric were reunited with their luggage and taken by rickshaw to the main railway station only half a mile away. The Mombasa railway station of 1925 was a basic construction: a simple facade with the station sign; then another notice indicated 'upper class passengers and luggage'. Just inside the station gates there were lists posted with each carriage number and the names of the occupants. The de Janzés' train left Mombasa station at four thirty in the afternoon to the sounds of applause and cheers from the platform and carriages. The engine pulled out across the causeway heading towards the mainland, then moved uphill through coconut plantations and mango trees, the elevation increasing incrementally with each mile.

This was the famous 'Lunatic Line' – the legendary railway built between 1895 (the first year of British rule in the Kenyan Protectorate) and 1901. Stretching from Mombasa on the east coast across nearly 600 miles to the shores of Lake Victoria in the west, the railway had first been proposed by the Imperial British East Africa Company but had been bedevilled by political controversy from the start. Back in London, there were questions about its cost (£5 million, about £450 million in today's money) and if there was actually any real need for it. Those in favour argued that the line would be a strategic move for the new British colony, a counterbalance to the imperial expansion being undertaken by the Germans in East Africa. Opponents argued that the line was a folly, built to prove the extent of British might and engineering ability rather than in response to a measurable need. The British radical politician Henry Labouchère dubbed the project the 'Lunatic Line', insisting that the railway was completely without purpose. The crux of his argument was that it crossed many hundreds of miles of completely empty and unoccupied lands en route to nowhere. His scathing poem about the project goes as follows:

What will it cost no words can express
What is its object no brain can suppose
Where it will start from no-one can guess
Where it is going to nobody knows.

What is the use of it none can conjecture
What it will carry there's none can define
And in spite of George Curzon's superior lecture
It is clearly naught but a lunatic line

The majority disagreed with Labouchère and building went ahead, continuing apace over a period of five and a half years. In the words of Albert Thomas Matson, who went on to become the health inspector for the Colonial Service in Kenya, this was 'the most courageous railway in the world' and along with the Orient Express and the Trans-Siberian Express, the Lunatic Line provided one of the world's great train journeys. Never before had a railway crossed such varied and often perilous terrain, spanning jungle, desert, mountains, plains, forest and swamplands, climbing from the coast to around 8,000 feet above sea level. Thirty-two thousand Indian workers were shipped in from the Subcontinent to lay its tracks, many of whom died of heatstroke and tropical diseases or were devoured by man-eating lions during construction. The track itself was only one metre wide and mostly single track to help facilitate the steepness of the climb. Thirty-five viaducts and one hundred and twenty bridges and culverts had to be built before it reached its end.

Wood-burning steam engines were British-made UR

35s, the type also used in India: they belched black smoke and frequent stops were required in order to refill their boilers with water. Despite this, well-to-do first-class passengers who boarded such trains in 1925 were treated with ample care. Alice and Frédéric dined in a grass-roofed hut after disembarking at Voi, some 150 miles uphill from Mombasa. Waiters were white-clad stewards from Goa, in India, who served up a menu of tinned salmon, meatballs, fruit and custard, and, for the first course, brown Windsor soup. (This beef and vegetable broth was very popular in Victorian and Edwardian times, especially on the railways, and was often said to have built the British Empire.) During dinner, attendants would carry the bedding into the carriages in order to make up the beds. On rejoining their carriage, Alice and Frédéric would have gone to their berth, closed their mosquito nets and opened their windows so as to enjoy the cool air coming in from the plains. First-class berths were comfortable, in the circumstances, and designed to accommodate two people, with private WCs and a small basin. Second-class berths were large, open affairs and could sleep four. Third-class carriages had simple slatted wooden benches and no beds at all. In 1925, the axles of the passenger carriages would have been badly sprung, causing an immense jolt each time the train's wheels hit a gap in the rail. The joke went that couples honeymooning in Kenya would never forget their time in one of the berths of the Lunatic Line.

During such a bumpy ride, sleep would have come fitfully if at all. Alice and Frédéric may have deliberately tried to stay awake, eager to see signs of wildlife from the window. Even so, the almost total blackness of the African night would have prevented any sightings. As the passengers dozed in their berths and seats, the train climbed through forest and red rock to the great plain that slopes from 1,000 feet above sea level to 6,000 feet at the foot of the Kenyan highlands. At Makindu, Alice and Frédéric joined their fellow passengers in an outdoor refreshment room for breakfast. Porridge, eggs and bacon and tea were the standard fare. By the time they returned to the train, dawn was breaking and the engine resumed its pace towards the Athi River. At six in the morning when the sun rose, Alice and Frédéric would have shared the delight of witnessing herds of giraffe, antelope, zebra and perhaps even elephants moving across the vast plains. At twelve thirty in the afternoon the train arrived at Nairobi Station, some 329 miles from Mombasa. Looking down at their clothes, Alice and Frédéric saw they were covered in a thin layer of red dust blown from the burnished rocks en route. They would have felt immensely weary from the journey and the thin air at such an altitude would have only added to their tiredness. By arrangement, no one was there to meet them. They knew that their friend Joss Hay would contact them later in the day at Nairobi's Norfolk Hotel, a favourite meeting place for Kenya's expatriate settlers and visitors. So they took two rickshaws and went to the Norfolk for hot baths. The Lunatic Line had delivered them to Nairobi twenty-four hours after their departure from Mombasa.

In 1907, after Winston Churchill returned from his visit to East Africa as Undersecretary of State for the Colonies, he brought back news of the line. He was impressed by it, describing it as 'one of the most romantic and wonderful railways in the world', and adding, 'The railway is already doing what it was never expected within any reasonable period to do, it is paying its way.' Indeed, by the time of Churchill's visit, the railway *had* begun to pay for itself. In a bid to justify the line's existence, the Commissioner for East Africa, Sir Charles Eliot, had invited settlers from the British colonies to farm the land surrounding the newly founded railway town of Nairobi. In this way, it would be possible to say the railway was serving the purpose of connecting these farmers and their goods with the coast, thereby silencing those critics who questioned the line's practical purpose. In other words, the British had built the line and then come up with a reason for its existence. Recruitment of farmers began in 1901 and the first pioneers started to arrive in 1903. They came from as far away as Canada and New Zealand, as well as from Great Britain, and although many from the British contingent were aristocrats, the majority were middle-class men and women who faced the enormous odds of farming this uncharted territory with little capital but great tenacity.

After the end of the First World War, a second wave of European settlers – made up mostly of ex-servicemen – arrived to farm the land and to help swell the numbers of whites in the area. The colony's foothold seemed assured and by the early 1920s, the settlers had established their own Parliament and Legislative Council. It was at this juncture that the early pioneers started to sit back and enjoy the fruits of their labours. They began to build large stone houses for themselves, with verdant lawned gardens and airy verandahs. They employed local servants to tend to their properties and staff their kitchens. This was the era of the 'English squires established on the equator', as Evelyn Waugh described them, and these moneyed residents were determined to translate the English way of life to Africa. Servants were taught how to be 'proper' butlers and chambermaids, how to lay tables with polished silver in the correct manner, and to serve and cook imitations of English cuisine. Meanwhile, their masters played polo, tennis and croquet, and held luncheons and tea parties. There was now an impressive level of comfort to the lives of the colonial settlers in Kenya.

Wealthy socialite travellers had begun to come to Kenya for adventure, romance and safaris, and many of them decided to stay. The undisputed ringleaders of this small but decadent new circle were the de Janzés' friends, Joss and Idina. As part of Idina's divorce settlement with her former husband, she had inherited 2,500 acres of farmland in the Wanjohi Valley north of Gilgil. The Hays had built a house on the land, calling it Slains after the Erroll family home in Scotland (sold by Joss's predecessor, the profligate nineteenth Earl of Erroll). Here, Idina began to throw house parties for visiting friends and local socialites. The flow of cocktails only served to fuel natural highs brought on by the extreme altitude of the highlands. Far from home, the Hays and their clique of friends found themselves freed from the restrictions of their families and society. Repressions were cast aside with abandon. Idina's parties would often last for days at a time and it was even rumoured that – at the hostess's insistence – every guest would have to sleep with someone other than the person they had arrived with before the party could finish. This liberated atmosphere was to give rise to the name 'Happy Valley'. It was also the heady realm which Alice and Frédéric were about to enter.

Joss arrived to meet his guests at the Norfolk Hotel on 25 October 1925. The three friends were reunited at the hotel's door, excited to be meeting again so far away from Paris. They would have spoken in a mixture of French and English. Joss explained he had left Idina behind at their home for a very good reason. She was pregnant and the journey to Nairobi was bumpy and arduous. Joss was driving his brand-new, 1922 model, long-bodied, open-top Hispano Suiza, a wedding present from Idina. It was a car of enormous power with an engine having six cylinders in line, a single overhead cam, and over 6 litres in capacity. The car's massive, semi-elliptic front and rear suspension had been designed to cope with rough Spanish roads, making the car ideal for the challenges of the steep and rutted Kenyan byways. Practicalities aside, there would have been few cars more glamorous than Joss's in 1920s Nairobi, its bonnet topped by a flying stork, 'La Cigogne Volante'. The man behind the wheel of the Suiza would have been just as imposing, his blond hair ruffled from the drive, his skin tanned from the Africa sun, and his body clad in a well-cut safari suit.

Joss had brought with him a Ford box-body car, a backup to the Suiza, driven by a Somali driver who carried a spear. The following morning after an early breakfast,

Joss's servant loaded up the two cabin trunks on the Ford. Joss, Frédéric and Alice climbed into the front bench seat of the Suiza. It would have been characteristic for Joss to insist that Alice sat in the middle between the two men, ensuring she was thigh to thigh with him for the journey to Wanjohi. The gear handle and handbrake of the car were to the right of the driver (who also sat on the right), so there was nothing to come between Alice and her attentive host. Joss set off at high speed, his preferred tempo. The roads leading out of Nairobi at this time were made of murram, a degraded stone gravel dug from nearby quarries that was crushed, then spread and rolled, making for a dusty ride, especially when going so fast. The Suiza quickly scaled the Kikuyu Escarpment, some 6,000 feet up and 20 miles from the city. Here, a heart-stopping sight awaited the travellers. Looking down from the precipice, Alice and Frédéric could see below them the sheer drop of the Great Rift Valley. This continental divide, a literal rift through the heart of Africa, stretches 4,000 miles from Mozambique to Northern Syria, and is one of the true marvels of the world. Herds of wild game roam the valley floor which is dotted with defunct miniature volcanoes, including Longanot or Mount Margaret and the double-headed Suswa (described by H. Rider Haggard in *King Solomon's Mines* as the 'Twin Bosoms of Cleopatra'). It would have been an exhilarating prospect for Alice and Frédéric, who had only recently left behind them the tightly gridded streets and boulevards of Paris.

Next the Suiza began the descent to the bottom of the valley. Driving downhill at such an incline was enough to put an enormous strain on any car. The Suiza's brakes, although powerful, would have burned out had Joss not shifted into second gear to brake his descent. The engine grew hot, and at the bottom of the decline, Joss refilled the radiator with water from the stream that crossed the road, fed by a shaded spring. Next, he raced across the road heading to the right turn that would take them back uphill towards Gilgil and the Wanjohi Valley. Again, the climb was steep on a road that was rougher and dustier than the rest, so that by the end of the drive, a fine layer of red murram dust covered all three passengers. Alice wore a hat, but even so, her hair was thick with red specks. Joss, ever attentive and gracious to women, especially a woman as wealthy and beautiful as Alice, reassured his guest that Idina had brought a French lady's maid to Kenya and that she would wash and dress Alice's hair for dinner that evening.

Everything was conspiring to intoxicate Alice: the hot sun, the high altitude, the breathtaking views, the glamour of riding in the Suiza next to this attractive and confident Englishman. The two cars sped down the private road to Kipipiri, overlooked on the left by the Aberdare Mountains, before sweeping into the drive of Joss and Idina's farm. Idina was waiting for them, dressed casually yet elegantly in trousers and a blouse, her preferred outfit while in Kenya. The whole household had turned out to meet the new houseguests: the No. 1 houseman, a cook, a kitchen 'toto' (Swahili for child) and a 'dhobi' (washerman), as well as the French maid Marie, who immediately took to Alice when she heard her speak

French. The house, which had been built to Idina's specification in 1923, had four bedrooms with bathrooms, an elegant drawing room with a large raised fireplace, a dining room and an office. The rooms were fitted out with imported antique English furniture, old silver, leather-bound books and grand family portraits of Idina's and Joss's mothers.

But the feature that would have impressed Alice the most would have been Idina's bathroom, which was adjacent to the master bedroom. It was ten feet by eight feet and made of green travertine marble. Hot water was piped in from three 44-gallon drums heated by a log fire outside the bathroom. The water was somewhat discoloured by the local iron and murram sediment, but it was refreshing and stimulating. Idina was in the habit of taking a bath before dinner, wallowing in steaming water with a cocktail in hand while holding forth for dinner guests who were invited to join her as she bathed, in the nude, of course. The bath ceremony was just one of the many unconventional rituals at Slains. Another custom was that of dining in pyjamas and a dressing gown. Alice had no pyjamas, but she found a pair laid out neatly on her bedroom pillow by Marie. Dinner was usually late – around eleven at night – but in deference to Alice and Frédéric's long journey it is likely that it was served earlier that first evening. The African cook had been well taught by Marie and could manage cheese soufflé and *oeuf en cocotte* and there was champagne to celebrate the de Janzés' arrival. Despite the prevalence of French wine and food, Alice would have felt herself as far away as possible from the formalities of Parfondeval and Paris.

The following day, Alice and Frédéric had their first sighting by daylight of Slains and its surrounding landscape. It has often been observed that the Kenyan highlands are reminiscent of the English and Scottish countryside – albeit on an epic scale. When the one-time editor of the *East African Standard*, George Kinnear, later visited Wanjohi, he, like so many visitors before and since, found himself in thrall to the landscape. His description of the valley gives an idea of the sight of the Aberdare Mountains that awaited Alice and Frédéric when they awoke that morning:

Every morning it takes the sun well nigh two hours to climb over the Aberdares and paint this valley with its rays and chase away the dew that cheats the drought. Many times I have stood shivering at dawn and watched the grey curtain of fading night lifted from the valley. The Aberdares stand like black bastions against the sun. Pockets of grey mist hide and reveal in turn. Here and there wisps of blue smoke rise lazily from hut and homestead. A silvery light steals down from the sky, but away over the Rift Valley the sky is already orange and yellow and a little pink. Suddenly the orchestra of the countryside plays the song of dawn and a dark hilltop is lit by a shaft of light. Even the streams run more noisily, chasing over the stones and leaping recklessly down the mountainside. Weirdly the light changes from silver to soft gold as the sun relentlessly climbs up the mountain; and then soars over the mountain ridge and restores all the colour to the flowers and the trees and to every living thing. Here is a lovely garden radiant with masses of flowers: there are several ponds and water always running back to the mountain stream from whence man had led it higher up the valley.

That morning, Alice and Frédéric were indeed treated to views of rolling hills layered in early-morning mists, the mountain peak of Kipipiri rising from the clouds, a great waterfall in the distance, and dense forests of cedar. Breakfast would have included porridge and fresh cream from a nearby dairy. Joss and Idina were intent on owning their own dairy, and were breeding Guernsey cattle to enable them to do so. After breakfast, Alice and Frédéric participated in another Slains ritual – the early-morning ride. Together with Joss, they rode out on three Somali ponies, with Idina staying at home due to her pregnancy. Although in France Alice had been forced to ride on the left side, in Kenya she was free to ride astride. These early-morning rides would have thrilled her: the beauty of the vistas, the unpopulated landscape, the sense of breadth and possibility, and above all the chance to see wild animals at close proximity. When she spied monkeys gambolling in the trees, she expressed a longing to own one as a pet. Joss and Frédéric duly obtained a tame monkey and gave it to her. Alice christened him Roderigo and he seldom left her side; she carried him shoulder high everywhere she went.

Alice would have cut a striking figure in Kenya, monkey at her ear. True to form, she had brought with her a sophisticated collection of Paris fashions and shoes, which she continued to wear, especially whenever she visited Nairobi. At Slains, however, she began to sport the cord trousers and loose blouses preferred by Idina. Like Coco Chanel, who had already shocked French society by wearing men's clothes, Idina and Alice carried off their masculine look with immense elegance. Alice also had several sets of khaki safari outfits made for her by Ahmed the tailor in Nairobi to her own design, complete with wide-brimmed hats and calf-high leather mosquito boots to protect her ankles from bites. Alice probably wore her boots only when visiting lower altitudes, however, as mosquitos generally cannot survive Wanjohi Valley's cold nights and high altitudes.

During their stay, Idina would take Frédéric and Alice by car to the nearby town of Gilgil to collect their mail. Letters from Aunt Tattie and Frédéric's mother, Moya, were soon arriving care of the Post Office filled with news about the children. Alice would write back, regaling the children with tales of her morning rides and the beauty of the African countryside. She described for them the scurrying warthogs and how they would suddenly stop, their tails sticking straight up in the air. She told them about the sweet little dik-dik (tiny antelope with cloven feet) and about the monkeys, especially Roderigo. But despite her eagerness to communicate with her family in France, the truth was that Alice was relieved to be away. She had never been comfortable in her role as a mother. As a child, she had been abandoned, once as a result of her mother's death, and again when she was removed from her father.

On some level, she must have been very comfortable with the idea of her children being cared for by Aunt Tattie — after all, this had been her own experience as a child.

The de Janzés remained in Kenya for three months, a month longer than originally planned. During that time they met most of the key players in Kenya's white settler community. Alice's charm and good looks captivated many. One of her most important social conquests was Hugh Cholmondeley, third Baron Delamere, known to everyone as 'D'. Thirty years her senior, the baron took a shine to Alice's beauty and her deep-voiced, American drawl. He also liked the fact that she was able to hold her drink, quaffing brandy and soda or pink gin with ease. Acceptance by D counted for a lot in the colonial community of the 1920s. Lord Delamere was the undisputed leader of the Kenyan settlers. He had arrived in Kenya in 1901, plunging his considerable personal wealth and energies into 100,000 acres of land near Njoro and encouraging his aristocratic friends in England to join him. Delamere, like his fellow settlers of all classes, had many setbacks in the beginning, particularly with the cattle he had imported, which quickly caught diseases and died. Over time, he learned to dip his herds to protect them from flies. He also mastered the art of growing wheat, employing a horticulturalist to develop a new variety of grain that would withstand local conditions. He began ranging his sheep on the edge of the Kinangop (a lower ridge of the plateau en route to the Wanjohi Valley) where conditions were clement and where his flocks soon thrived. D's tireless experimentation in farming often brought him to the brink of bankruptcy, but the wisdom of his experiences, which he shared with the other farmers in the area, is the reason that a colony flourished in the highlands at all. Later, when the settlers needed to defend themselves against the restrictive regulations of colonial officialdom, it was D who led the charge.

So much has been written about the Happy Valley crowd and their penchant for parties that it can come as something of a surprise to discover that most of its members were actually extremely diligent farmers, Joss and Idina included. At the time of Alice's arrival in Africa, Joss was meeting regularly with leading ranchers and farmers, such as D and Sir Francis Scott, seeking to learn from their long experience. Scott, the second son of the Duke of Buccleuch, was another Englishman who was instrumental in establishing effective farming techniques in the highlands. A former Coldstream Guards officer, he had arrived in Kenya with the wave of ex-servicemen settlers after the war, building himself a magnificent home called Deloraine near Nanyuki. Together with D, he was only too delighted to help a fellow old Etonian such as Joss establish himself in the valley.

Alice got to know the other farmers in the area. On her morning rides she came upon a Tudor-style house, Satima Farm, named after one of the Aberdare peaks, just to the south of Slains. The house belonged to Geoffrey Buxton, who farmed the surrounding 2,500 acres. Geoffrey Charles Buxton had been born in Thorpe, Norwich in 1879. He was a close friend of Denys Finch Hatton, the adventurer who was immortalized by Karen Blixen in *Out of Africa* (1937). Both Buxton and Finch Hatton had attended Eton, like so many of the settlers, Delamere and Joss included. Buxton had first arrived in Kenya in 1910 but when the Great War commenced, he returned to the UK and obtained a commission in the Coldstream Guards in 1916 and was awarded a territorial decoration after being mentioned in dispatches. On his return to Kenya, he devoted himself to farming. In fact, it was Buxton who had first lured Finch Hatton to the area, telling his friend that he had discovered 'Shangri La on the equator'. Unlike Idina, who entertained in pyjamas, socializing at Buxton's was a much more formal, black-tie affair, in the style of an English country mansion. Although he later married, at the time of Alice's arrival in Africa Geoffrey was still a bachelor, albeit rather a serious one.

Other immediate neighbours included the Honourable David Leslie-Melville, the second son of the Earl of Leven and Melville, and his wife, Mary, the granddaughter of Lord Portman. The Leslie-Melvilles were married in 1919 and arrived in Kenya soon afterwards, farming 5,000 acres. Their house was a broad and rambling affair, decorated in the English fashion with antiques, silver, family portraits and even a grand piano. Then there was Bill Delap and his wife, Bubbles, who owned Rayetta, a small pyrethrum farm. Pyrethrum was a valuable new crop and a natural pesticide grown by many of the farmers in the area, Idina included. Bill was a jealous and difficult man whose first wife – according to rumour – 'messed around with the troops'. After he married Bubbles he built a drawbridge around his house and threatened to shoot unannounced visitors. The Delaps kept themselves to themselves, and the Happy Valley set were evidently perfectly in step with this arrangement.

Thanks to Alice's friendship with Lord Delamere the de Janzés were also getting to know the crowd that gathered at the exclusive Muthaiga Club in Nairobi. The club had been founded by a group of settlers who had wanted somewhere to socialize away from the existing Nairobi Club, a place where they were likely to run into government officials with whom they were often at war. The new club opened on New Year's Eve 1913, with D as its first president, and soon gained a loyal and elite membership. Well-bred settlers were drawn like moths to the magnificent Muthaiga, its cellar filled with fine French wines, its well-appointed rooms offering comfort and elegance, along with the opportunity to socialize with friends over an infinite number of cocktails. Race weeks took place twice a year, at Christmas and in midsummer, during which times the Muthaiga overflowed with revellers — balls were held every evening, with members dressed to the nines, and the dancing lasted until dawn. Alice and Frédéric had been made temporary members of Muthaiga soon after their arrival, ensuring that they found themselves at the very centre of colonial social life. Full membership would follow by virtue of D's backing.

For the last two months of the de Janzés' stay in Kenya, Frédéric hired a Ford car so that they would be able to drive to the Muthaiga and explore the surrounding area without relying on Idina or Joss to chauffeur them around. It was on one of their regular visits to Nairobi that they were introduced to Roy and Margaret Spicer, a couple recently arrived from Ceylon. English-born Roy was serving as the Commissioner of Police for Kenya. His new wife was American and had a 9-year-old daughter from a previous marriage. Frédéric was delighted to strike up a friendship with the Kenyan Head of Police, but the strongest bond was between Alice and Margaret. Alice found she had much in common with this well-dressed 32-year-old mother: like Alice, Margaret was from the United States but had spent time in Europe and spoke fluent French, having been educated in Montreux. Margaret was often invited to stay at Slains, where she kept Alice, Frédéric, Joss and Idina in fits of laughter with her imitations. Margaret had a talent for mimicry: she would impersonate the people she'd encountered on the boat trip out and the pompous manners of the Nairobi government officials.

It was during visits to Slains that Alice taught Margaret how to play the ukulele. The two women would often entertain Joss, Idina and their guests after dinner with popular and traditional American songs. Alice and Margaret had complementary voices: Alice had a rather deep and husky contralto voice and Margaret, who had trained as a soprano in Florence, possessed a higher and sweeter one. The two women would sit together on the descending lawn in front of the house as if on a stage. Guests would drive their cars into a half-circle facing them, switching on headlights to illuminate the scene. One of Alice and Margaret's duets was the following folk song from the Deep South:

There is an old log cabin and it's a beautiful place
In that old log cabin, there is my baby waiting for me.
And it won't be long, until I hear that song
Ringing in the fields of cotton and I'll rejoice
When I hear that voice saying Bab-y
Oh yeah, there is an old log cabin . . .

They also performed George Gershwin hits such as 'Swanee' and 'Oh, Lady Be Good!' as well as duets in French. Such performances became much talked about amongst the settler society of the times, and Alice would be asked to play and sing wherever she went.

It was through Roy and Margaret that the de Janzés first came into contact with the Governor of Kenya, Sir Edward Grigg, and his wife, Joan. Roy Spicer had already won the respect of the handsome and commanding governor: Edward Grigg approved of Roy's impressive service record during the First World War (he had been awarded the Military Cross in France) and of his highly effective reorganization of the Kenya Police force, especially its African section. Roy's morale-boosting innovations were much admired and included attention to officers' dress and the newly coined Kenya Police motto 'Salus Populi' (the Latin motto means 'Service to the People' and it is still used today, although translated into Swahili). Roy also created cricket and football teams for the officers and developed Kenya's first mounted police force, all of which helped to give the right impression to the enthusiastic governor. Although the governor's wife, Joan, had become friends with Margaret, she did not share Margaret's enthusiasm for

Alice. Word had reached Lady Grigg that Alice had a decadent side and the very prim and proper Joan was insistent that wives had to conduct themselves in a ladylike fashion if they were to be admitted into her circle at Government House. Margaret, however, managed to endear herself to Joan, despite being a divorcee, and was never excluded from official gatherings.

While Alice spent a good deal of time with Margaret, her closest ally in Kenya was Idina. The two had much in common. Although Idina was six years older and lacked Alice's unimpeachable good looks – the former being known for her trademark weak chin – both women shared a fashionable elegance, an active disrespect for convention, and a passion for the Wanjohi Valley. It soon became clear that they had something else in common, namely their attraction to Joss. After Alice's arrival in Africa, she found herself increasingly attracted to Idina's handsome husband. For his part, Joss returned the compliment, flirting publicly with Alice at every opportunity. Idina was unperturbed by her husband's latest infatuation. In fact, she may have even encouraged Joss to set his sights in Alice's direction. The Hays had always maintained an open relationship, and the heavily pregnant Idina may have felt that at this time Joss should be permitted his affairs. The advantage of Alice was that she would respect Idina's precedence and would never attempt to rub her nose in it. Alice was someone who got along just as well with women as men, often making friends with the wives of her male friends. In many ways, Alice and Idina's mutual attraction to Joss became a bond between the two women.

We do not know exactly when Joss and Alice first consummated their relationship, but it seems that this happened at some point during Alice's first visit to Kenya. Although their affair wasn't openly acknowledged at this point – and neither Joss nor Alice sought to leave their spouses as a result – their on-again-off-again relationship would continue for the next two decades. In hindsight, their liaison has an air of inevitability about it. Alice was unfulfilled in her marriage, looking for excitement and escape: her relationship with Frédéric was stable, but far from passionate. For his part, Joss had always been magnetically attracted to wealthy and beautiful married women. Clandestine encounters between Alice and Joss would have taken place whenever Idina and Frédéric happened to be out at the same time, and the rarity of such opportunities would have only added to the excitement. By all accounts, Joss was an accomplished lover, known for his ability to bring a woman to climax easily: it is entirely possible that Alice experienced a kind of sexual awakening with him. For his part, Frédéric put a brave face on Alice's flirtation and subsequent affair with Joss. He was even heard to refer to Joss on more than one occasion as 'the boyfriend'. Frédéric had lived with Alice's moods for such a long time, it seems he was inclined to go along with anything that might make his unpredictable wife a little happier.

It was true that since their arrival in Kenya, Alice's health had improved enormously. For the first time in years, she was happy – her heavy moods had almost completely lifted. As the African trip began to draw to a close,

Alice realized she was dreading her return to Paris and her life there. It was at this juncture she made up her mind to buy a permanent home in the highlands. Frédéric's need to appease Alice was such that he agreed to help her purchase land in the Wanjohi Valley. The de Janzés arranged for a meeting with the Leslie-Melvilles and Geoffrey Buxton to talk about purchasing Wanjohi Farm, adjacent to Geoffrey's property. The acreage was small, only 600 acres, but could be easily managed and was ideal for growing pyrethrum. Frédéric and Alice would be able to employ the local Kikuyu farmers, who had smallholdings dotted about the area, to plant and harvest the crops. The de Janzés learned that the land was owned by Sir John Frecheville Ramsden, known as 'Chops', a local builder of settler houses. Before long, Frédéric was putting wheels in motion to buy Wanjohi Farm from Chops, driving to Nairobi to see Mr Barrat at the firm of Shapley, Schwartze and Barrat (the Hays' legal advisers). By the end of 1925, a deal had been struck and Alice began making plans to build a new house on the site. The de Janzés' future home would be situated about seventy-five yards from the Wanjohi River, facing a bend where a deep pool formed. There was a small manager's house on the land (still there to this day) that would provide the de Janzés with temporary accommodation while they supervised construction. Although Alice was anxious to start the building work, she would have to wait until the title for the land had been transferred and legal arrangements processed by the lawyers. This would not be completed until June of the following year.

The de Janzés stayed on with the Hays through Christmas and New Year, experiencing the customary revelry of Nairobi's race week. By January 1926, Idina had given birth to a daughter, Dinan, in Nairobi. It was at this point that Alice and Frédéric decided to go back to France, at least temporarily, to see their children. Alice refused to be parted from her pet monkey, Roderigo, and so she took him with her on the liner to France, successfully disembarking with him at Marseilles. On their arrival in Paris, the de Janzés were reunited with their children who must have been delighted at the sight of their mother with an African monkey perched on her shoulder. Nolwen and Paola, now ages three and a half and twenty months respectively, were staying with Aunt Tattie at her rather grand apartment on the rue de la Pompe. Their parents had been away for five months, an interminably long time for young children. Although Nolwen would have recognized her parents immediately, little Paola would have already grown completely accustomed to life with Aunt Tattie.

Meanwhile, Aunt Tattie was not at all happy about the arrival of Roderigo in her elegant home. Terrified that the monkey would ruin her furniture, she suggested that they all go and stay at the de Janzés' rue Spontini apartment. That January, Alice, Frédéric, their children, a French nanny, the monkey and a grand piano took up residence in the rue Spontini. Not surprisingly, Roderigo wreaked havoc. The children loved him, but the nanny was up in arms – every day the monkey would knock over another vase or ornament as he leapt from sofa to sofa. (We can only imagine what an African monkey made of being transplanted to the confines of a sophisticated Paris apartment.) For Alice, Roderigo was a living connection to Africa, to the Wanjohi Valley, and to her friends there, Joss in particular. Throughout her life, Alice would continue to show a greater attachment to her pets than she did to her two daughters. Although she was doubtless pleased to see Nolwen and Paola, she was also determined to leave them again as soon as possible to return to Africa.

After only a few weeks in Paris, the de Janzés received a cable from their lawyer, Barrat, to say that completion of the Wanjohi Farm acquisition could take place in Nairobi as soon as they returned to Kenya. By mid-February, after only a few weeks in France, they were ready to leave again. Both Alice and Frédéric feared that Alice's moods would return if she stayed in Paris a moment longer. Frédéric had kitted himself out with powerful rifles and a shotgun in preparation for going on safari – he was looking forward to hunting game on his return. Alice, meanwhile, packed up crates of linen, silver, books and other household essentials for their new African home. Based on her experience of living with the Hays, she knew exactly what was needed to make the place comfortable and personal. Her linen was exceptionally beautiful, with the de Janzé coat of arms embroidered on every sheet, pillowcase, hand-towel and table napkin. Pictures, lamps and carpets were also included in the de Janzés' luggage as well as a few pieces of antique French furniture to lend refinement to their drawing room. With four vast crates in the hold and some new Paris clothes in a cabin trunk, they said goodbye to their daughters once more.

For half the year, Nolwen and Paola would be installed in Château Parfondeval in Normandy, with Moya, their devoted grandmother. For the rest of the year they would be in Paris with Alice's Aunt Tattie. This second trip to Africa marked the beginning of what was to become for Alice a total separation from her children. Perhaps it was Alice's instinct – and in this respect she may have judged correctly – that Moya and Aunt Tattie would simply be better mothers to the girls. Evidently, Alice lacked the maternal instincts that her aunt and Moya so naturally felt for Nolwen and Paola. Alice had been severely shaken by both her daughters' births, enduring post-natal depressions that had only recently been relieved by her escape to Africa. Like many women of her generation and class, Alice would have found it not at all unusual to be living at a distance from them. Wealthy families of the period were often divided in this way – with parents overseas while their offspring stayed at home to be looked after by relatives or sent to boarding school. (Idina and Joss would also arrange for their daughter, Dinan, to be brought up by a relative, in this case Idina's sister in England, while they remained in Africa.) Later in life, both Nolwen and Paola always maintained that they adored their mother and did not resent her desertion. Perhaps they understood why Alice had to live away from them, and were pleased to see her happy. Nonetheless, they must have missed her deeply at times, anticipating and longing for her letters and return.

After the long journey from Europe, Alice and Frédéric arrived in Nairobi again. The de Janzés signed the documents for Wanjohi Farm in March 1926. The certificate of title reads as follows:

> Title I. R. 1494
> Frédéric le Comte de Janzé and Alice la Comtesse de Janzé, both of Gilgil in the colony of Kenya, pursuant to the transfer dated the 9th day of March 1926 registered at the Registry of Titles at Nairobi as I.R. 1052, are now the proprietors as owners of the fees subject to such encumbrances as are notified by memorandum written hereon to the conditions contained in the said transfer etc. – etc.

Alice lost no time persuading Chops to build her a house, on the site she had marked out. She also needed him to fix up the small manager's house at the rear of the property so that she and Frédéric could move in there immediately. With the help of Idina, Alice drew plans for Chops to follow. The lines of the house would be similar to those of so many of the settlers' houses in the area. It was to be built on a single level in the shape of a fat 'H' with stone foundations that were visible to a height of three feet. There would be cedar half-logs cladding the sides, a cedar roof and a square verandah. The house would overlook the Wanjohi River at its rear and the long silvery waterfalls of the Satima Peak in the Aberdare Mountains at the front. Inside, walls would be plastered and some basic wiring would be installed with a generator housed in the servants' quarters. Two wings would be devoted to bedrooms, with Alice's bedroom on the left as you faced the verandah and more bedrooms and bathrooms on the right. In the centre of the house, there was going to be a long drawing room with a central stone fireplace. A central chimney would also serve the dining room with its large pantry off to one side. As was traditional, the kitchen would be separate from the house – food would be cooked there and, when it was ready to serve, brought to the pantry in the main house. After the title for the land was transferred to the de Janzés on 2 June 1926, building work finally began.

On her return to Africa, Alice went about adding to her menagerie. To protect her dogs from night-time marauders she had an open wire kennel constructed near to her temporary living quarters. Here she also kept her baboon, Valentino. Joss lent the de Janzés two Somali ponies that were housed at Geoffrey Buxton's stables across the river. Every morning, Alice continued to ride out before breakfast through the morning mists with Frédéric, her new greyhound Fairyfeet running alongside. Frédéric recorded stories from these morning rides in his book of pen portraits about Africa, *Tarred with the Same Brush* (1929). The book – which is dedicated to one of its characters, 'Delecia', a pseudonym for Alice – describes one ride in particular which helps to paint a picture of Alice's close relationships with her animals. One morning, Delecia/Alice goes out riding alone with her greyhound for company. Her pony bolts, leaving Delecia/Alice winded but uninjured beneath a cluster of trees. The greyhound panics and tears off in the opposite direction. A few minutes later, the dog returns to his mistress, deeply scarred and bleeding after catching a paw blow to her side and front legs from a lion. The dog has saved her life. Greatly shaken, she walks home leading her pony and hound. Back at the farm, she bathes the poor dog and bandages his wounds, nursing him all day and into the night.

Looking at the photographs of Alice during this time, it is possible to see the degree to which she was evidently invigorated by her surroundings. In her Paris photos, Alice often looks pale and has a haunted expression. In the Kenyan photos, she radiates ease. The eyes look out to the horizon, her face tanned across her broad cheekbones. Alice told friends that she had never felt happier in her life. Her dreaded depressions had lifted: she felt cured, as though she had taken a miracle draught of smelling salts. In fact, there is a scientific explanation for this new stabilization of her moods. Kenya is on the equator, blessed with intensely bright light year round. Studies have shown that sufferers of cyclothymia often demonstrate a marked improvement in mood after being exposed to bright light therapy: it is thought that sunshine stimulates the pituitary and pineal glands, effecting the release of mood-altering hormones. Doctors all the way back to Hippocrates have recommended natural light as a cure for unhappiness – for her part, Florence Nightingale found patients recovered more rapidly when kept in sunny wards. Adding to the beneficial effect of so much sunshine, the Wanjohi Valley is 6,000 feet above sea level, and at such a height, alterations in psychology, behaviour and cognitive functioning are common. Then there was the sheer uplifting beauty of the place. Evelyn Waugh, who visited Kenya in 1931, described well the effect that the highlands have on those who visit. 'There is a quality about it which I have found nowhere else but in Ireland, of warm loveliness and breadth and generosity,' he wrote. 'It was not a matter of mere liking, as one likes any place where people are amusing and friendly and the climate is agreeable, but a feeling of personal tenderness. I think almost everyone in the highlands of Kenya has very much this feeling, more or less articulately.' He went on to evoke the particular quality of the light: 'Brilliant sunshine quite unobscured, uninterrupted in its incidence; sunlight clearer than daylight; there is something of the moon about it, the coolness seems so unsuitable. Amber sunlight in Europe; diamond sunlight in Africa. The air fresh as an advertisement for toothpaste.' In Kenya, those combined effects of sunshine, altitude and landscape continued to positively affect Alice's mental chemistry.

In other words, it was easy to be happy in Happy Valley. The de Janzés would drive over to Slains every day in their new 1925 Straight Six Buick with a drop head and spare wheels. They variously entertained their neighbours, the Leslie-Melvilles and Geoffrey Buxton. Alice had her new house to plan and her animals. There was the thrill of her occasional liaisons with Joss to add to her pleasures. Her life in Paris was fading to a distant memory. She no longer felt trapped by her role as countess and by her marriage. Certainly, she missed her daughters, but they were to be visited on a regular basis and Alice decided that as soon as her house was built and furnished she would return to see them. She wrote long descriptive letters for Aunt Tattie to read out loud to her girls, always starting 'My Darlings', giving news of her house, and her new servants, and including little stories about Roderigo and the other animals.

Perhaps for the first time since her early childhood, Alice was actually at peace. Then, as so often happens when a person finally achieves a degree of contentment in life, Alice was about to fall in love.

4

Raymund and the Coup
de Foudre

A month after the de Janzés' return to Kenya, a new
face appeared on the Happy Valley scene. It was that
of Raymund de Trafford, a 26-year-old English aristocrat. Darkly handsome, slender and the youngest son
of Sir Humphrey de Trafford, third baronet, Raymund
could trace his ancestors back to the eleventh century and
the time of King Canute. By all accounts, Raymund could
also be described as something of a cad, a man who had
already left a trail of broken hearts stretching from Mayfair
to Buenos Aires and back again. Some years later, Evelyn
Waugh, who visited Raymund at his farm in Kenya,
described him as a 'bachelor farmer', adding 'though perhaps he is more typically bachelor than farmer'.

Raymund had been brought up in the rather starchy

environment of a Catholic English country home at the turn of the century before being sent away to boarding school, as was customary. He was educated at St Anthony's, a Catholic school in Eastbourne, and at the Oratory at Edgbaston (often described as the 'Catholic Eton'). At the age of eighteen, he entered the Royal Military College of Sandhurst and was gazetted as an ensign in the Coldstream Guards (1st Battalion) on 20 December 1918, thereby narrowly avoiding probable slaughter in the trenches of France. He left the army on 27 February 1924, after serving in the British Army of occupation in Constantinople. In his final year of army service he developed asthma and was told by his doctors to go abroad for his health. He embarked on a tour of South America beginning in 1925, spending time in both Uruguay and Argentina, where the dry climate proved conducive to his weak lungs. In South America, he learned to cut cattle on ranches, went boar shooting in Uruguay with one Aaron Ancharenas la Barras and was entertained by a family of wealthy polo-playing ranchers named Basualdos in Argentina. On his return to London early in 1926, Raymund decided to travel on to Kenya, with another dry climate and a popular destination for so many Englishmen of his age and class. As the youngest de Trafford son, he was a victim of primogeniture, meaning that his eldest brother would inherit the family estate. Although Raymund received regular payments from the family coffers, it was expected that he would begin to make his own money at some point, especially now that his health had improved.

He decided to try his hand at farming and business in East Africa. The prospect of big-game hunting was also a considerable lure, but other factors helped his decision. He had heard much about the Kenya highlands from fellow members at the London club White's, to which he was elected in 1922. Apparently, there were groups of English aristocrats living in decadent fashion in a place called the Wanjohi Valley. Raymund would have heard tales of drunken parties, wife-swapping and general debauchery. The joke would have gone around at White's, 'Are you married, or do you live in Kenya?' Given Raymund's appetite for alcohol and women, Wanjohi would have sounded like absolute heaven. Soon after his return to London from South America, he started to make preparations for his departure. Raymund could have begun his journey to Kenya from Southampton, but this would have taken him through the Bay of Biscay to Gibraltar, a route that could be rough, sick-making and even dangerous. Instead, like many English passengers bound for Africa, he chose to leave from Marseilles, after which the route to Mombasa was comparatively smooth sailing. Raymund took the train to Marseilles in early April of 1926, boarding the SS *General Duchayne* bound for Kenya on the 15th. He arrived in Nairobi via the Lunatic Line about four weeks later, and was seen soon after his arrival on the verandah of the Mombasa Club with a pretty fellow passenger, who probably succumbed to his charms on board the ship.

Next, Raymund set about finding himself a home in the highlands. Although he was not an Etonian – like so many of the upper-class settlers in Kenya of the time – he brought with him an impressive list of introductions from his father and friends in England. First he called on Lord Delamere and Sir Francis Scott, the two most prominent expatriate farmers in the region. He also went to see Geoffrey Buxton, a former Coldstream Guards officer. Soon after his arrival, Raymund settled on buying a maize farm near Njoro called Kishobo. Here he employed a manager to run the farm, purchased a lorry and rented a Buick car. There was already a house on Raymund's newly purchased land, albeit a fairly basic one, but he improved it, furnishing it for the most part with his extensive collection of books which he had brought out in crates. Photos of Raymund from this period show an immaculately dressed young man, slim-framed and athletic, with dark hair and a winning smile, his hat often set at a rakish angle. Needless to say, he soon established a reputation as something of a lothario amongst the small community of settlers – doubtless relishing his own notoriety. Raymund's primary interest, however, was hunting of another variety. Big-game safaris in Africa had been fashionable amongst aristocratic Europeans since the turn of the century, and by the time Raymund arrived in Kenya, Denys Finch Hatton, the most famous of the white hunters in Kenya, had just begun his new business venture escorting wealthy clients into the wilderness on safari. Raymund was keen to join in.

By June of 1926, Raymund had heard of Joss and Idina and their friends the de Janzés, but he had yet to meet them. When he called on Geoffrey Buxton early in June, he asked Geoffrey to engineer a meeting with Frédéric in particular. Raymund was anxious to undertake his first safari and had heard that Frédéric was also keen. What's more, Raymund was intrigued to meet the count for another reason. Although mostly self-educated, Raymund considered himself well read, and he had heard that Frédéric was a writer. Geoffrey arranged for Raymund to meet the de Janzés along with Joss and Idina at Satima Farm that June. Some years later, Raymund related to Margaret Spicer the details of his first meetings with Alice. He remembered Alice standing by the fireplace in Geoffrey's drawing room looking up over a glass of champagne, her grey eyes vivid and lit by the fire. He also recalled the next time he saw her, which was the following day. After staying the night with Geoffrey, Raymund decided to drive over to Slains to discuss a hunting safari with Frédéric. At Idina's insistence, Raymund stayed for lunch, which gave him the opportunity to study Alice in daylight. Raymund recalled in particular Alice's hair, which was beautifully arranged around her face, and her tight sweater, emphasizing her breasts. She had made up her eyes to kill. He also noticed that she drank spirits easily and was unaffected by them.

In later years, Alice would tell friends that she met Raymund 'on a lion hunt'. With her well-developed sense of drama, she had evidently decided that 'lion hunt' had a better ring to it than 'introduced by mutual friends'. In any case, Alice was immediately drawn to this good-looking unmarried arrival, with his polished conversation and tales of South American adventures. It was, for both parties, a mutual attraction of powerful proportions. Raymund resolved to find some way to see Alice alone. It transpired that he did not have to wait long for the opportunity. Frédéric was leaving on a safari the following week and there was no room for Raymund on this occasion. Instead, the count suggested another date in August and gave Raymund instructions as to how to obtain an elephant licence. While Frédéric was away, Raymund set to work arranging a secret rendezvous with Alice in Nairobi. She agreed to meet him there so they could then travel together down the coast near Mombasa.

For Alice, this entailed a double deception. Not only did she need to keep the trip secret from Frédéric, she also had to make sure that Joss would not find out. Since her return to Africa, Alice had resumed her affair with Joss and she sensed that he would not be keen on this new dalliance with Raymund. Idina was no fool, however, and when Raymund and Alice returned from their trip, Idina confronted her friend. Although Idina is often seen as Happy Valley's high priestess of free love, in fact, she was happiest when relationships were within her control – she may even have taken Alice's new affair as a kind of infidelity to Joss. Suffice to say, she sensed that the happy foursome of the de Janzés and the Hays had just been disturbed. Idina duly informed Alice that she was not pleased about Raymund and did not like him.

Undeterred, Alice returned to Wanjohi Farm to oversee the work on her new house and to welcome her husband back from his safari. Despite the reappearance of Frédéric, Raymund set about redoubling his attentions to

Alice, becoming a frequent visitor to Wanjohi Farm. As the de Janzés did not have a telephone, he would drive down unannounced in his box-bodied Ford. An accomplished amateur photographer, Raymund took many pictures of Alice during this period. In one portrait, Alice is standing chest-deep in the waves during a clandestine trip to the coast, her eyes obscured by a wide-brimmed sun hat, her swimming costume pulled down around her shoulders, revealing bare shoulders and torso. She exudes happiness, health and sex appeal. During the initial stage of this new romance, Alice continued her meetings with Joss, although her primary interest was now Raymund. Alice's new interest was unattached and could potentially help her escape from her situation with Frédéric, whereas Joss had never offered her any long-term commitment or a route out of her failing marriage.

Besides, Joss's eye was already wandering elsewhere. The object of his attention was Mary Ramsay-Hill, sometimes known as 'Molly' – a pale-skinned 33-year-old beauty with a red-lipsticked mouth and matching lacquered nails. At the time of her first meetings with Joss, Mary was already married and living with her husband, Cyril, in the ostentatious Spanish palace that he had built for her on the nearby shores of Lake Naivasha. This impressive structure and its mistress enthralled Joss, even if Mary's origins were dubious. Born in London in 1893, she was often referred to as 'Miss Boots' because it was rumoured that her fortune was from the chemist chain. In fact, her father was a bankrupted London clerk, who had lost all his money by the time Mary was fifteen (the exact source of Mary's wealth is not known). Cyril was her second husband: she had married her first at sixteen. Now she set her sights on Joss, or at least he set his sights on her. The attraction was mutual – he was lured by her money, lavish home and sexual experience. She was drawn by his title, good looks and considerable reputation as a lover. For both parties, the liaison may well have also helped to provide a route out of marriages that were turning bad.

With Joss directing his attentions elsewhere and Alice engrossed with Raymund, Frédéric was faced with a new dynamic. While the affair between Joss and Alice had never threatened the status quo, Alice's attraction to Raymund was altogether more destructive. If Frédéric guessed what was going on, he said nothing. Alice's moods were powerful and potentially destructive and Frédéric may have preferred to remain silent in order to preserve the relative peace. What's more, the de Janzés could still find plenty of common ground when it came to their animals. At this point their menagerie included Alice's baboon Valentino, a marmoset monkey, Fairyfeet the greyhound and a mongrel dog called Monster. Alice's prize pet, however, was her lion cub. Frédéric had discovered the cub one morning while out riding alone on his pony. In his description of the incident from his book *Tarred with the Same Brush*, about his adventures in Africa, he wrote: 'I had only a fleeting impression of a yellow streak darting out at us from behind a rock.' Frédéric and his pony eventually came to a halt, the poor horse trembling with fear. Frédéric guessed that he had just been saved from a lion's charge, so he decided to tie up the pony in order to see if he could locate the den. He approached the area from the opposite side and managed to get a glimpse of a lioness and her cubs. The next day he took Alice with him and they watched through binoculars from a safe distance. In the coming days, the couple frequently returned to the area, approaching to within fifty yards of the den. They could see four cubs inside. The lioness greeted these visits with low growls, but she did not attack.

Two weeks later, Alice and Frédéric received an unexpected visit from an Indian maharaja, his two young princes and an older man, an aide-de-camp or vizier. They explained that they were on safari and were hoping for lunch. Frédéric and Alice were happy to provide. After the meal, the maharaja invited the de Janzés to view his trophies – gazelles, kongonis (large antelope), and a great kudu (another species of antelope) as well as two lion skins pegged out in the sun. Frédéric enquired as to where the lions had been killed. 'Oh, quite near,' he was told. 'Among some kopjes (small hills) a few miles from here.' Frédéric asked, 'But didn't you see the cubs?' 'Oh no, they were all alone; the lioness charged from some rock piles after letting us get within fifty yards.' Frédéric was furious and immediately went to saddle up his pony. He found the poor lion cubs in a small cave. They had been starved for three days. One was dead. Frédéric brought the three remaining cubs back to the farm, but one more died in the night. He wrote: '. . . it is an unpardonable crime to shoot females of any species'. The maharaja's party was invited to stay the night, but the atmosphere between the de Janzés and their guests was strained and the visitors left the following morning.

Alice and Frédéric doted on the cubs, feeding them on tinned milk and raw meat. These new visitors were ravenous, sleeping together in a basket; two round, fat balls of fluff. Christened Samson and Judah, they were soon introduced to the other members of Alice's menagerie. They got along well with the dogs, and even the monkeys, particularly Valentino the baboon, who elected himself the cubs' keeper, and cuffed both of them if they got out of line. One night, when the cubs were older, Judah escaped and was never seen again. Samson, however, became a household pet. He was playful and often naughty, and possessed great character. In the evenings, he would often wander into the house and lay his head on the laps of his master and mistress. There is an iconic photograph of Samson and Alice taken by Raymund, in which Alice is sitting on the verandah with Samson draped across her knees – a Madonna and child with the cub playing the part of the infant. The cub's tail is hanging down to Alice's toes and his paws are bigger than her hands. He must have weighed at least fifty pounds, and was easily old enough to do some harm, but Alice appears completely unperturbed. She is wearing a loose shirt and baggy trousers, a large felt hat on her head, gazing into the middle distance with the look of a woman who has come into her own. The photo was sent to her children – whom Samson had literally replaced – and Frédéric's mother, Moya, as well as to Alice's father, William.

Although Alice and Frédéric adored their pets, their own relationship was becoming increasingly untenable. In his series of quasi-autobiographical stories about Kenya, *Vertical Land* (1928), Frédéric presented an accurate, if poignant, assessment of their marriage via the fictionalized relationship of 'Delecia' and 'Ned' (Alice and Frédéric). The names of the de Janzés' pets were not changed. The narrator is a new arrival in Kenya and is called 'Bob':

After a long trek down, and the motor ride from Meru, I reach Nairobi fagged out. Washed and bathed, I'm carried off to Muthaiga for a drink.

As we drive up we are passed by a low-bodied Buick, piled with luggage and boys. 'Ah – they are the Happy Valley crowd,' says the Colonel at my side. We stop and park the car behind theirs. 'Salaam! Mon colonel!' the boy cries, all dusty faced, orange shirt turned to brown. 'Hello, Delecia!' the Colonel calls, as the girl gets out, dark haired under a broad terai, in grey slacks and green jumper, small and dainty with firm, pointed chin and wide spaced grey eyes, much personality. We all meet and sit on the verandah for a drink. – 'You don't know Samson! – Oh, Ned, please get Samson.' He drags his long supple form from the deepest chair with a sigh of ennui, goes to the car, bringing back a four months' old lion cub.

'I never travel without him, but I've also got Roderigo and Bill Sikes, also Samson's pal, Gillie, the Airedale.'

They are all brought for inspection, the two monkeys tiny, and clinging like moths. Roderigo is sweet, but Delecia warns he is not very gentlemanly in his habits.

She talks and tells the Colonel all the gossip. Ned stalks off to the bar. He seems so nervous and jumpy, cannot stay still, wanders from group to group. Delecia tells of his accident with the elephant: 'His nerves are terrible and he will go hunting in the forest with only one good arm.' She smiles, 'He's difficult at times.'

'And, Delecia, do play to us to-night.'

'Well, maybe, but not at the club, and we must have dinner, a wash and thousands of drinks. I'm feeling completely passed out now. I'm going to my room, do send Ned along soon, he'll only get cross if he stays too long in the bar.'

'A great pity,' murmurs the Colonel as she goes. 'A great girl, Delecia, but she cares too much for her pets and he cares too much for her.'

Despite his growing sense that he was losing the woman he loved, Frédéric must have accepted his new rival's appearance with a degree of equanimity, because that August, the two men agreed to go on a four-week safari together. Frédéric invited Alice to join them and all three began making the necessary arrangements. On 20 August 1926, Raymund purchased a licence to shoot two elephants at a cost of £45. They engaged a white hunter to guide them and began to gather the necessary equipment for the trip.

A safari was perhaps not the best idea in the circumstances. Alice, Frédéric and Raymund would be spending both days and nights for a whole month in extremely close proximity to one another and without respite. Raymund would doubtless make frequent attempts to spend time alone with Alice and to persuade her to leave Frédéric. Meanwhile, Frédéric could be in no doubt of Alice's feelings for Raymund, and would have to stifle his husband's sense of hurt pride continually. Any underlying tensions were bound to erupt in the isolated environment of the wilderness.

Even in the weeks leading up to the safari, frictions between Raymund and Frédéric began to surface. There were frequent disputes, usually about literature, fuelled by drink and altitude. Too gentlemanly to argue outright over Alice, they elected to fight about books instead. Both of them moved in literary circles and considered themselves intellectual. Raymund had attended military school rather than university, but could nonetheless be dogmatic when it came to literary matters, readily defending his wide knowledge of the classics and his favourite nineteenth-century authors. He was indifferent to Shelley, loathed Byron, but loved William Thackeray, George Eliot and Charles Dickens. Frédéric, on the other hand, was a legitimate intellectual, a graduate of Cambridge University with a degree in English, and a friend and contemporary of Proust. He venerated in particular Honoré de Balzac, Gustave Flaubert and Charles Baudelaire. Exactly what took place during the trip itself is unknown but it is hard to imagine that the dynamic between the three participants was anything but fraught. It is perhaps not surprising that Alice decided to depart a week early and return to Wanjohi Farm without her husband or lover, anxious to leave the men to their own devices. Frédéric wanted to push on north to Uganda. Raymund was torn between going back with Alice – thereby ensuring he could have time alone with her – or going on with this next leg of the adventure. It is characteristic of Raymund that he put hunting first. He had been told that there were gorillas in the Ugandan forests near Lake Victoria and the Congo and had already decided that he would supplement his farming and family allowance by capturing live animals and selling them to European zoos. At the time, live gorillas fetched extremely high prices in Europe. Raymund elected to plough on.

Alice made her way home with a driver and a servant. It was mid-September, and building work on her house was almost finished. The Indian builders had moved quickly, working from dawn until dusk. In her three weeks away, the house had been transformed. Alice was able to unpack the rest of her crates and move furniture and beds into position. Idina was there to advise. Idina's French maid Marie made curtains. Soon, Wanjohi Farm House began to look like home. But it was no longer a home Alice wished to share with Frédéric. Alone, she had time to think. She confided in Idina, telling her friend that she was contemplating divorce. Although Idina disliked Raymund, she did not find this news in the least bit shocking. After all, she was a veteran divorcee. 'If Raymund makes you happy darling, then that's what you must do,' she advised. 'But for heaven's sake, don't leave us; do come and live here near us in your angelic little valley.' Next Alice drove to Nairobi in order to discuss matters with Margaret Spicer. Margaret warned Alice to be careful. The Spicers liked and admired Frédéric; they had met Raymund, knew of his reputation and were wary. Alice returned to Wanjohi, but not before ordering some extra furniture from a Scottish joiner called Mr Macrae who made excellent Georgian-style furniture for colonial homes. In more ways than one, Alice was attempting to set her house in order.

Even though Alice had sought Margaret's advice, it was becoming increasingly clear to her that she was not going to follow it. Frédéric and Raymund were due back very soon and Alice began to steel herself for their arrival. To her surprise, Frédéric returned alone. Raymund had remained in Uganda, trying to negotiate a game-capturing safari for which he needed special assistance and crates. It should have been Alice's first inkling that she was unlikely to be Raymund's first priority; instead, she reassured herself that it would not be long before he pitched up again. Meanwhile, there was obviously something terribly wrong with Frédéric. He was gaunt and complaining of fever. Alice sent him straight to bed, then drove to Nakuru to contact a doctor. The doctor offered the diagnosis of a severe and dangerous type of malaria, dosed Frédéric with quinine and ordered Alice to apply cold, damp towels to her husband's legs to draw the heat down from his head and reduce his temperature. Not wanting to take the local doctor's word for it, Alice asked Idina about good doctors in Nairobi. Idina told her to drive directly to Nairobi to pick up Dr R. W. Burkitt, the famed Irish surgeon, who was known for his rough but effective treatment of malarial patients.

Burkitt's diagnosis was gloomy. Frédéric was suffering from the early signs of blackwater fever, a condition brought on by malaria and the dosing of quinine he had just received. Frédéric had contracted blackwater fever previously while serving as aide-de-camp in Morocco during the First World War, and had been invalided out of the French Air Force as a result. Once contracted, the disease can easily return if stimulated by a new bout of malaria and quinine. Frédéric's urine was beginning to turn black, a sure symptom of the disease. It was decided that the count should return to Paris for treatment. The doctor also recommended that Frédéric stay away from places where he might contract malaria in the future. Remaining in Kenya on any permanent basis was out of the question. Alice was faced with the following dilemma: should she return to Paris with Frédéric or stay in Kenya with Raymund? She was in love with Raymund, but Frédéric was her husband and he was dangerously ill.

Alice was honest with Frédéric. She informed him that she was not prepared to leave Kenya for good. The couple considered their options. Frédéric could return to France alone, leaving Alice to look after the menagerie. Or Alice could return to Paris with him for a temporary period, but then what would they do with the animals? They contemplated turning Samson loose, but he was only four or five months old, still an uneducated cub, and unable to fend for himself. Neither of them could bear the idea of losing Samson. The lion cub was so concerned about his master he was visibly moping, laying his great head on Frédéric's sick bed and insisting on sleeping there. Frédéric agreed to travel to France alone unless Alice could find someone to look after the pets. Valentino the baboon had recently escaped, taking his collar, chain and ground anchor with him one night when everyone was down in Nairobi on a Muthaiga Race Week binge. So that was one problem less. But Alice and Frédéric still needed someone to buy or shoot meat for the other animals. Geoffrey Buxton's manager, who lived next door, agreed to supervise. Before they left for France, the de Janzés threw a house-warming and farewell party. That evening, Wanjohi Farm swarmed with cars, servants and guests. Everyone brought a contribution in the form of drink: vodka, gin, wine, whisky and brandy. Dinner was laid out for twenty on the extended table in the dining room, and Samson wandered in and out. At one point in the evening, the lion cub snatched the tablecloth in his jaws and began nodding vigorously, eventually pulling the cloth off the table altogether and thereby sending glasses, knives, forks and plates crashing to the floor.

In the days that followed, Alice and Frédéric said a last goodbye to their friends and their animals, and went by car to Nairobi and then by train to Mombasa. Of his departure Frédéric wrote in *Tarred with the Same Brush*:

Ordered home – failing in health – miserable in mind. Much as I would greet a home leave of even a long period, just as much do I resent this ordering out of the colony. My heart is out here – with my house – my boys [servants] – my zoo . . . I would much rather die out here as they say I will, unless I return to temperate climes . . . I will rest in the shade of the [Mombasa] Club veranda, sipping pink gin – thinking, remembering, mostly Samson, his baby roundness; his affection which helped us through some hectic months of puppy hood, until he grew up to be a real man, fearless, quiet, understanding, a better friend than any of you could find in most men's lives.

Raymund, busy with his new business ventures, seemed hardly affected by Alice's departure. Even so, Alice was determined to shake herself free of Frédéric so that she could be with Raymund. She now had the travel time back to Paris in which to end her marriage. She needed to make clear to her devoted husband that after seeing him safely home, she intended to return to Kenya immediately. By the time the de Janzés reached Paris, Frédéric had agreed to Alice's conditions. They would remain good friends, but the marriage was over. Alice would ask her lawyer to file for divorce. Nolwen and Paola would remain in Frédéric's custody. On this matter Alice was adamant and Frédéric did not argue. Both girls had always been closer to their father than their mother. There was no question of Alice taking her daughters back with her to Africa. Yes, she loved her children, but if she did not feel well then how could she be a good parent to them? She could always return to Paris for visits. There is no doubt that Frédéric was heartbroken by Alice's decision to divorce. He loved her and was deeply attached to Kenya and to their animals. Now he was being banished, not only from Africa, but also from his wife's affections.

In Paris, the little girls were reunited with their parents, only to find their father sick and their mother on the verge of departure again. After only a month in Paris, Alice re-embarked at Marseilles for Kenya, leaving Frédéric in the care of his mother and placing Nolwen and Paola with Aunt Tattie. It was October of 1926. As a bizarre consolation prize, Alice promised Frédéric that she would bring Samson back to him in Paris before the end of the year. The count told her this would be impossible, but Alice was undeterred. Once again, she boarded the train to Nairobi at Mombasa. Alice was familiar with the route by now and she would have greeted the train's arrival at Voi with delight: dinner at the wayside station meant you had truly returned to Kenya. The menu was the same as it had been a year ago and Alice and the other old hands en route to Nairobi greeted each dish with acclamation: brown Windsor soup, tinned salmon, meatballs and fruit and custard. Alice was returning to Kenya alone and free of all obligations to her family, her husband, her children or her rank. Instead, she had a new husband in her sights; a new house; dozens of friends waiting for her in Wanjohi Valley; her animals, Samson, Fairyfeet, Monster, Roderigo, two more monkeys, and her dik-dik.

On her return to Kenya, Alice and Raymund officially became a couple, dining out together and sharing a bedroom. For the last three months of 1926, Alice spent most of her time with Raymund at Wanjohi Farm, channelling her energies into making improvements to her new home. She often visited Joss and Idina, whose notorious marriage had dwindled into a rather strained friendship by now. Raymund slithered over from his base in Njoro on a regular basis: it was not a long journey and there was a good road to Nakuru, and then on to Gilgil, before turning off to Wanjohi Valley. There is no doubt that with their dark good looks they made a striking pair, but while Alice's attraction to Raymund was developing into devotion, Raymund, although very keen on Alice, was instinctively more restrained. He was someone who would never be able to care about anyone quite as much as he did about himself. Nonetheless, Alice was determined to secure her divorce from Frédéric so that she could be free to remarry.

Alice was still resolved to return with Samson to France in December as promised and she enlisted Raymund's newfound expertise in capturing and transporting animals to help her accomplish this feat. There is a note in Margaret Spicer's diary that Raymund de Trafford dined and danced with Margaret at the Muthaiga Club on New Year's Day 1927. Alice is not mentioned. In fact, she had sailed in mid-December with Samson the lion cub and Roderigo the monkey, now on his second trip to France. Once back in Paris, Alice delivered the animals to the apartment at rue Spontini, where her daughters Nolwen and Paola were living with Frédéric and their nanny. When Aunt Tattie arrived for her regular visits, she would be greeted by a monkey climbing on the furniture, a lion in the living room and a baby Nile crocodile in the bathtub. It is not known whether Alice smuggled in this crocodile from Africa, or whether she had bought it in Paris. Certainly, Samson had the run of the rue Spontini apartment, because Paola, then two and a half, distinctly remembers riding on the cub's back while hanging on to his considerable ruff of a mane.

Alice remained in Paris for more than a month this time. One of the reasons for her delayed return to Africa was that Raymund was in England after having received word that his father had suffered a stroke. In February 1927, Alice told Moya and Aunt Tattie that she was moving out of the rue Spontini apartment to take a small pied-à-terre in rue Chalgrin: evidently she wanted to be free to receive Raymund without the encumbrances of her children, her husband and her animals. Alice's friends and family in Paris remained understandably concerned about this new relationship. Raymund was an unknown quantity, whereas Frédéric had proved himself to be loyal, devoted and tirelessly kind. But Alice was in love, she was a woman of means and she was determined. In Raymund's letters to Alice during this time, he cautioned her not to move so fast. Instead, Alice simply urged her lawyers to hurry through the divorce proceedings even faster, fearing that Raymund's interest was dwindling. She began to make plans for her wedding.

To his credit, Raymund had informed his family that he wanted to marry Alice. However, the de Trafford family, especially Raymund's brother, Humphrey, had grave reservations about this new relationship. As son and heir to the baronetcy, Humphrey was a much more conservative member of the de Trafford family than his wilder younger brother. The aristocratic de Traffords considered the countess far below their social status, despite her enormous personal fortune. Alice was American, still married and she had two children into the bargain. Above all, Raymund's family were strait-laced Catholics and did not approve of divorce. As far as Humphrey was concerned, Raymund had been instrumental in breaking up a Catholic marriage: scandalous behaviour in other words. Divorce was a mere technicality, meaning nothing in the eyes of God. Only the Pope could rule on an annulment, as he had done in the case of the de Traffords' sister, Violet, who had divorced her first husband, receiving an annulment in 1921. The mechanics of annulment were complicated. One argument was that annulment could be granted if the marriage had not been consummated. This obviously could not apply in the case of Alice and Frédéric who had two children. (Nolwen once asked her sister, Paola, in later years, 'How can mummy's marriage be annulled when we are her two children?') Another submission could be that the children had been unwillingly conceived. A large payment to the Pope (Pius XI) was also deemed to be a help. Alice's French lawyers provided a very competent submission, combining the argument of reluctant conception with a considerable offer of money.

The lawyers did not move fast enough, however. On Friday 25 March 1927, less than a year after their first meeting, Raymund visited Alice at her apartment in Paris in order to inform her that the relationship was over and that he was leaving the next day by the four o'clock boat train. His parents were threatening to cut him out of his inheritance and would stop his allowance altogether unless he ended the relationship immediately. The threat of disinheritance terrified Raymund: he relied on regular injections of the family's cash to fund his love of gambling, travel and luxury. Alice told him there was no need to worry about money. She had quite enough for both of them. Raymund explained that he could not turn his back on his family, his religion and his country. It was too much of a sacrifice. Alice reminded him that she had given up her husband and her children for him. Raymund could not be persuaded. He argued that if he continued his relationship with Alice, he would further jeopardize his father's health. He even went as far as to suggest that Alice would probably be better off going back to Frédéric.

After Raymund's departure, Alice was left in an unenviable position: she had abandoned her husband and children for a man who was now about to abandon her. Alice was a naturally unstable person, displaying a dangerous combination of vulnerability and determination. Faced with the sudden ending of the relationship with Raymund, she quickly began to unravel. That Friday evening, she visited Frédéric and her daughters at the rue Spontini apartment. Frédéric could see that Alice was distraught and he asked her what had happened. Alice told him about Raymund's announcement. Although Frédéric was already aware of Raymund's reputation and can hardly have been surprised, the count comforted Alice as best he could. Then, in an act that demonstrates Frédéric's impressive decency, he decided to defend the very woman who had rejected him. He went to see Raymund at his hotel, accusing his wife's lover of dishonourable cowardice and instructing him to marry Alice as promised. Frédéric's words, although well intentioned, had little or no effect. Later that same evening, Raymund arrived at Alice's apartment on the rue Chalgrin to inform her, yet again, that he was leaving. This offered Alice one more opportunity to change his mind. She begged him, shouted at him, tried to reason with him, offered him money, and even tried to seduce him. But to no avail. Raymund was determined to leave for London the next day. He told her that he had no source of income without his family's support and no intention of being kept by anyone else. He agreed to one more lunch to say goodbye the following day before he caught his train but nothing more.

That night, Alice decided there was no future she could imagine for herself without him. The best and only possible way out of this situation was also the most extreme. She barely slept. By Saturday morning, she was resolved. If she couldn't persuade Raymund to stay, she was going to have to take the most drastic action imaginable.

5

The Shooting at the Gare du Nord

On the morning of Saturday 26 March 1927, Alice awoke from a fitful sleep in the bedroom of her apartment at 20 rue Chalgrin. She got out of bed and began to prepare for lunch with Raymund. She dressed with great attention to detail; if this was to be their last meeting then she wanted to look her best. She had arranged to meet him at the Maison Lapérouse, a restaurant and *salon de thé* on the quai des Grands-Augustins, overlooking the Seine. That week, Alice was looking after a friend's Alsatian dog and she decided to take the animal with her, glad of the company. After a short cab ride along the banks of the Seine, she arrived at the Lapérouse. Alice and the dog made straight for a private dining room reserved especially for the meeting with Raymund. Lunch consisted of champagne, foie gras and salmon. Raymund must have been nervous but Alice was determined to lighten the mood and consequently the meal went smoothly as they ate and drank, laughing, and even joking together. So amusing was their meeting that Alice had to remind herself of the gravity of the situation: Raymund was planning to leave.

When lunch was over, Alice suggested they do some shopping before going to the station in time for Raymund's four o'clock train. She informed him that she had to run an errand for Frédéric at a nearby gun shop and suggested she could also buy a parting gift for Raymund there. The gun shop was on l'avenue l'Opéra, a short walk across the Pont Neuf and through the courtyards of the Louvre. The owner of the shop, a Monsieur Guinon, recognized Alice. She had visited with Frédéric to buy hunting equipment for their trip to Kenya in early 1925. For that reason, no special permits or licences were required for Alice's purchase. Raymund chose some knives and a twelve-bore shotgun. Alice elected to buy herself a small revolver – a 3.8 calibre Colt with pearl inlay handle and a box of nickel-plated bullets. The countess paid for the weapons and asked for them to be wrapped separately. She watched attentively as her gun was carefully enclosed in brown paper, with the box of bullets placed in the same bag.

The Gare du Nord was a cab ride away. When they arrived at the station, it was bustling with Saturday-afternoon shoppers on their way home to the suburbs. The boat train to Boulogne was waiting at Platform 1 at the far end of the station. Alice and Raymund made their way through the crowds, picking up some snacks from a *boulangerie* along the way. As Alice looked up at the station's enormous overhead clock, she would have realized that she had only a little time left. She told Raymund she would meet him on the train to say their farewells. Next she went to the Ladies to unwrap her gun from its parcel, load it with bullets and place it in her handbag. As she walked towards the boat train, Alice maintained her resolve. She had decided to die in Raymund's arms. Suicide was both a solution to her impossible predicament and a twisted restitution of justice. In other words, she would rather kill herself than allow herself to be abandoned by another man.

Alice boarded the train and found Raymund in his first-class compartment, stowing his luggage above his seat, ready to settle down with his newspaper for the journey ahead. He got up and moved towards Alice who was standing in the entrance to the first-class carriage.

'Do you really want to leave?' she asked him.

'Yes,' he replied.

The whistle blew and the train gave a jolt, signifying its imminent departure. Alice went for her gun, but at this moment, as she later described, she had a sudden change of heart. Why should Raymund continue to live without her? Why should he be allowed to go on with his life when hers was about to end? Alice leaned forward to kiss him, throwing one arm around his neck while removing the gun from her bag. Then she pressed the muzzle against Raymund's chest and pulled the trigger. He collapsed. Next Alice turned the gun on herself. Another crack. Witnesses reported that as she fell to the floor, she smiled.

Neither Alice nor Raymund remembered the furore that followed. The guards were summoned, someone was sent to call for an ambulance and within a matter of minutes train officials had boarded the train. The guards found the couple motionless and bleeding, their bodies half in and half out of the first-class compartment. Alice's Alsatian was growling so ferociously that it initially proved impossible to rescue the dying couple. Finally, someone threw a rock at the head of the dog so that the police were able to approach and remove the bodies from the train. Raymund was able to utter, 'It was she who fired,' while Alice's chief concern was with the Alsatian now lying unconscious on the platform. 'Take care of my dog!' she managed to gasp to an onlooker.

Alice and Raymund were taken to Lariboisière Hospital, directly adjacent to the Gare du Nord, where operations were performed to remove the bullets. The condition of both parties was desperate and there was a possibility that neither would live through the night. Raymund's family was notified and members of the de Trafford clan left the deathbed of their father to sit in the hospital's anteroom while the youngest son of the family slipped into a coma. An examination of Raymund's wound and clothing showed that the muzzle of the pistol had been pressed directly against his chest as he had leaned forward to kiss her goodbye. By a miracle, the bullet had missed his heart by a few millimetres and it is a tribute to the skill of the Parisian surgeons that he was revived at all. Meanwhile, Alice was faring slightly better. Her bullet had passed through her stomach before penetrating her lower abdomen.

The events at the Gare du Nord made headlines in the United States, France and Great Britain. The Fort Covington *Sun* in New York State printed the following account on 14 April 1927:

> America, France and England were all threatened in the tragedy in the Gare du Nord, Paris, when Countess de Janzé, estranged wife of Frenchman, shot Raymond [*sic*] V. de Trafford, scion of a promi nent British family, and then put a bullet through her own body. The countess was Alice Silverthorne of Chicago, cousin of J. Ogden Armour and well-known in American social circles. Her relations with De Trafford recently led her husband to file suit for divorce. For several days after the shooting it was believed both the countess and De Trafford would die, but latest reports are that they are out of danger.

Certainly, the novelist F. Scott Fitzgerald must have seen the newspaper reports. At the time, he was hard at work on his novel *Tender is the Night*, which would finally be published after many redraftings in 1934. In the novel, an American acquaintance of Dick and Nicole Diver, a woman called Maria Wallis, is depicted shooting an Englishman on a railway platform in Paris. She 'plunged a frantic hand into her purse: then the sound of two revolver shots cracked the narrow air of the platform'. The train stops and the man is carried away on a stretcher while the police take the woman away. Dick is at the station seeing a friend to the train and races to find out what has happened. He reports back to his group that Maria Wallis just shot an Englishman. Although Fitzgerald changed the setting of the shooting from the Gare du Nord to the Gare Saint-Lazare, Maria Wallis is unmistakably Alice: 'The young woman with the helmet-like hair'. The murder weapon, like Alice's, is '*très petit, vraie perle – un jouet!*'

The French police soon pressed charges against the countess, with the District Police Commissioner preparing a tentative indictment accusing her of attempted homicide. The task of bringing these charges against her was assigned to the prosecution. All charges were deferred, however, until the two principals of the shooting either succumbed to their wounds or recovered. Alice spent nearly six weeks at Lariboisière Hospital recovering enough to be transferred to the hospital ward of the all-women's prison, Saint-Lazare. The French authorities had already tried to interview her on several occasions. The first time her sole response was, 'I decline to give the reason for my act. It is my secret.' However, as the police started to interrogate her more thoroughly, she was forced to seek legal advice. In April she made the following statement: 'I was determined to die in his arms, and when the whistle blew, I suddenly changed my mind and resolved to take him with me into the Great Beyond. Slowly, very slowly, I loosened my grasp around his neck, placed the revolver between our two bodies and, as the train started, fired twice – into his chest and into my own body.'

Alice's use of the phrase 'Great Beyond' is significant. Death was the ultimate gesture for Alice, the one aspect of her existence over which she could have complete control. She had been brought up in the Presbyterian faith and so she would have been taught that when a person dies, his soul goes to be with God, where it waits for the final judgement. After the final judgement, souls are restored to bodies, eternal rewards and punishments are handed out and everything and everyone is 'refreshed and restored'. In other words, in heaven, Alice would finally be reunited with Raymund and with her long-departed mother. The existence of an afterlife was a credo to which Alice passionately subscribed. Ever since her adolescent suicide attempt she continued to wish to 'escape this world'. According to her friends and acquaintances, she frequently made use of expressions such as the 'other side' or 'the Great Beyond'.

For now, Alice found herself far from heaven. After her arrest, she was imprisoned in a cell in Saint-Lazare Prison on charges of attempted murder. The cell had hosted several notorious female criminals in the past, including Marguerite Steinheil, the former mistress of French President Felix Fauré. In 1908, Steinheil had been held at Saint-Lazare Prison for a year while she awaited trial for the double murder of her husband and stepmother. She tried to pin the blame on a gang of intruders and members of her household staff – stories that the judge called a 'tissue of lies'. Eventually she was acquitted. Another notorious former inhabitant of the same cell was Henriette Caillaux, the second wife of the Finance Minister of France,

Joseph Caillaux. She was imprisoned for shooting the editor of the French newspaper *Le Figaro* after he published a letter about her husband that portrayed the minister in an unflattering light. Although Henriette admitted her crime, her lawyers pleaded that she was the victim of 'uncontrollable feminine emotions' and that the shooting was in fact a 'crime passionnel'. The jury also acquitted her. Alice's other famous predecessor at Saint-Lazare was Mata Hari (born Gertrud Margarete Zelle), the Dutch-born exotic dancer who was arrested as a double agent by the French in 1917 and convicted of treason, possibly on trumped-up charges. She had agreed to spy for France but her employees had lost faith in her and accused her of working for the Germans. Unlike Steinheil and Caillaux, she was eventually sentenced to death by firing squad. Alice's fate remained in the balance. As the weeks slipped away, her attorneys worked furiously to secure her release. On 19 May 1927, after nearly six weeks in the prison ward, Alice was temporarily released on the proviso that she would remain in secluded convalescence until she was sufficiently healthy to appear in court. It was true that Alice had been badly wounded and her lacerated stomach needed constant care. Despite everything that had come to pass, the obvious place for her convalescence remained her husband's country residence, Château de Parfondeval. In official terms, Alice was still married. What's more, she had been the love of Frédéric's life for six years and she was still in close contact with his family. Château Parfondeval offered countryside peace, the attentions of the kindly Moya, and those of her favourite manservant, Edward, both of whom had a soothing effect on Alice's health and nerves. Although Alice claimed she did not fear death, there is no doubt she was terrified of imprisonment should she be convicted of attempted murder (or murder, should Raymund die).

During the nine months of convalescence before her court hearing, Alice rested at Parfondeval and wrote a number of letters to her friends and relatives. Despite the de Janzé family's generosity in looking after Alice during this time, they felt the 'scandale' deeply, and at Parfondeval, she was made only too aware of her estrangement. During this dismal period of her life, she also visited her apartment in Paris to collect clothes and books. Meanwhile, the gossip about Alice continued to circulate in Chicago, New York and London and she soon found out that her imprisonment had isolated her almost completely. Although she received correspondence from her father, Louise her stepmother, and close friends such as Paula de Casa Maury, other members of her acquaintance were evidently keen to put distance between themselves and the notorious countess. Joss visited London for his grandfather's funeral in July, but there is no evidence that he made contact with Alice at that time, and besides, by the end of 1927, he was already hatching plans to marry Mary Ramsay-Hill. Alice heard from Margaret Spicer that Margaret was planning a visit to London via Paris in December 1927 and wondered if they could meet? They never did.

Alice did, however, exchange multiple letters with

Raymund. Although his wounds were still causing him considerable pain, he had emerged from his coma and was well enough now to order his nurses about, barking at them to appear at his bedside 'at the double'. Contrary to popular expectation, he was not about to cut Alice out of his life. In fact, her dramatic act seems to have piqued his vanity. On 19 May 1927 he even went so far as to tell the *New York Times* that a reconciliation with Alice was on the cards, although that may have had something to do with wishing to appear noble in the eyes of the public.

And what of Frédéric? It seems he remained generous and loyal throughout the 'scandale' – although many would have recommended he keep his distance from Alice. He did the reverse, agreeing that his family home was the best place for her recovery. By now, he had begun work on *Vertical Land*, his book of pen-portraits of Africa – which would be published the following year – in which the female characters were directly inspired by his relationship with Alice. Like many who have been spurned, Frédéric continued to remain attached to his lost love, at least on the pages of his notebook. Alice makes her first appearance in the book as Anna-Christine Mason, a cousin of the narrator, Bob, who has just arrived in Kenya by boat. Like Alice, Anna has wide-set grey eyes, wavy hair and a distinctive voice. Frédéric wrote:

> . . . her arms are marvellous, from the orange tinted nails to the shoulders, not a trace of colour, not

marble, not white ivory; perhaps of some old ivory held for generations in long Chinese fingers. On one finger an opium smoker's ring of green jade, no other ornament. As the ordered cocktail comes, she takes off her hat, revealing deep grey eyes set wide apart, long black lashes and eyebrows so minute and regular they might have been painted on.

'Pale moon face' of the old Chinese ballads. The dark red lips nearly maroon, the wavy shingled hair – a marvellous work of nature, a more marvellous work of art; and that on board a ship after three weeks at sea!

I am stunned and during luncheon can only mumble and be very British while she talks vividly now in English, now in French.

Later in the evening I take her off, the whole ship's company seems to man decks to see her go; I'm getting back my footing and we talk in the Customs house, and we talk in the taxi, and we talk in the hotel, she sitting on the edge of a bed, while my boy unpacks her things.

I go away to change, my mind whirling with the charm of this child of eighteen. It does not seem possible. She knows everyone – about everything, she seems to have been everywhere, and her voice, that flat voice, without tone or pitch, like voices heard in Islam's bazaars, reciting verses of the Koran. It worms into your mind, fascinates your senses, envelops, numbs one! What is natural? What is art? What is training?

As we start out for Tudor House, across the island, for dinner, she insists, and we take bathing suits just in case.

The hibiscus, the jasmine, the Bougainville [*sic*] trail overhead. Light fishes served on brown and grey dishes. Pawpaws and mangoes on the table.

Her stories of India bazaars and Hill stations way up in the Himalayas, and . . . dinner is over.

Her amber fragrance goes to my head, all my British training and self repose has fled. I am throbbing in heart and mind.

Down to the beach and into the rippleless creek, the moon throwing flashes of blue fire into our wakes as we swim.

Suddenly I miss her, no longer at my side; and turning, startled, see her emerge, naked, silver on the shining beach. Madness! I rush in to be told in that cold flat voice that the night is for night hawks, and, as there is no one there to see, I should not have to worry.

She lies on the sand beautiful as some goddess, silver statue of some Athenian athlete, all length and suppleness, and yet as cold as white marble, frozen in some Nordic garden.

At last we go home; she tells me with a wandering smile to sleep well and have no dreams.

Frédéric's subsequent description of Anna-Christine's wilfulness is particularly revealing of Alice's petulant temperament:

Today there was a clash of wills, and I lost as I am now doomed to lose for ever; I was reserving seats on the train and she wouldn't 'be put in with some maybe bathed but certainly not washed female'. She insisted in travelling in a big compartment with me. I battled my best, but was undone.

After the conflict, in soothing tones, one hand on my feverish hand: 'Bob, it's no use; I always get my own way. I always take what I want and throw it away when I like; don't forget this ever, I hate repetition.'

We are now in the train. Dinner at the wayside station amused her; the lights are out, and through the panes of glass shadow landscapes dwindle by.

There is a certain humour in it all; what a defeat Aunt Anna-Belle is in for. At that moment soft lips touch mine, but cold! Arms stretch above my head round my shoulders.

Those pure arms I saw in that first meeting, that silver body of the beach.

'I take what I want and throw it away'. When shall I be thrown? Thrown by a child!

Frédéric was writing from harsh personal experience: 'I always get my own way'; 'I take what I want and throw it away' – such exclamations could have been taken directly from Alice's lips. Whatever his opinion of Alice, Frédéric evidently remained fascinated by his exotic and dangerous former wife.

Nolwen and Paola were now in the legal custody of their father, who continued to do his best to protect them from their mother's growing notoriety. The girls were living in the apartment in rue Spontini with their Portuguese nanny, the crocodile, the monkey and the oversized lion cub, but because of the animals, the nanny was threatening to leave. Her name was Denise de Milo-Viana and years later Paola would remember her as 'horrible'. Denise told Frédéric that if he wanted her to stay, the animals had to go. Frédéric duly removed the crocodile and transported the monkey to Parfondeval where he was placed in the care of Alice's butler. The lion was donated to the Jardin d'Acclimatation, the children's park in the Bois de Boulogne. While Alice convalesced at Parfondeval, Aunt Tattie took Nolwen and Paola to the Riviera where Alice briefly visited them in Nice. She spent only a short time there before returning to Normandy. Alice's lawyers had warned Moya that Alice must convalesce and be seen to do so, as this was the special condition of the court.

Now that it was certain that both parties in the shooting had recovered, the date was set for Alice's official charging. Nine months after the events at the Gare du Nord, on 23 December 1927, in the 12th chamber of the Police Correctionnelle, Alice was charged with 'wounding and causing bodily harm' to Raymund de Trafford. According to the newspaper *Le Figaro*, she came to the courtroom that day 'a thin little woman in a grey suit. Big, shiny, feverish eyes; high cheekbones; great charm and style' and with 'the guilty look of a naughty girl'. In a photograph of Alice taken that day, she is certainly as beautiful as ever, if extraordinarily pale, looking up at her lawyer – the well-known advocate Maître René Mettetal – with an expression that lies somewhere between fear and defiance. She is wearing a dark cloche hat that masks almost completely her bobbed hair. There are pearls around her neck and in her white-gloved hands she holds a black fur stole. Her dress is to the knee, revealing her legs in their elegant white stockings. In the courtroom, she had attracted a crowd. *Paris-Soir* reported that: 'There were many women in the 12th Chamber where M. Fredin (the most Parisian of Judges) is presiding. All that is fair enough; is this not a beautiful love story? – one of those stories which novelists put together in moving phrases.'

The following description of the court proceedings is a composite taken from the newspaper pages of *Paris-Soir*, as well as *Le Petit Parisien*, *Le Journal* and *L'Echo de Paris*, for 24 December 1927. Alice answered the examiner with 'yes' or 'no' mostly, speaking French with an American accent. The judges had heard about the circumstances leading up to the shooting, but were eager to learn more.

'You have abandoned your husband and children for M. Raymund de Trafford?'

'Yes.'

'Your children?'

'It's so hard to explain; but I only thought of myself.'

'You don't seem to realize the serious situation in which you find yourself.'

'Oh yes.'

The examiner, M. Fredin, wondered about the two of them buying the gun together.

'It was I who asked M. de Trafford to accompany

me to the gunsmith shop. I told him I had to run an errand for my husband.'

The judge could not stop himself from asking: 'And M. de Trafford believed you? In his place, in the situation in which you both found yourselves, I would not have been very comfortable at all.'

Alice smiled sadly and added: 'He had no reason to doubt me. He knew I did not want him to go. I was suffering, but I was sure that he was leaving me – in spite of what he wanted, because he couldn't do otherwise.'

The next question: 'If you didn't want him to leave, why did you buy a revolver?'

She replied: 'But it was to kill me, not him.'

'But you shot M. de Trafford while you were kissing him.'

'Not quite. I was holding my gun when he kissed me. I don't know what went on in my head. I saw, like a drowning woman, all the memories of my life. I wanted to kill myself, but at the last moment in a sort of trance, I fired on him!' Alice was speaking in French: '*Alors, vraiment. Je ne sais pas ce qui c'est passé dans ma tête. J'ai vu comme une femme se noie, dénier tous les souvenirs de ma vie.*'

M. Fredin looked exasperated. 'Then, I don't understand,' he said.

'I was unhappy. I wanted to kill myself,' Alice emphasized.

Here in the French courts in front of the jury and a packed courtroom, Alice admitted that she had often wanted to kill herself.

'Yes,' replied the judge. 'There are some extenuating circumstances in your favour. M. de Trafford had promised to marry you. He did not keep his word. I would also present you, elsewhere, as a gentle person, an excellent mother . . .'

Meanwhile, Raymund, who was not called as a witness in the trial but had insisted on appearing, was permitted to speak. He was described in the *Tribunal Gazette* as 'tall, strong and speaking bad French'. He delivered his testimony rather coldly and flatly: 'I am responsible,' he insisted. He hardly glanced at Alice, who in turn stared unblinkingly at the man she had come so close to killing.

Raymund went on to explain to the court: 'I had asked Mme. de Janzé to become my wife; she wanted to. But my family didn't want to.'

Raymund then recalled what had taken place at the gun shop.

'And what did you think?' he was asked about Alice's purchase of the revolver.

'Nothing. I was in another part of the shop.'

His memory of the crime itself was confused.

'Mme. de Janzé approached me and asked me if I really wanted to leave. I replied yes. Then I saw the revolver in her hand. I seized it at the handle. She had already fired.'

The salesman who sold the gun to Alice gave brief evidence and so did Dr Paul, the surgeon who had operated on both Alice and Raymund, saving their lives.

Alice's attorneys delivered their pleas of mitigation. M. Gandel was said to have pleaded 'indulgently', saying: 'The accused is a sick woman for whom doctors have found extenuating circumstances. She has been an excellent wife and admirable mother, until she met the person responsible for the crime . . . But one must not forget the other dignified man, who has forgotten and forgiven everything. I hope that they get back together again.' (He was referring of course to the Count de Janzé.)

Finally, M. Mettetal entered his plea on Alice's behalf, his voice full of compassion and feeling, hinting to the tribunal that this had been a 'crime passionnel'. It was a crime that the French understood very well: a crime committed for love. In the end, the tribunal was lenient and the judge ruled in Alice's favour. She was ordered to serve six months but was '*condamner avec sursis*', given a suspended sentence, allowing her to leave the court on temporary probation. She was also ordered to pay a fine of 100 francs (around £1), a pittance for a wealthy heiress like Alice and a fraction of what she would have paid under French law for shooting a deer out of season.

Alice was free to go. No sooner had she walked out of Paris's Police Correctionnelle Court on the 23rd of December than she began making plans to travel back to Kenya. In April 1929, President Gaston Doumergue fully pardoned her, but he was later criticized for having done so.

6

Freedom and Exile

After her release, Alice informed Frédéric that she was leaving immediatcly for Africa. Again, there was no question of her daughters going: they would remain in Paris, in their father's custody, as agreed in the terms of the divorce. The lion and the monkey, however, would be returning with her. Although Frédéric knew Alice could easily arrange for Roderigo's return from Parfondeval, he forbade her from removing Samson from the zoo. By now, the lion was nearly fully grown and, besides, it was unlikely that the zookeepers would give him up. The count appeased Alice by promising to visit Samson regularly to make sure that he was well cared for. Alice left Paris for Marseilles and sailed for Kenya with her monkey in the hold.

She arrived in Mombasa in January of 1928 and immediately caught the train to Nairobi before motoring up to her house in Wanjohi. After surveying her empty animal cage and living quarters, she went to stay with Joss and Idina, perhaps reluctant to spend time in isolation after the ordeal of the trial. Joss was about to announce that he was marrying Mary Ramsay-Hill. Idina, meanwhile, had begun a new affair, this time with 'Boy' Long, a good-looking rancher who had been invited to Kenya by Lord Delamere to manage his cattle at a place called Elmenteita in the Rift Valley. In other words, the happy dynamic formerly enjoyed by Joss, Idina and Alice had shifted considerably. Each day, Alice went up to her house to visit her farm. Her servants had remained on during her year-long absence, paid for by Geoffrey Buxton's manager, and her old car was driven out of its garage and revitalized. There was much to do.

Alice's return had coincided with the arrival of a giant plague of locusts in the region. No one had anticipated the invasion: Alice's smallholdings of maize were devastated, along with most of the arable farmland in the area. David and Mary Leslie-Melville and Geoffrey Buxton, whose farms were both nearby, had been similarly affected. To each of these neighbours and her wider circle she related the dramatic story of her absence and explained how sorry she was to have caused everyone so much embarrassment. In her time away from Kenya, Alice's legend had grown. At the Muthaiga Club, the regulars had begun referring to her as 'the Fastest gun in the Gare du Nord', a title that stuck. After her arrival, Alice's movements were eagerly documented by the Parisian fashion and gossip magazine *Boulevardier* which often included a newsletter from East Africa. The settlers were evidently a little proud of the notoriety that the glamorous countess had brought to the heady world of the 'white highlands'. In general, Alice's Kenyan friends were inclined to forgive her. They had always been suspicious of Raymund, never really accepting him into their circle, and may have privately suspected he had got what he deserved. Only two of Alice's old allies were not so readily available. Lord Delamere, Alice's loyal supporter after her arrival in Africa, was now preoccupied courting Lady Gwladys Markham, daughter of the Honourable Rupert Beckett. He would marry her in May 1928. And Margaret Spicer, one of Alice's closest friends in Africa, had returned to London to have a baby.

Alice was relieved to find herself for the most part welcomed back into the highlands circle. Her return was to be short-lived, however. In February of 1928, less than a month after her arrival, Alice was contacted by an immigration officer, and given notice that she must leave the country. Her passport was removed and 'prohibited immigrant' written across it. She was given twenty-eight days to make arrangements for her departure. Alice was a divorcee, living alone without a new husband. As a general rule, single women were not admitted into Kenya at all. If a woman was engaged to someone living in the region, she arrived and went straight to Mombasa Cathedral to be married before even embarking on the train to Nairobi (Margaret Spicer went through this exact rigmarole in order to qualify for entry on her arrival in 1925). It transpired that Alice had made a powerful enemy in Kenya during her last visit: the governor's wife, Lady Joan Grigg. Lady Grigg, the colony's self-appointed moral guardian, had never liked Alice and now saw her opportunity to get rid of her altogether. After the incident at the Gare du Nord it would have been easy for Lady Grigg to argue that Alice was a single, dangerous and unstable character and should not be allowed to disturb the sanctity of other married families living in the area. Lady Grigg had her husband's ear on this matter and Alice had no other recourse but to obey orders. Lord Delamere was otherwise engaged and she had no influential connections amongst the authorities to argue her case.

With enormous reluctance, she began to arrange for her passage and to pack her possessions. She saw her lawyers and authorized them to rent her house, in the hope that the tenants would keep the place in good order and employ her loyal servants. In the period prior to her departure she was with Joss often, and there is plenty of evidence that she slept with him at this time, despite his new attachment to Mary. This pattern of frequent separations and intermittent sexual reunions between Joss and Alice would continue for years to come. Certainly, the couple were seen together on the afternoon of 28 February 1928. On that day, Karen Blixen, the future author of *Out of Africa* – who had been living and farming in Kenya with her husband Baron von Blixen-Finecke since 1914 – related in a letter to her mother that she had been visited by Joss and Alice. Karen had been running errands

Alice in a pony and trap, aged seven, Buffalo, New York, shortly before her mother Juliabelle died on 2 June, 1907. (From the collection of Harry Hartshorne Jr.)

Fred Silverthorne in his Stoddard-Knighton nine-litre motorcar with uniformed chauffeur. (From the collection of Harry Hartshorne Jr.)

Portrait photo of Alice, aged eighteen, before she met Frédéric de Janzé. (From the collections of Harry Hartshorne Jr. and Guillaume de Rougemont)

Wedding of Frédéric and Alice in Chicago on 21 September, 1921. (From the collections of Harry Hartshorne Jr., Guillaume de Rougemont, and Pat Silverthorne)

Hunting at Château Parfondeval in Normandy, France, where Alice spent long weekends and summers from 1922 to 1925. (From the collection of Guillaume de Rougemont)

Paula Gellibrand dressed as a mannequin in 'a coat of white rainproof cloth trimmed in black wool'. Paula was Alice's closest female friend in Paris and later in Kenya. (From Paula Gellibrand's scrapbook)

S.S. Gascon, the ship of the Messageries Maritimes, on which Alice and Frédéric sailed from Marseilles to Mombasa, Kenya, on 17 September, 1925. (Image provided by Iziko Museums of Cape Town)

Alice with Lord Delamere and Raymund de Trafford at Delamere's house, 'Loresho', Nairobi, Kenya, 1926. (Courtesy of Sir Dermot de Trafford Bart.)

Alice and Joss Erroll in 1926. (From the collection of Sir Dermot de Trafford Bart.)

Lapérouse restaurant where Alice and Raymund met for lunch on 17 March, 1927. They shopped in the afternoon, with Alice purchasing a revolver and six bullets. Alice shot Raymund and herself at 4:30 P.M. on that day.

Alice in the Paris Correctional Court awaiting a verdict on the attempted murder of Raymund de Trafford, 23 December, 1927. (© Corbis)

Studio portrait of Alice with pearls, 1928, while in exile from Kenya. (From the collection of Frédéric Armand Delille)

Press photo of Alice with Raymund and bulldog Jimmy after their marriage in Paris on 22 February, 1932. The marriage lasted only three months.

Porto Luca Cottage in Muthaiga, Nairobi, rented by Alice. She slept here on the night of Joss Erroll's murder in January 1941. (Courtesy of the author)

Lady Diana Delves Broughton, née Caldwell, with her pet mongoose at the Marula Lane House at Karen, Nairobi, 1941

Marula Lane House at Karen, Nairobi. It was from this house that Joss Erroll departed on the night of 24 January, 1941, only to be murdered on his drive home. (Courtesy of the author)

Dickie Pembroke at Alice's house in Tiwi. This was a coastal property south of Mombasa. Dickie was Alice's last lover. (Courtesy of Noel Eaton-Evans)

The veranda side of Alice's house in Wanjohi Valley. This was where Alice died on Saturday, 27 September, 1941. (Courtesy of Noel Case)

in Nairobi when she met Joss, the newly entitled Lord Erroll – he had succeeded to the earldom on the death of his father that very month – and invited him home for tea. Joss asked if he might bring Alice along.

That same afternoon, Karen Blixen received some unexpected guests: Lady Lucie McMillan, the widow of American millionaire Sir William Northrup McMillan, and the McMillans' old friend Charles Bulpett, both long-time Kenya residents. With them were two American tourists who had just arrived by steamer in Nairobi. Karen gleefully describes the ladies in her letter to her mother as 'really huge and corpulent'. They had been driving around the countryside, hoping to see a lion, so they could regale their fellow passengers on the ship later on. The Americans were also eager to talk about 'all the dreadfully immoral people in Kenya, Americans too unfortunately'. The 'worst one of all' was Alice de Janzé, whose exploits at the Gare du Nord had made headlines in the United States. Aware that the main subject of discussion was due to arrive at any moment, Karen let her guests continue with their tirade. When the infamous Alice arrived, Karen took mischievous delight in making the requisite introductions, to the extreme embarrassment of the American visitors. Karen told her mother, 'I don't think that the Devil himself could have had a greater effect if he had walked in; it was undoubtedly better than the biggest lion, and has given them much more to talk to the fellow passengers about.'

Alice left Africa in April. Back in France, she took up residence in the apartment in rue Spontini. Hairdressers, manicurists and masseurs were summoned to revitalize her. She visited her children who were living with Frédéric. Along with the loss of Kenya, she had one more sadness with which to contend. Soon after she had left France, Frédéric had decided to visit the Jardin d'Acclimatation to see Samson. On his arrival, he was told that all the cats there had been transferred to a circus. Frédéric went to the circus immediately. There he found a magnificent black-maned Masai lion half-asleep in a cage at the back of a tent. In his account of the incident in his book *Tarred With the Same Brush* Frédéric wrote: 'At last he got up and my heart stood still with horror – down his right hand quarter ran a jagged scar, Z shaped. It couldn't be Samson, but no two lions could have that same scar!' Frédéric called out to him. The lion cocked an ear and stalked over suspiciously. Frédéric put his hand through the bars. The attendant called out, '*Vous êtes fou, monsieur, il est très dangereux!*' The lion suddenly rolled over on his side, his back against the bars. Frédéric scratched him on the forehead; the lion put out his immense red tongue and licked Frédéric's hand, purring gently, delighted to be petted in a way that was evidently so familiar to him. It was Samson. Frédéric went to see the lion every day for a week, determined to buy him back from the circus. On his last visit, Frédéric was happily scratching Samson's brow when a female trainer, later described by Frédéric as a 'fiend in pink tights', arrived unexpectedly. She cracked her whip at Samson, ordering him to perform a new trick. The poor lion was driven panting and crouching into the corner of his cage. When the trainer turned her head for a second, Samson sprang at her, landing his massive paw on the side of her skull. A revolver shot rang out, then another. Frédéric wrote:

> Somehow I found myself in the cage, my hand on Samson's shoulder. I felt him shudder and he collapsed on my feet, knocking me over. I got up from under him and took his great head on my lap; a trickle of blood flowed from the side of his jaw onto me, then down to the floor; he tried one or two manful licks and snuggled his great shaggy head into my lap; he died in my arms – content, I hope, on the heart of a friend.

If Frédéric had permitted Alice to take Samson back to Kenya, the lion would have survived. We do not know if Alice reproached her former husband for his decision, but it is clear that she would have been deeply affected by the death of her beloved pet, especially as it coincided with her painful exile from Kenya.

On a happier note, it was during this time that Alice resumed her friendship with Paula de Casa Maury (née Gellibrand). Paula was in the process of separating from her husband, the Marquis de Casa Maury, and by the end of 1928 they had parted ways (de Casa Maury went on to marry Freda Dudley Ward, formerly mistress of Edward the Prince of Wales). Alice and Paula, as two newly single women, now had even more in common than ever. They accompanied one another on various adventures during this time: the following year, they decided on the spur of the moment to go to South America on a cargo boat with only two private cabins. Alice maintained her title of countess and, like the Marquise Paula, enjoyed playing the part of the beautiful, scandalous, titled divorcee. There is no doubt that the two women attracted a great deal of male interest wherever they went. In addition they could share their passionate interest in fashion. Alice eagerly began wearing her skirts short above the knee, and décolletée evening gowns hung from thin straps on her shoulders. Paula had become a fashion icon in Paris and was beginning to create her own clothes. 'It was a desire to have an occupation in life, instead of wandering from one tea party to another,' Paula later said of her designs, adding, 'I am tired of the eternal complaint that English women do not know how to wear their clothes.'

Alice was evidently inspired by Paula's new enterprise because it was after her return to Paris that she decided to invest in the fashion business herself, buying a substantial shareholding in the designer Jean Patou's Paris salon. Patou had opened his salon in 1919 and was making a name for himself as a haute couture designer, creating not only gowns but also sportswear for women, bathing suits in particular. He had already expanded into the American market, having dressed film stars such as Mary Pickford and Louise Brooks. On a visit to New York in 1925, he was so impressed by the long-legged American girls he encountered there that he auditioned 500 young women, choosing six of them to accompany him back to Paris as models (a masterful publicity stunt). In 1919, however, he was still struggling and Alice, along with her friend Idina, decided to help bail him out. Under the two women's sponsorship, Patou could begin to develop his new perfumes and other sidelines to help subsidize his couture line, a business model that fashion designers continue to follow to this day. Alice, Idina and Paula would both wear Patou and direct their influential friends to the salon.

Despite this new business distraction, Alice was restless. Although her time in Paris enabled her to explore her interest in fashion and play a more active part in the lives of her children, her focus remained on Raymund. She was in frequent contact with him and began visiting him regularly in England. It was as if by threatening to leave her, Raymund had triggered a need in Alice to hold on to him at all costs. The shooting had been her first attempt to prevent him from leaving. Now she resolved to get him back for good. Her sense of their relationship as unfinished business continued to blind her to his considerable character flaws. It is tempting to draw comparisons between Raymund and her father. Both men were unreliable, irascible, profligate, and compulsive gamblers and womanizers – which may go some way to explaining Raymund's continuing appeal for Alice. It is possible that her inability to countenance rejection by Raymund had its roots in her adolescence: one thinks of how Alice was forcibly removed from her father's care as a teenager, and wonders if she was revisiting and trying to rectify this trauma in her relationship with Raymund.

In June of 1927, less than three months after the shooting at the Gare du Nord, Alice and Frédéric had been granted a divorce. The marriage was officially annulled by Pope Pius XI in August of 1928. At this point, there was no longer anything to prevent a legal Catholic union with Raymund. What's more, if she could persuade Raymund to become her husband, she would be permitted to return to Kenya without delay, a high priority for Alice. But first, she needed the de Trafford family's blessing. In London, Alice called on Raymund's brother Rudolph at his house in Westminster. Rudolph's son, Dermot de Trafford, the future sixth baronet, recalled a visit from Alice during this period. Dermot's room and nursery were at the top of the house: Alice climbed all the stairs and warmly greeted him, explaining to his French governess that she was a friend of the family. Dermot remembered Alice telling the governess about her life in Africa and her animals there. (Afterwards, the governess remarked unkindly to Dermot that Alice's French was not very good.) Alice visited Rudolph and Dermot on more than one occasion, even going to stay with the de Traffords at their country home, Clock House, Cowfold, Sussex, where she signed the visitors' book with a flourish. Meanwhile, Raymund went back to Kenya at the end of 1928 to receive his other brother Humphrey, who had decided to see Raymund's farm and to meet a few old friends. That a single man like Raymund could travel freely to Kenya in this way must have rankled Alice and left her feeling doubly bereft.

By the end of 1928 Alice had decided that she would have to obtain a more permanent base in London if she was going to be a frequent visitor there. To this point, she had been staying in London's Ritz Hotel when in town, but at the beginning of 1929 she moved into an apartment block on fashionable Berkeley Street in Mayfair. Her half-sister, Patricia Silverthorne, and her stepmother, Louise Silverthorne, had recently moved into the same building. Louise and Pat had left the United States in 1919 following a drama in which the local sheriff had arrived at the family home in Sharon, Connecticut, to confront William Silverthorne. Pat remembers her father sitting downstairs puce in the face. Pat was sent to bed. In the morning, bags were packed and mother and daughter departed. When asked about this incident many years later, Pat refused to give full details, only revealing that, 'The chauffeur was the informer.' At such a distance, it is difficult to speculate on the nature of William's crime, but suffice to say that his behaviour was inappropriate enough that his wife and daughter sailed for France only a few days later.

Pat completed her education in Florence before being brought to London by Louise, who was determined to introduce her into English society. This was a tricky prospect for an Italian-educated American girl with no fixed abode or society sponsorship. Early in 1929, Alice, Pat and Louise found themselves living as neighbours. Alice had never been particularly close to Pat, but she had always got on well with Louise; however, she was careful to keep a certain distance from both women in public. 'With my reputation and the scandal surrounding me, I would not wish to spoil Pat's chances of meeting the right people,' she explained. Whenever Alice came over from Paris, they would breakfast together and it was during this period that Pat and Louise were often privy to Alice's unpredictable tempers and moods. On one occasion of Pat's recollection, Alice had been eagerly awaiting the day's mail, perhaps hoping for a letter from Raymund who had returned again to Kenya. That day, a single letter came and Alice opened it, only to find a large dividend cheque. Alice threw it to the ground, eyes welling with disappointment and disgust: 'I don't want all this damn money,' she told Pat. 'It doesn't buy happiness.'

Often Alice would walk alone up Berkeley Street at lunchtime, meeting a friend at the Ritz bar, where she would drink vodka cocktails spiked with absinthe. She was on the verge of her thirties, and her beauty, rather than waning, was maturing as the next decade of her life approached. Although a whisper of scandal accompanied her wherever she went, the countess was much in demand. Most Thursday evenings she could be found sitting at a table near the entrance of the Embassy Club in Old Bond Street, the famously exclusive London dance club. Thursday evening was the most fashionable night of the week, when the Embassy's dance floor swam with royalty, socialites and celebrities. The walls were painted in a soft green, with pink sofas placed against them, and low-level lighting was provided by twin candelabras fitted low on the walls. At the Embassy, Alice socialized with a small circle of Kenya connections that included, when he was in London, Denys Finch Hatton. Alice was also seen regularly with the club's most illustrious members, Edward, Prince of Wales – who would later abdicate the throne in order to marry Wallis Simpson – and his decadent younger brother, Prince George, the future Duke of Kent. Prince George kept up a long line of affairs with both men and women throughout his short life (he was killed in an aeroplane crash in Scotland in 1942). Alice could often be seen at the 'Royal Box', a table on the right at the front of the club, usually the rowdiest table in the room. Another member of the Embassy set was banking heiress Poppy Baring, christened Helen, daughter of Sir Godfrey Baring of Baring banks, and one of Prince George's many consorts. Gloria Vanderbilt, the widow of railroad heir Reginald Vanderbilt and mother of the future jeans designer, was also a regular. Kiki Preston, the drug-addicted great-niece of Reginald's mother, Alice Vanderbilt, could also be found there. Known as 'the girl with the silver syringe', she was the woman Prince George had fallen in love with on a trip to Kenya in 1928.

The novelist Barbara Cartland's description of Thursdays at the Embassy evokes something of the glamour of the female members of the club:

The faces of the women dancing and sitting round the room have an almost monotonous beauty. They all have large eyes with mascaraed eyelashes, full crimson mouths, narrow aristocratic noses and fine bones. Their hair, cut short and styled close to their well-shaped heads, is like exquisite satin, shiny and neat. Everything about them is neat and the expensive perfection of simplicity. Their skins are white — very white, the only exception being the warm golden loveliness of Lady Plunket as she floats by in the arms of Prince George. Dorothe is the first person to be sun-tanned, and she has whispered to me that in the winter she keeps the same colour by applying diluted iodine to her skin.

It was at the Embassy that Alice and Prince George discovered their mutual love of French bulldogs. Alice had come into possession of a bulldog called Jimmy; Prince George had a bitch of equal breeding. It was decided that the two dogs should be married. To demonstrate Jimmy's eligibility, Alice flew privately from Paris to London with him and her two children. Paola remembers being pulled across Regent's Park by Jimmy on his long leather lead. The prince must have approved of Alice's hound because, despite quarantine regulations, the royal bitch was boxed and flown over to Paris to mate with Jimmy the next time she was in season. Twenty guests toasted the canine consummation with champagne at Alice's rue Spontini apartment and the dogs were decorated with orange blossom. While guests got drunk, Jimmy and his consort were locked in a bedroom. At one point, Alice decided to see how they were getting along, whereupon she discovered that Jimmy was facing 'south' and the prince's dog was facing 'north'. Horrified, Alice rang her vet, informing him, 'My dog is killing the Prince's poor girl!' The vet advised her to remain calm, assuring her that in twenty minutes all would be well.

When not arranging wedding parties for pets, Alice continued her campaign to secure a marriage of her own. After Raymund returned from one of his Kenya trips, Alice whisked him away to the South of France where he could indulge his love of gambling. Raymund had always been a keen gambler. He belonged to six clubs in London, including Buck's and White's, where he regularly lost money. *Reynolds Illustrated News* reported that he had lost

£7,000 playing cards in London in the course of one year. Occasionally, he got lucky. Soon after leaving the army, he had visited Deauville in France and cleared £5,000 winnings in a week's play. While in Cannes with Alice, Raymund scored an even bigger win. As he later recounted to Margaret Spicer, he had been playing roulette and betting on 0 and 0, 1, 2 and 3. When 0 came up twice running, followed by 3, which was half covered by 0, he won many thousands of francs. Inspired, Raymund piled on the chips and won even more. Sensibly, Alice encouraged him to cash in his chips: the amount he received exceeded his total allowance for the year. Later, Pat Silverthorne – who met Raymund only once and took an immediate dislike to him – would describe this incident as the time he 'broke the bank at Monte Carlo' (in fact, the win took place at Cannes).

Alice was not the only member of the Happy Valley set in the process of remarrying. As soon as Joss's divorce from Idina was made absolute at the beginning of 1930, he married Mary Ramsay-Hill on the 8th of February of that year at St Martin's Register Office in London. Soon afterwards the couple returned to Kenya and set themselves up in the sumptuous former Ramsay-Hill residence, which Mary had secured in her divorce settlement from her former husband. Frédéric remarried that same year. The wedding took place on 9 January 1930 at the Church of Saint-Pierre-de-Chaillot in Paris. His bride was Genevieve Ryan (née Willinger), another American and the widow of Thomas Jefferson Ryan, a prominent New York lawyer and politician. Not to be outdone, Idina would also wed before the end of 1930. Her fourth husband, Donald Haldeman – born in England and educated at Eton – was the son of an American shirt maker. Their nuptials took place in Steyning, Sussex on 22 November 1930. After a honeymoon in the United States, the couple returned to Kenya, where Donald had already made a name for himself as a white hunter.

All these weddings galvanized Alice's resolve. Despite Raymund's evident flaws, she continued her campaign. After almost four years of Alice trying to persuade him to marry her, Raymund finally relented. In 1931, the couple announced their engagement.

7

The Bride in Black
and White

By the end of 1931, Raymund had convinced his family that there was no longer anything to prevent him from marrying Alice. Her marriage to Frédéric had been annulled by the Pope, which meant that, as far as the Catholic Church was concerned, Alice had never been married at all. Humphrey and Rudolph gave their consent and secret plans were hatched for a discreet wedding to be held in Paris early in the new year. Raymund must have been anxious to avoid publicity. He was still conscious of his family's underlying disapproval of his relationship with Alice, and the ongoing scandal of the Gare du Nord shooting. Humphrey was warning him to keep the wedding a low-profile affair. Alice was more realistic. She felt that the presence of the press at the nuptials was inevitable and that only so much could be done to control the coverage of the event. In fact, she hoped that the ensuing publicity might actually mitigate the 'scandale' in the eyes of the public and silence the lingering recriminations surrounding her relationship with Raymund.

Alice and Raymund decided to get married in the wealthy Parisian suburb of Neuilly. Alice busied herself with the preparations. She needed to find a dress to wear for the ceremony that would be both chic and appropriate. Alice knew she would be photographed extensively and she enlisted Paula de Casa Maury's help in selecting a suitably striking outfit. Paula advised Alice to wear black. 'I am not in mourning!' was Alice's response. 'You can hardly wear white,' Paula replied. A compromise was reached: Alice would wear black *and* white. Her former employer, M. Arnot, created Alice's wedding outfit at his shop on rue Saint-Florentin. Arnot made a close-fitting black cloak with black and white feathers, worn over a tight broad black tail jacket with white gauntlets and an ermine collar. Under the cloak and jacket was a black frock with a white insert, and to top it off, a dramatic black hat. The colour scheme matched Alice's black and white bulldog Jimmy to perfection. Jimmy would accompany Alice to the ceremony. The dog was given a special shampoo in honour of the occasion.

The wedding took place on 22 February 1932 in a room adjoining the historic Salle des Fêtes (where the treaty of Neuilly between Bulgaria and the Allies had been signed in 1919) in Neuilly town hall. The deputy Mayor performed the short service in French. The bride was resplendent in black and white with her bulldog Jimmy at her side. Raymund wore a dark suit and a white shirt and tie and sported a bowler hat. The witnesses were Rudolph de Trafford and Paula de Casa Maury. As with her first marriage, Alice's father did not attend. Neither did her two children, who were with Frédéric in Paris. Alice was later described as 'charming and smiling', and apparently she signed the register with 'a firm hand'. (Even though the register was an official document, usually available to the public, in this instance, it was carefully removed and put away in anticipation of the pack of press waiting outside.) When the brief formalities were over, Raymund escorted the guests down a side staircase and Alice meanwhile slipped away down another. She then caught a waiting car and drove off separately to Paula's residence in Neuilly, where a small reception was held.

That night a religious ceremony was performed in the Church of Saint Pierre at Neuilly. This time Alice wore a white veil. The wedding was widely reported in the French, American and British press. On 23 February, the *New York Times* printed the following pithy headline: 'American Woman Weds Man She Shot'. On the wedding day itself, London's *Evening News* gave the event front-page coverage with the headlines 'Black and White Bride' and a subheading of 'Coat, Hat and Dog to Match'. The *Evening Standard* went with 'Romance of Happy Valley' in large type and a subtitle of 'Mr Raymund de Trafford Marries Former Countess'. The *Star* printed: 'Locked Room Wedding' and 'Mr Raymund de Trafford's Bride Takes Her Bulldog'. The *Daily Telegraph* was more discreet, covering the story on page nine with a photograph of the couple and a short caption. (At least three reporters spelled Raymund's first name incorrectly. It must have happened all his life. He was Raymund, not Raymond.)

It is true that the majority of Alice's friends and relatives found her fixation on Raymund impossible to understand: for six years now, she had refused to let go of the idea of marrying a patently unpleasant man who clearly had few redeeming characteristics. Even Raymund's closest friends were never particularly complimentary about him, referring to him as '*tête brûlée*' or hothead. After Evelyn Waugh returned from Kenya in 1931, he wrote a letter to Lady Dorothy Lygon in which he described Raymund as 'very nice but SO BAD. He fights and fucks and gambles and gets DD [disgustingly drunk] all the time.' Alice, meanwhile, had continued to overlook Raymund's bad behaviour, clinging to the hope that the relationship would improve if only she could marry him. Now that she was Raymund's wife, she had a new British passport to boot, presented to her by the British Embassy in Paris. It declared she was a 'British Subject by Marriage' which also meant that she could return with Raymund to Kenya.

But first there was the honeymoon, which Alice and Raymund spent in Monte Carlo and Cannes. The newly-weds settled down at the Hôtel de Paris in Monte Carlo where Alice installed them in a grand suite overlooking the harbour. No expense was spared, and each day passed in preparation for the night ahead. Raymund, of course, made straight for the casino and its Salon Privée where he proceeded to play roulette at the high table until the early hours. Unlike his luck in Cannes, his losses during the honeymoon were considerable and Alice funded him throughout. He was placing maximum bets on numbers 'en plein' which never came up. Alice was understandably distressed – after all, he was playing with her money – and they quarrelled. Although Alice must have been aware of Raymund's more unappealing qualities before the wedding, it was in Monaco that she began to have some idea of the full extent of his failings. Marriage, it seems, was having the effect of bringing out the worst extremes of Raymund's character. This was a man so completely unsuited to being a husband that it makes one wonder why he agreed to marry Alice. But Alice had been extraordinarily persistent, and there were the small matters of her beauty and wealth, both of which would have been powerful incentives for someone as vain and profligate as Raymund. He may have also had a lingering sense of 'honour' about the woman he had jilted in very public circumstances.

Before the honeymoon was over, Raymund decided his luck might take a turn for the better if they had a change of venue. They moved along the coast to the casino at Cannes, where he had been successful in the past, and where they stayed in the equally majestic accommodations of the Carlton Hotel, with its grand terrace facing the corniche. Raymund's luck did indeed change in Cannes and he won back at least half of his considerable losses in Monte Carlo. His mood improved and Alice diverted the discussion to Kenya, reminding Raymund that she hoped to return there as soon as possible. The couple flew to

London in late March 1932, staying initially at Rudolph de Trafford's home in Cowfold, Sussex. Here the rows continued. Alice was determined to return to Kenya. Raymund would not be told what to do. Although Alice had hoped that the presence of Raymund's family would tame her new husband's temper, this was not the case. Alice confided their problems to Rudolph, but it did nothing to alleviate the rancour.

The more Alice tried to talk about returning to Kenya, the more Raymund retreated from the marriage in general. By April of that year, Alice decided it would be best to go away for a while without him. The couple had been married barely two months when she made plans to take the waters at the Thermia Palace spa in Piestany, Slovakia, with her new sister-in-law, Mrs Keith Menzies. Raymund's sister – christened Violet Mary – was a little older than Alice, having been born in 1893. Like Alice, she had been divorced from her first husband, receiving an annulment from the Pope in 1921. She married Colonel Keith Menzies in 1922. The new sisters-in-law agreed that a trip abroad would allow Raymund a cooling-off period. Built in 1912, the Thermia Palace was famous for its curative thermal spring waters, healing mud pool and luxurious art nouveau accommodations. It was a place frequented by Hollywood film stars, European royalty and Indian maharajas alike. Alice and Violet booked in for a complete course.

While in Slovakia, Alice wrote a letter dated 8 May 1932 to her Uncle Sim (Simeon Chapin) who was still the trustee of her fortune and her financial adviser. Alice wanted to thank him for his wedding present and for his letter of good wishes. She also wrote that she was 'suffering considerably from my "tummy"'. Alice's self-inflicted bullet wound to her abdomen continued to trouble her and the injury seems to have been exacerbated by stress and overexertion. Years later, her eldest daughter, Nolwen, remembered that her mother underwent multiple operations over the years and was rarely free of abdominal pain. In Alice's letter to Uncle Sim, she put a brave face on her ailment as well as her new marriage, even managing to explain away the fact that she was travelling without Raymund only two months after the wedding. After five years of being independent, she wrote, she couldn't imagine being married 'to anyone who had no respect for one's privacy . . .' Obviously, Alice did not wish to confide her marital problems to Uncle Sim because she went on to say that her new marriage was harmonious precisely because Raymund never interfered with her plans and she never interfered with his. After Slovakia, she would join Raymund in Paris. Despite Alice's valiant effort to give Uncle Sim the impression that all was well with the marriage, matters with Raymund had grown untenable. When Alice returned from Slovakia, she met him for lunch at a pavement cafe in Paris. Onlookers reported to the American gossip columns that Alice and Raymund were in the middle of a very vocal fight when Raymund picked up his champagne-brandy cocktail – decorated with a glacé cherry – and threw it in Alice's face. Alice, her face dripping with drink and a cherry sticking to the little black veil on her hat, was seen to reach for her handbag to retrieve a compact. Raymund apparently misinterpreted Alice's movement, assuming that she was going for her gun again. Terrified, he made off down the street. Alice wasted no time, contacting her lawyers and advising them that she wanted an immediate legal separation. She agreed to buy Raymund a first-class passage to Australia, and to fund him sufficiently to stay there for a considerable length of time.

Raymund took the money and left for Australia as instructed. Mere months after the wedding, Alice was alone again. Determined to return to Kenya, even without Raymund, she travelled to London to pack up her flat in Berkeley Street and went once more to see Rudolph de Trafford. Rudolph seems to have taken pity on his sister-in-law as she stayed with him throughout August of 1932 (according to his visitor's book). Alice also managed to make contact with a visiting white hunter from Kenya who was arranging a safari for members of the Vanderbilt family. The planned hunting trip would take the party into the Congo from the west coast of Africa and towards the Ugandan border. Alice offered to pay her way if she could tag along, with the idea that she would cross over to Uganda and then get a train down from Kisumu on Lake Victoria to Nairobi. The Vanderbilts were delighted to have this interesting American girl as part of their entourage and so Alice packed her bags.

She said goodbye to Nolwen and Paola, who were now aged ten and eight years old respectively, promising them she would return for regular visits. Although Alice had been living in Europe for almost six years, her daughters

were so accustomed to their mother's regular disappear-
ances that this one would not have seemed very different
from all the others. Alice de Trafford, as she was now
known, entered Kenya via the Congo and Uganda with her
new British passport and went straight to the newly
appointed governor, Sir Joseph Byrne, who had assumed
office the previous year. Lady Joan Grigg was no longer in
a position to block her return, and so Alice presented her
letters of support (one from Frédéric de Janzé himself).
Sir Joseph granted her the right to stay. It was 1933, and
Alice had been away since 1928. With her ferocious determination and an unrelenting desire to get what she
wanted, Alice had managed to find her way back to Kenya
again.

Part Two

8

Return to Happy Valley

Whenever Alice arrived in Nairobi from Europe it was her habit to go immediately to stay with Joss and Idina at Slains. But this was 1933 and Happy Valley was much changed. Joss and Idina had separated in 1928 and Slains had been sold while the divorce was still in progress. And so instead of making her way to Slains on her arrival, Alice went immediately to Idina's new home, Clouds, about six miles up the road from Wanjohi Farm on Mount Kipipiri (a Masai word meaning rain). Here she took up temporary residence in one of Idina's three guestrooms while Mr Barrat, the lawyer, gave notice to the family renting Alice's farm. Clouds was another settler house laid out in the typical manner, with a large central drawing room opening up on to a sixty-degree verandah where Idina often dined with her many guests. Along with her new residence, Idina had a new husband: in 1930 she had married an American, Donald Haldeman, but the union was an unhappy one, with Idina intent on carrying on her usual affairs. Donald's money came from a clothing manufacturing business and after one of the couple's blazing rows Idina was heard on the verandah of Clouds wailing: 'You makers of shirts, how can you understand us who have been wanton through the ages!' Another legend has it that Donald shot at the tyres of a car owned by one of Idina's boyfriends in protest.

Joss, meanwhile, could be found living in great style at Oserian, built on the beautiful shores of Lake Naivasha, where hippos roamed freely at night. The house had been awarded to his new wife, Mary, as part of her divorce settlement and was a much crenellated and domed North African-style castle, complete with minarets. Here Joss had installed squash courts and a swimming pool, and he bred polo ponies and hosted matches every week. Locals called Oserian the 'Djinn Palace' and although it did indeed look like an oversized Aladdin's lamp, the pun on 'gin' was intentional. Through the years, plenty of alcohol was consumed at Oserian, most of it by Mary who was developing a serious dependency. The poor woman desperately wanted to conceive a child, and when this did not happen, she fell back on her favourite black velvet cocktails. It didn't help that Joss and Mary's closest neighbours were Kiki and Gerry Preston: Kiki was the 'girl with the silver syringe', the American socialite whose conquests included Prince George, the Duke of Kent. Addicted to heroin, Kiki is said to have introduced Mary to the habit.

What did Joss see in Mary? The general consensus was that he had married her for her money.

At the time of Alice's return to Kenya, Joss had begun another new chapter in his life. Kenya's governor, Sir Joseph Byrne, had recently nominated Joss for the position of Councillor on the Naivasha District Council. Meetings, speech-giving and the responsibilities of public office now became part of Joss's regular routine. Of course, Joss was happy to see Alice – she continued to exert a powerful attraction for him and he had a talent for keeping on good terms with former mistresses – but he was busy. Not surprisingly, Mary wasn't inclined to tolerate Joss's extra-marital activities with the same laissez-faire as Idina. As a result, Alice's time with Joss would have been limited. The other lynchpin in Alice's Kenyan social life, Lord Delamere, had died in November 1931. Overall, the mood amongst Alice's friends was considerably less frivolous than it had been in the 1920s. Along with the rest of the world, the colony was entering a recession. Everyone, Alice included, was a little older, and without Joss and Idina to anchor her friendships or D as her champion, she would have felt adrift. What's more, she no longer had Frédéric or Raymund to partner her in social situations: as an unaccompanied woman, even in the relatively free-wheeling atmosphere of the highlands, there was only so much she could do alone.

Determined to make the best of things, Alice set about making a new life for herself. In her absence, her house in Wanjohi had been let to an English family called Case. The Cases had land in the area and were building their house

slightly north of Alice's Wanjohi property. They were serious farmers and pioneers, not in the least socially
ambitious, and as such they had little interest in their
wilder, grander neighbours. Their daughter, Noel, was in
her twenties, and determined to run a good establishment. While Alice had been away, she had created a proper
garden on the property (something Alice had overlooked),
laying out lawns and a rose garden. She had installed new
curtains and comfortable sofas in the house and generally
trained the servants who, under Alice's tenure, had grown
used to operating without instruction. Under Noel – the
household staff were smartly decked out in long white
kanzus and red hats and the cook could make European
dishes – Wanjohi Farm had been quite transformed. Now
that Alice was back, Noel Case asked if she could remain
at Wanjohi as an employed housekeeper, and Alice happily
agreed – Noel possessed the necessary household and
managerial skills that Alice so sorely lacked. When it came
to settling bills and paying staff, Alice's lack of acumen was
appalling: this was never due to meanness or lack of funds,
it was simply that she had no desire to deal with such mun-
dane matters. The title deed of Wanjohi shows that on
several occasions, close friends such as Geoffrey Buxton
and Idina were paying for Alice's outstanding bills and
taking a charge on Wanjohi Farm until Alice handed over
the amounts in question. Once the furniture had been
reinstated from the manager's house, Noel moved in and
ran the main house and kitchen. Alice bought herself a
new Plymouth car and hired a driver who was to remain
with her for the rest of her years: his name was Ruta (he

was of the Kalengin tribe, and therefore known as 'Arap Ruta'). Alice brought her maid over from France, rounding out the new order at Wanjohi.

As always, Alice began acquiring pets. On her return, she adopted a little dachshund, called Minnie, who became her particular favourite. She acquired a Rhodesian ridgeback hunting dog, often called the African lion dog for its ability to keep lions at bay by barking. Also included in her menagerie was a magnificent pet eland or East African antelope that roamed her grounds freely. Alice's days at Wanjohi were spent playing backgammon, riding, walking her dogs, reading and drinking. She socialized with her neighbours, striking up a friendship with Fabian Wallace, an old friend of Joss's from Eton. Openly homosexual and strikingly handsome, Fabian lived on a small but well-appointed farm at the entrance to the Wanjohi junction near Gilgil where he grew pyrethrum. As well as being a remittance man, Fabian was also something of an epicure: he loved fine food and had his own cigarettes specially made for him in St James's Street, London, which were sent out to Kenya in boxes of a hundred. Another new friend was Pat Fisher, who had a cottage not far from Kipipiri, which she occupied while helping her husband, Derek, manage Sir John 'Chops' Ramsden's cattle on an estate near Clouds. Pat later remembered Alice's potent home-made cocktails, which included a whisky sour that was doused with grenadine and fresh lime and took immediate effect. Together with Idina, these new friends provided Alice with a much-needed social outlet on her return to Wanjohi Farm.

Just as Alice was establishing herself in Kenya, however, the recent past came back to haunt her. Towards the end of 1933, Raymund emerged on the scene. The couple were still legally married, but even so, Alice had not expected to hear from Raymund so soon. She had put up the money for him to travel to Australia, on the proviso that he did not return for some time. Instead, it seems he had so alarmed his Australian host and hostess in Melbourne with his general debauchery that he had thought it best to leave, deciding to return to Kenya in a bid to revive his relationship with Alice. She fended him off to the best of her ability, but she often had to run to Idina for protection. One evening, Raymund arrived at Alice's farm having driven over from his farm at Njoro. He was already drunk and threatening, demanding dinner and accommodation. Alice allowed him to take a bath before giving him something to eat, but when Raymund failed to appear at the dinner table, the French maid put her head around the bathroom door, only to find him drunk and asleep in the bath. 'Madame, one small push of the head under the water,' noted the maid to Alice, 'and all your troubles will be over.'

Then, in the new year, Alice received very sad news. Frédéric had died suddenly in Baltimore, Maryland, on 24 December 1933. He was in the United States on assignment, writing a series of syndicated articles for the French papers on economic conditions, but had fallen ill soon after his arrival. Two weeks later, he died of a septic infection complicated by meningitis. By his side was his new American wife, Genevieve, who had been married to

Frédéric for nearly four years. Frédéric was only thirty-seven. Nolwen and Paola were eleven and nine, respectively, at the time of their father's tragic death. Although they had been in Frédéric's custody after the divorce, it was decided that they should remain in the able care of Alice's Aunt Tattie now that their father was gone. Alice's reaction to this loss is not recorded, but there is no doubt that she would have felt it deeply: Frédéric had been a loyal husband and good friend, not to mention a devoted father to her two children. Even so, her reaction must have been tempered by her desire to keep in abeyance difficult memories of her own early loss of a parent: although she made sure to write to Nolwen and Paola, she did not return to France to attend the funeral nor to comfort her two children in this immediate period after Frédéric's death. Many years later, Alice's housekeeper, Noel, would remember that Alice almost never spoke of her past or her children during this time, nor did she keep any photographs of the family at Wanjohi, not even of her two daughters. On one occasion, Alice mentioned to Noel that her father was in a home in the United States and that it was costing her a lot of money but, otherwise, she continued to promote the illusion that she was a woman without ties or a past.

What is clear is that she did not neglect Nolwen and Paola entirely. In this period after their father's death she sent letters and later made visits to France to see her daughters. In 1931, the Imperial Airways flying service had begun a regular schedule from Southampton to Kisumu on Lake Victoria, which meant that Alice could travel back and forth to Europe without enduring a month-long sea voyage. Flights were swift, if expensive, usually only stopping at Alexandria for refuelling. Paola later remembered being taken out to restaurants in Paris by her mother who would regale her children with stories of animals and Africa. Paola remembers that on one occasion, Alice was convinced that an African waiter serving them hot chocolate was from Kenya, and so she tried to give her order in Swahili. In fact, the waiter was from Algeria and spoke fluent French. According to Nolwen, Alice had a delightful sense of humour, willingly laughed at herself and was a good leg-puller. She was, Nolwen said, '*très pince-sans-rire* [very deadpan] despite that dreamy gaze of hers which was due to her extreme near-sightedness'.

Despite her regular visits to Europe, Alice had already given up her apartment in London and was beginning to expand her residences in Africa. She acquired a new cottage, called Portaluca, conveniently located in the Muthaiga area, close to the centre of Nairobi, which made it ideal for socializing with her city friends and for those times when she felt unduly isolated at Wanjohi. Alice's new pied-à-terre was approached by a secluded drive, surrounded by a garden terrace. The main living room formed a central tower in the house, with two bedrooms on one side and a maid's bedroom on the other. During her stays at Portaluca, her driver, Ruta, and her French maid would accompany Alice. The house was conveniently located close to the Muthaiga Club, which she could only visit on Raymund's membership. Entry was a tricky proposition for a single woman: the bar was for men only, as was membership in general. Alice found herself having to sign her name 'de Trafford' despite the fact that she was doing everything in her powers to put a distance between herself and her estranged husband.

During this period of her life, she also began to look for a house on the coast. Most people from the Wanjohi area – upcountry people as they are known – regularly spend a few weeks at the coast every year as a respite from the high blood pressure induced by living at 6,000 feet above sea level. Alice set about exploring the Diani area, south of Mombasa, where she discovered an old coastal house at a place called Tiwi. The house, also called Tiwi, was small and in disrepair, but it was close to a quiet beach lined with palm trees and facing the Indian Ocean. Sunshine was tempered by ocean breezes and the nights were magical, lit by moon and stars and lulled with the gentle lapping of waves. Alice quickly negotiated a rent for the house, hired two local servants and proceeded to do it up, surrounding it with bougainvillea. Water was drawn from an old Arab well and the outside 'long drop' was the only available latrine: it consisted of a grass-roofed hut with an eight-foot pit, fitted with a wooden box to overhang the pit. While Tiwi wasn't particularly smart or comfortable, it was idyllic, and Alice loved staying there and hosting friends. There was plenty of fresh fish and seafood to eat, along with tropical fruits such as paw paw, mango, pineapple and watermelon. The house had four bedrooms, but Alice, who was never good with numbers, often invited too many guests for the existing space. On one occasion, she was forced to add more bedrooms at short notice;

such was the haste with which the rooms were assembled that none of them were symmetrical, nor were they interconnected with the original house. At all three of her houses, Alice kept an especially big and luxurious bed for herself. The guest beds, however, were notoriously hard and uncomfortable. And so Alice began a new chapter in her life, moving between her three residences frequently. Back at Wanjohi Farm, Noel Case would often be driven to distraction by her mistress's impulsive behaviour. Alice never thought to give notice of when she would be leaving or returning, often disappearing for days on end. Part of this secrecy was probably based on general carelessness and a need to avoid Raymund, but it also had to do with the general air of privacy that Alice cultivated during this time.

As for her relations with Joss, these were complicated by the fact that Alice did not approve of his recent political attachments. In April 1934, Joss had flown back to London with Mary, spending the summer there. It was during this trip that he became a card-carrying member of the British Union of Fascists. Sir Oswald Mosley – known as Tom – had founded the Union in 1932 and had been an acquaintance of Joss's since the early 1920s when the two men had first met. Now, with a worldwide depression entrenching, support for Mosley's brand of staunch protectionism was growing, especially amongst members of the English upper classes. The cause was a controversial one from the start. In June of 1934, only a month after Joss's initiation into the Union, Mosley's blackshirted stewards clashed violently with police and hecklers in

London, causing an outcry and damaging the party's already dubious image. The Union never recovered and was unable to gather sufficient support to play a part in the general election the following year. But Joss was convinced of the rightness of Mosley's solutions, especially in terms of their application to the economic difficulties being experienced in the colonies. If the threat of foreign markets could be removed and trade within the British Empire developed into an economic stronghold, Joss reasoned, then the possibilities for Kenya would be enormous. In Mosley's thrall, he spent the following months attending rallies, meetings and parties, appearing at the annual Blackshirt Cabaret Ball of 1934 with the Union's badge in silver on his sporran. By the time he returned to East Africa in August, he had been made Mosley's delegate in Kenya.

The timing of Joss's political conversion couldn't have been worse when it came to garnering support for the fascist cause in the settler community of Kenya. By the middle of 1934, Kenya itself was feeling the direct threat of fascist forces. The Italian fascist leader Benito Mussolini had stationed his armies on the Abyssinian border with Italian Somaliland. It was believed that British Kenya, which bordered Abyssinia, could well be the next line of attack. Up to this point, Abyssinia had managed to fend off her aggressors, remaining one of the few independent states in European-ruled Africa, but everyone was beginning to feel nervous about Mussolini's intentions in East Africa. In October of 1935, a border incident between the Abyssinians and the Italians gave Mussolini the opportunity he had been waiting for: with the League of Nations failing to intervene, Mussolini and his troops pushed back the Abyssinian army, taking Addis Ababa on 5 May 1936. Abyssinia's young leader, Haile Selassie, was forced to flee to Jerusalem via the Suez Canal and Haifa with the help of the British, taking with him 150 cases of silver coins so heavy that the sailors could carry only one case at a time. As head of the Coptic Church he was given a sensational reception in the Holy City. Mussolini's troops were now even closer to Kenya's northern border.

None of these events would have gone unnoticed by Alice, but unlike Joss, her politics inclined her strongly to the left. During one of her mother's trips to Paris in 1936, Nolwen, then aged fourteen, was sternly cautioned by Alice for expressing a preference for the fascist leader Francisco Franco over the Republicans in Spain. 'My mother rebuked me with restraint but real indignation in being wrong thinking about the Civil War in Spain. She was fervently republican. I, on the other hand, had been told how the Communists pumped up the bellies of innocent nuns with bicycle pumps . . .' This was evidently not the only political situation about which Alice had a definite point of view. Alice's eldest daughter also admitted to being 'alarmed by my mother' on several other occasions – 'not for fear of being shot by her, or because of some latent undercurrent of violence which I might perceive in her, but because I was inclined to much forthrightness in expressing opinions . . . Poor mama! Luckily there was Paola who cared nothing for religion or politics and preferred animals above all.'

It was during the same trip to Europe that Alice extended her visit to include a rare trip to see her father in Myrtle Beach, South Carolina. William Silverthorne was in ill health. In 1925, he had married again, a woman called Myrtle Plunkett, 'in order to have a nurse to look after him', according to his daughter Pat Silverthorne. William was nearing seventy and had only a few years to live – perhaps Alice sensed that this would be one of her last opportunities to see him. Father and daughter had remained in contact via their correspondence and – as Alice had suggested to Noel Case – she was helping to foot his medical bills. But even so, the visit does not seem to have constituted much in the way of a reconciliation between father and daughter. It was too late for that. Again, Alice left for Africa, putting a distance of many thousands of miles between herself and her troubled past. She was thirty-seven and living an independent life, one she had chosen for herself, removed from America and Europe, without a husband, shored up in her beautiful African houses with her books and her cocktails, a woman apart.

9

The Gathering Storm

In 1936, Joss and Mary moved into a bungalow in Nairobi, close to Alice's own pied-à-terre in the Muthaiga area. Alice and her old boyfriend became neighbours again, as they had been during the days of Slains. Despite Joss's political leanings, it was true that he remained one of the few constants in Alice's life. Their intermittent love affair had weathered their respective marriages to Idina and Frédéric, and the divorces thereafter, Alice's runaway romance with Raymund, her trial and imprisonment, her exile from Kenya, and her subsequent marriage and separation from Raymund, not to mention Joss's numerous other affairs and his marriage to Mary. In 1936, however, Mary's health was worsening and she needed to be near a hospital and her doctors. What's more, Joss was planning to stand for election to the Legislative Council, and so he needed to have a more permanent base in the capital than his usual rooms at the Muthaiga Club. With Joss living in such close proximity to Alice, it would have been impossible for him to resist the occasional secret meeting with his old flame, a habit that had been established for so many years. Alice had always made herself available to Joss and she continued to do so.

In that same year, in his role as Lord High Constable of Scotland, Joss was expected to take his place in the coronation procession of the new king, Edward VIII. Then came the abdication crisis, during which Edward declared he would rather marry a divorcee – Mrs Wallis Simpson – than ascend the throne. The coronation of Edward's brother, George Albert, was delayed until May of the following year. Alice would have followed these events keenly: Edward was one of her old friends from her Embassy Club days in London. When Joss did finally return from the coronation, in 1937, it was announced that he would stand for the Kiambu constituency in the forthcoming elections. Kiambu was at the very heart of the Kikuyu tribe, about eight miles from Nairobi, and had its own club, mainly supported by local coffee planters. Joss Erroll was duly elected and sworn in on 8 April 1938. By now, he had put his affiliations with Oswald Mosley behind him, celebrating along with the rest of his expatriate friends when the Munich crisis was averted in September of 1938. When Chamberlain arrived in London waving a non-aggression pact signed by Hitler, there was a new optimism that 'peace for our time' was not only possible, but a certainty.

Towards the end of 1938, Alice had good news of a more personal nature: she received word that her old friend Paula Gellibrand would be arriving in Kenya before the end of the year. After divorcing the 'Cuban Heel', the Marquis de Casa Maury, Paula had married William Allen in Paris but the marriage lasted only a year. (Bill Allen worked for British Intelligence – and would in time visit Kenya in the run-up to the outbreak of war in 1939.) For her part, Alice had finally become officially divorced from Raymund in October of 1937. The two women were single again and Paula, who wanted to try living in Kenya, decided to stay with Alice for a time. The friends proceeded to make the most of one another's company, living at Wanjohi and riding out each morning with Alice's dogs. The warmth of the relationship between these two attractive women is obvious from photographs they took of one another at Wanjohi Farm. Taking turns holding the camera, wearing identical short-sleeved gingham shirts and cord trousers – a boyish look that Alice cultivated and that the stylish Paula had evidently adopted since arriving in Kenya – they posed with Alice's dogs. There were frequent trips to the beach house at Tiwi in Alice's new 1938 DeSoto car, her old Plymouth having proven too uncomfortable for the frequent eight-hour trips along the hot and dusty murram road south from Nairobi to Mombasa. By contrast, the DeSoto had a straight-six-cylinder engine with enormous wheels and excellent suspension: it effectively steam-rolled rough roads, making driving in Kenya an altogether smoother experience. The front windscreens were split and could be opened by two handles on either side, keeping passengers both cool and comfortable. The two friends and Alice's little dog Minnie would have made an elegant sight as they motored from the city to the highlands and to the beach.

This happy time together was to be short-lived, however. One evening, Idina invited Alice and Paula over to Clouds for dinner and to stay the night. Idina had recently separated from her husband, Donald, and had taken up with Flight Lieutenant Vincent Soltau of the Royal Air Force, who would soon become her fifth husband. That evening, Boy Long – the handsome rancher and one of Idina's former conquests – was amongst the guests. He was recently divorced from his first wife, Genesta, and became immediately smitten with Paula. Paula returned the compliment and the couple wasted no time in marrying. The wedding took place towards the end of 1938. Boy's actual name was Edward Caswell Long, but he had been called Boy for as long as anyone could remember. Genesta once said of her former husband: 'Life with Boy was electric. I think he was the handsomest man I have ever seen, with infinite charm but "difficult".' Boy was certainly a flamboyant dresser, with a penchant for wearing stetson hats and colourful Somali shawls. Together with Paula, one of the most fashionable women in Europe, they made a striking pair. But although Alice was delighted that Paula had found her true love, Paula's marriage registered as a loss. Later, in 1941, she would write in a letter '. . . Paula is gone in a way. Our way of life lies apart and her big, bold paramour has changed her nature a little.'

With Paula otherwise engaged, Alice began seeking out the company of new female friends. In 1938, she met Patsy Bowles at the Muthaiga Club. Barely out of her teens, Patsy had married one of Alice's doctors, Roger Bowles, a man sixteen years her senior. Patsy was happy to let Alice take her under her wing and in the coming years the pair would often join one another for drinks or dinner around town, often accompanied by two other girlfriends, Rose Delap and Noreen Pearson. Patsy later confirmed that Alice retained all of her beauty during this later period of her life and that her distinctive wide-set grey eyes continued to captivate. Although it was clear that Alice had depressive tendencies and was dramatic into the bargain, she was nonetheless excellent company, someone who thrived in social situations, who was quick to laugh and adored a good party. Certainly Alice continued to rely on strong cocktails to mitigate her moods, but Patsy was certain that her friend was too intelligent to use drugs. She also confirmed that Alice never spoke of her family or of Paris during their friendship. By now, Alice's American accent was barely discernible – after all her years away from her native country, she spoke in the almost neutral tones of one who has left her home nation long ago.

Patsy also remembered Alice's rather odd taste in reading material. Over the years, in part thanks to two literary husbands, Alice had collected a large library. Towards the end of the 1930s, however, she began collecting volumes on medical problems, psychology and the occult. Patsy recalled one of these books in particular, *A Journey Round My Skull* (1938) by the Hungarian author Frigyes Korinthy (which has since been declared a masterpiece of medical autobiography). Korinthy's memoir tells the fascinating if grisly story of his brain tumour and the operation he had on it with only a local anaesthetic. Noel Case also recalled Alice's 'morbid mind' and 'books on horrible diseases' and how Alice would repeatedly ask Noel to mark out one place after another for her future grave site. According to Noel, Alice would sit on her verandah at Wanjohi Farm gazing at the river bend opposite her house, and pointing to the bank beside the deep pool as one possible burial place. Then she would change her mind and point to a completely different location: the iris beds on the edge of the 'cut' which she had made to take the stream water right round the edge of her house and garden. Perhaps the traumas that Alice had never managed to acknowledge fully – her mother's death, her father's abandonment – were beginning to manifest themselves in these morbid obsessions. Or perhaps as she grew older, Alice merely sensed that her years were numbered.

The new year would not be a particularly happy one for many of the inhabitants of Happy Valley. Locusts would devastate crop production, droughts were imminent and the news from Europe continued to go from bad to worse. Despite Chamberlain's pact with Hitler, war now seemed unavoidable and the colonists began making nervous preparations. In February Joss took on his new role as deputy director of the Central Manpower Committee, his patriotism trumping any lingering fascist allegiances (unlike many of his right-wing contemporaries, he was now fervently opposed to Chamberlain's appeasement of Hitler).

Joss's new job involved, for the most part, planning for the necessary distribution of military and civilian manpower and, as such, kept him well occupied. He was often away for weeks at a time, travelling throughout the Kenyan countryside mobilizing somewhere in the region of 2,000 European settlers. Despite his marital problems and considerable professional commitments, he still found time to see Alice – his offices, by coincidence, were located right next door to her Muthaiga cottage.

Always eager for a new conquest, however, Joss was also turning his attentions elsewhere. Phyllis Filmer was the wife of Percy Filmer, the managing director of the Shell company in East Africa who had arrived in Nairobi in 1935. No one in Joss's circle quite understood his fascination with Phyllis; she was considered rather dumpy and ordinary, at least by the standard of his more glamorous previous wives and mistresses. Even so, Joss continued to seek her out. Rumour has it that he was once discovered making love to her before dinner on the billiard table at the Norfolk Hotel. Alice would doubtless have not felt threatened by someone as unexciting as Phyllis – a small, rather conventional-looking blonde with none of Alice's flair – but it is safe to assume that the affair would have rankled nonetheless.

To make matters worse, Alice's health was in decline. In March of 1939, she visited her favourite doctor, William Boyle, complaining of stomach pains. The injury she had sustained during the shooting at the Gare du Nord often bothered her, but it is also possible that she was developing the first symptoms of ovarian cancer. Dr Boyle arranged to have her hospitalized and a drain was inserted. As soon as she was well enough, Alice flew up to Nakuru in an ambulance plane with a nurse, and went home to Wanjohi Farm. By now, Alice's devoted housekeeper, Noel, had left Wanjohi and Alice began to rely increasingly on Flo Crofton for help running her household. Flo was the daughter of a former Kenyan Governor, General Edward Northey, and was married to Dick Crofton, a white hunter living near Gilgil. After Alice's return from the hospital, Flo agreed to look after the house so that Alice could leave Kenya to visit her children in France. Despite her recent operation, Alice was determined to make the trip, aware that if war was declared, it might be one of her last opportunities to see Nolwen and Paola for some time. On 16 March 1939, she wrote to Aunt Tattie in France that the large rubber drain had been removed from her stomach, replaced by a gauze one which the nurse would remove in small pieces each day. It was still hard for Alice to sit up, and so her doctor had attempted to convince her that she should stay for another week to build up her strength for the journey home, advice that Alice had decided to ignore. She admitted to feeling greatly unsettled by the German army's recent march into Prague, but despite her anxiety about events in Europe, she went on to say that she was making all the necessary travel arrangements. It is revealing that Alice's greatest concern in the letter was not for her children, but her fear that passage on British ships might be restricted if war broke out and that she might somehow be prevented from returning to Africa. If all went well, she hoped to visit friends in Athens on her way home in June, travelling on a Belgian line. 'I do hope and pray there will be no war,' she wrote. 'Heaven knows what happens to our homes in such a case.'

Alice arrived in Paris in late March, as planned, remaining there for two months in order to spend time with Nolwen and Paola. Soon after her arrival, however, she decided to change her travel plans. She began to make arrangements to return to Kenya via Belgian West Africa, rather than by way of Athens. The Congo interior was a place that her friend Idina had visited two years previously, venturing deep into the rainforests to see the indigenous pygmy tribes. In the 1930s, there were still many thousands of pygmies living in the region – Idina must have returned to Wanjohi and regaled Alice with stories of her trip because now Alice became determined to see the pygmies for herself. Although Alice had also visited the Congo during her 1932 safari with the Vanderbilts, she had not been able to visit the tribes as her American host was interested only in hunting. And so on 29 March 1939, just after her arrival in France, Alice wrote to her Uncle Sim in New York to ask for funds from her 'Fifth Avenue Account' to be processed, so that a letter of credit of $2,400 and a further $400 in travellers' cheques could be provided for her Congo trip. She wrote that she intended to leave on the 4th of June, travelling across Central Africa all the way to Kenya. The trip would last in the region of four months. For two months she would be in places so remote that she would be unable to send or receive mail or cables. She asked that her cheques should be cashable in the Congo towns of Matadi, Kinshasha and Stanleyville, as those were the places where she 'will be quite alone, and between the first and last place mentioned, out of all communication'.

The decision to travel to the Congo was extraordinarily bold and, some would say, even dangerous. She would be venturing far into Central Africa, a single woman, alone, unwell, with Europe on the verge of war and – as she underlined in her letter to Uncle Sim – travelling to a remote area where she would be unable to make contact with the outside world. The tribal region she was to visit was 300 miles south-east of Stanleyville, now Kisangani, the provincial capital of the Tshopo Province and itself the furthest navigable point upstream from the capital Kinshasa. Certainly her doctor strongly advised against her going. But Alice was determined and, after leaving Paris, she sailed for West Africa. In some senses, the adventure was an act of defiance – Alice had always been headstrong and prone to making impulsive decisions – but perhaps it also represented her continuing need to live on her own terms during this period of her return to Happy Valley as a single woman, without Frédéric, Raymund, Joss, or her American or French families. In any event, Alice survived her extraordinary expedition, and returned to Wanjohi towards the end of the summer of 1939.

On her return, there was news of her ex-husband. Raymund had left Kenya in disgrace after getting very drunk one night at his farm in Njoro and striking one of his employees, whom he injured very badly. The matter was taken up by the police and the local district officer. To avoid any further scandal, Raymund was asked to depart for England immediately. Back in England, something altogether more serious had happened: he had been driving from a race meeting in Cheltenham and accidentally killed a woman cyclist. There had been a witness in the car – someone he had offered a lift to on his way back to London – and this person testified that Raymund was under the influence of drink when the accident occurred. On 7 June 1939, just after Alice left France for the Congo, Raymund was given three years' penal servitude for manslaughter. In sentencing him at the Gloucester Assizes, Justice Charles said, 'You have been found guilty – and very properly found guilty – of as bad a case of manslaughter by driving a car in a criminally negligent manner as I can well imagine. You drove like a lunatic. The sentence I pass upon you must necessarily, not only from a punishment point of view, but as a deterrent to others, be severe.'

Raymund was sent to Parkhurst Prison on the Isle of Wight, one of the toughest and most secure prisons in Great Britain. Escape was known to be impossible – water between the island and the mainland was unswimmable, multi-currented and with four strong tides every twenty-four hours. Alice must have taken pity on Raymund because she wrote to him often during this time and he replied. Evidently she remembered her own time in prison and how Raymund had been one of the only people to write to her while she was there. Despite everything that had taken place, she felt sorry for him. At the time of Raymund's incarceration, Parkhurst housed some of

Britain's most hardened criminals, including at least four leading IRA militants and several forgers. With his charm and ability to turn matters to account, Raymund had already discovered how to do his time in reasonable comfort. He made arrangements via the warders for extra provisions, including his favourite foie gras; he learned how to place bets on the horses, and to get the results. He also learned to communicate with his fellow Catholic convicts, who were IRA members, talking to them during exercise without moving his lips. His cell was scrubbed and washed out by other inmates who were keen to earn a few extra pounds, an arrangement which Raymund was able to honour. As usual, he read voraciously and had an ample supply of books, not only from the prison library, but also from friends who brought them in to him on a regular basis.

Then, in September of 1939, a month after Alice returned to Kenya, war was declared in Europe. Alice's two children were taken to the United States where they remained at Aunt Tattie's house in Chicago for the duration of the conflict. Although Alice was removed from hostilities on Wanjohi Farm, the war had one immediate consequence for her: she was no longer able to travel freely to see her children. In November, she wrote to her daughters via Aunt Tattie, unsure if any of her letters would ever arrive. At this time, airmail letters sent from Kenya could be delivered only to the countries of the British Empire. Alice worried that it might be years before her letters reached their destination, 'if they're not sunk on route'.

Enclosed with this particular letter was an article about Wanjohi Valley written by George Kinnear, editor of the *East African Standard* newspaper and a friend of Alice's. Alice asserted that George was a good writer and that his description of the valley and the mountains was apt. Of the stunning Wanjohi Valley, Kinnear wrote poignantly, 'The trees and the streams and the great mountains, the cattle and the sheep and the horses, the plump, chattering Kikuyu women picking daisies in the fields are still at peace.' While Alice always included descriptions of Africa such as these for her children to read, Nolwen and Paola were never invited to join her in Kenya. Now, with the advent of war, this would have been impossible, even if Alice had wished it.

In her letter to Aunt Tattie just before the war, Alice suggested that she had signed up as a Red Cross volunteer, but there is no evidence that she ever served in this capacity. For his part, Joss, like many of the colonists, was deeply engrossed in the war effort. He had been given a temporary commission in the Kenya Regiment as a second lieutenant, quickly rising to Assistant Military Secretary. There were fears that after the plagues of locusts and the recent drought, Kenya would simply be unable to produce enough food to feed its populace, especially with so many young and able male farmers being called up for the army. Events in Abyssinia continued to make the conflict feel very close to home: everyone knew that Mussolini would probably ally himself with Hitler and the invasion of British Kenya would be the logical next step. Colonial troops had already been assembled on the northern borders and there were plans to have parts of the highlands evacuated in the event of an invasion. Joss was very much involved in these arrangements.

A month after the outbreak of war, Joss's wife, Mary, who had been virtually housebound since the summer, finally succumbed to her illnesses. The cause of death given was kidney failure. She was buried that October at St Paul's Church in Kiambu, eight miles outside Nairobi and the main town in her husband's constituency. Alice did not attend. The money Mary had left she willed to Joss, but after the extravagances of their marriage, the amount was far from substantial. After Mary's death, Alice confided to her neighbour, Pat Fisher, that she would like to get back together with Joss. Evidently, this did not happen. Although short of cash and thrown off kilter by Mary's death, Joss was disappearing into his work and social activities, while also continuing his affair with Phyllis Filmer. He was ever more engrossed in his wartime duties. The following year, in June 1940, Mussolini declared war on Great Britain and the threat of Kenya's invasion by the Italians redoubled. Bombings were expected and Nairobi was blacked out in anticipation of air attacks; sandbags surrounded official buildings, and hundreds of new military personnel flooded the city.

Meanwhile, Alice's ever-delicate grasp on her moods was worsening. Like many people suffering from cyclothymia, the symptoms of her illness were becoming more severe as she grew older, her mood swings more pronounced and her unhappy periods lasting for a longer time. The effect of the light and altitude of the highlands was failing to work its magic as it had done in the past. It has been shown that various psychosocial factors – for example stressful circumstances, complicated living conditions and personal difficulties – can play a large part in exacerbating symptoms of the disease. Alice, who had been dogged by depression since adolescence, now had to deal with the considerable stresses of wartime, solitude, illness and middle age (she had just turned forty). Over the years, she had learned to ameliorate her condition with alcohol and used barbiturates to help her sleep. Now she seldom woke up before noon. Alice was entering an altogether disquieting time, with the outbreak of war foreshadowing the beginning of her sad decline.

10

The New Elements

In 1940, Alice was given her own chance to play a role in the war effort. In his capacity as Assistant Military Secretary Joss had decided that his old friend Lizzie Lezard (real name Julian Joseph Lezard) of the King's African Rifles should be stationed at Wanjohi Farm in order to undertake intelligence work in the area. Alice knew the Wanjohi Valley and its residents well and could help Lizzie report back on any local events that smacked of subversion. Alice was excited at the prospect of serving as an intelligence gatherer. For his part, Joss was evidently making a protective gesture towards his old girlfriend. Alice was alone and isolated at Wanjohi. Lizzie, meanwhile, had a reputation as a joker, someone who was excellent company. Joss was correct in his assumption that the pair would get along: Lizzie and Alice became good friends and, for a time, lovers.

Lizzie was Jewish, a striking-looking man of thirty-eight at the time of his arrival in Kenya, with hooded blue eyes and a mass of curly black hair. Born in Kimberley, South Africa, in 1902, he attended Cambridge University where he studied law between 1918 and 1922. He was a talented tennis player who captained the University Lawn Tennis Team and later represented South Africa with distinction in Davis Cup matches. When Alice first met him, he had recently separated from his wife, Hilda Wardell. She had filed for divorce after tiring of funding Lizzie's gambling, which resulted in considerable losses. With war imminent, he joined the military, where his quick-wittedness and poise attracted the attentions of the Field Intelligence Services. He was immediately commissioned as a lieutenant and posted to the Sudan before being reassigned to Kenya. Lizzie was known for his talent with women: he was a good listener and perceptive, usually in a humorous way, but always with enough flattery thrown in that his girlfriends would instinctively feel 'Here at last is someone who really understands me – the real me.' He also had a habit of speaking his mind. Throughout the first drive to Wanjohi, he complained bitterly to Alice about the abysmal road conditions. It was pouring with rain that day and the DeSoto was slithering from side to side as Alice battled to negotiate cavernous water-filled potholes. 'Stop the car!' Lizzie is said to have cried out. 'I can't take any more of this. I don't want to be a pioneer in Kenya. I'd rather be a bloody shit in London!'

Despite this unpromising start, Lizzie went on to enjoy his stay at Wanjohi, conducting his field intelligence duties during the day and playing hours of backgammon each evening with his hostess. Most likely he lost often as Alice was an expert at the game. Lizzie's natural diagnostic ability would have drawn his new girlfriend into telling him about herself, especially as her trust in him increased. Alice may also have enjoyed their more intimate relations: during his time in London, Lizzie had earned a reputation as an accomplished lover and he was always the first to boast of his skills. 'You see, I was regarded as rather intellectual and interesting, and that gave me a special position,' he would explain. 'Yes! I used to be London's ethereal lover!' According to Pat Cavendish O'Neill, in her memoir *A Lion in the Bedroom* (2004), Lizzie was also in possession of an exceptionally long penis which he sometimes produced while playing bridge: he would announce 'Full house', and everything went on display. Whether this knowledge had reached the ears of Idina, we do not know, but it is possible that she had heard something because on a visit to Clouds, Lizzie was prevailed upon to play the 'sheet game'. This unusual after-dinner game involved stringing up a sheet with holes in it across the living room. Half a dozen men could stand on one side with their penises through the holes and an equal number of women would stand on the other side, selecting their favourite appendage by calling out a number. Lizzie often joked that he had been the 'Number 3 lover in London in 1934' and so there would have been plenty of cries of 'Three!' from the women in attendance that evening. After his stay with

Alice, Lizzie returned to Nairobi where he took up residence at Joss's two-bedroom cottage in Muthaiga, continuing to fulfil his field intelligence duties, while still finding time to show off his serves at the Muthaiga Tennis Club. The brief relationship with Alice petered out, naturally and without rancour.

Then, one night at the Muthaiga Club Alice met another military man stationed in Nairobi. He was Richard (Dickie) Pembroke, a charming and good-looking Coldstream Guards officer who had been transferred to Kenya in 1939. Alice immediately marked him out as a possible conquest now that her affair with Lizzie was over, but to her dismay Dickie turned his attentions elsewhere. His object of interest was a cool blonde with blue eyes called Lady Diana Delves Broughton, who arrived from London in November of 1940. At the time of Diana's appearance in Nairobi, she was newly married to Sir Henry Delves Broughton, the eleventh baronet of Doddington – known as Jock, an imposing man with slicked-back dark hair who walked with a limp due to an old war wound. At twenty-seven, she was thirty years younger than Jock, and had been his mistress for five years when she agreed to travel with him to Africa. Although the timing of this emigration might seem unusual, in fact, Jock was entitled to land under the 1919 Soldiers Settlement Scheme and saw his departure to Kenya as a way of being useful in some way to the war effort. By the time the Delves Broughtons reached Cape Town towards the end of October 1940, Jock's divorce from his first wife was official and the couple were married in Durban on the 5th of

November. Before the two married, they agreed on the following unusual terms: if Diana wished to separate, Jock would let her go.

Although Diana evidently adored her new title of Lady Delves Broughton, she was not so enamoured with Jock. The issue of marriage had been forced because it would have been extremely difficult for Diana to gain entry into Kenya as an unmarried woman. After disembarking from the train at Nairobi, the newlyweds took up temporary residence at the Muthaiga Club where Diana made it clear to the members of this male-dominated establishment that she was very much available. For his part, Dickie was smitten with the glamorous Diana, but Diana was less enthused. Although Dickie was wealthy – having inherited his money from his grandfather, Edward Pembroke, Chairman of the Baltic Exchange – he, unlike Jock, lacked a title. Although the affair was over before it had begun, Dickie's attentions to Diana proved to be of immense annoyance to Alice, who found herself rebuffed in favour of Diana. Alice had never had any problem attracting men before. When she had first arrived in Kenya in 1925, it had been Alice who was the new girl in town, gaining the attention of all the prominent men of the settler community, Joss included. But this was 1940. Alice had turned forty the previous September and although her beauty was still very much in evidence, her looks could not last for ever. To make matters worse, she was in ill health and becoming increasingly reliant on alcohol and sleeping pills. She could only watch as this younger interloper drew the gazes of the most attractive and available men in Nairobi.

Everything about Diana conspired to irritate Alice. Not only was Diana younger, she was Alice's exact opposite in terms of looks and temperament, blonde and extrovert whereas Alice was dark and complex. While Diana was obviously voluptuous, Alice was delicately slender (her Kikuyu servants nicknamed their mistress 'Wacheke', meaning 'the thin one'). Simply put, Diana had the kind of blatant sex appeal that often inspires an instinctive dislike in other women. Alice was also alert to Diana's social ambitions. Diana had been born into a solidly middle-class English family – in her younger years, she had been a working girl, serving for a time as a hostess in a somewhat seedy cocktail bar called the Blue Goose in London. Although Diana had hoped to meet a wealthy and titled husband, instead she managed to marry a piano player called Vernon Motion: the marriage had lasted less than a year when husband and wife discovered that neither had any money. When Diana met Sir Jock Delves Broughton at the Blue Goose in 1935, she wasted no time in becoming his mistress. Now she seemed to be casting around for another titled lover amongst the pool of available Nairobi men. Alice detected Diana's underlying ambition and found it distasteful. After her time as a French countess, Alice knew exactly what it was like to be judged by one's pedigree (or lack thereof) and she had developed a considerable antipathy for those who valued titles over substance. Writing to Raymund in Parkhurst she described Diana as a 'new element' who had upset the delicate balance of a number of relationships within the close circle of Kenya society.

In the end, Alice did not have to wait long for her chance with Dickie. Diana quickly rejected Dickie on the grounds that he was 'dull', clearing the way for Alice to begin a relationship with the handsome guards officer. Dickie was thirty-six at the time of his affair with Alice. Unlike Raymund, another ex-officer in the Coldstream Guards, he took a certain pride in his status as gentleman soldier. His manners were polished and his courtesy to all, including Alice's staff, made him both popular and respected. In many ways, this new boyfriend constituted another Frédéric figure in Alice's life – someone who was dependable and loyal but lacking in the spark that ignited her relationships with Raymund or Joss. For Dickie's part, the affair with Alice offered him newfound happiness after a very difficult period in his own life. Born in Epsom on 18 December 1904, he attended Malvern School and entered the Military Academy at Sandhurst on 30 August 1924. On passing out he was offered a commission in the Coldstream Guards, which he accepted, beginning a career of steady promotion. But just prior to his arrival in Kenya, Dickie had begun an affair with a fellow officer's wife. As punishment, he was put on temporary leave, seconded to the Colonial Office and made a Brigade Major in the King's African Rifles. Such a turn of events constituted an enormous embarrassment for Dickie, who took his military career extremely seriously, and he was anxious to make amends. He retained his Coldstream cap star and always wore his Coldstream Guards uniform and buttons during his time in Kenya. After the disappointment of being seconded and then cast aside by Diana, Dickie quickly embraced the relationship with Alice, spending more and more time with her, not just at Wanjohi but also at her cottage in Nairobi and the beach house at Tiwi where they were photographed together. But even though Alice had succeeded with Dickie, a rivalry with Diana had been established.

Imagine Alice's growing dismay, then, when it became clear that Diana was beginning a very public affair with Joss. By Christmas of 1940, Joss and Diana were seen regularly dancing together at the Muthaiga Club, their bodies locked together in a way that many of the club members considered indecent. Diana evidently found Joss irresistible: his good looks, high ranking in settler society and title of Lord High Constable of Scotland made him extremely attractive to her. A mutual infatuation was underway. Alice sensed that the relationship with Diana was different. Joss was consumed with Diana in a way that Alice had never witnessed before. Still smarting from the Dickie–Diana affair, Alice felt herself dropped by her old friend Joss. Again, she wrote to Raymund about her fury regarding Diana's appearance on the scene.

Jock Delves Broughton, meanwhile, seemed to be accepting his new wife's infidelity with a degree of good humour. Joss and Jock were friends: they had attended the same school, Eton, and had been enjoying one another's company now that they were living in the same part of the world. That December, the Delves Broughtons had moved into a large house in Marula Lane, in Nairobi's Karen district, and Joss would often visit both of them there. The Delves Broughtons' close neighbour in Karen,

Derek Erskine, spent a good deal of time with the three of them during the last few months of 1940. Another old Etonian, albeit one with politically liberal leanings, Derek had arrived in Kenya in the early thirties to become the news announcer for the Kenya Broadcasting Service (but because he had a lisp and was unable to pronounce his r's, he mangled his introduction – 'This is the Naiwobi Bwoadcasting Sewvice' – and soon quit the job). After starting up a bakery with his wife, Elizabeth, he went on to form a successful grocery business. In later years, Derek always maintained that Jock was surprisingly tolerant of the liaison between Joss and Diana. Derek recollected that on one occasion Jock was looking out of his library window, which overlooked the swimming pool at Marula Lane. That day, Diana was swimming in the nude. Joss was standing beside the pool and holding up a towel, ready for her exit. Jock opened his library window and shouted jokingly, 'Joss! It's my turn to dry Diana today!' According to Derek, the relationship between the two men was always grown-up and good-spirited, regardless of Jock's hurt feelings. There was a sense of 'no grudges' between these two men who shared the same alma mater and had been brought up to believe that 'all's fair in love and war'.

As 1941 began, it was becoming increasingly clear to Jock that his wife was in love with Joss. Like Alice, Jock could only look on as yet again Joss and Diana danced publicly and amorously with one another at the Muthaiga Club. What's more, Jock was receiving anonymous letters. The first read 'You seemed like a cat on hot bricks at the club last night. What about the eternal triangle? What are you going to do about it?' The next one was even more unpleasant in its insinuation: 'There is no fool like an old fool. What are you going to do about it?' In mid-January, Jock decided that he would take it upon himself to confront his wife and her lover in order to discover their true intentions. As was later revealed in his trial, Jock went first to Diana, asserting his right to know the nature of her feelings for Joss. Diana did not lie: she told Jock that she was in love with Joss, saying, 'It's something I cannot help.' Jock then suggested that Diana come away with him for a few months, in order to allow for a cooling-off period. If she still felt the same way about Joss after time away, he would agree to a separation. 'I promise you, Diana, I will stand by it,' he said. 'But let us give our marriage a longer trial.' Diana would not consent.

Next Jock went to visit Joss at his Nairobi bungalow, demanding that he also reveal his intentions. 'I take no notice of gossip,' Jock declared, 'but it has been clear to me for some time that you are in love with Diana. I have spoken to her and she says she is in love with you too.' Joss was truthful: he told Jock that he was 'frightfully in love' with Diana although he hadn't realized she felt the same way until now. Jock reiterated that he wanted to take Diana away for a number of months. 'If she still believes she is in love with you and wants a divorce to marry you, Joss, I'll make no objection.' When Joss pointed out it was unlikely that Diana would agree to such a plan, Jock tried another tactic, begging Joss to allow him the chance to make something of the marriage: 'Won't you arrange to leave Nairobi? Perhaps if you apply to do service else-where, they will let you go.' Again, Joss declined, citing his attachment to Diana and pointing out that, apart from anything else, he could not go away, as there was a war on. Jock gave it one last try, demanding that Joss reveal how he intended to support Diana. 'You've got practically noth-ing apart from your pay and allowances,' he reminded Joss. 'I know Diana would not take a penny of the money I've settled on her if you two were to be married. She is the straightest person I know where money is concerned.' Joss's reply did not reveal his own concern about Diana's financial situation: 'Of course, I would not expect her to take it nor would I live on her money. But we'll manage somehow.'

Jock's attempt to save his marriage had resolutely failed. He told Diana he had no choice but to go ahead with a divorce. Later, at his trial, he would say, 'I made up my mind to bow to the inevitable. The only thing for me to do was to cut my losses and go, say, to Ceylon. Perhaps I would return to Kenya in a few months. She might then no longer be in love with Erroll.' Jock still held out a final glimmer of hope that Diana's infatuation would peter out, and that 'all might still come right in the end'. It was at this point Jock wrote to a friend, Jack Soames, to inform him that Joss and Diana were in love, and that he was going to 'cut his losses' and leave. 'There's nothing for me to live in Kenya for,' he wrote. According to Lizzie Lezard, who also gave evidence at the trial, Joss had informed him that 'Jock could not have been nicer. He had agreed to go away. As a matter of fact, he has been so nice that it smells bad.'

On the morning of Thursday the 23rd of January, Jock sent word to his lawyer that he wished to begin divorce proceedings. Over lunch, he informed Diana of his decision and told her that he would soon be leaving for Ceylon. That evening, the Delves Broughtons were expected at the Muthaiga Club where they were to meet Joss and another friend, June Carberry. When Jock arrived, Joss and Diana were already lounging on a sofa, limbs entwined. The evening constituted an odd celebration of sorts: champagne was ordered and Jock even went so far as to toast his wife and her lover. He held his glass aloft and in a loud voice declaimed: 'To Diana and Joss. I want to wish them every happiness in the future and may their union be blessed with an heir. To Diana and Joss.' Everyone in the room could hear his words. Jock was deliberately making a great show of giving up his wife. Later he would say, 'The dinner party was a most cheerful affair. Mine was an attitude of complete resignation in view of the circumstances I had encountered. There was nothing else to be done. I realized it.' After dinner, Joss and Diana decided to go off dancing at the nearby Claremont nightclub, with Jock stipulating that Diana should be returned home by 3 a.m. Dickie Pembroke was at the Muthaiga Club that night and when he returned to Alice's Portaluca bungalow, he informed her of the extraordinary celebration he had witnessed that evening.

The Delves Broughtons' friend June Carberry later testified that she had remained at the bar with Jock while he drank a quantity of brandy. 'We've only been married three months,' he told June, 'and look how it is for me now.' When he left with June at 1.30 a.m., Jock came close to passing out from too much drink and the sudden impact of fresh air. Jock and June left for Karen, arriving at the Delves Broughton residence at 2 a.m. June, who was staying at the house, went to her room. Shortly afterwards, Jock put his head round her door to say goodnight. He was wearing his dressing gown. Fifteen minutes later, Joss and Diana pulled up at the Karen house in the Buick that Joss had borrowed, as his own car was out of order. Diana's maid was there to greet them. Joss said goodbye. Diana cautioned him to 'drive carefully'. Everyone knew that Joss always drove too fast. June and Diana chatted for a while before Diana went to bed.

11

The Murder of Lord Erroll

After saying goodbye to Diana, Joss drove back in the direction of his Muthaiga bungalow. It was after two in the morning and the road ahead would have been hard to make out. In accordance with blackout regulations, Joss's headlights were half-shaded, and he would have been forced to lean forward in his seat to see his way. Despite the lack of visibility, there is no doubt that he was driving at his usual top speed. He would have been keen to get home. It was late, he was tired, and he needed to be at his desk first thing in the morning. Although Joss almost always lived up to his reputation as a philanderer, he rarely neglected his professional duties.

Joss soon approached the intersection of the Ngong–Nairobi road, where he was intending to turn right, which would have taken him back towards Nairobi and Muthaiga, where his cottage was located. Only so much is known for certain about what happened next. What we do know is that he was persuaded to stop his car well before the crossroads. Two shots were then fired at him at close range. One bullet missed but the other entered his neck under his left ear, passing through the base of his skull and killing him instantly. Next, Joss's body either fell or was pushed under the dashboard of the car. The Buick then rolled or was pushed off the road so that its front wheels were hanging precariously over a gravel pit by the side of the verge. The person who fired the shots fled the scene.

It did not take long for Joss's body to be discovered. At around 3 a.m., two African dairy workers (milk boys) driving along the Ngong–Nairobi road saw the Buick which appeared to have swerved off the road. As the milk boys came closer, they could see that the car's headlights were still on and that blood was spattered on the windscreen. There was a man in the car but it was difficult to see who this might be as he was crouched down on the floor beneath the dashboard. The milk boys drove immediately to the nearest police station at Karen to sound the alert. Two constables arrived at the scene. Again it was assumed that some kind of accident had taken place. Another set of tracks could be seen in the mud, heading off in the direction of Nairobi. Perhaps this was a case of hit and run. At 8.15 a.m. an ambulance arrived and the body was taken out of the car so that a government pathologist could examine it. The man was obviously dead: rigor mortis had begun to set in and there was blood clotted around his left ear. At this point, someone recognized the body as that of Joss Erroll.

Word spread quickly. Back at Joss's bungalow, Lizzie Lezard was awakened by a hysterical Diana. She had heard that Joss had died in a car accident and she was inconsolable. After gathering up what she wanted of Joss's possessions – his pyjamas included – Diana departed in floods of tears. Next to visit the bungalow was Idina, Joss's former wife, in search of the Erroll family pearls, which she hoped to pass on to her daughter Dinan. The pearls were nowhere to be found. Lizzie realized that it now fell to him to inform the other woman in Joss's life, Alice. He drove the short distance to the Portaluca cottage where he found Alice ensconced with Dickie. Here he repeated the news that Joss had died in a car accident. Alice's reaction was immediate. While Diana and Idina had chosen to race to Joss's home to retrieve his possessions, Alice had a very different idea. She asked to be taken to the mortuary. She wanted to see Joss. Lizzie agreed to this request and drove her there himself.

Together, Alice and Lizzie were permitted to view Joss's body, which was laid out on the mortuary slab. What could have been Alice's thoughts at the sight of him? Joss had been a key figure in her life for almost twenty years. Her on-again-off-again relationship with him had weathered their many marriages, divorces and affairs. Now he was gone, his body stretched out, his pale features drained of all animation and life. But if Alice had come to say a final 'goodbye', this was not the word she chose to use. Instead, she bent down, put her lips on Joss's, kissed him passion-ately and declared: 'Now you are mine for ever.'

The visit to the mortuary and her declaration while there were the first of many bizarre reactions from Alice in the aftermath to Joss's death.

Later in the day, Joss's body was taken to be examined by a pathologist, Dr Vint. When the clotted blood behind the left ear was cleaned away, Vint could see that Joss had been shot in the neck and at close range. The bullet had passed through the neck below his left ear and was lodged in the right side of his neck. Joss was right-handed, so it would have been impossible for the wound to have been self-inflicted. He had been murdered. There were black powder marks around the wound, which meant that the killer had most likely been sitting in the passenger seat or standing on the car's running board when he or she took aim. Later that afternoon, another .32 calibre bullet was found under the accelerator pedal of the Buick. Joss must have ducked the first bullet, but the second shot killed him on impact. Dr Vint estimated that the murder had taken place between 2.30 and 3 a.m. He also suggested that the body might have been pushed into its curious position beneath the steering wheel so that someone else – the killer or an accomplice – could then drive the car off the road. The car itself was virtually undamaged and the mechanic who examined it asserted that the car was being driven at no more than 8 miles an hour when it had stopped. The gear lever was almost, although not quite, in top position, an oddity. In the front of the car was further evidence: a bloodstained hairpin.

Despite Vint's revelation that Joss had most definitely been shot, the newspapers were duly informed that Lord Erroll had died in a car accident. Assistant Inspector Arthur James Poppy, formerly of the Metropolitan Police, London, and head of the Nairobi Criminal Investigation Department, had been immediately assigned to the case, but he deliberately chose to keep the truth under wraps for twenty-four hours until more details could be ascertained. It seems that the police were keen to stave off speculation until more was known: after all, Joss was a high-ranking official and a well-known British aristocrat into the bargain. This was an investigation that needed to be handled with diplomacy and care. Joss's funeral took place the following day on 25 January 1940 at St Paul's Church in Kiambu, Lord Erroll's constituency. Here he was buried next to his wife, Mary, his headstone inscribed with the following words:

In loving memory
of
Josslyn Victor Hay,
twenty second Earl of Erroll,
Hereditary High Constable of Scotland,
born 11th Day of May 1901,
met his death on 24th Day of January 1941.
Thy will be done.

The funeral was well attended. Most of Kenya's official-dom was present, including the governor, Sir Henry Moore, as well as an impressive line-up of military and governmental representatives. Alice had composed herself enough to make an appearance amongst the other mourners. Jock Delves Broughton arrived late. Diana was too upset to attend but she had given her husband a note to drop into the coffin. Almost everyone who was present was still under the impression that Joss had been killed tragically in a car accident. This made sense. Joss had always driven too fast and recklessly. Alice even went so far as to suggest to Jock that perhaps Joss had suffered from heart trouble and that this could have been the cause of his death.

It wasn't until the day of the inquest, in the afternoon of Monday the 27th, that the news broke that Joss had been 'probably murdered' and that an investigation was underway to find the killer. Assistant Inspector Poppy was known to be thorough and expert, but the odds were stacked against him from the start. Many aspects of the crime scene had already been carelessly bungled. Joss's body had been removed from the car before exact measurements of the position of the body could be ascertained. The car had been washed out before fingerprints could be taken. No one had thought to put a rope around the Buick and so a second set of tyre tracks going off in the direction of Nairobi had been trampled into the mud by the police before they could be correctly recorded. With hard evidence in short supply, Poppy was going to have to rely on psychological factors, and a great deal of supposition, to determine the identity of the murderer.

Of course, the most obvious suspect was Jock Delves Broughton. It was common knowledge that Joss had been having an affair with Diana and in the eyes of most Jock was immediately cast as the cuckolded husband, seeking revenge on the man who had stolen his wife. In the coming weeks, Assistant Inspector Poppy drew up a list of suspects with Jock high on the list. Poppy's suspicions were heightened further when he went to visit Jock at his house in Karen. Here he discovered a fire burning in a pit in the garden with remnants of a bloodstained golf stocking in the ashes. The blood type, although human, could not be established, and, strangely, Jock could neither explain the presence of the stocking nor why it had blood on it.

Other names on Poppy's list included that of Phyllis Filmer's husband, Percy. He too fitted the description of jealous husband but his secretary confirmed his whereabouts on the night of the murder, and besides, he just 'wasn't the type'. And what of Diana? She was the last person to have seen Joss alive and possibly had some hidden motive for wanting him dead. But Poppy could not conceive what such a motive might be and Diana's obvious distress at the death of her lover seemed to rule her out. Although many in the settler community later hissed 'murderess' behind Diana's back – and it was later rumoured that she had killed Joss in a fit of pique after he refused to marry her – it is hard to imagine her motive for doing away with the man she evidently hoped to wed. Also, in practical terms, it would have been very difficult for Diana to kill Joss. After saying goodbye to him, she had chatted with June Carberry for some time before going to bed. In order to shoot Joss, Diana would have had to make the drive to the crime scene in an impossibly short amount of time.

Then there was Alice. Of all Joss's many former mistresses, no one was more unsettled by his love affair with
Diana than Alice. More importantly, she had known that
Joss would be coming home from Marula Lane before 3
a.m. Alice's lover, Dickie Pembroke, had been at the
Muthaiga Club the night of the murder and had overheard
Jock say to Joss, 'Bring Diana back before 3 o'clock,
there's a good fellow.' Dickie had duly related this to Alice
on his return to her cottage that evening. In a further
strike against her innocence, Alice had a history: she had
already been convicted of attempted murder in Paris, after
the shooting of Raymund at the Gare du Nord. When
Poppy's men questioned the erstwhile countess, however,
they discovered that she had an airtight alibi. Dickie
Pembroke swore that Alice had been in bed with him at
her Portaluca cottage for the duration of the night of the
murder. Alice's name was removed from the list.

In the period after Joss's death, Alice's state of mind was
precarious to say the least. Fate had decreed that the two
most important men in her life would die within a week
of one another, Joss on the 24th of January and William
Silverthorne, her father, on the 30th of January. William,
nearly seventy-four at the time of his death, was buried in
Savannah, Georgia, where he had been living. Alice did not
contemplate attending the funeral. Apart from the fact she
was unable to travel because of the war, she was consumed
with the events of Joss's murder investigation. We do not
know her reaction to the news that William had passed
away, but we can only assume that his death, coming so
soon after Joss's murder, placed even more pressure on

her already fragile equilibrium. Alice's relationship with her father had always been central to her unhappiness and now the lifelong rift between father and daughter had been made perpetual, dangerously mirroring her separation from her beloved Joss.

With Alice and Diana discounted as suspects, the police refocused their attentions on Jock. If they could find the murder weapon and link it to Jock – or at least identify that one of his guns had fired the bullets that had been recovered from Joss's body and car – then they would have sufficient evidence to charge him. The Karen house and its grounds were duly searched but nothing was found. After Jock was questioned further, it turned out that his two revolvers had been stolen the Tuesday before the murder. Poppy was immediately suspicious. The stolen pistols were a Colt .32 revolver and a Colt .42. Joss had been shot with a .32 calibre bullet. Had Jock deliberately arranged for the guns to go missing prior to the murder to divert attention from himself? It was also discovered that Jock had shot rounds from his revolvers at his friend Jack Soames's farm. Bullets taken from Soames's shooting range were examined and deemed to match those found in Joss's car and body.

Poppy felt certain he had found his man. Jock had the motive to kill and also seemed to have owned the gun that could well have been the murder weapon. Even so, the police still had to ascertain how Jock could possibly have left the house at Karen and then returned there without anyone hearing his movements. June Carberry was prepared to testify that she had seen Jock at 2 a.m. and again at 4 a.m. The shooting had taken place before 3 a.m., but the staircase at Karen creaked loudly and Diana, June and the maid had not heard anyone going downstairs, driving away or coming back between two and four that morning. Could Jock have climbed down the drainpipe at the side of the house or over the side of the balcony? Did he lie in wait for Joss, driving away with him until they were at a far enough distance to accomplish the shooting without anyone hearing the shots? Was Jock capable of the physical prowess required to climb out of the house and walk the two miles back home from the scene of the shooting? This was a man who walked with a limp and had a fractured wrist that would have severely impeded his climb and ability to walk long distances. Jock also suffered from night blindness and had been advised by his doctors not to drive after dark. As a further impediment, he had drunk excessively that night, as June would attest.

Despite shaky evidence Jock was arrested on 14 March 1941. Jock's words to Poppy at the time of his arrest were, 'I'm sorry. You've made a big mistake.' That evening, he was placed in a cell at the Nairobi police station and the following day, he was charged with Joss's murder at the residents' magistrate's court. Immediately afterwards, he was sent to Nairobi Kilimani Prison and given his own cell (where he was permitted to order the food of his choice from the nearby Torrs Hotel). By mid-April, the magistrate had ruled that the Crown had a prima facie case of murder.

Although Diana was grief-stricken over Joss's death, she proved herself to be a loyal wife, visiting Jock in prison on a regular basis. One of Jock's most frequent visitors, however, was Alice. She took him supplies – books in particular – counselled him and tried to cheer him up. She told him he could not possibly be found guilty. Indeed, what evidence was there? Alice was fixated on the idea that Jock might be found guilty, and repeatedly told Pat Fisher how worried she was that this might come to pass. Why would Alice have taken such keen interest in this man's imprisonment while remaining convinced of his innocence? She had never had any desire to befriend Jock before, and his marriage to Diana would only have marked him out as 'off limits'. It is possible that Alice merely sympathized with Jock: she had spent time in prison and knew how it felt to be socially ostracized as a result. Or was something else altogether preying on her mind?

If Jock was found to have committed the murder, it was likely that he would be hanged. As with her peculiar visit to the mortuary, Alice's attentiveness to Jock seems strange to say the least.

12

The Trial of Jock Delves Broughton

On the advice of Jock's solicitor, Lazarus Kaplan of the law firm Kaplan and Stratton, Diana flew to South Africa to see if she could hire Henry Harris 'Harry' Morris KC, who was the leading South African defender of the times. Not only was Morris a brilliant cross-examiner, he was also a noted ballistics expert. Diana must have been persuasive because Harry Morris accepted the job of defending Jock Delves Broughton, at the cost of £5,000, a very large sum for the day. While in South Africa, Diana took the opportunity to buy herself a large number of new outfits and her wardrobe soon became a matter of note in the Nairobi newspaper, the *East African Standard*. On day one of Jock's trial, she arrived dressed dramatically in widow's black and diamonds. The ensuing trial lasted for twenty-seven days, extending over a period of five weeks, the longest on record for Central Africa. But nonetheless – as the *Standard* gleefully reported – Diana never wore the same outfit twice.

The trial of Jock Delves Broughton began on 26 May 1941 in the Supreme Court of Kenya in Nairobi. Chief Justice of Kenya Sir Joseph Sheridan presided. Mr Walter Harrigan KC prosecuted for the Crown. Henry Harris Morris KC defended. A large crowd of Broughton supporters attended each day – all seats were taken. Diana was not the only female mourner for Joss in the packed courtroom. Idina came each day: she and Joss had remained friends until the end. Accompanying Idina was Joss's girlfriend Phyllis Filmer, who had returned from South Africa after hearing the terrible news. Since the murder, Idina and Phyllis had become fast friends, grieving for Joss together, to the point where Phyllis even moved in with Idina at Clouds. Then there was Alice. Although she was never called upon to give evidence, she attended the trial daily, always arriving early to secure a good seat, beautifully turned out, as if in competition with the other women in the courtroom. According to Harrigan's secretary, Peggy Pitt, Alice made copious notes throughout the trial.

Proceedings began with the prosecutor for the Crown, Walter Harrigan, making his powerful opening address. Harrigan reminded the men and women of the jury that 'motive' should guide their verdict: Sir Delves Broughton had killed the Earl of Erroll because the latter had stolen his wife. 'We shall try to establish that Erroll died from a bullet in the brain fired from a revolver which, at any rate, had been in Broughton's possession three days before,' Harrigan declared.

Next, Harry Morris set about laying the groundwork for Jock's defence. Morris wanted to show that it would have been impossible for Broughton to climb down the drainpipe or over the balcony of the Karen house before climbing into the car with Joss that night. '. . . Sir Delves consumed a quantity of liquor at the Muthaiga Club on the night of January 23rd and was under its influence by the time he returned to Karen,' Morris advised. 'He was extremely tired as well and night blindness prevented his driving his car after dark, let alone in a wartime blackout. He also has a broken wrist, the result of a car accident some years ago.' Equally, the two-mile walk back to the house after the shooting would have been extremely challenging for Jock. Friends of Broughton's – including Jack Soames and June Carberry – gave evidence of Jock's good nature and general equanimity when it came to Joss and Diana's affair. Soames described his friend as neither 'quick tempered [n]or passionate'. June portrayed him as 'courteous, considerate and most cheerful, with a sense of humour, and not at all jealous.' Morris also cited the anonymous letters that had been sent to Broughton before Erroll's murder as proof that Joss had many enemies – former mistresses and cuckolded husbands included – who might have wanted to stir up bad feeling between Jock and Joss during this time. Morris even hinted that the murder might have been politically motivated: Joss had been a sometime member of the British Union of Fascists after all.

Lizzie Lezard was called in as a witness. Described in court as 'Lieutenant Julian Lezard', he related the conversation he had had with Joss the day before the murder during which Joss had told Lizzie how 'nice' Jock was being about the whole affair. Dickie Pembroke also gave evidence, having been brought in by the Crown in order to rule out Alice as a possible suspect. Dickie clearly loathed playing his part in such a public event, although he duly confirmed that Alice had been in bed with him on the night of the murder.

The Crown's case therefore rested on the following supposition: Jock Delves Broughton had killed Joss Erroll with a bullet fired from the Colt .32 revolver allegedly stolen a few days before the murder. In order to affirm Jock's innocence, Harry Morris knew that he had to prove that the bullets fired from Jock's revolver at Soames's shooting range were different from the ones used to commit the murder. For the prosecution, Harrigan brought in two ballistics specialists to show that the bullets fired at Joss and the bullets discovered on the shooting range had been fired from the same gun. According to both specialists, all the bullets in question had right-hand rifling grooves and therefore were from the same equipment. It was at this moment that Morris knew he could win his case.

It had already been ascertained that Joss had been shot with five-grooved bullets. Morris knew that Jock's Colt was a six-grooved revolver. He had cabled the Colt company in the United States to confirm this fact.

'It stands to reason,' Morris proposed, 'that you cannot get a five-grooved bullet out of a six-grooved gun. And the missing Colts were six-grooved, were they not?' The bal-listics specialist on the stand was forced to agree. Morris had it on the record: the bullets and the supposed murder weapon did not match. The Crown was forced to drop its line of argument that Jock had arranged for the Colts to be stolen in order to cover up the murder.

Now it was Jock's turn to give evidence and be cross-examined. This process took place over a period of six days.

'Sir Delves,' Morris began. 'Did you have anything to do, directly or indirectly, with the death of the Earl of Erroll?'

'Certainly not,' came the reply. Jock went on to mention his limp, his fractured wrist and his night blindness. He described himself as devoted to his wife, Diana. He told the story of their recent marriage and the pact that they had made before the wedding, that if Diana wanted a separation, he would let her go.

Morris then asked Jock if he had been prepared to sac-rifice his marriage in order to secure his wife's happiness.

'I realized that she had all her young life in front of her,' Jock replied. 'I have not. The only thing, therefore, was for me to cut my losses and go away to Ceylon.'

He went on to describe in some detail the events pre-ceding the murder, his evening at the Muthaiga Club and how he returned home at 2 a.m. before going to bed.

'I do not mind how many men fall in love with my wife as long as she does not fall in love with them,' he explained. 'She never gave me the slightest cause for jealousy till she started going out with Erroll. This, I admit, came as a bit of a shock and I did my best to persuade her to come to Ceylon with me. But she did not want to.'

On the prosecution side, Harrigan needed to show that Jock's line of argument was implausible.

'Do you seriously mean that if you suspect a man of making love to your wife, you are incapable of making it clear to him you would like him to desist?' he asked.

'Before you know for certain,' Broughton replied, 'that your wife is in love with another man, or a man is in love with your wife, I think it would be an extremely foolish thing to do. Once you know, you have to do one of two things – either give up the contest and go away, or have a frightful row and tell the other man you won't have it. As we had a pact and my wife was thirty years younger, I felt bound to honour it. Otherwise what's the use in making it?'

To clinch his case, Morris brought in another small-arms expert who confirmed that the bullets used to shoot Joss could not have come from Jock's Colt revolver. More witnesses spoke about Jock's general good temper and his difficulties with walking long distances at any great speed.

Finally, Morris made his closing remarks. Referring back to Harrigan's original supposition that motive would guide the jury in their verdict, he spoke definitively: 'We live in an age of mathematics and machinery. The appeal is no longer to the hearts and to the passions of men. The appeal is to their reasoning power.' It was not the responsibility of the defence to come up with the true identity of the murderer, Morris asserted, it was up to the Crown to show, beyond reasonable doubt, that Jock Delves

Broughton had murdered Lord Erroll. Morris reminded the jury that the murder weapon had never been found and that the bullets from Jock's gun did not match that found in the Buick and the one in Joss's body. The Crown needed to prove that Jock had shot Joss with bullets from a five-grooved gun on the morning of the murder. The Crown could not prove this. Also, there was no evidence that Jock had left the Marula Lane house on the night of the murder. What remained of the case against Jock? The motive of jealousy? Morris reminded the jury of Jock's equanimity in the matter of his wife's affair.

'There is no proof he uttered a single threat against Erroll's life at any time. Habit, gentlemen, is a compelling thing. Breeding is powerful and tradition omnipotent . . . You are asked to believe, gentlemen, that Sir Delves Broughton suddenly became transformed into a cold-blooded, crafty individual who decided after his interview with Erroll, to slaughter him . . . I can only make this submission to you gentlemen: it is incredible.'

Morris concluded his summing up with the following words: 'The evidence does not support the conclusion that Sir Delves Broughton had a hand in the murder, directly or indirectly. You cannot find him guilty of this crime.'

Next it was Harrigan's turn to conclude. He informed the jury that the bullets needn't have come from a Colt revolver. It was possible that Broughton had used another gun. Besides, the Crown's ballistics experts had spent many months researching and verifying the bullets at the shooting range and the bullets found at the crime scene and had confirmed these were the same. It was clear to him,

Harrigan informed the jury, that Jock had decided to murder his rival. He had arranged to have the revolvers vanish, reporting the burglary to the police to distract attention.

'I have already suggested, and I repeat, this was a faked burglary,' insisted Harrigan.

Harrigan then moved on to the central question of motive. Jock had every motive to kill the man who had taken away his wife. During the period leading up to the murder Jock had acted the part of a husband happily conceding his wife to another man and done so 'magnificently'. As to Jock's disabilities, Harrigan reminded the jury that Jock had recently returned from hunting big game. 'He has stalked lion. He uses an elephant gun. There was nothing wrong with his walking or powers of endurance on the hunting expedition to the Masai Reserve.' As for his night blindness, Harrigan suggested that Jock had simply made up this particular impediment to suit his story.

'The Crown has put forward jealousy as the principal motive for this crime,' declared Harrigan. 'In your deliberations, gentlemen, you will consider human nature. None are exempt from passion or temptation . . .'

Harrigan finished his conclusion just before six on the evening of the 1st of July 1941. Three hours later, at nine o'clock, the jury filed back in. Jock stood to receive the verdict.

'Not guilty.'

Harry Morris's expertise in ballistics had indeed ensured Jock's acquittal. It had not been proven beyond reasonable doubt that Jock was the murderer. For his part, Jock thanked the Chief Justice and turned to face his jubilant supporters, Alice included. Diana had stayed away from the courtroom that day (at Jock's insistence in case of a guilty verdict). Morris, who had returned to South Africa, wrote the very next day to tell Jock he had been certain of his innocence from the beginning, and that Jock had been an exemplary witness. Copies of the letter were made and sent to Jock's many acquaintances, in case they should be in any doubt of his blamelessness. In his reply to Morris's letter, Jock wrote: 'I can never thank you enough for saving my life. Apart from what it means to me there is a deep debt of gratitude my family owe you for clearing my name.'

Alice had followed every moment of the courtroom proceedings with compulsive attention, making jottings in her notebook, investing so much in the outcome of the trial. Now a 'not guilty' verdict had been given, just as she'd prayed for and predicted.

13

The Case for Alice

If Jock was innocent, then who shot Lord Erroll?
No other suspect was ever tried for Joss's murder.
It was wartime after all and, after the furore of the trial,
Walter Harrigan in particular was keen to play down the
scandal which many in Kenya's colonial community had
found extremely embarrassing. The Kenya police duly
dropped their investigations. At the time of writing, nearly
seventy years have passed and yet the Erroll murder
remains officially unsolved. The many 'unexplained details
of the case' – as they are described in *White Mischief*, James
Fox's classic work about the mystery – continue to tanta-
lize the amateur sleuth. Who was the owner of the hairpin
found in the car? What happened to the murder weapon?
Why had the Buick rolled off the road with the lights left

on and the ignition switched off? What was the exact position of Joss's body under the dashboard and why was he crouched there?

It is no surprise that a succession of respected authors have been drawn to the rich territory of such a notorious uncracked case. What *is* surprising is that two of the most distinguished of these writers, both Fox and Errol Trzebinski, Joss's biographer, agree that Jock Delves Broughton was indeed to blame. Fox believes Jock was motivated by jealousy and that Harry Morris simply confused the jury with his ballistics jargon. Trzebinski concluded that Jock was a pawn but that MI6 operatives were entrusted with Joss's assassination. Yet when one examines what is known about Jock's character, weighing this with Harry Morris's persuasive case for his acquittal, along with the technical evidence presented by the defence and the lack of a murder weapon, it becomes difficult to disagree with the jury's verdict of 'not guilty'. The Crown's case failed and with good reason. The mismatch of the bullets and the weapon clinched the case for Morris, but even so the idea that Jock had murdered Erroll never really felt right. This was a man in his late fifties who had difficulties with walking and who was visibly drunk on the night of the murder. Yet in order to shoot Joss he would have had to climb down a drainpipe or over a balcony before walking the two miles home. The police plodded to the conclusion of Jock's guilt on the grounds that he must have been 'jealous' but Jock was a man who had learned how to live with his losses. As he said at his trial, he was accustomed to losing. He had lost in life before – his wife had divorced him after going off with her lover – and as a gambler who regularly bet and lost huge sums on the horses, Jock knew how to be sporting about such things. He had written Diana off as a bad but unavoidable business.

The Kenya Police never even considered the possibility of a professional hit by an MI6 team, although Harry Morris did raise the idea at Jock's trial. In this respect, I am inclined to agree with the Attorney General, Walter Harrigan QC, who said of this particular supposition: 'If a jury could believe that, I have nothing more to say.' There were many prominent men in 1939 and 1940 who were pro-Oswald Mosley, and quite a few from Scotland, yet none of them became the victims of assassination plots. The Duke of Montrose was an avid Mosley supporter, as was the military scientist J.F.C. Fuller and the novelist Henry Williamson. Charles Stewart Henry Vane-Tempest-Stewart, seventh Marquis of Londonderry, visited Germany in 1936 and was entertained by Hermann Goering and Joachim von Ribbentrop; Adolf Hitler himself gave a dinner in the marquis's honour. Hitler, on the other hand, *was* a target for MI6 and had he been eliminated in 1939 the course of history might have been very different. But Lord Erroll? A man who had been a member of the British Union of Fascists for only a few months? Not worth bothering about. Joss had presented no danger to Britain or to its colonies and, if suspected, he could easily have been watched.

The lack of a clear suspect other than Jock was

evidently very much on the mind of Harry Morris during the course of the trial. Morris knew he would have to convince the jury that someone else was responsible for the crime. In summing up, he asked the jury to consider a number of alternatives. It was possible that Lord Erroll – once a card-carrying member of the British Union of Fascists – might well have been the victim of a political plot. Equally, a jealous husband could have been to blame. If not a husband, then it could well have been one of Joss's former girlfriends, seeking revenge. 'Hell hath no fury like a woman scorned,' Morris reminded the jury.

In fact, Morris had good reason for supposing that one of Joss's lovers might well be responsible for the murder. Shortly after Morris's arrival in Nairobi for the trial, he had received two anonymous letters. The first note read: 'Under separate cover I have written to the Chief Magistrate, Kenya, asking him why the murderer of Joss Erroll, a relative of mine by marriage, was not looked for in the proper quarter. Sir Delves Broughton is not the murderer . . . (the name of a leading socialite and Nairobi personality was given) murdered him in a fit of jealousy.'

The second read:

Have you found out what lady (?) had the privilege of the late Lord Erroll's affections before he fell in love with Lady Broughton? I think if you put a good detective on the job to find out and follow this lead, you will be pleased . . .

Lord Erroll would stop his car if such a woman (he knew) signalled that she wanted to speak to him. The rest would be easy . . . If she could not have Erroll herself, no one else would.

Think it over – two birds with one stone. I'm sure Sir Delves didn't do it . . .

Morris took the notes to the police, but the identity of their mysterious author could not be ascertained. The notes were never seen again. Fortunately, Henry Morris kept records and these were reprinted in *Genius for the Defence*, Benjamin Bennett's biography of Morris, published in 1959.

So who was the mysterious leading socialite and Nairobi personality mentioned in the notes? Joss's other love interest was Phyllis Filmer but she was out of the country at the time of his murder, and, besides, she could hardly be described as a 'leading socialite and Nairobi personality'.

The description fits Alice perfectly. Alice was a central figure in the Nairobi social scene. She was ferociously jealous of Joss's relations with Diana. She had certainly enjoyed 'the privilege of the late Lord Erroll's affections before he fell in love with Lady Broughton'. Joss would certainly have stopped his car if he had seen her in the road. What's more, Alice *knew* that Joss would be driving back to his bungalow from Marula Lane on the night of the murder at around 3 a.m. because Dickie Pembroke had told her so. It was thanks to Dickie that Alice also learned that Jock had given his blessing to Diana and Joss's union that very evening. The idea that Diana might now be free to marry Joss can only have sent Alice into a 'fit of jealousy'. Nothing caused Alice more anguish than when the men in her life attempted to reject her. 'I always get my own way'; 'I take what I want and throw it away.' These were the ominous words that Frédéric had used to give voice to Alice's wilful destructiveness in his book, *Vertical Land*. 'If she could not have Erroll herself, no one else would,' wrote the author of the anonymous notes.

There is no doubt Alice had the motive and the knowledge. She also had the nerve. In 1927 she had turned her gun on Raymund when he tried to break off their engagement. She had been tried for his attempted murder and found guilty of a 'crime passionnel'. In other words, she was entirely capable of acting on her passionate impulses. She was a brave and competent shot, someone who seldom left home without a revolver. According to Margaret Spicer, Alice had first owned a gun in Chicago when she was eighteen years old, given to her by her mobster boyfriend 'for her own protection'. This Colt-type weapon was an American pocket revolver: hammerless with automatic extraction, nickel-plated and .38 calibre. Alice bought one very like it in Paris, with its pearl inlay handle, just prior to shooting Raymund. In Kenya, she kept such a revolver on her bedside table. But what of her alibi, Dickie? It is possible that Dickie slept through Alice's departure and her return on the night of the murder. Even if he had heard Alice leaving or coming back, he certainly loved her enough to want to protect her. When questioned by the police, he would have been anxious to minimize his association with the Erroll case so that he could be reinstated into the Coldstream Guards as soon as possible. Either he lied to the police for Alice's sake – and in order to preserve what remained of his already tarnished reputation – or he was telling the truth. Alice had simply managed to leave and then return without waking him.

That night, Alice could have easily taken her revolver from the bedside table and soundlessly climbed into her car, and then sped away. Her route would have been swift and without traffic. Turning left out of Portaluca, she would have driven downhill over the Nairobi River and then past the Catholic church until she reached Ainsworth Bridge and the Da Rajah House, where she and Frédéric had visited the Spicers many times during 1926. At Ainsworth Bridge, Alice would have turned left to pass the Norfolk Hotel before reaching the Ngong road, which led to the Karen road and its intersection with Marula Lane. She could have parked her car on the Karen road at this point and doused her lights to save the battery. She knew that a car being driven by Joss would be coming down this road sometime before or around 3 a.m. Checking her revolver, she would have made sure it was fully loaded. When a pair of half-shaded headlights appeared over the horizon ahead, Alice would have opened the door of her car and walked into the middle of the road, waving her arms as she did so. Joss would have immediately recognized Alice's slim figure illuminated by the Buick's headlights. He probably would have slowed to a full stop but with the engine still running, his foot on the clutch and the top gear still engaged. The Buick was right-hand drive so Joss would have needed to lean across the long front bench seat in order to open the passenger window to speak to Alice. With his foot still on the clutch, the length of his body would have been almost parallel with the seat.

At this point, Alice would have pulled out her pistol and fired. Undeterred by the first miss, she would have immediately pulled the trigger again, letting loose a second bullet. This one met its mark, entering Joss's neck just below his ear. On the bullet's impact, Joss would have slipped from his stretched-out position, falling in a crumpled heap under the dashboard, his left foot coming off the clutch. With the engine still ticking over, and with top gear engaged, the car would then have inched forward. The huge torque of the engine could have permitted the Buick to move without stalling, and Alice would have watched the car turning slightly right and going over the embankment into the ditch on the right-hand side of the road, where it came to rest, stopping with the headlights still ablaze and the key still in the ignition.

In this scenario, both Joss's position under the dashboard and the position of the car with its wheels over the verge are explained. The second pair of wide car tracks found at the scene of the crime, going off in the direction of Nairobi, is also explained: Alice's car was a DeSoto, which had enormously wide tyres. Could the hairpin found in the car have belonged to Alice? And what of the ignition and the headlights? The car was apparently discovered with its lights on but the ignition off. It is my guess that the first constables who arrived at the scene attempted to turn the lights off by switching the ignition key to the 'off' position. In fact, the lights were operated independently but the light switch was broken and could not be operated without pliers. Hence when the car was later examined, the lights were on and the ignition off. A larger question is why Alice didn't try to kill herself that night, just as she had attempted to do at the Gare du Nord after shooting Raymund. Did she go as far as to press the gun to her own head on the night of the murder? Did she lose courage, too horrified by what she had already accomplished? Did the thought of the loyal Dickie draw her back to the Portaluca Cottage? For whatever reason, after committing her horrible crime, Alice would have climbed into her car and raced back to bed where Dickie was waiting. She could not have been absent for more than one and a half hours. As for her revolver, she could have easily disposed of it during the following days. Alice's Muthaiga cottage, her beach house and Wanjohi Farm were never searched by the police.

If Alice *did* shoot Lord Erroll, this would certainly help explain her reactions in the aftermath of Joss's murder. It would explain her decision to see his dead body on the morning of his death: she would have needed to be sure that she had succeeded. This would also explain why she was so completely involved in the outcome of Jock Broughton's trial. If Jock had been found guilty, he would probably have been hanged and in all likelihood Alice would have felt bound to confess in order to save him. No wonder she visited Jock so frequently in his cell, reassuring him that she had perfect faith in his innocence. She knew that he was innocent because she herself was guilty. If Jock had been convicted, Alice would have had Jock's death — as well as Joss's — on her conscience.

14

❧ ❦

A Green Bedroom Full of Flowers

Both during the trial and after the verdict, Alice spent as much time as possible with Dickie Pembroke, leaning on him with an increasing devotion. While she remained gripped by every detail of the Erroll case, Dickie could not share her interest. He had been highly uncomfortable about giving evidence in court: after the disgrace of being placed on leave from the Coldstream Guards, he was acutely sensitive when it came to matters of his reputation. It was agonizing for him to have his name associated with the general ignominy surrounding Joss's murder. Although Dickie loved Alice, his clear priority was to rejoin his regiment in North Africa where the 3rd Battalion Coldstream Guards was stationed at this time. Even before the start of the trial, he had made his application to HQ in

London to be reposted. While Dickie waited to hear whether he would be accepted back into his regiment, the possibility of his departure only served to increase Alice's attachment to him. As with all the men in her life – Raymund and Joss included – Alice would always experience her greatest passions for those who were attempting to leave her.

In June 1941, with Jock's trial still in progress, Dickie's application for transfer was granted and he was asked to travel to Cairo where he was to be made acting Regimental Lieutenant Colonel. He left on the 24th of July, only a few weeks after Jock's acquittal. Alice knew there was every possibility Dickie would see action and be killed and so she put off saying goodbye to him for as long as possible, travelling with him as far as Kampala, Uganda, before bidding him farewell. In Dickie's luggage was a letter Alice had written to him before his departure from Wanjohi: poignantly, she had wanted him to have something to open on his arrival in Cairo. Very few of Alice's letters have been preserved, but the ones she wrote to Dickie during the war were kept. They are immensely revealing of this woman during a period of her life when she was struggling with grief, separation, solitude, uncertainty, depression and physical illness, not to mention possible culpability in a murder. Despite Alice's predicament, the letters are marked by tenderness, and a self-knowing humour.

The first letter to Dickie is dated the night before his departure, 23 July 1941. Alice wrote in it that it seemed ridiculous to be writing a letter to someone who was still sitting in front of her. Even so, Alice said, she would rather give him something to read when he arrived in Cairo than for him to wait weeks for a letter to arrive in the mail. She told him that she'd had a lovely week with him, and that she hoped she could manage to say goodbye the next day in decent fashion. She went on in a less stoical vein: 'I can't imagine the immediate future at all . . . all of you are gone or going and my self-pity wells up when I realize that I can follow no one.' Alice's close circle was certainly diminished. Joss was dead. Idina had moved to her coastal house north of Mombasa. Lizzie Lezard had been posted to Cairo. Alice's closest friend in Kenya, Paula, was absorbed in her marriage to Boy Long. Even Alice's French maid had been dispatched back to France at the beginning of the war. Alice could count on her neighbour Pat Fisher, her friends Patsy Bowles and Noreen Pearson, and her housekeeper, Flo, for companionship. But she often found herself spending long days alone. Another letter to Dickie, this one undated – but which must have been written soon after his departure – offers more evidence as to her precarious state of mind during this time: '. . . the fact of you going away in these uncertain times, even for only a short time, as we hope, is pure and absolute pain . . .'

After Dickie's departure, Alice's health certainly took an immediate turn for the worse and in early September of 1941, she had a hysterectomy. Her regular doctor, William Boyle, performed the operation at a hospital in Nairobi. Since he first attended to her in 1932, Dr Boyle had taken a special interest in Alice and the two had long since established a flirtatious rapport. Years later, Boyle's daughter, also called Alice, would recall that her father was 'rather in love with Alice de Trafford'. While it would have comforted Alice to know that Dr Boyle would perform the operation, she remained terrified of the recovery period. In her next letter to Dickie – whom she knew was facing much graver dangers in North Africa – she managed to keep her tone light, at least initially. She spoke of the matron and the nurses, all of whom she knew from previous visits, greeting her warmly. Flo had travelled down to Nairobi with her, a trip that was marred by the fact that they had two punctures and only one spare tyre. Alice observed that now she had arrived at the hospital her operation was cheerfully referred to as 'the op' by the nurses, accompanied by much pillow-thumping and towel-shaking. But she also wrote of events that took place before she left for Nairobi. Immediately before her departure, Alice made the extraordinary decision to put down her beloved dachshund, Minnie. The reason Alice gave Dickie was that her poor dog had begun to panic every time she was put in the car and that recently the hysteria had worsened. Unable to bear Minnie's distress, Alice gave her pentobarbital, a short-acting barbiturate (often given the trade name Nembutal). Alice could have taken Minnie to a vet, and yet she chose to do this herself. For someone who loved her animals as much as Alice, it seems a desperate act, one that reveals her increasingly morbid state of mind during this time. Her choice of language in the letter was equally chilling. Alice said she 'killed' Minnie, and that she felt as if she had 'committed a murder'. She went on in an even more sinister vein. She remembered

Dickie once counselling her that 'life must go on'. Life need not go on, Alice observed: 'In Joss's case someone decided that, in Minnie's case I did, and the length of our own lives lies entirely within our own hands (unless someone else gets at us first!).'

Alice buried Minnie in the iris beds at Wanjohi Farm, at the edge of the 'cut' she had made to take the stream water right around the edge of her house and garden. After her operation, Alice returned to Wanjohi to recover. It has been suggested that Alice was suffering from ovarian cancer. However, Patsy Bowles (who was married to Alice's second doctor) recalls that although her womb was removed, no cancer was discovered. On 15 September 1941, Alice was well enough to attend an all-girls lunch with Patsy and Noreen Pearson, along with another friend, Rosie Delap.

Years later, Patsy would recall Alice's mysterious words that day: 'If you have an obsession or a very deep wish,' Alice informed her friends, 'or even two wishes which you dream about and want – they often happen. The first of my wishes has happened. I wonder if the second one will occur?'

If Alice did shoot Lord Erroll, then presumably her first wish had been to commit the murder. Her second wish would also soon come to pass.

After lunch, Alice asked her driver, Arap Ruta, to take her to the small church of St Paul's in Kiambu, where Joss was buried. At the far side of the graveyard, she found his headstone with that of his wife Mary close behind. This was not the first time that Alice had visited the gravesite:

since Joss's burial, she had made regular trips to Kiambu to put flowers on his resting place.

In her next letter to Dickie, written two days later on 17 September, she described her visit, and how pleased she had been to see new pots of flowers on his grave, which in recent times had been neglected. She also wrote about the difficulties of her recuperation. Although her surgical wound had healed, she remained extremely weak and ill. The matron had told her to expect to feel depressed, but not to let that get her down, advice that Alice wryly brushed aside. 'What these periods of depression will be like, plus the ones I get anyway, I can't imagine . . .' she wrote, adding that she felt 'desolate beyond words' now that Minnie was gone.

As September progressed, Alice's forty-second birthday was looming. In frail health and failing spirits, she must have dreaded its arrival. To make matters worse, her neighbour Pat Fisher was hosting a joint birthday party with Phyllis Filmer. Alice had never much cared for Joss's old flame and, not surprisingly, she decided to back out of the birthday party at the last moment. Flo Crofton was dispatched to Kipipiri with the excuse that Alice was unwell. After Flo's departure, Alice took to her bed and ingested a dose of Nembutal, the same barbiturate she had fed to Minnie.

A few days later, on 27 September 1941, Alice sent Flo off to Olkalau, a small town near to Wanjohi Farm, to do some shopping and collect mail. She told her African staff not to disturb her. This wasn't at all unusual as Alice usually breakfasted in bed and didn't get up until about

11 a.m. Then she went out into her garden and collected armloads of flowers. Back in her bedroom, she decorated her room, placing the flowers on her bed and furniture. Her large bedroom was painted with green oil and water paint mixed together, an effect that was both peaceful and striking, especially with the added decoration of the flowers. Alice then attached the names of close friends to her furniture, including the large Knole settee brought from France (one of her favourite possessions), and two large African drums, which served as side tables near her substantial bed.

She had already written five letters. Two of these were to her children, one was a suicide note and one was addressed to the police. The other was to Dickie and was sent to him in Cairo. She described the beauty of the African morning as she sat writing to him by a pool in her garden, surrounded by the sunshine, colourful flowers and a sense of peace. She told Dickie she loved him and predicted that he would find it very hard to understand her actions. Even so, she said, he should know that she believed she was doing the right thing. Then she revealed that the reason she had found it so hard to say goodbye in Uganda was that she knew it would be their last goodbye. Alice ended the letter with the following words to Dickie: 'I simply can't write again, and there is nothing more to say.'

Alice locked her bedroom door and wrapped a large bandage around her chest. By now, it had begun to rain. She put on her best nightdress and climbed into bed. Next she swallowed 10 grammes of Nembutal, a huge dose. She placed her revolver to her heart. Before she slipped out of consciousness completely, she pulled the trigger. Alerted by the sound of rasping breathing noises coming from Alice's bedroom, one of her African servants forced the door open only to discover a terrible scene. By the time Flo returned from Olkalau, Alice was near death.

Flo drove out to Kipipiri where there was a telephone and called Dr Boyle who was in his surgery in Nairobi. Boyle knew his own car was too small and slow to drive up to the heights of Wanjohi so he borrowed Dr Bowles's powerful Lincoln and raced up to Alice's house in the pouring rain. He arrived to find Alice was dead. At her bedside, Dr Boyle discovered the painting that she had labelled and left for him. She must have known he would come. The oil, possibly painted by the Russian-American surrealist Pavel Fedorovich Tchelitchew, shows three figures done in several shades of blue. On the back Alice had written teasingly to her favourite doctor: 'To the one who is too frolicsome . . .', a final joking gesture of sorts.

Dr Boyle knew he must now carry out his legal duties. A coroner's inquest would be required. He found Alice's five letters which he handed over to the police before lodging a death certificate at the coroner's office.

Alice was buried at the side of the river on Wanjohi Farm, near to the place where her dog Minnie had been laid to rest. Her staff, together with Pat Fisher and Flo Crofton, attended her funeral. In one of her suicide notes, Alice had asked that a cocktail party be held at her grave, but it was not to be. Most of her other friends stayed away, dispersed by war or ill health. In her final years, many friends had fallen away. Alice's grave was left unmarked, as was often the case in this part of the world – the local Kikuyu believed that the white settlers died with their wealth still upon them, and they often dug up graves in search of money and jewellery.

The coroner duly investigated the circumstances surrounding Alice's death and an inquest was held on Thursday 9 October 1941 at Gilgil. At the inquest, the doctor submitted the letters found at Alice's deathbed along with his report: by law, suicide notes have to be submitted to the authorities and the coroner. Dr Boyle gave his evidence, but the hearing was adjourned pending the result of the post-mortem. In December 1941, the hearing was again delayed 'owing to certain witnesses being in Mombasa', namely Alice's housekeepers, Flo Crofton and Noel Case. When the inquest was reconvened on 21 January 1942, the coroner, who had been unable to locate the missing witnesses, stated that he did not wish to prolong the inquiry, so he brought the hearing to a close. In his statement, he asserted, 'Alice de Trafford took her own life on 27th September 1941' and that 'the proximate cause of her death was shock and internal haemorrhage from a gunshot wound. It is clear that the deceased's taking of her own life was intentional, and there is no evidence of mental instability . . .'

There is no doubt that Alice's suicide was intentional. She had planned her death carefully. She had said goodbye to Dickie for the last time. She had tested the Nembutal on Minnie first, ensuring that her dog would not survive her. She had visited Joss's grave to pay her final respects.

She had written letters to her children and amended her will, assigning her furniture and other items to her friends. She had prepared her bedroom and the manner of her death. Above all, she made sure that she would not fail and that this suicide attempt would be final.

Alice's two daughters – now nineteen and seventeen respectively and living in Chicago with Aunt Tattie – learned of their mother's suicide from a newspaper headline announcing her death. They had not seen Alice in two years due to the war. Alice had always lived at such a great distance from them that it must have been easy for Nolwen and Paola simply to imagine their mother going on with her life in Wanjohi, with her animals and her stories. Although Alice's daughters had never visited their mother in Africa, the terms of her will contained a belated invitation. Nolwen and Paola were to inherit Wanjohi Farm and her house on condition that they come to live in Kenya and look after the place for five years, spending eight months each year there. As Nolwen later pointed out, these were impossible terms for two adolescent girls during wartime. In the event that her daughters were unable to live at Wanjohi, Alice's African estate was to go to a fatherless child of eight, the daughter of Noreen Pearson. Noreen's husband had died in the war, and Alice had evidently decided to take pity on this young child who had recently lost her father. Nolwen later recalled that, 'Alas, the child who inherited was taken away to Washington, her mother having remarried in Kenya an American Officer. So, the Wanjohi Farm was sold on the girl's 21st birthday. My mother's wishes all to the wind.'

In the coming years, Wanjohi Farm was given over to the authorities, becoming the Satima Primary School for Girls.

After their mother's death and the end of the Second World War, Nolwen and Paola left Chicago and returned to France. Nolwen had taken a course in Maryland with the Women's Army Corps and she joined the Free French Army in 1944 as a diplomatic liaison officer. On 23 September 1948 she married Lionel Armand-Delille and together they had two children, Frédéric and Angélique. In the 1950s, Nolwen embarked on a career in fashion, becoming the president of the Incorporated Society of London Fashion designers, which would have no doubt delighted her stylish mother. After divorcing Armand-Delille, Nolwen married twice – first to Edward Rice and then to the art historian Kenneth Clark. She died at the family château, Parfondeval, in 1989. Paola married twice, first to Walter Haydon and next to John Ciechanowski. She had two sons, Guillaume and Alexander. She died in 2007. Both Alice's daughters remained loyal to their mother's memory throughout their lives. Their apparent lack of resentment must be some indication of their good feeling towards her, despite their long separations from her, and of Aunt Tattie's excellent care of them in Alice's absence. Sadly, Nolwen and Paola never did visit Alice's beloved Wanjohi Valley. The only de Janzé member of the family to have seen Alice's farm to this day is Nolwen's daughter, Angélique Fiedler. On a visit there in 2004, Angélique was so taken by the breathtaking beauty of the place that she set about negotiating with the authorities to have the school renamed the 'De Janzé Primary School'. Angélique is now seeking to endow the school to enhance its prosperity and future, in memory of her grandmother.

Dickie Pembroke received word of Alice's death while posted in Egypt. He was devastated by the news. Undoubtedly he had had it in mind that if he survived the war he would return to Kenya and marry Alice, but this was not to be. Throughout the rest of the war, he carried Alice's letters in the left-hand breast pocket of his battle uniform, along with his AB64 (the document denoting his number and rank). In March 1943, Dickie's battalion entered Medenine in Tunisia where the British won a decisive victory against Field Marshal Rommel, one of the finest German generals of the Second World War. Towards the end of armed conflict, Dickie returned to England, later going on to the War Office where he was granted the status of full Colonel in 1951. His medals and awards included the 39/45 Star; the Africa Star; the Defence Medal and an OBE. After marrying a Mrs Dermot Pakenham in 1950, he left the army and embarked on a career in the bill-broking business. He died in Upham, Hampshire, in 1967 at the age of sixty-three. Brigadier H.R. Norman, formerly of the Coldstream Guards, wrote an obituary for Dickie Pembroke in which he described him as 'the most modest of men', someone who had the gift of creating friendships with all sorts of people, old and young.

Lizzie Lezard also outlived Alice. On arriving in Cairo in late 1941, he began boarding with several other bachelor officers, one of whom was the future diplomat and translator of Turgenev, Charles Johnston. Later, Johnston would immortalize Lizzie and their time in Cairo in his book, *Mo and Other Originals* (1971), where Lizzie appears as Monty Malan, a bon vivant who spends all day lounging in bed, being brought trays of chicken sandwiches, and whisky and sodas by his servant, Mo. In 1943, Lezard, who had recently completed his parachute training, was dropped near Monte Carlo, where he fell heavily and broke his back, henceforth becoming known as 'The man who broke his back at Monte Carlo.' Lizzie was rescued and hidden by the local Free French until the arrival of the Americans, at which point he returned to London on a steamer and was welcomed home a hero. He was next heard of living in a butler's room at the top of the Ritz Hotel, leading an extremely active social life, before taking a flat in Eaton Square. In 1958, he went into hospital for a minor operation where he died very suddenly from shock on 21 August at the age of fifty-six. Charles Johnston wrote in Lizzie's obituary: 'It was as if a vital source of light and warmth in our lives had been violently put out.'

Raymund de Trafford was released from Parkhurst Prison in 1941, having survived the air raids on the Isle of Wight during the Battle of Britain. He soon reported to his former regiment of the Coldstream Guards, hoping to rejoin, but he was turned down and his application for a commission with the Rifle Brigade was also refused. Eventually, in 1942, after having missed three years of service during the war, he was permitted to join the Pioneer Corps as a lieutenant. Raymund was posted to

Morocco where he worked conscientiously as the commander of a platoon of engineer workers, digging drains and building bridges. He remained in North Africa until 1945 when he was honourably discharged, having attained the rank of Captain. After the war, Raymund was awarded two medals. He also resumed his previous lifestyle, hunting, gambling, womanizing and visiting friends, including the writers Evelyn Waugh, Maurice Baring and Robert Graves. (When Baring died at the end of 1945, Raymund was named as his literary executor.) In 1950, he met Eve Drummond, whom he married the following year. The day after the couple's wedding announcement appeared in *The Times* on 21 May 1951, congratulatory telegrams arrived along with demands from six separate bookmakers. Raymund and Eve went to live in Ireland, but the marriage did not last long. Raymund used his asthma and worsening emphysema as an excuse to visit Robert Graves in Majorca, leaving Eve behind. Robert, who was very fond of Raymund, took him in almost permanently at his house in Deià on the Spanish island. In May of 1971, Raymund was visiting London when he suffered a fatal stroke. He was seventy-one years old. He is buried in the Catholic cemetery in Monks Kirby, Warwickshire. On his headstone is written 'Liber Scriptus Proferetur in quo totum continetur', a verse from the Catholic requiem mass which translates as 'The written book will be brought in which all is contained'. Dermot de Trafford, the sixth baronet and Raymund's nephew, has said of his uncle, 'He behaved badly, but he knew how to behave well.' Raymund left an estate worth £212.02.

Jock Delves Broughton sailed to Ceylon and India after the end of his trial for Joss's murder, staying until later that year. Diana was at his side. On their return to Kenya in 1942, they rented Joss's former home, Oserian, for a time: Diana said that it brought her solace to be surrounded by a place Joss had loved. The Delves Broughton marriage lasted until the end of the year, at which point Jock returned to England. Despite his acquittal, he had continued to be dogged by speculation and ignominy. Soon after his return he took a fatal overdose of morphine at the Adelphi Hotel in Liverpool, dying on 5 December 1942, a little more than a year after Alice's suicide.

Diana Delves Broughton stayed on in Nairobi, where she was more or less completely ostracized by the settlers, many of whom had come to blame her for Joss's death. Undeterred, she proceeded to marry one of the wealthiest men in Kenya, Gilbert Colvile, in 1943 (a month after Jock's suicide). Gilbert bought Oserian for Diana, and the couple went on living there until their divorce in 1955. At this point, Diana had already met and fallen in love with Thomas Pitt Hamilton Cholmondeley, fourth Baron Delamere, the son of the famed highland settler and third Baron Delamere, Alice's old friend D. Tom and Diana married in 1955. Despite Gilbert's divorce from Diana, he still left her his entire estate on his death, making her a very wealthy woman. When Tom died of heart failure in 1979, Diana was sixty-six years old, at which point she took an apartment behind the Ritz Hotel in London, staying there for a few months each year. The rest of her time was spent in Kenya, attending Nairobi races or fishing at Kilifi where she acquired a home called Villa Buzza. She died of a stroke on 7 September 1987 at the age of seventy-four. Her body was flown back to Nairobi and buried at Ndabibi between the graves of Gilbert and Tom. The inscription on her grave reads 'Surrounded by all I love'.

Alice's great friend Paula Long, née Gellibrand, also maintained her ties to Kenya. She and her husband, Boy, lived on their ranch, Nderit, at Elmenteita, where they farmed cattle, close to the lake whose shores are fringed with pink flamingos. It was an appropriately dramatic setting for this flamboyant couple: in the hills above the house is a place called Eburu, where hot steam emerges from splits in the rocks. After Boy's death in 1955, Paula left Elmenteita and returned home to England, where she lived at Henley-on-Thames, in Oxfordshire. Late in her life, she began to suffer with dementia and she died at the Priory, a private psychiatric hospital in London, in 1986 at the age of eighty-eight. She is buried in the small Oxfordshire village of Nettlebed.

After Alice's death, Idina went on living and farming at Clouds. Until the end of the war, Phyllis Filmer lived there too and Idina was evidently glad of the company – her husband of the time was the fighter pilot Vincent Soltau, and he was almost permanently away. What's more, during the course of the war she suffered the losses of her first and third husbands (Euan and Joss) and her two sons from her first marriage, David and Gee. By 1945, she had a nervous breakdown, brought on by grief. Her doctors advised her to seek relief from living continuously at so many thousands of feet above sea level and she left

Clouds for a time for her bungalow at Mtapwa Creek. Mtapwa is about ten miles north of Mombasa, on the banks of a long sea inlet. Here she planted a lushly beautiful tropical garden. After divorcing her fighter-pilot husband, Idina reverted to her maiden name, Sackville, promising never to marry again. In 1950, she met James Bird, known as Jimmy Bird or James the Sixth in honour of his position as the sixth 'husband' in Idina's life, although the pair were never officially married. He became her constant companion, despite the fact that he was something of a drunk and known to prefer men to women. 'I've worn out five husbands and the sixth is on his last legs,' Idina was often heard to say. In 1952 she had a hysterectomy, due to having been diagnosed with uterine cancer. Despite the operation, her cancer returned. After refusing to go back to the hospital Idina fell into a coma, dying at Mtapwa in 1955 at the age of sixty-two. Idina had once told her neighbour there, the essayist Edward Rodwell, that she knew the identity of Joss's killer and that she would tell Rodwell the name before she died. She never did.

And so one by one, the protagonists in the Erroll saga passed away, taking what they knew of the mystery of his murder to their graves.

Epilogue

The Missing Letter and the Great Beyond

In 1998 I had begun to cast around for information on Alice de Janzé, in the hope that I might write her biography. I was keen to track down Alice's former housekeeper Noel Case, who had helped run Wanjohi Farm after Alice's return to Kenya in 1933. I felt she must have great insight into Alice's life there, and that she could well prove essential to my research. By now, I had begun to suspect that Alice was responsible for the Erroll murder, but I needed to know more about her psychology and movements in order to be sure. I was already in contact with the writer Errol Trzebinski, who was at that time hard at work on her biography of Joss Erroll, *The Life and Death of Lord Erroll*. It was Trzebinski who put me in contact with a woman named Alice Boyle. Alice Boyle was the daughter of Dr

William Boyle, the physician who had raced to Alice de Janzé's bedside after her fatal suicide attempt. Trzebinski told me that Alice Boyle was in close contact with Noel Case and could perhaps put us in touch. Even so, Trzebinski warned me, I should not hold out too much hope of an interview. Apparently Noel was refusing to talk to anyone (even her own nephew) about her days with Alice de Janzé at Wanjohi Farm.

I obtained a telephone number for Alice Boyle (now Mrs Alice Fleet) and invited her to lunch at my house in London. I was met by an attractive woman in her fifties, with dark hair and a lively and capable air. As we began to speak – firstly about Noel Case and then about Dr Boyle – I realized that this Alice was shy and even a little defensive, especially when it came to talking about her father. Over lunch, she revealed to me that she was still in possession of the blue oil painting that Alice de Janzé had left to Dr Boyle at the time of her death. Later I learned that Alice Boyle was certain her father must have had some kind of an affair with Alice – who was his favourite patient – possibly before his marriage in 1936. It was only after our fifth or sixth meeting that Alice Boyle revealed information to me that cast the story I was researching in a startling new light.

'You know, my mother told me all about Alice's confession letter,' said Alice Boyle, obliquely, one day over lunch in London. She seemed to assume that I already knew about the existence of such a letter. I began to question her further, trying to suppress the true degree of my curiosity, in case it should disturb the telling of her story.

When Alice Boyle was eleven, she informed me, her mother, Ethnie, had told her that Alice de Janzé had left a confession letter addressed to the police before her death along with her suicide notes. Dr Boyle had shown his wife these letters before submitting them to the coroner's office. Ethnie Boyle had seen the confession letter with her own eyes and had told her daughter all about it. Alice Boyle continues to stand by the clear memory of her mother's words: Alice de Janzé confessed to shooting Lord Erroll in a letter. When I went back to my copy of James Fox's *White Mischief*, I even found a reference to this vital piece of evidence: 'She [Alice] left several notes. One was to the Police – its contents were never released,' wrote Fox.

So, if a confession did indeed exist, whatever happened to this missing letter? It is true that its contents were never released and the Kenya Police deny that there is any record of the note existing in their archives. Although Dr Boyle definitely submitted the note at the original coroner's inquest, the letter has since disappeared. Certainly, its contents were not disclosed at the inquest. What happened to the missing note? It is possible that the confession letter never reached the Kenya Police in the first place. It is my guess that the coroner was so shocked at the implications of Alice's confession that he directed the note to the personal attention of the Attorney General, Sir Walter Harrigan K.C. Harrigan was the Attorney General from 1933 to 1944, and prosecutor for the Crown at the trial of Jock Delves Broughton. Harrigan would doubtless have been extremely alarmed by the letter's contents. He would have weighed the implications carefully, bearing in mind that the Crown's case against Jock had failed and that numerous suggestions had been made both during and after the trial (some in writing) that the murder had been carried out by a discarded mistress. Rather than open up a can of worms, Harrigan could easily have decided to suppress the confession, justifying his decision on the grounds that he was stabilizing speculation about a controversial murder. To protect himself, he could have sent the confession out of the country in the diplomatic bag to London for safe keeping with a memorandum explaining his actions.

I soon discovered that I was not the only one to have learned of Alice's confession letter. Alice Boyle had recently revealed her story to Gordon Fergusson. At the time, Fergusson was in the process of writing a history of the Tarporley Hunt Club, entitled *The Green Collars*. Tarpoley, founded in 1762, is the oldest hunt club in England and once counted Jock Delves Broughton amongst its members (in fact he was the only member of the club ever to have been tried for murder). As a result, Fergusson was familiar with the Erroll case. When he met Alice Boyle socially in 1993, she told him the story about her mother and the confession letter. Fergusson felt he had information that would finally and definitively clear Jock's name and so he published his findings in *The Green Collars* in 1993. When Fergusson's book came out, the Peterborough column in the *Daily Telegraph* picked up the story, publishing it under the headline: 'Tarporley Man Puts the Finger on Alice'. This led to a little flurry of correspondence in the paper. 'No!'

replied J.N.P. Watson, a cousin of Dickie Pembroke. 'Alice was deeply in love with Pembroke and was in bed with him at the time of the murder.' Watson went on to argue that, apart from her alibi, it would have been 'quite out of character for Alice to have hidden in the back of Erroll's car in order to shoot him, or to have killed him up on the road'. But there is no doubt that Alice had the 'motive, means, and mentality for murder', wrote Fergusson, adding that her alibi was 'one that any woman could have arranged'.

During my investigations, I came across other clues further implicating Alice. In *White Mischief* James Fox wrote that after the trip to the morgue on the morning of Joss's death, Lizzie Lezard always suspected Alice as 'the murder fitted in with her morbid preoccupations'. Fox even went so far as to suggest that Alice might have confessed the murder to Lizzie. 'In later years Lezard was untypically evasive on the subject,' Fox wrote. Then there was Betty Leslie-Melville's memoir about her time in Kenya, *The Giraffe Lady*, published in 1997. Betty's mother-in-law, Mary Leslie-Melville, was once Alice's neighbour in the Wanjohi Valley. In *The Giraffe Lady*, Betty recounts the time she asked her mother-in-law who she thought had shot Lord Erroll. Mary replied without hesitation: 'My Dear, I do not *think* who may have killed him, I *know*.'

It was Mary's firm belief that Alice had shot Lord Erroll. Betty wrote:

Alice knew that Erroll was due to have dinner at Muthaiga Club on the fateful night. Mary also knew that Alice was aware of the road Lord Erroll would take to drive back from Karen afterwards. So Mary's theory was that Alice had waited at the cross road where the murder took place. The sight of her on the road would have stopped him. She would then have walked up to the car and shot him in the head. Afterwards she drove home.

And Mary claimed to have actual proof. A few years after Erroll's killing, Mary's headman was fishing rocks out of the little river that separated Mary's property from Alice's Wanjohi Farm in order to repair the road. Here he found a gun buried under one of the rocks. He took it to Mary. According to Mary, this gun was the exact make and calibre of the missing revolver used to shoot Joss. Mary concluded that Alice must have thrown it there after returning from shooting Joss on the night of his murder.

'What did you do then?' Betty asked, astonished.

'Nothing,' Mary replied. 'Erroll was dead. Alice was dead. What good would it have done to tell anyone?'

Mary led Betty to the hall cupboard in her Nairobi house, unlocked the door and showed her the revolver in question, just hanging there. By the time I read these words, Mary Leslie-Melville had long since died and the whereabouts of this supposed murder weapon was unknown. But its existence, as described by Betty, added further fuel to my theories.

With the clues provided by Alice Boyle and by Mary's story, I became convinced that it was Alice who had murdered Joss. Still, several questions remained in my mind.

Why would Alice have killed the man she loved? Wouldn't it have made more sense to kill her rival, Diana?

In 1998, I finally succeeded in calling on Alice's former housekeeper, Noel Case (then Mrs Eaton-Evans). Noel was white-haired by this time, in her eighties and living with her husband, Tom, at Diss in Norfolk. I had already sent various questions to her through Alice Boyle, and contrary to all my expectations, I was received hospitably by both Noel and her husband. We talked at length that day, exchanged letters, and when I called on her again a year later she offered me photographs of her time at Wanjohi Farm along with various letters pertaining to Alice's life there.

During my first interview with Noel I asked her if she thought it was Alice who had murdered Lord Erroll.

'It could have been Alice who shot Erroll,' Noel replied thoughtfully. 'Why she would want to do this is a mystery because she was madly in love with Erroll and surely it would have been more motivating to kill Diana and not Erroll. But, on the other hand, with her belief in the occult and her firm belief about the other side, it is possible that she thought that if she could send Erroll to heaven, where he might just have qualified for entry, she could join him there.'

In the French courts, when Alice was being tried for attempted murder, she had told the judge that she had shot Raymund because she wanted to join him in the 'Great Beyond'. If she did kill Joss then this desperate act must be seen in the same context. Alice had always believed in an afterlife. She had been brought up in the

Presbyterian faith. She took as gospel that when you die, your soul goes to be with God, where it enjoys God's glory and awaits the final judgement. The Presbyterian Scots Confession states: 'The chosen departed are in peace, and rest from their labours . . . they are delivered from all fear and torment . . .' Alice took for granted that after her death, she would be reunited with her loved ones, and that all her pain would be washed away. 'Now you are mine for ever,' she told Joss in the mortuary.

By killing herself, Alice completed what she had begun on the night of Joss's murder. Hence her strange words to Patsy Bowles just days before her death: 'If you have an obsession or a very deep wish, or even two wishes which you dream about and want – they often happen. The first of my wishes has happened. I wonder if the second one will occur?'

Her first wish was to kill Joss. Her second wish was to kill herself so that she could be reunited with him in the Great Beyond. Her own suicide had always been part of the plan, and yet she held off, unable to finish the job. Perhaps it was Dickie's devotion that kept Alice alive for the subsequent eight months after the murder. It was only after Dickie left for Cairo that she could no longer put off the inevitable.

As Alice's fatal dose of Nembutal took hold just a few months later, what were her final thoughts? Had she forgiven Joss for forsaking her? Had she forgiven herself for his murder? Did she think only of Joss as she approached her own death or also of her long-lost mother and estranged father, both waiting for her, she believed, on the other side? She had even ensured that her beloved dog Minnie would be there too. The revolver lay on her heavily bandaged bosom, its muzzle pointed at her heart. One squeeze of the trigger and she would finally be free. This time, she did not falter.

Author's Note

There was a set of compelling reasons and coincidences for writing about Alice de Janzé.

One of my first encounters with Alice's story was through her erstwhile husband, Raymund de Trafford. I was a schoolboy, living with my family at Yarmouth, on the Isle of Wight. It was wartime, shortly after the Battle of Britain, the famous aerial conflict between British and German air forces that took place in the skies above the south-east of England during 1940. One of the UK's largest radar stations was located on the Isle of Wight at Ventnor, and as a result, many thousands of tons of bombs had been dropped on the surrounding area during the conflict. On one occasion, a stick of bombs narrowly missed our home, destroying the house next door. Later,

I witnessed a German ME109 shot down on the farm opposite and I bicycled to the scene. The German pilot survived and was taken to nearby Parkhurst Prison.

Parkhurst was where Raymund was incarcerated throughout 1940. When he was released the following August – his sentence had been reduced due to good behaviour – he made immediately for our home at Yarmouth, where he knew he would be welcomed by my mother, his friend Margaret Spicer. It was six in the morning when he arrived at our door. My father had sent a car for him. The cook and maid were up early and gave him a very good breakfast of toast, eggs and bacon and coffee. I was at home from school for the summer. I remember Raymund's grey-looking, badly shaven face. He talked and talked. He spoke as if delivering a monologue: rattling off the names of numerous people from his Kenya days; describing his prison life; complaining about being left out of the war. He also spoke about Alice. This was a name that was familiar to me because it often came up in family conversation – my mother and Alice being friends from their Kenya days. Although Raymund was divorced from Alice by the time of his release, he was evidently still in contact with her because I distinctly remember him describing Alice's fury at the entry of Diana Delves Broughton into the tight-knit Happy Valley circle.

Before his departure at around eleven that morning my mother asked him, 'What are you going to do now?'

'I have written 4,500 words about my life in Parkhurst Prison,' Raymund replied. 'And I shall offer it to the *Sunday Dispatch*. But my family will pay me more not to publish. So that will set me up for a bit.' Even as a young boy, I could detect Raymund's aggression and toughness. He did not take much notice of me and concentrated such charm as he had on my mother. I do not think he liked my father.

As can be imagined, the appearance of an ex-convict at the breakfast table was extremely exciting for a young boy and I can still picture Raymund puffing out his cheeks before exhaling his cigarette smoke. After breakfast, he announced he was off to nearby Cowes where he would stay with his old friend Poppy Baring, the banking heiress, at her family's country seat. It was Cowes Week on the Isle of Wight and the annual yachting regatta was taking place despite the war. Raymund would doubtless have enjoyed the magnificent vantage of the Barings' Nubia House, with its views on to the silvery waters of the Solent, where, even in wartime, hundreds of boats had gathered for the regatta. Many years later, while researching this book, I met Raymund's nephew, Sir Dermot de Trafford, who told me that after Cowes Week, Raymund had travelled to London, returning to his club, White's, to see if he could locate any familiar faces. Raymund's contemporaries, however, had all been called up for the war and the club's venerable elder members refused to acknowledge this recently released prisoner. The story goes that Raymund went up to an elderly and extremely bald senior member of White's, who was sunk deep in his chair with his *Times* held high in the air. When the man refused to as much as look at him, Raymund smacked him on his bald pate, and declared, 'Hoity toity!' The room broke up with laughter.

Although I remained fascinated with Raymund, it was his appearance at my family's home that marked the point when my mind became concentrated on Alice's existence. Later, as a young man, I had my own first-hand glimpse into her world. It was 1950, and I was stationed in Kenya for two years to work for the British oil company Shell. The Erroll murder was almost a decade old but it was still a subject of fascination for those I encountered and I became intrigued. One day, I decided to motor up to Kipipiri on the peak beside Wanjohi Valley to see if I could find Idina Sackville at Clouds. I had already heard tales of Idina's infamous house parties in those early days of Happy Valley so I approached with a degree of curiosity mixed with trepidation. When Idina opened the door I introduced myself. She was then in her late fifties and had a strong upper-class English accent and an impressively girlish figure. She greeted me with great enthusiasm and questioned me closely about my mother and my father, whom she remembered. She also wanted to know whether I was related to the Spicers of Spye Park in Wiltshire into whose family her sister, Avice, had married (in fact, we are distantly connected). When Idina invited me to stay the night I accepted.

That evening, the moon was serving as an overhead lamp; a cool breeze swept down from the Aberdare Mountains behind the house and dinner was served at 11 p.m., as was customary in the carefree world that Idina had created for herself. After dinner was over, my hostess then turned to me and said, 'After I go to my bedroom, I shall wait ten minutes and then switch off the generator.

So that is all the time you have in which to undress and go to bed.' In my room I found a new pair of silk pyjamas laid out on my pillow, together with a bottle of brandy, a glass and a lighted candle on the bedside table. I lay in bed and watched for the electric lights to dim. Ten minutes later, as I was dozing off, I heard the door handle turn. Who could want to enter my room at such a time? Was it to be Idina herself? I pulled up the sheet to my neck and waited in dread anticipation. It was not Idina but Jimmy Bird, Idina's live-in companion. That evening he was obviously the worse the wear for drink and had possibly mistaken my bedroom for his own; I told him to leave, which he did quickly, and I locked my door. That night, I learned that when in Happy Valley, a locked door is a valuable defence against late night intruders.

Later that month, I visited Thomson's Falls and went to the hotel there for lunch. (Thomson's Falls is not far from the road entrance to the Wanjohi Valley.) While waiting in the lobby, I was approached by a man of medium stature whose faded fair hair, almost orange in colour, was brushed to both sides over his ears in elegant quiffs. He introduced himself as Fabian Wallace and asked if I happened to be Paul Spicer. He said he had heard from Idina that I was in the area and asked if I were free for lunch. I gladly accepted and followed him in my car to his nearby house, which was set in a well-kept garden. There was a river at the end of the lawn, swept by weeping willow trees and bamboo. I sat on his verandah sofa, which was covered in newly laundered white linen, eagerly awaiting the luncheon. I was very hungry. I remember the menu because the first course was a hot consommé with a superb flavour. A servant wearing white gloves and dressed in a long white kanzu or robe, topped by a tall red hat called a 'tarboosh', served us. The second course was blue trout cooked in the French style, the fish having been caught from the stream below. After lunch, we sat back on the verandah sofa and drank coffee. Fabian produced a thick white carton of cigarettes with a 'By Appointment' insignia on the lid: inside were one hundred perfect hand-rolled cigarettes imported from St James's Street, London, each unusually fat cigarette containing Fabian's favourite blend of Virginia tobacco. I was young, earning very little money and readily impressed by the delightful comfort of the surroundings in which I found myself, if a little concerned that Fabian might make advances towards me (in fact, he did not). Unfortunately, we did not speak of Alice during that memorable lunch, although Fabian had been Alice's neighbour and had known her well in the years immediately preceding her death.

The world that Fabian and Idina inhabited would change irrevocably in the course of the 1950s. Land disputes had already become a source of increasingly bitter conflict among the local Kikuyu and white settler farmers. While a small number of Kikuyu landowners consolidated their farms and ingratiated themselves with the colonial administration, by the early 1950s almost half of all Kikuyus had no land claims at all. Such glaring disparity led to division among the Kikuyu and extreme resentment towards the settlers. Oath-swearing ceremonies took place throughout Kenya: those participating believed that if they broke with their promises, they would be killed by supernatural forces. In the beginning, tribe members swore to acts of civil disobedience but as time went on their rituals demanded that they fight and kill the Europeans. In 1952, the Mau Mau rebellion began in earnest and the British administration declared a State of Emergency. Settlers took to carrying loaded revolvers wherever they went and placing them on the table at dinner, the time of day when many attacks took place. Spurred on by reports of extreme violence and brutality, the British government sent troops to assist the colonists, although by the end of the conflict, the number of native Kenyans killed far exceeded that of the European casualties. When the core Mau Mau leader, Dedan Kimathi, was captured in 1956, it signalled the end of the rebellion and victory for the British. The brief era of Happy Valley, however, was most definitively over. What's more, the days of British rule in Kenya were also drawing to a close. The first elections for Africans to the Legislative Council took place in 1957 and when the Kenya African National Union led by Jomo Kenyatta formed a government in 1963, the stage was set for Kenyan independence.

During the Mau Mau period, which coincided with my first visit to Kenya, I also got to know Derek Erskine and his family. Derek was a neighbour of Jock and Diana Delves Broughton in Nairobi. I met Derek through his son, Francis, who befriended me on my arrival in Kenya and who was later awarded a Military Cross for his bravery while fighting the Mau Mau rebellion in the forests of the Aberdares. Derek was a businessman and his grocery firm, Erskine & Duncan Ltd, handled several exclusive accounts from the UK including Marmite and Bronco toilet paper. I remember the daily teatime assembly at Derek's house, Riverside, where toast and Marmite were the preferred fare. After tea, Derek and I would ride out across the Kikuyu Reserve on the same route that Jock Broughton had once taken on his hacking sessions. I had purchased an Arab polo pony called Rashid el Haroun from Juanita Carberry (in 1999 Juanita would publish a memoir of her childhood in Wanjohi Valley entitled *Child of Happy Valley*). During these evening rides, Derek talked much about life and business, explaining the difference between capital and income, how to embark on investment, and the workings of the gilt markets in London. Much to my fascination, he also spoke at length about Alice de Janzé. He remembered Alice's hatred for Diana Broughton. He recalled that despite Diana's infidelity, Jock and Joss were the best of friends: the two men would josh each other about 'whose turn it was to dry Diana today' when she went swimming nude in the pool at the Broughtons' house in Marula Lane. It was Derek's opinion that Jock had been a very good sport when it came to Diana's affair with Joss.

A man of strong opinions in general, Derek was determined to promote a multiracial society in Kenya, which sadly made him extremely unpopular amongst the white settlers at the time. When I arrived in Kenya, Derek had recently befriended Jomo Kenyatta, a Kikuyu-born schoolmaster who would be arrested by the British authorities and unfairly charged with 'managing and being

a member' of the Mau Mau Society. Derek fought passion-
ately for Kenyatta's release and, in 1960, he travelled to
London where he joined the African delegates at Lancaster
House to demand Kenyatta's freedom and Kenya's independence from the British. On Derek's return to Nairobi
he was met by a group of angry settlers at the airport and
one threw thirty pieces of silver at him for his 'treason'.
Such opposition only strengthened Derek's certainty
about the rightness of the cause of African independence.
In 1963, when Kenyatta became Kenya's first president,
the story goes he wanted to pass two laws: the first law
was to stop all beating in schools; the second was to 'Make
Derek Erskine a Lord!' Derek was later knighted by the
Queen at Kenyatta's request. I make these digressions
to give a sense of Derek's integrity and the likelihood
that his recollections and opinions of Alice, Joss, Jock and
Diana were especially reliable.

It was through Derek Erskine's daughter Petal – a Royal
Academy of Dramatic Arts-trained actress – that I met
Danièle Waterpark, wife of Lord Waterpark, who lived at
Equator Farm in Subukia, Kenya. (I once went to stay
there and acted as bodyguard to Lord Waterpark's mother
Countess Enid Kenmare during a Mau Mau skirmish in
the district.) Many years later, in 1990, it was Danièle, a
Parisienne, who became a great provider of contacts
in Paris as I undertook research into Alice's life. Danièle
introduced me to Alice's grandson, Frédéric Armand-
Delille, who is the owner of Parfondeval, the Normandy
château where Alice spent much of her early married life.
By coincidence, Petal had her own link to the Erroll case.

She was married to Lee Harrigan, son of Walter Harrigan, the former Attorney General of Kenya, prosecutor of Jock Delves Broughton for the murder of Lord Erroll, and possibly the man who had suppressed Alice's confession note.

Later, in 1970, with Kenyatta still presiding, I would find myself living in Kenya for a second time. I had been asked to travel to Kenya to become Managing Director for an international group's holding in East Africa. On this trip I was accompanied by my wife, June, and our two children. The house provided for me by the company was in Marula Lane. It was the same house that Jock Delves Broughton had secured after his new marriage to Diana in 1940 and where they were living at the time of Joss's murder. My wife and I immediately dubbed the place 'Murder House'. A Swiss couple devoted to chamber music had originally built the house. The black cotton soil underlying the cement foundation was unstable and therefore the whole structure was given to slippage, causing cracks at one end that had to be continually patched up. Much of the decor had been influenced by Diana whose bedroom had an en suite bathroom done up with the pink tiles that had last been fashionable in the 1930s. My wife and I called it the 'Brighton bathroom', as it looked to us like the kind of thing you might see at the famously salubrious Brighton Metropole Hotel in England. (The Metropole was where errant husbands would go to stay with a prostitute, thereby giving 'evidence' of adultery for divorce proceedings.) Jock's bedroom was next door to Diana's – it has been said that they never slept in the same room during their brief marriage. This room also had its own peculiar bathroom: the bath was surrounded on three sides by mirrors and there was also one on the ceiling above the bath. The reasons for such self-imposed voyeurism must be left to the imagination. Downstairs were three main rooms and a cloakroom near the entrance. The sitting room was long and dominated at one end by a fireplace. It was here that Joss and Diana had had their last conversation before he was shot. Across the hall were two front rooms, a dining room and an extra sitting room. One dining-room window looked out over the small round pool where Diana used to go skinny-dipping and which we filled with sand to provide a play pit for the children. At the back of the house were servants' quarters and a deep well, which provided fresh water for the house and was driven by a compression pump or ram; as well as the stables, one of whose loose boxes was once used to accommodate Pantaloon, a piebald polo pony. The stairs in the house did indeed creak — as the police investigation had revealed — but only halfway down.

When I first took up residence at Murder House, almost thirty years had passed since Alice's and Joss's deaths, but there were aspects of life in Nairobi that both would have found familiar. The Muthaiga Club was still a centre of social life for expatriates. Polo clubs were in full swing (I played in Nairobi, Gilgil and Nanyuki). Race days in Nairobi were still very popular occasions. And people still spoke about the Erroll case. It was during this trip that I first met Dickie Pembroke, who was Alice's last lover. I had heard much about him from my colleague, Colin Mackenzie, a professional cattleman from Rhodesia who was a director of the company I worked for at that time. One day in 1971, Colin came to visit me at Marula Lane, bringing Dickie with him. Dickie had returned to Kenya to retrace all the places he had lived with Alice and to remember their times there. The meeting was brief. Dickie gazed about him in a nostalgic sort of way and wandered around the garden, musing about the time some thirty years before when he had spent every day for five months with Alice before rejoining his regiment in North Africa to fight the Afrika Korps all the way back to Tunisia during the Second World War.

There is one more character in Alice's story to whom I am also closely connected: Geoffrey Buxton, Alice's Wanjohi neighbour and the man who had introduced Alice and Raymund in 1926. My mother got to know Geoffrey very well in 1928, which was how I became his godson. I still possess a King Charles II silver tankard he gave me. Engraved on its base are these words: 'For Paul Spicer from his Godfather G. Buxton.' Sadly, I never met Geoffrey.

All these coincidences and connections led me to the creation of this book. After I retired from business in 1994, I began to follow Alice's path around the world. I visited her house and farm in Kenya and her grave there. I met Dave Allen, a local bush pilot, and Senior Chief William Kinuthia, who helped me to identify her burial place. (The spot lies somewhere beside the banks of the Wanjohi River, close to a deep pool and near to where she had buried her dog Minnie in the iris beds.) I discovered Alice's Nairobi cottage, now a massage spa, and her 'golden' beach house at Tiwi on Kenya's south coast. I lunched with her grandson at Château de Parfondeval in Normandy. I trailed her story to Chicago, and to London and Paris as well. Over a period of ten years I gained first-hand impressions of Alice from those who knew her. In my portrait of her I have relied heavily on the reminiscences of her housekeeper for many years, Noel Eaton-Evans (née Case, now deceased). Other vital evidence came from Alice's close friend Patsy Chilton (formerly Bowles), who survives. I was fortunate to have in my possession the written recollections of my mother. I also interviewed Alice's then surviving daughter, Paola, as well as her half-sister Pat Silverthorne and her cousin Harry Hartshorne. I was lucky enough to speak to her grandchildren, Frédéric Armand-Delille, Guillaume de Rougemont, and Angélique Fiedler. Other vital insights came from Alice Boyle. Her revelation about Alice's confession letter assured me that I had a story to tell. Vi Case, Errol Trzebinski, Juanita Carberry, and Lee Harrigan also contributed enormously. My thanks go to all these people for helping me make this portrait of Alice as detailed and as conclusive as possible.

Cast of Characters

William (Bill) Allen
Married Paula Gellibrand in 1930 after her divorce from Marquis de Casa Maury. Eventually became head of British Secret Service in Ankara.

Lolita Armour
Daughter of J. Ogden Armour and Alice's second cousin. She introduced Alice to Chicago socially and was the matron of honour at her wedding to Frédéric de Janzé on 21 September 1921.

Poppy Baring
Daughter of Sir Godfrey Baring of Nubia House, Cowes, Isle of Wight. She became a mistress of the Duke of Kent

for several years. Raymund de Trafford knew her well – he went to stay with her soon after his release from prison.

Mr Barrat
Alice's lawyer in Kenya, he was a principal of the firm Shapley, Schwartze and Barrat. He processed the acquisition of Wanjohi Farm from Sir John Ramsden, who had agreed to sell to the de Janzés.

Karen Blixen
Author of *Out of Africa*. Born Karen Dinesen, she married Baron Blor Blixen. She became Denys Finch Hatton's closest friend and lover in Africa. Her original house in Karen, Kenya, has been restored and opened to the public as the Karen Blixen Museum.

Patsy Bowles
Married to Dr Roger Bowles, Alice's physician. She befriended Alice in 1938.

Roger Bowles
Alice's sometime physician, although not her main doctor.

Phyllis Boyd
Alice's sister-in-law. Married to Henri de Janzé, Frédéric's younger brother. She studied at the Slade School of Art in London and a direct descendant of Mrs Jordan and King William IV.

Alice Boyle

Only daughter of Dr William Boyle, Alice's main physician. She was told by her mother, Ethnie, about Alice de Janzé's letter in which Alice confessed to the shooting of Joss Erroll.

William Boyle

Studied at Cambridge and the London Hospital before arriving in Kenya. He married Ethnie Byrne, daughter of Sir Joseph Byrne, Governor of Kenya (1931–1937). He was Alice's favourite doctor and he attended the scene of her death, where he collected her last letters on 27 September 1941.

Diana Delves Broughton

Arrived in Kenya in November 1940, newly married to Sir Henry John ('Jock') Delves Broughton. She had become Jock's mistress at the age of twenty-two, when he was fifty one. Her maiden name was Caldwell. Diana began her affair with Joss Erroll within a month of her arrival in Kenya, at which point she decided to leave her husband. Diana went on to marry Gilbert Colvile and then Thomas Cholmondeley, the fourth Baron Delamere.

Sir Henry John ('Jock') Delves Broughton (the eleventh baronet of Doddington)

Known as Jock, he arrived in Kenya in 1940 and became the prime suspect in the murder of Lord Erroll. He was married to Diana Delves Broughton, who left him after beginning an affair with Lord Erroll. Jock was tried and acquitted of the murder. He committed suicide in December 1942 at the Aldephi Hotel in Liverpool.

R.W. Burkitt
Famous Irish surgeon renowned for his rough treatment of malarial patients. He diagnosed Frédéric de Janzé when he contracted blackwater fever.

Geoffrey Buxton
Arrived in Kenya in 1910. Born in Norwich and brought up at the Buxton family home, Dunston. He acquired 2,500 acres in the Wanjohi Valley and was the first settler to own land there. In 1926 he introduced Raymund de Trafford to Alice de Janzé at a dinner party at his Tudor-style house.

Sir Joseph Byrne
Governor and Commander-in-Chief of Kenya (1931 to 1937). He readmitted Alice to Kenya and permitted her renewed residence there in 1933. His daughter Ethnie married Dr William Boyle, Alice's doctor.

Marquis de Casa Maury
A Cuban-Castilian Count (full name Pedro José Isidiro Manuel Ricardo Mones Maury). He married Alice's great friend Paula Gellibrand in 1923 in London. Divorced in 1928, he married Freda Dudley Ward, former mistress of Edward, Prince of Wales, in 1937.

Noel Case

At age twenty, she visited the Wanjohi Valley and located Alice's farm, which was for rent. After Alice's departure due to an expulsion order, Noel moved into the farm with her parents. Noel became Alice's housekeeper in 1933 when the latter returned from exile. She later married Tom Eaton-Evans.

Father Casey

The priest in Chicago who initiated Alice into the Catholic faith before her marriage to Frédéric de Janzé on 21 September 1921.

Emery David Chapin

Married Marietta Armour, daughter of Danforth Armour. The two daughters from this marriage were Juliabelle (mother of Alice) and Alice 'Tattie' Chapin, aunt of Alice and guardian of Nolwen and Paola.

Simeon B. Chapin (Uncle Sim)

Successful financier and stockbroker on Wall Street and Alice's uncle. Took the lead in making Alice a ward of court.

Hugh Cholmondeley (the third Baron Delamere)

Lord Delamere, better known as 'D', was a pioneer Kenyan settler who developed cattle ranching and wheat growing in the Rift Valley. Made close friends with Alice de Janzé in 1925.

Flo Crofton

Became Alice's housekeeper after Noel Case retired to get married. She was the daughter of General Northey, a previous Governor of Kenya. She married Dick Crofton, a white hunter living near Gilgil.

Bill and Bubbles Delap

Owners of 'Rayetta' farm in the Wanjohi Valley and neighbours of Alice and Frédéric.

Gaston Doumergue

President of France in 1927. Alice's sentence for the attempted killing of Raymund de Trafford was six months in prison (suspended sentence) but a total pardon was granted by President Doumergue in 1929.

Edward

Sent to France by Alice's Aunt Tattie, he served as butler to the de Janzés at Parfondeval. A skilled photographer and conjuror.

Derek Erskine

Friends with Alice, Joss Erroll, and Jock and Diana Delves Broughton. Successful grocer and entrepreneur in Kenya. Firm advocate of multiracialism. Knighted by Queen Elizabeth II at the request of Jomo Kenyatta (first President of Kenya).

Phyllis Filmer

Occasional mistress of Joss Erroll and wife of Percy

Filmer, the managing director of Shell in East Africa. Lived with Idina at Clouds after Lord Erroll's death in 1941.

Monsieur Fredin

Alice's examiner in the 12th Chamber of the Police Correctional Court on 23 December 1927 during her trial for the attempted killing of Raymund de Trafford.

Monsieur Gandel

One of two attorneys representing Alice at her trial. He pleaded for Alice 'indulgently'.

Paula Gellibrand

Close friends with Alice in Paris. Fashion icon in the 1920s. Photographed by Cecil Beaton and often described as the most beautiful woman in Europe. She married the Marquis de Casa Maury and then William Allen. Later she went to Kenya where she married 'Boy' Long.

Prince George (Duke of Kent)

Fourth son of King George V. He made friends with Alice at the Embassy Club in London in the late 1920s. His black and white bulldog mated with Alice's bulldog 'Jimmy' in Paris.

Robert Graves

Author of numerous books including *Good-bye to All That* and *I Claudius*. Befriended Raymund de Trafford who went to live with him in Deià, Majorca after his second marriage collapsed.

Sir Edward Grigg
Governor of Kenya (1924–1931). Responsible for Alice's expulsion from Kenya in 1928.

Lady Joan Grigg
Wife of Sir Edward. Strong advocate of marital stability within the Kenya European community. Believed Alice was a threat to married society and so persuaded her husband to issue a prohibited immigrant order against her in February 1928.

Monsieur Guinon
The owner of the gun shop in avenue l'Opéra, Paris, where Alice bought the pearl-handled Colt revolver with which she shot Raymund de Trafford.

Sir Walter Harrigan
Attorney General in Kenya from 1933 to 1944. His prosecution of Jock Delves Broughton for the murder of Lord Erroll failed. He may have suppressed Alice's letter of confession which stated that she had killed Lord Erroll.

Josslyn Victor (Joss) Hay, Lord Erroll
Married Lady Idina Gordon (née Sackville) in 1923 and went to live with her in Kenya. Upon the death of his father, he became the twenty-second Earl of Erroll in 1928. Married Mary Ramsay-Hill in 1930. Alice's long-term lover after they met in 1925. Began affair with Diana Delves Broughton in 1940. Shot in mysterious circumstances in January 1941.

Alice de Janzé

Born Alice Silverthorne. Moved to Paris where she met her first husband, Count Frédéric de Janzé. Travelled to Kenya where she met and fell in love with Josslyn Hay and Raymund de Trafford. Married and divorced de Trafford after having attempted to shoot him in 1927 at the Gare du Nord. Committed suicide in September 1941, eight months after Joss's murder.

Count François Louis Léon de Janzé

Father of Frédéric and Henri. Married Moya Hennessy.

Frédéric de Janzé

Eldest son of Count François Louis Léon de Janzé. Married Alice Silverthorne in 1921. After his divorce he married Genevieve Willinger Ryan in 1930. Died suddenly while on assignment in the United States. Author of two books about Kenya, *Vertical Land* and *Tarred with the Same Brush*.

Henri de Janzé

Younger brother of Frédéric. Married to Phyllis Boyd.

Moya de Janzé

Married to Count François Louis Léon de Janzé. Mother of Frédéric and Henri. Her mother was a Mather of the United States. Her maiden name was Hennessy. Her sister Nora was godmother to Alice's first daughter, Nolwen, and married Lord Methuen of Corsham Court.

Nolwen de Janzé

Firstborn daughter of Frédéric and Alice de Janzé. She first married Lionel Armand-Delille, then Edward Rice, and then Baron Clark of Saltwood Castle, father of Alan Clark MP.

Paola de Janzé

Second daughter of Frédéric and Alice de Janzé. Married Walter Haydon and later John Ciechanowski. Paula Gellibrand was her godmother.

Lazarus Kaplan

Solicitor who helped Henry Harris 'Harry' Morris to defend Jock Delves Broughton during his trial for the murder of Lord Erroll.

Jomo Kenyatta

First President of Kenya. Supreme leader of Kenya's independent democracy and promoter of a multiracial society. Creator of the rallying cry of 'Harambee' meaning 'All pull together'. Close friend of Derek Erskine, whose knighthood he requested.

Betty Leslie-Melville

Author of *The Giraffe Lady*, about her life in Kenya. Married to 'Jock' Leslie-Melville whose mother, Mary Leslie-Melville, was an immediate neighbour to Alice in the Wanjohi Valley. Betty wrote in her autobiography that her mother-in-law was certain that Alice had shot Lord Erroll.

Mary Leslie-Melville

Farmed 5,000 acres in the Wanjohi Valley with her husband, the Honourable David Leslie-Melville. Neighbour to Alice. Assisted Alice in buying Wanjohi Farm from Sir John Ramsden. Found a gun that matched the missing Erroll murder weapon in a stream dividing her farm from Alice's.

Julian Joseph ('Lizzie') Lezard

Arrived in Kenya in 1940. Went to stay with Alice at Wanjohi Farm on Lord Erroll's instructions to conduct government surveillance work. Briefly Alice's main lover.

Edward Caswell ('Boy') Long

Invited by Lord Delamere to manage his cattle in the Rift Valley. Married Genesta Heath in 1924. Had brief affair with Idina Hay. Married Paula Gellibrand in 1938.

Marie

French maid and housekeeper to Idina Hay in 1925. Most helpful to Alice on her first arrival in Kenya.

Louise Mattocks

Alice's stepmother. Married William Silverthorne in Paris shortly after the death of Alice's mother, Juliabelle (Louise's cousin). She had several children by William, including Patricia, who was born in 1915.

Henry Harris ('Harry') Morris, KC

Well-known senior counsel based in South Africa. Hired by Diana Delves Broughton to defend her husband, Jock, at his trial (on Lazarus Kaplan's instruction). An expert on ballistics, he obtained an acquittal in the trial.

Alice May (Aunt Tattie)

Born Alice Chapin, she was the sister of Alice's mother, Juliabelle. Married Francis May of the Mays department store chain. Became joint guardian of Alice when Alice was made a ward of the court at the instigation of her brother, Simeon Chapin (Uncle Sim). Also served as long-term guardian of Alice's daughters, Nolwen and Paola.

René Mettetal

Alice's main lawyer in Paris and her defence counsel in her trial for the attempted murder of Raymund de Trafford. Procured her ultimate pardon from the President of France and put the case for her marriage annulment to Pope Pius XI.

Noreen Pearson

Friend of Alice in Nairobi. Had a daughter whom Alice admired – Alice stated in her will that her farm was to go to Noreen's daughter if her own children failed to take over Wanjohi Farm after her death.

Richard (Dickie) Pembroke

Alice's lover in 1940–1941. Testified in court that Alice had been with him on the night of Lord Erroll's murder. Carried Alice's letters with him in the desert campaign against the Afrika Korps in North Africa.

Pope Pius XI

Granted an annulment of Alice's marriage to Frédéric de Janzé in August 1928. Pope from 1922 to 1939.

Mary ('Molly') Ramsay-Hill

Divorced her husband, Cyril Ramsay-Hill, in order to marry Lord Erroll in 1930. Lived with Joss at Cyril's former home, Oserian, on the shores of Lake Naivasha. Her personal wealth was rumoured to have come from Boots, the chemist chain.

Sir John Frecheville 'Chops' Ramsden

Landowner and builder of settler-type houses in the Wanjohi area. Owned Wanjohi Farm prior to the de Janzés' purchase. Built their house for them under Alice's supervision.

Arap Ruta

Alice's chauffeur from 1933 onwards. Member of the Kalengin tribe. Remained with Alice until her death.

Lady Idina Sackville

Much-married founder of the Happy Valley set. Daughter of Albert Sackville, the eighth de la Warr. Married Josslyn Hay in 1923 and had four other husbands as well. Her house Clouds was the centre of Alice's social life after her return to Kenya in 1933.

Sir Francis Scott (the third baronet)

Pioneer settler based near Nanyuki. Made friends with Joss Hay.

Juliabelle Silverthorne
Alice's mother, who died when Alice was seven years old. She was the daughter of Emery David Chapin and Marietta Armour.

Patricia (Pat) Silverthorne
Alice's half-sister. Daughter of William Silverthorne by his second marriage to Louise Mattocks.

William Silverthorne
Alice's father, a businessman in Chicago, Buffalo and New York City. Married Juliabelle Chapin and then, shortly after Juliabelle's death, Louise Mattocks. All but disappeared from Alice's life after she was made ward of court by Juliabelle's family. Married for a third and fourth time late in life to Iris Cottell and Myrtle Plunkett.

Margaret Spicer
Friend to Alice. Mother of the author of this book. American-born and Swiss-educated. Married Roy Spicer in 1926 in Kenya. Died at Hampton Court in 1953 in the grace-and-favour apartment granted to her by Queen Elizabeth II.

Roy Spicer
Father of the author of this book. Son of Bullen Spicer and Adele von Besser. Scholar at St Paul's School, London. Fought in the First World War, wounded and gassed. Awarded the MC. Became Commissioner of Kenya Police

(1925–1931). Friends with Alice and Frédéric de Janzé. Later he was Inspector General of the Palestine Police (1931–1937). Joined the Allied Administration during the Second World War and as a full Colonel became Governor of Rome.

Sir Dermot de Trafford (the sixth baronet)
The current baronet is the son of Rudolph de Trafford and the nephew of Raymund.

Sir Humphrey de Trafford (the third baronet)
Father of Raymund de Trafford. Upon his death in January 1929, he was succeeded by his son Humphrey, who became the fourth baronet.

Raymund de Trafford
After arriving in Kenya, he became Alice's lover. He almost died when she shot him at the Gare du Nord in Paris in 1927. Went on to marry and divorce Alice. Later married Eve Drummond.

Sir Rudolph de Trafford (the fifth baronet)
Brother of Raymund and best man at Alice's marriage to Raymund in 1932. He became the fifth baronet upon the death of his brother Humphrey in 1971.

Fabian Wallace
Close friend of Alice's after her return to Kenya in 1933.

Evelyn Waugh
Renowned author who stayed with Raymund de Trafford in Kenya in 1931 and wrote about his visit in a travel book, *Remote People* (1931). Among his many other books are *Decline and Fall* and *Brideshead Revisited*.

Bibliography

Books

Aschan, Ulf. *The Man Whom Women Loved: The Life of Bror Blixen*. New York: St Martin's Press, 1987.

Brenan, Gerald. *Personal Record 1920–1972*. London: Jonathan Cape, 1974.

————. *Best of Friends: The Brenan-Partridge Letters*. London: Chatto & Windus, 1986.

Brinton, Christian. *The Ambrose McEvoy Exhibition*. New York: Redfield-Kendrick-Odell, 1920.

Cameron, Roderick. *Equator Farm*. London: William Heinemann, 1955.

Carberry, Juanita. *Child of Happy Valley: A Memoir*. London: William Heinemann, 1999.

Carrington, Noel, ed. *Mark Gertler: Selected Letters*. London: Rupert Hart-Davis, 1965.

The Church of Scotland Women's Guild of St. Andrew's. *Kenya Settlers Cookery Book and Household Guide.* Nairobi: East African Standard, 1928.

Connolly, Cyril. *Enemies of Promise.* London: Routledge & Kegan Paul, 1938.

Cooper, Artemis. *Cairo in the War: 1939–1945.* London: Hamish Hamilton, 1989.

Curtis, Arnold, ed. *Memories of Kenya: Stories from the Pioneers.* Nairobi: Evans Brothers, 1986.

Dinesen, Isak. *Letters from Africa 1914–1931.* Edited by Frans Larson; translated by Anne Born. London: Weidenfeld & Nicolson, 1981.

———. *Out of Africa.* London: Putnam, 1937.

Farrant, Leda. *Diana, Lady Delamere and the Lord Erroll Murder.* Nairobi: Publishers Distribution Services, 1997.

———. *The Legendary Grogan: The Only Man to Trek from Cape to Cairo: Kenya's Controversial Pioneer.* London: Hamish Hamilton, 1981.

Farwell, Byron. *The Great War in Africa: 1914–1918.* New York: W. W. Norton, 1987.

Fisher, Clive. *Cyril Connolly: A Nostalgic Life.* London: Macmillan, 1995.

Fox, James. *White Mischief.* London: Jonathan Cape, 1982.

Furneaux, Rupert. *The Murder of Lord Erroll.* London: Stevens & Sons, 1961.

Garnett, David, ed. *Carrington: Letters and Extracts from Her Diaries.* London: Jonathan Cape, 1970.

Gerzina, Gretchen. *Carrington: A Life of Dora Carrington, 1893–1932.* London: John Murray, 1989.

Goldsmith, Lady Annabel. *Annabel: An Unconventional Life.* London: Weidenfeld & Nicolson, 2004.

Graves, Robert. *Good-bye to All That.* London: Jonathan Cape, 1929.

Green, Johnnie. *The Legendary Hispano Suiza.* London: Dalton Watson, 1977.

Gregory, Joseph Richard. *Under the Sun: A Memoir of Dr. R. W. Burkitt, of Kenya.* Nairobi: English Press, 1952.

Grigg, E.W.M. *Kenya's Opportunity: Memories, Hopes and Ideas.* London: Faber & Faber, 1955.

Hamilton, Genesta. *A Stone's Throw: Travels from Africa in Six Decades.* London: Hutchinson, 1986.

Hartley, Aidan. *The Zanzibar Chest: A Memoir of Love and War.* London: HarperPerennial, 2004.

Hayes, Charles. *Oserian: Place of Peace.* Nairobi: Rima, 1997.

Hertz, Noreena. *The Silent Takeover: Global Capitalism and the Death of Democracy.* London: Arrow, 2002.

Hibbert, Christopher. *Africa Explored: Europeans in the Dark Continent.* London: Allen Lane, 1982.

Hill, Jane. *The Art of Dora Carrington.* London: Herbert Press, 1994.

Huxley, Elspeth. *The Flame Trees of Thika: Memories of an African Childhood.* London: Chatto & Windus, 1959.

———. *Nine Faces of Kenya.* London: Collins Harvill, 1990.

———. *Out in the Midday Sun: My Kenya.* London: Chatto & Windus, 1985.

———. *The Sorceror's Apprentice: A Journey Through East Africa.* London: Chatto & Windus, 1949.

————. *White Man's Country*. London: Macmillan, 1935.

Huxley, Elspeth, and Arnold Curtis, eds. *Pioneer's Scrapbook: Reminiscences of Kenya, 1890–1968*. Nairobi: Evans Brothers, 1980.

Jamison, Kay Redfield. *Touched with Fire: Manic Depressive Illness and the Artistic Temperament*. New York: Simon & Schuster, 1993.

Janzé, Frédéric de. *Tarred with the Same Brush*. London: Duckworth, 1929.

————. *Vertical Land*. London: Duckworth, 1928.

Jewell, J.H.A. *Mombasa and the Kenya Coast*. Nairobi: Evans Brothers, 1987.

Johnston, Charles. *Mo and Other Originals*. London: Hamish Hamilton, 1971.

Kenyatta, Jomo. *Facing Mount Kenya*. London: Mercury Books, 1938.

Kohler, Peter C. *Sea Safari*. Abergavenny, Wales: P.M. Heaton, 1995.

Leigh, Ione. *In the Shadow of the Mau Mau*. London: W.H. Allen, 1954.

Leslie-Melville, Betty. *The Giraffe Lady: The Autobiography of Betty Leslie-Melville*. Baltimore: Upland Publishing, 1997.

Lewis, Jeremy. *Cyril Connolly: A Life*. London: Jonathan Cape, 1977.

Lovell, Mary S. *Straight On Till Morning: The Biography of Beryl Markham*. London: Hutchinson, 1987.

Marco Africa (publisher). *Who's Who in East Africa*. 1968

Markham, Beryl. *The Splendid Outcast: The African Stories*

of Beryl Markham. Edited by Mary S. Lovell. London: Hutchinson, 1987.

Matheson, Alastair. *Land of Wide Horizons: An Illustrated Guide to East Africa*. London: MacDonald, 1962.

McEvoy, Ambrose. *Contemporary British Artists*. New York: Charles Scribner's Sons, 1924.

Miller, Charles. *Battle for the Bundu: The First World War in East Africa*. New York: Macmillan, 1974.

Mitford, Nancy. *The Pursuit of Love*. London: Hamish Hamilton, 1945.

Morton, James. *The Who's Who of Unsolved Murders*. London: Kyle Cathie, 1994.

Mosley, Nicholas. *Rules of the Game: Sir Oswald and Lady Cynthia Mosley, 1896–1933*. London: Secker & Warburg, 1982.

Nicholls, C. S. *Elspeth Huxley: A Biography*. London: HarperCollins, 2002.

O'Neill, Pat Cavendish. *The Lion in the Bedroom*. Sydney: Park Street Press, 2004.

Osborne, Frances. *The Bolter: Idina Sackville – the woman who scandalized 1920s society and became White Mischief's infamous seductress*. London: Virago, 2008.

Ostrovsky, Erika. *Eye of Dawn: The Rise and Fall of Mata Hari*. New York: Macmillam, 1978.

Pakenham, Thomas. *The Scramble for Africa*. London: Weidenfeld & Nicholson, 1992.

Pasley, Fred D. *Al Capone: The Biography of a Self-Made Man*. London: Faber & Faber, 1930.

Pavitt, Nigel. *Kenya: The First Explorers*. London: Aurum Press, 1989.

Pearson, John. *Wild Life and Safari in Kenya*. Nairobi: East African Publishing House, 1967.

Porter, Henry. *Remembrance Day*. London: Orion, 1999.

Ricciardi, Lorenzo, and Mirella Ricciardi. *African Rainbow: Across Africa by Boat*. London: Ebury Press, 1989.

Ridgeway, Rick. *The Shadow of Kilimanjaro: On Foot Across East Africa*. New York: Henry Holt, 2000.

Rodwell, Edward. *The Mombasa Club*. Nairobi: Rodwell Press, 1988.

Rutherston, Albert, ed. *Contemporary British Artists: Ambrose McEvoy*. New York: Charles Scribner's Sons, 1924.

Sandford, Christine. *Ethiopia Under Haile Selassie*. London: J.M. Dent, 1946.

Schoenberg, Robert J. *Mr. Capone*. New York: William Morrow, 1992.

Scott, Pamela. *A Nice Place to Live*. Salisbury, England: Michael Russell, 1991.

Taylorson, A. W. *Revolving Arms*. London: Herbert Jenkins 1967.

Thesiger, Wilfred. *My Kenya Days*. London: HarperCollins, 1994.

Tomalin, Claire. *Mrs Jordan's Profession: The Story of a Great Actress and a Future King*. London: Penguin, 1994.

Trench, Charles Chenevix. *Men Who Ruled Kenya: The Kenya Administration 1892–1963*. London: Radcliffe Press, 1993.

Trzebinski, Errol. *The Kenya Pioneers*. London: William Heinemann, 1991.

————. *The Life and Death of Lord Erroll: The Truth Behind*

the Happy Valley Murder. London: Fourth Estate, 2000.

————. *The Lives of Beryl Markham.* London: William Heinemann, 1993.

————. *Silence Will Speak.* London: Grafton Books, 1985.

Vatican Council. *Dignitas Connubii.* Vatican City: Libreria Editrice Vaticana, 2005.

Wagner, Rob L. *Classic Cars.* New York: MetroBooks, 1996.

Wahrman, Dror. *Michael's Jerusalem: The New Guide.* Edited by Michael Shichor. Tel Aviv: Inbal Travel Information, 1993.

Waugh, Evelyn. *Remote People: A Report from Ethiopia and British Africa, 1930–1931.* London: Duckworth, 1931.

Wheeler, Sara. *Too Close to the Sun: The Life and Times of Denys Finch Hatton.* London: Jonathan Cape, 2006.

Wills, Colin. *Who Killed Kenya?* London: Dennis Dobson, 1953.

Privately Published Sources

Cartland, Barbara. 'Firsts'. Last entry dated 1997.

Silverthorn Family Newsletter, 1986.

Newspapers and Periodicals

Baltimore Sun

Le Boulevardier

Bystander

Chicago Tribune

Daily Express

Daily Mail
Daily Mirror
Daily Sketch
East African Standard
L'Echo de Paris
New York Times
News of the World
Paris-Soir
People
Le Petit Parisien
Reynolds Illustrated News
Star
Sunday Express
Sunday Pictorial
Tatler
Telegraph
The Times

Acknowledgements

Dave Allen Exceptional bush pilot with superb skills in navigation and low flying. For discovering Wanjohi Farm from the air and then delivering me there.

Frédéric Armand Delille, son of Nolwen de Janzé and owner of Château de Parfondeval. For his hospitality at his country house in Normandy, for allowing me to inspect the family photograph albums in the Plum Room, and for the loan of two photographs of Alice on display in his main sitting room at Parfondeval.

Alice Boyle, daughter of Dr William Boyle, Alice de Janzé's doctor in the last years of her life and the key witness regarding the letter of confession left at Alice's bedside on her death. For her constant friendship and help on the story of Alice de Janzé.

Richard Britten-Long For all his help with photographs of Paula Gellibrand and Augustus John.

Dame Barbara Cartland For her correspondence and supply of 'Firsts' and for the details she provided about the Embassy Club and who went there on Thursday evenings.

Juliet Cassidy For six years of continuous research and help on rewrites, and for her visits to Paris, Normandy, and particularly Chicago, where she would discover details about Alice's early life. A meticulous researcher and scribe. But perhaps her greatest asset apart from her academic prowess is her splendid personality.

Causeway Resources For providing numerous press cuttings.

Eve Charles A very talented editor. For her mastery of the English written word and deep understanding of the subject, and for giving a high polish to the story I had crafted.

Patsy Chilton, former wife of Dr Roger Bowles. For detailed written notes about her meetings with Alice at the Muthaiga Club, Nairobi in 1939.

Paola Ciechanowski, Alice's younger daughter. For our

friendly meetings in Londinières and endless chats, for the memories she provided of her mother, and for our correspondence over five years.

Sir Toby Clarke For his introductions in Chicago.

Dick Crofton For his guidance regarding the military records of Dickie Pembroke and Raymund de Trafford (both Coldstream Guards officers).

Tom Eaton-Evans Husband of Noel Case. For providing help and acting as a liaison.

Sir Derek Erskine For his continuous friendship since 1950 and for many insights into life in Kenya in 1930.

Francis Erskine, Derek's son. For his hospitality on our visit to the Wanjohi Valley.

Patrizia Erskine, Francis Eskine's daughter-in-law. For being good enough to accompany me to Alice's home in the Wanjohi Valley.

Petal Erskine, Derek's daughter. For her many memories of her father.

Dr Peter Fenwick, neuropsychiatrist. For his detailed comments on Alice's probable mental state and his explanation of the difference between bipolar disorder and cyclothymia.

Captain Gordon Ferguson, the secretary of the Taporley Hunt Club and author of *The Green Collars*, a history of England's oldest hunt club. Gordon included an addendum in an edition of *The Green Collars* about Alice's confession to the shooting of Joss Erroll. He also recommended that I seek out Barbara Cartland about the Embassy Club.

Angélique Fiedler, Alice's granddaughter. For her heartfelt and protective interest in the de Janzé name; and for making letters from her mother (Nolwen) and Alice available to me.

Christy Fletcher and Grainne Fox My wonderful agents at Fletcher & Company, for their superlative precision and competence in bringing the Alice story to its completion.

William Gachanja For tracing the location of settlers' farms in the Wanjohi Valley.

Madame Genèvieve François-Poncet A great friend of Frédéric Armand Delille's father. For her help in arranging for me to meet Frédéric.

Michael Harley For acting as a liaison in Kenya.

Aidan Hartley, author of *The Zanzibar Chest* (2004). For his advice and well-chosen introduction to Emma Parry and with thanks to Claire, Aidan's wife, for her apt and perceptive comments.

Doreen Hartley, mother-in-law of the current owner of Giraffe Manor, formerly owned by the Leslie-Melvilles. For making me aware of *The Giraffe Lady* by Betty Leslie-Melville, with its revelation of Alice's possible culpability.

Harry Hartshorne Jr, the grandson of Simeon Chapin. For his help that resulted in the supply of several unique early photographs taken in the United States and for his welcoming hand on our visit to New York.

Margaret Hayes, the widow of the author of *Oserian*, Charles Hayes. For kindly obtaining four reels of tape recording every issue of the *Boulevardier* publication. Her husband's book *Oserian* covers a century of Kenya's social history including some details concerning Alice de Janzé.

Dr Noreena Hertz, author of *The Silent Takeover: Global Capitalism and the Death of Democracy*. For introducing me to Juliet Cassidy and for persuading me to write for two hours a day.

Robin Hollister For his insight into the making of *Out of Africa*, and for his enlightened comments on the making of *The Constant Gardener*, a film set in Kenya.

Joanne Grady Huskey, author, educator and wife of an American diplomat. For accompanying the author on his first visit to Alice's house in the Wanjohi Valley.

Senior Chief William Kinuthia, a resident of the Wanjohi Valley whose house is near Alice de Janze's former home there. He was kind enough to coordinate my visit.

Robin Long For his help and his many memories of his stepmother Paula Gellibrand Long.

Patricia McGuigan (neé Silverthorne), Alice's half-sister. For her extensive help and her memories of Alice while in London.

Lord Montagu of Beaulieu For identifying and describing Mr Silverthorne's enormous Stoddard-Dayton motor car.

Clare Naylor Vivacious and intelligent author of seven books. For her encouragement. It was her enthusiasm for the Alice story and her professionalism that led me into the world of writing.

Martha Nyman For discovering and bringing to my notice the sensational photograph of Alice in the Correctional Court in Paris.

Frances Osborne For her friendship and cooperation while writing her second book, *The Bolter*, a biography of her great-grandmother Lady Idina Sackville, who married Joss Hay, Earl of Erroll.

Emma Parry The most competent literary agent that

anyone could wish for. Inspirational and clever in her deal-ings with neurotic authors.

Henry Porter, author of the novel *Remembrance Day* and one-time London editor of *Vanity Fair*. For listening to the Alice story and for encouraging me to make the Gare du Nord event one of the key chapters in this book.

P.J. Ransley For enabling me to trace the original deed plan of Alice's home in the Wanjohi Valley.

Arnold Raphael For listening early on and lending his support in my research. It was he who made me aware of the crime documentary by Rupert Furneaux.

Guillaume de Rougement, Alice's grandson. For providing me with detailed notes that he wrote down at the bedside of his mother, Paola, in Londinières, Normandy. These notes contained information about Alice, and the de Janzé family. A very remarkable man with the finest collection of beetles (Coleopterus) in the world, and who speaks Aramaic (the language of Jesus Christ).

Kerri Sharp, my editor in the UK. For her inspiring enthusiasm about the Alice story and her essential role in producing this edition of the book.

Sir Sacheverell Reresby Sitwell For supplying a bril-liant photograph of Lizzie Lezard, who had been a friend of his mother's, and frequently stayed at her country home.

Penny Smith, a secretary who has laboured mightily with six years of research correspondence and numerous drafts of the manuscript. For her aptitude and loyalty.

Yaniv Soha, Charles Spicer's editorial assistant. For his dedicated help and first-class capability in the art of bringing a book to completion.

Charles Spicer, my editor in the United States. For all his help and perceptive understanding of this biography; for his enthusiasm and wit, and for his in-depth knowledge of publishing.

Dermot de Trafford, Raymund de Trafford's nephew. For the loan of his uncle's personal photograph album compiled in Kenya in 1926, and for his help in describing Raymund's life after the war.

Errol Trzebinski, a great and well-known writer, who has made Kenya a special subject of study. Her biography of Joss Erroll, *The Life and Death of Lord Erroll: The Truth Behind the Happy Valley Murder* (2000), has proved to be invaluable. For her enthusiasm about this project, and for generously giving me both ideas and help.

Ronnie Ward of Lake Forest, near Chicago, for his liaison work in that part of the world.

Acknowledgements

Danièle Waterpark For being French, for taking me to the Bibliothèque Nationale in Paris, for finding French newspaper coverage of the Gare du Nord event, and for providing instant translations. I am also grateful to her for introducing me to Frédéric Armand Delille, the son of Nolwen de Janzé; for inviting me to stay at her daughter Caroline Goulding's house in Le Touquet and driving me to Normandy to visit the Château de Parfondeval and Paola in Londinières, and for introducing me to Angélique Fiedler, Alice's granddaughter.

Michael Watson For his enlightened comments about his cousin Dickie Pembroke.

Rupert Watson For his research in Kenya.

The Honourable Vicky Westrop For providing a family album showing pictures of Phyllis de Janzé (née Boyd) in later years.

Index

Index

Index

The Temptress

Index